Stephen Crane (November 1, 1871 – June 5, 1900) was an American poet, novelist, and short story writer. Prolific throughout his short life, he wrote notable works in the Realist tradition as well as early examples of American Naturalism and Impressionism. He is recognized by modern critics as one of the most innovative writers of his generation. The ninth surviving child of Methodist parents, Crane began writing at the age of four and had published several articles by the age of 16. Having little interest in university studies though he was active in a fraternity, he left Syracuse University in 1891 to work as a reporter and writer. Crane's first novel was the 1893 Bowery tale Maggie: A Girl of the Streets, generally considered by critics to be the first work of American literary Naturalism. He won international acclaim in 1895 for his Civil War novel The Red Badge of Courage, which he wrote without having any battle experience. (Source: Wikipedia)

Literary works:
Maggie: A Girl of the Streets (1893)
The Red Badge of Courage (1895)
The Black Riders and Other Lines (1895)
George's Mother (1896)
The Third Violet (1897)
The Open Boat and Other Tales of Adventure (1898)
War is Kind (1899)
Active Service (1899)
The Monster and Other Stories (1899)
Wounds in the Rain (1900)
Great Battles of the World
The O'Ruddy (1903)
The Monster. London
Last Words. London
Whilomville Stories

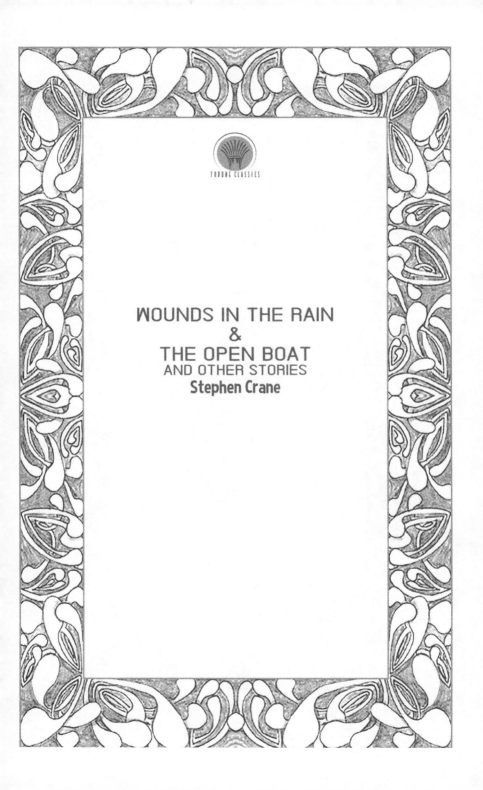

THRONE CLASSICS

WOUNDS IN THE RAIN
&
THE OPEN BOAT
AND OTHER STORIES
Stephen Crane

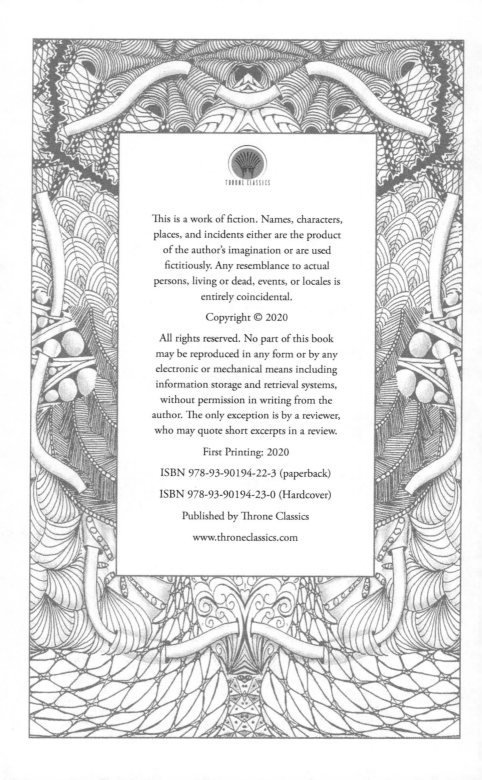

First Printing: 2020

ISBN 978-93-90194-22-3 (paperback)

ISBN 978-93-90194-23-0 (Hardcover)

Published by Throne Classics

www.throneclassics.com

Contents

WOUNDS IN THE RAIN
&
THE OPEN BOAT
AND OTHER STORIES

WOUNDS IN THE RAIN

THE PRICE OF THE HARNESS

I

Twenty-five men were making a road out of a path up the hillside. The light batteries in the rear were impatient to advance, but first must be done all that digging and smoothing which gains no encrusted medals from war. The men worked like gardeners, and a road was growing from the old pack-animal trail.

Trees arched from a field of guinea-grass which resembled young wild corn. The day was still and dry. The men working were dressed in the consistent blue of United States regulars. They looked indifferent, almost stolid, despite the heat and the labour. There was little talking. From time to time a Government pack-train, led by a sleek-sided tender bell-mare, came from one way or the other way, and the men stood aside as the strong, hard, black-and-tan animals crowded eagerly after their curious little feminine leader.

A volunteer staff-officer appeared, and, sitting on his horse in the middle of the work, asked the sergeant in command some questions which were apparently not relevant to any military business. Men straggling along on various duties almost invariably spun some kind of a joke as they passed.

A corporal and four men were guarding boxes of spare ammunition at the top of the hill, and one of the number often went to the foot of the hill swinging canteens.

The day wore down to the Cuban dusk, in which the shadows are all grim and of ghostly shape. The men began to lift their eyes from the shovels and picks, and glance in the direction of their camp. The sun threw his last lance through the foliage. The steep mountain-range on the right turned blue and as without detail as a curtain. The tiny ruby of light ahead meant that the ammunition-guard were cooking their supper. From somewhere in the world came a single rifle-shot.

Figures appeared, dim in the shadow of the trees. A murmur, a sigh of quiet relief, arose from the working party. Later, they swung up the hill in an unformed formation, being always like soldiers, and unable even to carry a spade save like United States regular soldiers. As they passed through some fields, the bland white light of the end of the day feebly touched each hard bronze profile.

"Wonder if we'll git anythin' to eat," said Watkins, in a low voice.

"Should think so," said Nolan, in the same tone. They betrayed no impatience; they seemed to feel a kind of awe of the situation.

The sergeant turned. One could see the cool grey eye flashing under the brim of the campaign hat. "What in hell you fellers kickin' about?" he asked. They made no reply, understanding that they were being suppressed.

As they moved on, a murmur arose from the tall grass on either hand. It was the noise from the bivouac of ten thousand men, although one saw practically nothing from the low-cart roadway. The sergeant led his party up a wet clay bank and into a trampled field. Here were scattered tiny white shelter tents, and in the darkness they were luminous like the rearing stones in a graveyard. A few fires burned blood-red, and the shadowy figures of men moved with no more expression of detail than there is in the swaying of foliage on a windy night.

The working party felt their way to where their tents were pitched. A man suddenly cursed; he had mislaid something, and he knew he was not going to find it that night. Watkins spoke again with the monotony of a clock, "Wonder if we'll git anythin' to eat."

Martin, with eyes turned pensively to the stars, began a treatise. "Them Spaniards——"

"Oh, quit it," cried Nolan. "What th' piper do you know about th' Spaniards, you fat-headed Dutchman? Better think of your belly, you blunderin' swine, an' what you're goin' to put in it, grass or dirt."

A laugh, a sort of a deep growl, arose from the prostrate men. In the meantime the sergeant had reappeared and was standing over them. "No rations to-night," he said gruffly, and turning on his heel, walked away.

This announcement was received in silence. But Watkins had flung himself face downward, and putting his lips close to a tuft of grass, he formulated oaths. Martin arose and, going to his shelter, crawled in sulkily. After a long interval Nolan said aloud, "Hell!" Grierson, enlisted for the war, raised a querulous voice. "Well, I wonder when we will git fed?"

From the ground about him came a low chuckle, full of ironical comment upon Grierson's lack of certain qualities which the other men felt themselves to possess.

II

In the cold light of dawn the men were on their knees, packing, strapping, and buckling. The comic toy hamlet of shelter-tents had been wiped out as if by a cyclone. Through the trees could be seen the crimson of a light battery's blankets, and the wheels creaked like the sound of a musketry fight. Nolan, well gripped by his shelter tent, his blanket, and his cartridge-belt, and bearing his rifle, advanced upon a small group of men who were hastily finishing a can of coffee.

"Say, give us a drink, will yeh?" he asked, wistfully. He was as sad-eyed as an orphan beggar.

Every man in the group turned to look him straight in the face. He had asked for the principal ruby out of each one's crown. There was a grim silence. Then one said, "What fer?" Nolan cast his glance to the ground, and went away abashed.

But he espied Watkins and Martin surrounding Grierson, who had gained three pieces of hard-tack by mere force of his audacious inexperience. Grierson was fending his comrades off tearfully.

"Now, don't be damn pigs," he cried. "Hold on a minute." Here Nolan asserted a claim. Grierson groaned. Kneeling piously, he divided the hard-tack with minute care into four portions. The men, who had had their heads together like players watching a wheel of fortune, arose suddenly, each chewing. Nolan interpolated a drink of water, and sighed contentedly.

The whole forest seemed to be moving. From the field on the other side of the road a column of men in blue was slowly pouring; the battery had creaked on ahead; from the rear came a hum of advancing regiments. Then from a mile away rang the noise of a shot; then another shot; in a moment the rifles there were drumming, drumming, drumming. The artillery boomed out suddenly. A day of battle was begun.

The men made no exclamations. They rolled their eyes in the direction of the sound, and then swept with a calm glance the forests and the hills which surrounded them, implacably mysterious forests and hills which lent to every rifle-shot the ominous quality which belongs to secret assassination. The whole scene would have spoken to the private soldiers of ambushes, sudden flank attacks, terrible disasters, if it were not for those cool gentlemen with shoulder-straps and swords who, the private soldiers knew, were of another world and omnipotent for the business.

The battalions moved out into the mud and began a leisurely march in the damp shade of the trees. The advance of two batteries had churned the black soil into a formidable paste. The brown leggings of the men, stained with the mud of other days, took on a deeper colour. Perspiration broke gently out on the reddish faces. With his heavy roll of blanket and the half of a shelter-tent crossing his right shoulder and under his left arm, each man presented the appearance of being clasped from behind, wrestler fashion, by a pair of thick white arms.

There was something distinctive in the way they carried their rifles. There was the grace of an old hunter somewhere in it, the grace of a man whose rifle has become absolutely a part of himself. Furthermore, almost every blue shirt sleeve was rolled to the elbow, disclosing fore-arms of almost incredible brawn. The rifles seemed light, almost fragile, in the hands that were at the end of these arms, never fat but always with rolling muscles and veins that seemed on the point of bursting. And another thing was the silence and the marvellous impassivity of the faces as the column made its slow way toward where the whole forest spluttered and fluttered with battle.

Opportunely, the battalion was halted a-straddle of a stream, and before it again moved, most of the men had filled their canteens. The firing increased. Ahead and to the left a battery was booming at methodical intervals, while the infantry racket was that continual drumming which, after all, often sounds like rain on a roof. Directly ahead one could hear the deep voices of field-pieces.

Some wounded Cubans were carried by in litters improvised from hammocks swung on poles. One had a ghastly cut in the throat, probably from a fragment of shell, and his head was turned as if Providence particularly wished to display this wide and lapping gash to the long column that was winding toward the front. And another Cuban, shot through the groin, kept up a continual wail as he swung from the tread of his bearers. "Ay—ee! Ay—ee! Madre mia! Madre mia!" He sang this bitter ballad into the ears of at least three thousand men as they slowly made way for his bearers on the narrow wood-path. These wounded insurgents were, then, to a large part of the advancing army, the visible messengers of bloodshed and death, and the men regarded them with thoughtful awe. This doleful sobbing cry—"Madre mia"—was a tangible consequent misery of all that firing on in front into which the men knew they were soon to be plunged. Some of them wished to inquire of the bearers the details of what had happened; but they could not speak Spanish, and so it was as if fate had intentionally sealed the lips of all in order that even meagre information might not leak out concerning this mystery—battle. On the other hand, many unversed private soldiers looked upon the unfortunate as men who had seen thousands maimed and bleeding, and absolutely could not conjure any further interest in such scenes.

A young staff-officer passed on horseback. The vocal Cuban was always wailing, but the officer wheeled past the bearers without heeding anything. And yet he never before had seen such a sight. His case was different from that of the private soldiers. He heeded nothing because he was busy—immensely busy and hurried with a multitude of reasons and desires for doing his duty perfectly. His whole life had been a mere period of preliminary reflection for this situation, and he had no clear idea of anything save his obligation as an officer. A man of this kind might be stupid; it is conceivable that in remote cases certain bumps on his head might be composed entirely of wood; but those traditions of fidelity and courage which have been handed to him from generation to generation, and which he has tenaciously preserved despite the persecution of legislators and the indifference of his country, make it incredible that in battle he should ever fail to give his best blood and his best thought for his general, for his men, and for himself. And so this young officer in the shapeless hat and the torn and dirty shirt failed to heed the wails of the wounded man, even as the pilgrim fails to heed the world as he raises his illumined face toward his purpose—rightly or wrongly, his purpose—his sky of the ideal of duty; and the wonderful part of it is, that he is guided by an ideal which he has himself created, and has alone protected from attack. The young man was merely an officer in the United States regular army.

The column swung across a shallow ford and took a road which passed the right flank of one of the American batteries. On a hill it was booming and belching great clouds of white smoke. The infantry looked up with interest. Arrayed below the hill and behind the battery were the horses and limbers, the riders checking their pawing mounts, and behind each rider a red blanket flamed against the fervent green of the bushes. As the infantry moved along the road, some of the battery horses turned at the noise of the trampling feet and surveyed the men with eyes as deep as wells, serene, mournful, generous eyes, lit heart-breakingly with something that was akin to a philosophy, a religion of self-sacrifice—oh, gallant, gallant horses!

"I know a feller in that battery," said Nolan, musingly. "A driver."

"Dam sight rather be a gunner," said Martin.

"Why would ye?" said Nolan, opposingly.

"Well, I'd take my chances as a gunner b'fore I'd sit way up in th' air on a raw-boned plug an' git shot at."

"Aw——" began Nolan.

"They've had some losses t'-day all right," interrupted Grierson.

"Horses?" asked Watkins.

16

"Horses and men too," said Grierson.

"How d'yeh know?"

"A feller told me there by the ford."

They kept only a part of their minds bearing on this discussion because they could already hear high in the air the wire-string note of the enemy's bullets.

III

The road taken by this battalion as it followed other battalions is something less than a mile long in its journey across a heavily-wooded plain. It is greatly changed now,—in fact it was metamorphosed in two days; but at that time it was a mere track through dense shrubbery, from which rose great dignified arching trees. It was, in fact, a path through a jungle.

The battalion had no sooner left the battery in rear when bullets began to drive overhead. They made several different sounds, but as these were mainly high shots it was usual for them to make the faint note of a vibrant string, touched elusively, half-dreamily.

The military balloon, a fat, wavering, yellow thing, was leading the advance like some new conception of war-god. Its bloated mass shone above the trees, and served incidentally to indicate to the men at the rear that comrades were in advance. The track itself exhibited for all its visible length a closely-knit procession of soldiers in blue with breasts crossed with white shelter-tents. The first ominous order of battle came down the line. "Use the cut-off. Don't use the magazine until you're ordered." Non-commissioned officers repeated the command gruffly. A sound of clicking locks rattled along the columns. All men knew that the time had come.

The front had burst out with a roar like a brush-fire. The balloon was dying, dying a gigantic and public death before the eyes of two armies. It quivered, sank, faded into the trees amid the flurry of a battle that was suddenly and tremendously like a storm.

The American battery thundered behind the men with a shock that seemed likely to tear the backs of their heads off. The Spanish shrapnel fled on a line to their left, swirling and swishing in supernatural velocity. The noise of the rifle bullets broke in their faces like the noise of so many lamp-chimneys or sped overhead in swift cruel spitting. And at the front the battle-sound, as if it were simply music, was beginning to swell and swell until the volleys rolled like a surf.

The officers shouted hoarsely, "Come on, men! Hurry up, boys! Come on now! Hurry up!" The soldiers, running heavily in their accoutrements, dashed forward. A baggage guard was swiftly detailed; the men tore their rolls from their shoulders as if the things were afire. The battalion, stripped for action, again dashed forward.

"Come on, men! Come on!" To them the battle was as yet merely a road through the woods crowded with troops, who lowered their heads anxiously as the bullets fled high. But a moment later the column wheeled abruptly to the left and entered a field of tall green grass. The line scattered to a skirmish formation. In front was a series of knolls treed sparsely like orchards; and although no enemy was visible, these knolls were all popping and spitting with rifle-fire. In some places there were to be seen long grey lines of dirt, intrenchments. The American shells were kicking up reddish clouds of dust from the brow of one of the knolls, where stood a pagoda-like house. It was not much like a battle with men; it was a battle with a bit of charming scenery, enigmatically potent for death.

Nolan knew that Martin had suddenly fallen. "What———" he began.

"They've hit me," said Martin.

"Jesus!" said Nolan.

Martin lay on the ground, clutching his left forearm just below the elbow with all the strength of his right hand. His lips were pursed ruefully. He did not seem to know what to do. He continued to stare at his arm.

Then suddenly the bullets drove at them low and hard. The men flung themselves face downward in the grass. Nolan lost all thought of his friend. Oddly enough, he felt somewhat like a man hiding under a bed, and he was just as sure that he could not raise his head high without being shot as a man hiding under a bed is sure that he cannot raise his head without bumping it.

A lieutenant was seated in the grass just behind him. He was in the careless and yet rigid pose of a man balancing a loaded plate on his knee at a picnic. He was talking in soothing paternal tones.

"Now, don't get rattled. We're all right here. Just as safe as being in church.... They're all going high. Don't mind them.... Don't mind them.... They're all going high. We've got them rattled and they can't shoot straight. Don't mind them."

The sun burned down steadily from a pale blue sky upon the crackling woods and knolls and fields. From the roar of musketry it might have been that the celestial heat was frying this part of the world.

Nolan snuggled close to the grass. He watched a grey line of intrenchments, above which floated the veriest gossamer of smoke. A flag lolled on a staff behind it. The men in the trench volleyed whenever an American shell exploded near them. It was some kind of infantile defiance. Frequently a bullet came from the woods directly behind Nolan and his comrades. They thought at the time that these bullets were from the rifle of some incompetent soldier of their own side.

There was no cheering. The men would have looked about them, wondering where was the army, if it were not that the crash of the fighting for the distance of a mile denoted plainly enough where was the army.

Officially, the battalion had not yet fired a shot; there had been merely some irresponsible popping by men on the extreme left flank. But it was known that the lieutenant-colonel who had been in command was dead—shot through the heart—and that the captains were thinned down to two. At the rear went on a long tragedy, in which men, bent and hasty, hurried to shelter with other men, helpless, dazed, and bloody. Nolan knew of it all from the hoarse and affrighted voices which he heard as he lay flattened in the grass. There came to him a sense of exultation. Here, then, was one of those dread and lurid situations, which in a nation's history stand out in crimson letters, becoming a tale of blood to stir generation after generation. And he was in it, and unharmed. If he lived through the battle, he would be a hero of the desperate fight at ——; and here he wondered for a second what fate would be pleased to bestow as a name for this battle.

But it is quite sure that hardly another man in the battalion was engaged in any thoughts concerning the historic. On the contrary, they deemed it ill that they were being badly cut up on a most unimportant occasion. It would have benefited the conduct of whoever were weak if they had known that they were engaged in a battle that would be famous for ever.

<u>IV</u>

Martin had picked himself up from where the bullet had knocked him and addressed the lieutenant. "I'm hit, sir," he said.

The lieutenant was very busy. "All right, all right," he said, just heeding the man enough to learn where he was wounded. "Go over that way. You ought to see a dressing-station under those trees."

Martin found himself dizzy and sick. The sensation in his arm was distinctly galvanic. The feeling was so strange that he could wonder at times if a wound was really what ailed him. Once, in this dazed way, he examined his arm; he saw the hole. Yes, he was shot; that was it. And more than in any other way it affected him with a profound sadness.

As directed by the lieutenant, he went to the clump of trees, but he found no dressing-station there. He found only a dead soldier lying with his face buried in his arms and with his shoulders humped high as if he were convulsively sobbing. Martin decided to make his way to the road, deeming that he thus would better his chances of getting to a surgeon. But he suddenly found his way blocked by a fence of barbed wire. Such was his mental condition that he brought up at a rigid halt before this fence, and stared stupidly at it. It did not seem to him possible that this obstacle could be defeated by any means. The fence was there, and it stopped his progress. He could not go in that direction.

But as he turned he espied that procession of wounded men, strange pilgrims, that had already worn a path in the tall grass. They were passing through a gap in the fence. Martin joined them. The bullets were flying over them in sheets, but many of them bore themselves as men who had now exacted from fate a singular immunity. Generally there were no outcries, no kicking, no talk at all. They too, like Martin, seemed buried in a vague but profound melancholy.

But there was one who cried out loudly. A man shot in the head was being carried arduously by four comrades, and he continually yelled one word that was terrible in its primitive strength,—"Bread! Bread! Bread!" Following him and his bearers were a limping crowd of men less cruelly wounded, who kept their eyes always fixed on him, as if they gained from his extreme agony some balm for their own sufferings.

"Bread! Give me bread!"

Martin plucked a man by the sleeve. The man had been shot in the foot, and was making his way with the help of a curved, incompetent stick. It is an axiom of war that wounded men can never find straight sticks.

"What's the matter with that feller?" asked Martin.

"Nutty," said the man.

"Why is he?"

"Shot in th' head," answered the other, impatiently.

The wail of the sufferer arose in the field amid the swift rasp of bullets and the boom and shatter of shrapnel. "Bread! Bread! Oh, God, can't you give me bread? Bread!" The bearers of him were suffering exquisite agony, and often they exchanged glances which exhibited their despair of ever getting free of this tragedy. It seemed endless.

"Bread! Bread! Bread!"

But despite the fact that there was always in the way of this crowd a wistful melancholy, one must know that there were plenty of men who laughed, laughed at their wounds whimsically, quaintly inventing odd

21

humours concerning bicycles and cabs, extracting from this shedding of their blood a wonderful amount of material for cheerful badinage, and, with their faces twisted from pain as they stepped, they often joked like music-hall stars. And perhaps this was the most tearful part of all.

They trudged along a road until they reached a ford. Here under the eave of the bank lay a dismal company. In the mud and in the damp shade of some bushes were a half-hundred pale-faced men prostrate. Two or three surgeons were working there. Also, there was a chaplain, grim-mouthed, resolute, his surtout discarded. Overhead always was that incessant maddening wail of bullets.

Martin was standing gazing drowsily at the scene when a surgeon grabbed him. "Here, what's the matter with you?" Martin was daunted. He wondered what he had done that the surgeon should be so angry with him.

"In the arm," he muttered, half-shamefacedly.

After the surgeon had hastily and irritably bandaged the injured member he glared at Martin and said, "You can walk all right, can't you?"

"Yes, sir," said Martin.

"Well, now, you just make tracks down that road."

"Yes, sir." Martin went meekly off. The doctor had seemed exasperated almost to the point of madness.

The road was at this time swept with the fire of a body of Spanish sharpshooters who had come cunningly around the flanks of the American army, and were now hidden in the dense foliage that lined both sides of the road. They were shooting at everything. The road was as crowded as a street in a city, and at an absurdly short range they emptied their rifles at the passing people. They were aided always by the over-sweep from the regular Spanish line of battle.

Martin was sleepy from his wound. He saw tragedy follow tragedy, but they created in him no feeling of horror.

A man with a red cross on his arm was leaning against a great tree.

Suddenly he tumbled to the ground, and writhed for a moment in the way of a child oppressed with colic. A comrade immediately began to bustle importantly. "Here," he called to Martin, "help me carry this man, will you?"

Martin looked at him with dull scorn. "I'll be damned if I do," he said. "Can't carry myself, let alone somebody else."

This answer, which rings now so inhuman, pitiless, did not affect the other man. "Well, all right," he said. "Here comes some other fellers." The wounded man had now turned blue-grey; his eyes were closed; his body shook in a gentle, persistent chill.

Occasionally Martin came upon dead horses, their limbs sticking out and up like stakes. One beast mortally shot, was besieged by three or four men who were trying to push it into the bushes, where it could live its brief time of anguish without thrashing to death any of the wounded men in the gloomy procession.

The mule train, with extra ammunition, charged toward the front, still led by the tinkling bell-mare.

An ambulance was stuck momentarily in the mud, and above the crack of battle one could hear the familiar objurgations of the driver as he whirled his lash.

Two privates were having a hard time with a wounded captain, whom they were supporting to the rear, He was half cursing, half wailing out the information that he not only would not go another step toward the rear, but that he was certainly going to return at once to the front. They begged, pleaded at great length as they continually headed him off. They were not unlike two nurses with an exceptionally bad and headstrong little duke.

The wounded soldiers paused to look impassively upon this struggle. They were always like men who could not be aroused by anything further.

The visible hospital was mainly straggling thickets intersected with narrow paths, the ground being covered with men. Martin saw a busy person with a book and a pencil, but he did not approach him to become officially a member of the hospital. All he desired was rest and immunity from nagging. He took seat painfully under a bush and leaned his back upon the trunk. There he remained thinking, his face wooden.

V

"My Gawd," said Nolan, squirming on his belly in the grass, "I can't stand this much longer."

Then suddenly every rifle in the firing line seemed to go off of its own accord. It was the result of an order, but few men heard the order; in the main they had fired because they heard others fire, and their sense was so quick that the volley did not sound too ragged. These marksmen had been lying for nearly an hour in stony silence, their sights adjusted, their fingers fondling their rifles, their eyes staring at the intrenchments of the enemy. The battalion had suffered heavy losses, and these losses had been hard to bear, for a soldier always reasons that men lost during a period of inaction are men badly lost.

The line now sounded like a great machine set to running frantically in the open air, the bright sunshine of a green field. To the prut of the magazine rifles was added the under-chorus of the clicking mechanism, steady and swift, as if the hand of one operator was controlling it all. It reminds one always of a loom, a great grand steel loom, clinking, clanking, plunking, plinking, to weave a woof of thin red threads, the cloth of death. By the men's shoulders under their eager hands dropped continually the yellow empty shells, spinning into the crushed grass blades to remain there and mark for the belated eye the line of a battalion's fight.

All impatience, all rebellious feeling, had passed out of the men as soon as they had been allowed to use their weapons against the enemy. They now were absorbed in this business of hitting something, and all the long training at the rifle ranges, all the pride of the marksman which had been so long alive in them, made them forget for the time everything but shooting. They were as deliberate and exact as so many watchmakers.

A new sense of safety was rightfully upon them. They knew that those mysterious men in the high far trenches in front were having the bullets sping in their faces with relentless and remarkable precision; they knew, in fact, that they were now doing the thing which they had been trained endlessly to do, and they knew they were doing it well. Nolan, for instance, was overjoyed. "Plug 'em," he said: "Plug 'em." He laid his face to his rifle as if it were his mistress. He was aiming under the shadow of a certain portico of a fortified house: there he could faintly see a long black line which he knew to be a loop-hole cut for riflemen, and he knew that every shot of his was going there under the portico, mayhap through the loop-hole to the brain of another man like himself. He loaded the awkward magazine of his rifle again and again. He was so intent that he did not know of new orders until he saw the men about him scrambling to their feet and running forward, crouching low as they ran.

He heard a shout. "Come on, boys! We can't be last! We're going up! We're going up." He sprang to his feet and, stooping, ran with the others. Something fine, soft, gentle, touched his heart as he ran. He had loved the regiment, the army, because the regiment, the army, was his life,—he had no other outlook; and now these men, his comrades, were performing his dream-scenes for him; they were doing as he had ordained in his visions. It is curious that in this charge he considered himself as rather unworthy. Although he himself was in the assault with the rest of them, it seemed to him that his comrades were dazzlingly courageous. His part, to his mind, was merely that of a man who was going along with the crowd.

He saw Grierson biting madly with his pincers at a barbed-wire fence. They were half-way up the beautiful sylvan slope; there was no enemy to be seen, and yet the landscape rained bullets. Somebody punched him violently in the stomach. He thought dully to lie down and rest, but instead he fell with a crash.

The sparse line of men in blue shirts and dirty slouch hats swept on up the hill. He decided to shut his eyes for a moment because he felt very dreamy and peaceful. It seemed only a minute before he heard a voice say, "There he is." Grierson and Watkins had come to look for him. He searched their faces at once and keenly, for he had a thought that the line might be driven down the hill and leave him in Spanish hands. But he saw that everything was secure, and he prepared no questions.

"Nolan," said Grierson clumsily, "do you know me?"

The man on the ground smiled softly. "Of course I know you, you chowder-faced monkey. Why wouldn't I know you?"

Watkins knelt beside him. "Where did they plug you, old boy?"

Nolan was somewhat dubious. "It ain't much. I don't think but it's somewheres there." He laid a finger on the pit of his stomach. They lifted his shirt, and then privately they exchanged a glance of horror.

"Does it hurt, Jimmie?" said Grierson, hoarsely.

"No," said Nolan, "it don't hurt any, but I feel sort of dead-to-the-world and numb all over. I don't think it's very bad."

"Oh, it's all right," said Watkins.

"What I need is a drink," said Nolan, grinning at them. "I'm chilly— lying on this damp ground."

"It ain't very damp, Jimmie," said Grierson.

"Well, it is damp," said Nolan, with sudden irritability. "I can feel it. I'm wet, I tell you—wet through—just from lying here."

They answered hastily. "Yes, that's so, Jimmie. It is damp. That's so."

"Just put your hand under my back and see how wet the ground is," he said.

"No," they answered. "That's all right, Jimmie. We know it's wet."

"Well, put your hand under and see," he cried, stubbornly.

"Oh, never mind, Jimmie."

"No," he said, in a temper. "See for yourself." Grierson seemed to be afraid of Nolan's agitation, and so he slipped a hand under the prostrate man, and presently withdrew it covered with blood. "Yes," he said, hiding his hand carefully from Nolan's eyes, "you were right, Jimmie."

"Of course I was," said Nolan, contentedly closing his eyes. "This hillside holds water like a swamp." After a moment he said, "Guess I ought to know. I'm flat here on it, and you fellers are standing up."

He did not know he was dying. He thought he was holding an argument on the condition of the turf.

VI

"Cover his face," said Grierson, in a low and husky voice afterwards.

"What'll I cover it with?" said Watkins.

They looked at themselves. They stood in their shirts, trousers, leggings, shoes; they had nothing.

"Oh," said Grierson, "here's his hat." He brought it and laid it on the face of the dead man. They stood for a time. It was apparent that they thought it essential and decent to say or do something. Finally Watkins said in a broken voice, "Aw, it's a dam shame." They moved slowly off toward the firing line.

In the blue gloom of evening, in one of the fever-tents, the two rows of still figures became hideous, charnel. The languid movement of a hand was surrounded with spectral mystery, and the occasional painful twisting of a body under a blanket was terrifying, as if dead men were moving in their graves under the sod. A heavy odour of sickness and medicine hung in the air.

"What regiment are you in?" said a feeble voice.

"Twenty-ninth Infantry," answered another voice.

"Twenty-ninth! Why, the man on the other side of me is in the Twenty-ninth."

"He is?... Hey, there, partner, are you in the Twenty-ninth?"

A third voice merely answered wearily. "Martin of C Company."

"What? Jack, is that you?"

"It's part of me.... Who are you?"

"Grierson, you fat-head. I thought you were wounded."

There was the noise of a man gulping a great drink of water, and at its conclusion Martin said, "I am."

"Well, what you doin' in the fever-place, then?"

Martin replied with drowsy impatience. "Got the fever too."

"Gee!" said Grierson.

Thereafter there was silence in the fever-tent, save for the noise made by a man over in a corner—a kind of man always found in an American crowd—a heroic, implacable comedian and patriot, of a humour that has bitterness and ferocity and love in it, and he was wringing from the situation a grim meaning by singing the "Star-Spangled Banner" with all the ardour which could be procured from his fever-stricken body.

"Billie," called Martin in a low voice, "where's Jimmy Nolan?"

"He's dead," said Grierson.

A triangle of raw gold light shone on a side of the tent. Somewhere in the valley an engine's bell was ringing, and it sounded of peace and home as if it hung on a cow's neck.

"And where's Ike Watkins?"

"Well, he ain't dead, but he got shot through the lungs. They say he ain't got much show."

Through the clouded odours of sickness and medicine rang the dauntless voice of the man in the corner.

THE LONE CHARGE OF WILLIAM B. PERKINS

He could not distinguish between a five-inch quick-firing gun and a nickle-plated ice-pick, and so, naturally, he had been elected to fill the position of war-correspondent. The responsible party was the editor of the "Minnesota Herald." Perkins had no information of war, and no particular rapidity of mind for acquiring it, but he had that rank and fibrous quality of courage which springs from the thick soil of Western America.

It was morning in Guantanamo Bay. If the marines encamped on the hill had had time to turn their gaze seaward, they might have seen a small newspaper despatch-boat wending its way toward the entrance of the harbour over the blue, sunlit waters of the Caribbean. In the stern of this tug Perkins was seated upon some coal bags, while the breeze gently ruffled his greasy pajamas. He was staring at a brown line of entrenchments surmounted by a flag, which was Camp McCalla. In the harbour were anchored two or three grim, grey cruisers and a transport. As the tug steamed up the radiant channel, Perkins could see men moving on shore near the charred ruins of a village. Perkins was deeply moved; here already was more war than he had ever known in Minnesota. Presently he, clothed in the essential garments of a war-correspondent, was rowed to the sandy beach. Marines in yellow linen were handling an ammunition supply. They paid no attention to the visitor, being morose from the inconveniences of two days and nights of fighting. Perkins toiled up the zigzag path to the top of the hill, and looked with eager eyes at the trenches, the field-pieces, the funny little Colts, the flag, the grim marines lying wearily on their arms. And still more, he looked through the clear air over 1,000 yards of mysterious woods from which emanated at inopportune times repeated flocks of Mauser bullets.

Perkins was delighted. He was filled with admiration for these jaded and smoky men who lay so quietly in the trenches waiting for a resumption of guerilla enterprise. But he wished they would heed him. He wanted to talk about it. Save for sharp inquiring glances, no one acknowledged his existence.

Finally he approached two young lieutenants, and in his innocent Western way he asked them if they would like a drink. The effect on the two young lieutenants was immediate and astonishing. With one voice they answered, "Yes, we would." Perkins almost wept with joy at this amiable response, and he exclaimed that he would immediately board the tug and bring off a bottle of Scotch. This attracted the officers, and in a burst of confidence one explained that there had not been a drop in camp. Perkins lunged down the hill, and fled to his boat, where in his exuberance he engaged in a preliminary altercation with some whisky. Consequently he toiled again up the hill in the blasting sun with his enthusiasm in no ways abated. The parched officers were very gracious, and such was the state of mind of Perkins that he did not note properly how serious and solemn was his engagement with the whisky. And because of this fact, and because of his antecedents, there happened the lone charge of William B. Perkins.

Now, as Perkins went down the hill, something happened. A private in those high trenches found that a cartridge was clogged in his rifle. It then becomes necessary with most kinds of rifles to explode the cartridge. The private took the rifle to his captain, and explained the case. But it would not do in that camp to fire a rifle for mechanical purposes and without warning, because the eloquent sound would bring six hundred tired marines to tension and high expectancy. So the captain turned, and in a loud voice announced to the camp that he found it necessary to shoot into the air. The communication rang sharply from voice to voice. Then the captain raised the weapon and fired. Whereupon—and whereupon—a large line of guerillas lying in the bushes decided swiftly that their presence and position were discovered, and swiftly they volleyed.

In a moment the woods and the hills were alive with the crack and sputter of rifles. Men on the warships in the harbour heard the old familiar flut-flut-fluttery-fluttery-flut-flut-flut from the entrenchments. Incidentally the launch of the "Marblehead," commanded by one of our headlong American ensigns, streaked for the strategic woods like a galloping marine dragoon, peppering away with its blunderbuss in the bow.

Perkins had arrived at the foot of the hill, where began the arrangement of 150 marines that protected the short line of communication between the main body and the beach. These men had all swarmed into line behind fortifications improvised from the boxes of provisions. And to them were gathering naked men who had been bathing, naked men who arrayed themselves speedily in cartridge belts and rifles. The woods and the hills went flut-flut-flut-fluttery-fluttery-flut-fllllluttery-flut. Under the boughs of a beautiful tree lay five wounded men thinking vividly.

And now it befell Perkins to discover a Spaniard in the bush. The distance was some five hundred yards. In a loud voice he announced his perception. He also declared hoarsely, that if he only had a rifle, he would go and possess himself of this particular enemy. Immediately an amiable lad shot in the arm said: "Well, take mine." Perkins thus acquired a rifle and a clip of five cartridges.

"Come on!" he shouted. This part of the battalion was lying very tight, not yet being engaged, but not knowing when the business would swirl around to them.

To Perkins they replied with a roar. "Come back here, you —— fool. Do you want to get shot by your own crowd? Come back, —— ——!" As a detail, it might be mentioned that the fire from a part of the hill swept the journey upon which Perkins had started.

Now behold the solitary Perkins adrift in the storm of fighting, even as a champagne jacket of straw is lost in a great surf. He found it out quickly. Four seconds elapsed before he discovered that he was an almshouse idiot plunging through hot, crackling thickets on a June morning in Cuba. Sss-s-swing-sing-ing-pop went the lightning-swift metal grasshoppers over him and beside him. The beauties of rural Minnesota illuminated his conscience with the gold of lazy corn, with the sleeping green of meadows, with the cathedral gloom of pine forests. Sshsh-swing-pop! Perkins decided that if he cared to extract himself from a tangle of imbecility he must shoot. The entire situation was that he must shoot. It was necessary that he should shoot. Nothing would save him but shooting. It is a law that men thus decide when the waters of battle close over their minds. So with a prayer that the Americans would not

31

hit him in the back nor the left side, and that the Spaniards would not hit him in the front, he knelt like a supplicant alone in the desert of chaparral, and emptied his magazine at his Spaniard before he discovered that his Spaniard was a bit of dried palm branch.

Then Perkins flurried like a fish. His reason for being was a Spaniard in the bush. When the Spaniard turned into a dried palm branch, he could no longer furnish himself with one adequate reason.

Then did he dream frantically of some anthracite hiding-place, some profound dungeon of peace where blind mules live placidly chewing the far-gathered hay.

"Sss-swing-win-pop! Prut-prut-prrrut!" Then a field-gun spoke. "Boom-ra-swow-ow-ow-ow-pum." Then a Colt automatic began to bark. "Crack-crk-crk-crk-crk-crk" endlessly. Raked, enfiladed, flanked, surrounded, and overwhelmed, what hope was there for William B. Perkins of the "Minnesota Herald?"

But war is a spirit. War provides for those that it loves. It provides sometimes death and sometimes a singular and incredible safety. There were few ways in which it was possible to preserve Perkins. One way was by means of a steam-boiler.

Perkins espied near him an old, rusty steam-boiler lying in the bushes. War only knows how it was there, but there it was, a temple shining resplendent with safety. With a moan of haste, Perkins flung himself through that hole which expressed the absence of the steam-pipe.

Then ensconced in his boiler, Perkins comfortably listened to the ring of a fight which seemed to be in the air above him. Sometimes bullets struck their strong, swift blow against the boiler's sides, but none entered to interfere with Perkins's rest.

Time passed. The fight, short anyhow, dwindled to prut ... prut ... prut-prut ... prut. And when the silence came, Perkins might have been seen cautiously protruding from the boiler. Presently he strolled back toward the marine lines with his hat not able to fit his head for the new bumps of wisdom that were on it.

The marines, with an annoyed air, were settling down again when an apparitional figure came from the bushes. There was great excitement.

"It's that crazy man," they shouted, and as he drew near they gathered tumultuously about him and demanded to know how he had accomplished it.

Perkins made a gesture, the gesture of a man escaping from an unintentional mud-bath, the gesture of a man coming out of battle, and then he told them.

The incredulity was immediate and general. "Yes, you did! What? In an old boiler? An old boiler? Out in that brush? Well, we guess not." They did not believe him until two days later, when a patrol happened to find the rusty boiler, relic of some curious transaction in the ruin of the Cuban sugar industry. The patrol then marvelled at the truthfulness of war-correspondents until they were almost blind.

Soon after his adventure Perkins boarded the tug, wearing a countenance of poignant thoughtfulness.

THE CLAN OF NO-NAME

I

Unwind my riddle.

Cruel as hawks the hours fly;

Wounded men seldom come home to die;

The hard waves see an arm flung high;

Scorn hits strong because of a lie;

Yet there exists a mystic tie.

Unwind my riddle.

She was out in the garden. Her mother came to her rapidly. "Margharita! Margharita, Mister Smith is here! Come!" Her mother was fat and commercially excited. Mister Smith was a matter of some importance to all Tampa people, and since he was really in love with Margharita he was distinctly of more importance to this particular household.

Palm trees tossed their sprays over the fence toward the rutted sand of the street. A little foolish fish-pond in the centre of the garden emitted a sound of red-fins flipping, flipping. "No, mamma," said the girl, "let Mr. Smith wait. I like the garden in the moonlight."

Her mother threw herself into that state of virtuous astonishment which is the weapon of her kind. "Margharita!"

The girl evidently considered herself to be a privileged belle, for she answered quite carelessly, "Oh, let him wait."

The mother threw abroad her arms with a semblance of great high-minded suffering and withdrew. Margharita walked alone in the moonlit garden. Also an electric light threw its shivering gleam over part of her parade.

There was peace for a time. Then suddenly through the faint brown palings was struck an envelope white and square. Margharita approached this envelope with an indifferent stride. She hummed a silly air, she bore herself casually, but there was something that made her grasp it hard, a peculiar muscular exhibition, not discernible to indifferent eyes. She did not clutch it, but she took it—simply took it in a way that meant everything, and, to measure it by vision, it was a picture of the most complete disregard.

She stood straight for a moment; then she drew from her bosom a photograph and thrust it through the palings. She walked rapidly into the house.

II

A man in garb of blue and white—something relating to what we call bed-ticking—was seated in a curious little cupola on the top of a Spanish blockhouse. The blockhouse sided a white military road that curved away from the man's sight into a blur of trees. On all sides of him were fields of tall grass, studded with palms and lined with fences of barbed wire. The sun beat aslant through the trees and the man sped his eyes deep into the dark tropical shadows that seemed velvet with coolness. These tranquil vistas resembled painted scenery in a theatre, and, moreover, a hot, heavy silence lay upon the land.

The soldier in the watching place leaned an unclean Mauser rifle in a corner, and, reaching down, took a glowing coal on a bit of palm bark handed up to him by a comrade. The men below were mainly asleep. The sergeant in command drowsed near the open door, the arm above his head, showing his long keen-angled chevrons attached carelessly with safety-pins. The sentry lit his cigarette and puffed languorously.

Suddenly he heard from the air around him the querulous, deadly-swift spit of rifle-bullets, and, an instant later, the poppety-pop of a small volley sounded in his face, close, as if it were fired only ten feet away. Involuntarily he threw back his head quickly as if he were protecting his nose from a falling tile. He screamed an alarm and fell into the blockhouse. In the gloom of it, men with their breaths coming sharply between their teeth, were tumbling wildly for positions at the loop-holes. The door had been slammed, but the sergeant lay just within, propped up as when he drowsed, but now with blood flowing steadily over the hand that he pressed flatly to his chest. His face was in stark yellow agony; he chokingly repeated: "Fuego! Por Dios, hombres!"

The men's ill-conditioned weapons were jammed through the loop-holes and they began to fire from all four sides of the blockhouse from the simple data, apparently, that the enemy were in the vicinity. The fumes of burnt powder grew stronger and stronger in the little square fortress. The rattling of the magazine locks was incessant, and the interior might have been that of a gloomy manufactory if it were not for the sergeant down under the feet of the men, coughing out: "Por Dios, hombres! Por Dios! Fuego!"

III

A string of five Cubans, in linen that had turned earthy brown in colour, slid through the woods at a pace that was neither a walk nor a run. It was a kind of rack. In fact the whole manner of the men, as they thus moved, bore a rather comic resemblance to the American pacing horse. But they had come many miles since sun-up over mountainous and half-marked paths, and were plainly still fresh. The men were all practicos—guides. They made no sound in their swift travel, but moved their half-shod feet with the skill of cats. The woods lay around them in a deep silence, such as one might find at the bottom of a lake.

Suddenly the leading practico raised his hand. The others pulled up short and dropped the butts of their weapons calmly and noiselessly to the ground. The leader whistled a low note and immediately another practico appeared from the bushes. He moved close to the leader without a word, and then they spoke in whispers.

"There are twenty men and a sergeant in the blockhouse."

"And the road?"

"One company of cavalry passed to the east this morning at seven o'clock. They were escorting four carts. An hour later, one horseman rode swiftly to the westward. About noon, ten infantry soldiers with a corporal were taken from the big fort and put in the first blockhouse, to the east of the fort. There were already twelve men there. We saw a Spanish column moving off toward Mariel."

"No more?"

"No more."

"Good. But the cavalry?"

"It is all right. They were going a long march."

"The expedition is a half league behind. Go and tell the general."

The scout disappeared. The five other men lifted their guns and resumed their rapid and noiseless progress. A moment later no sound broke the stillness save the thump of a mango, as it dropped lazily from its tree to the grass. So strange had been the apparition of these men, their dress had been so allied in colour to the soil, their passing had so little disturbed the solemn rumination of the forest, and their going had been so like a spectral dissolution, that a witness could have wondered if he dreamed.

IV

A small expedition had landed with arms from the United States, and had now come out of the hills and to the edge of a wood. Before them was a long-grassed rolling prairie marked with palms. A half-mile away was the military road, and they could see the top of a blockhouse. The insurgent scouts were moving somewhere off in the grass. The general sat comfortably under a tree, while his staff of three young officers stood about him chatting. Their linen clothing was notable from being distinctly whiter than those of the men who, one hundred and fifty in number, lay on the ground in a long brown fringe, ragged—indeed, bare in many places—but singularly reposeful, unworried, veteran-like.

The general, however, was thoughtful. He pulled continually at his little thin moustache. As far as the heavily patrolled and guarded military road was concerned, the insurgents had been in the habit of dashing across it in small bodies whenever they pleased, but to safely scoot over it with a valuable convoy of arms, was decidedly a more important thing. So the general awaited the return of his practicos with anxiety. The still pampas betrayed no sign of their existence.

The general gave some orders and an officer counted off twenty men to go with him, and delay any attempt of the troop of cavalry to return from the eastward. It was not an easy task, but it was a familiar task—checking the advance of a greatly superior force by a very hard fire from concealment. A few rifles had often bayed a strong column for sufficient length of time for all strategic purposes. The twenty men pulled themselves together tranquilly. They looked quite indifferent. Indeed, they had the supremely casual manner of old soldiers, hardened to battle as a condition of existence.

Thirty men were then told off, whose function it was to worry and rag at the blockhouse, and check any advance from the westward. A hundred men, carrying precious burdens—besides their own equipment—were to pass in as much of a rush as possible between these two wings, cross the road and skip for the hills, their retreat being covered by a combination of the two firing parties. It was a trick that needed both luck and neat arrangement. Spanish columns were for ever prowling through this province in all directions and at all times. Insurgent bands—the lightest of light infantry—were kept on the jump, even when they were not incommoded by fifty boxes, each one large enough for the coffin of a little man, and heavier than if the little man were in it; and fifty small but formidable boxes of ammunition.

The carriers stood to their boxes and the firing parties leaned on their rifles. The general arose and strolled to and fro, his hands behind him. Two of his staff were jesting at the third, a young man with a face less bronzed, and with very new accoutrements. On the strap of his cartouche were a gold star and a silver star, placed in a horizontal line, denoting that he was a second lieutenant. He seemed very happy; he laughed at all their jests, although his eye roved continually over the sunny grass-lands, where was going to happen his first fight. One of his stars was bright, like his hopes, the other was pale, like death.

Two practicos came racking out of the grass. They spoke rapidly to the general; he turned and nodded to his officers. The two firing parties filed out and diverged toward their positions. The general watched them through his glasses. It was strange to note how soon they were dim to the unaided eye. The little patches of brown in the green grass did not look like men at all.

Practicos continually ambled up to the general. Finally he turned and made a sign to the bearers. The first twenty men in line picked up their boxes, and this movement rapidly spread to the tail of the line. The weighted procession moved painfully out upon the sunny prairie. The general, marching at the head of it, glanced continually back as if he were compelled to drag behind him some ponderous iron chain. Besides the obvious mental worry, his face bore an expression of intense physical strain, and he even bent his shoulders, unconsciously tugging at the chain to hurry it through this enemy-crowded valley.

V

The fight was opened by eight men who, snuggling in the grass, within three hundred yards of the blockhouse, suddenly blazed away at the bed-ticking figure in the cupola and at the open door where they could see vague outlines. Then they laughed and yelled insulting language, for they knew that as far as the Spaniards were concerned, the surprise was as much as having a diamond bracelet turn to soap. It was this volley that smote the sergeant and caused the man in the cupola to scream and tumble from his perch.

The eight men, as well as all other insurgents within fair range, had chosen good positions for lying close, and for a time they let the blockhouse rage, although the soldiers therein could occasionally hear, above the clamour of their weapons, shrill and almost wolfish calls, coming from men whose lips were laid against the ground. But it is not in the nature of them of Spanish blood, and armed with rifles, to long endure the sight of anything so tangible as an enemy's blockhouse without shooting at it—other conditions being partly favourable. Presently the steaming soldiers in the little fort could hear the sping and shiver of bullets striking the wood that guarded their bodies.

A perfectly white smoke floated up over each firing Cuban, the penalty of the Remington rifle, but about the blockhouse there was only the lightest gossamer of blue. The blockhouse stood always for some big, clumsy and rather incompetent animal, while the insurgents, scattered on two sides of it, were little enterprising creatures of another species, too wise to come too near, but joyously raging at its easiest flanks and drilling the lead into its sides in a way to make it fume, and spit and rave like the tom-cat when the glad, free-band fox-hound pups catch him in the lane.

The men, outlying in the grass, chuckled deliriously at the fury of the Spanish fire. They howled opprobrium to encourage the Spaniards to fire more ill-used, incapable bullets. Whenever an insurgent was about to fire, he ordinarily prefixed the affair with a speech. "Do you want something to eat? Yes? All right." Bang! "Eat that." The more common expressions of the incredibly foul Spanish tongue were trifles light as air in this badinage, which was shrieked out from the grass during the spin of bullets, and the dull rattle of the shooting.

But at some time there came a series of sounds from the east that began in a few disconnected pruts and ended as if an amateur was trying to play the long roll upon a muffled drum. Those of the insurgents in the blockhouse attacking party, who had neighbours in the grass, turned and looked at them seriously. They knew what the new sound meant. It meant that the twenty men who had gone to the eastward were now engaged. A column of some kind was approaching from that direction, and they knew by the clatter that it was a solemn occasion.

In the first place, they were now on the wrong side of the road. They were obliged to cross it to rejoin the main body, provided of course that the main body succeeded itself in crossing it. To accomplish this, the party at the blockhouse would have to move to the eastward, until out of sight or good range of the maddened little fort. But judging from the heaviness of the firing, the party of twenty who protected the east were almost sure to be driven immediately back. Hence travel in that direction would become exceedingly hazardous. Hence a man looked seriously at his neighbour. It might easily be that in a moment they were to become an isolated force and woefully on the wrong side of the road.

Any retreat to the westward was absurd, since primarily they would have to widely circle the blockhouse, and more than that, they could hear, even now in that direction, Spanish bugle calling to Spanish bugle, far and near, until one would think that every man in Cuba was a trumpeter, and had come forth to parade his talent.

VI

The insurgent general stood in the middle of the road gnawing his lips. Occasionally, he stamped a foot and beat his hands passionately together. The carriers were streaming past him, patient, sweating fellows, bowed under their burdens, but they could not move fast enough for him when others of his men were engaged both to the east and to the west, and he, too, knew from the sound that those to the east were in a sore way. Moreover, he could hear that accursed bugling, bugling, bugling in the west.

He turned suddenly to the new lieutenant who stood behind him, pale and quiet. "Did you ever think a hundred men were so many?" he cried, incensed to the point of beating them. Then he said longingly: "Oh, for a half an hour! Or even twenty minutes!"

A practico racked violently up from the east. It is characteristic of these men that, although they take a certain roadster gait and hold it for ever, they cannot really run, sprint, race. "Captain Rodriguez is attacked by two hundred men, señor, and the cavalry is behind them. He wishes to know——"

The general was furious; he pointed. "Go! Tell Rodriguez to hold his place for twenty minutes, even if he leaves every man dead."

The practico shambled hastily off.

The last of the carriers were swarming across the road. The rifle-drumming in the east was swelling out and out, evidently coming slowly nearer. The general bit his nails. He wheeled suddenly upon the young lieutenant. "Go to Bas at the blockhouse. Tell him to hold the devil himself for ten minutes and then bring his men out of that place."

The long line of bearers was crawling like a dun worm toward the safety of the foot-hills. High bullets sang a faint song over the aide as he saluted. The bugles had in the west ceased, and that was more ominous than bugling.

It meant that the Spanish troops were about to march, or perhaps that they had marched.

The young lieutenant ran along the road until he came to the bend which marked the range of sight from the blockhouse. He drew his machete, his stunning new machete, and hacked feverishly at the barbed wire fence which lined the north side of the road at that point. The first wire was obdurate, because it was too high for his stroke, but two more cut like candy, and he stepped over the remaining one, tearing his trousers in passing on the lively serpentine ends of the severed wires. Once out in the field and bullets seemed to know him and call for him and speak their wish to kill him. But he ran on, because it was his duty, and because he would be shamed before men if he did not do his duty, and because he was desolate out there all alone in the fields with death.

A man running in this manner from the rear was in immensely greater danger than those who lay snug and close. But he did not know it. He thought because he was five hundred—four hundred and fifty—four hundred yards away from the enemy and the others were only three hundred yards away that they were in far more peril. He ran to join them because of his opinion. He did not care to do it, but he thought that was what men of his kind would do in such a case. There was a standard and he must follow it, obey it, because it was a monarch, the Prince of Conduct.

A bewildered and alarmed face raised itself from the grass and a voice cried to him: "Drop, Manolo! Drop! Drop!" He recognised Bas and flung himself to the earth beside him.

"Why," he said panting, "what's the matter?"

"Matter?" said Bas. "You are one of the most desperate and careless officers I know. When I saw you coming I wouldn't have given a peseta for your life."

"Oh, no," said the young aide. Then he repeated his orders rapidly. But he was hugely delighted. He knew Bas well; Bas was a pupil of Maceo; Bas invariably led his men; he never was a mere spectator of their battle; he was known for it throughout the western end of the island. The new officer had early achieved a part of his ambition—to be called a brave man by established brave men.

"Well, if we get away from here quickly it will be better for us," said Bas, bitterly. "I've lost six men killed, and more wounded. Rodriguez can't hold his position there, and in a little time more than a thousand men will come from the other direction."

He hissed a low call, and later the young aide saw some of the men sneaking off with the wounded, lugging them on their backs as porters carry sacks. The fire from the blockhouse had become a-weary, and as the insurgent fire also slackened, Bas and the young lieutenant lay in the weeds listening to the approach of the eastern fight, which was sliding toward them like a door to shut them off.

Bas groaned. "I leave my dead. Look there." He swung his hand in a gesture and the lieutenant looking saw a corpse. He was not stricken as he expected; there was very little blood; it was a mere thing.

"Time to travel," said Bas suddenly. His imperative hissing brought his men near him; there were a few hurried questions and answers; then, characteristically, the men turned in the grass, lifted their rifles, and fired a last volley into the blockhouse, accompanying it with their shrill cries. Scrambling low to the ground, they were off in a winding line for safety. Breathing hard, the lieutenant stumbled his way forward. Behind him he could hear the men calling each to each: "Segue! Segue! Segue! Go on! Get out! Git!" Everybody understood that the peril of crossing the road was compounding from minute to minute.

VII

When they reached the gap through which the expedition had passed, they fled out upon the road like scared wild-fowl tracking along a sea-beach. A cloud of blue figures far up this dignified shaded avenue, fired at once. The men already had begun to laugh as they shied one by one across the road. "Segue! Segue!" The hard part for the nerves had been the lack of information of the amount of danger. Now that they could see it, they accounted it all the more lightly for their previous anxiety.

Over in the other field, Bas and the young lieutenant found Rodriguez, his machete in one hand, his revolver in the other, smoky, dirty, sweating. He shrugged his shoulders when he saw them and pointed disconsolately to the brown thread of carriers moving toward the foot-hills. His own men were crouched in line just in front of him blazing like a prairie fire.

Now began the fight of a scant rear-guard to hold back the pressing Spaniards until the carriers could reach the top of the ridge, a mile away. This ridge by the way was more steep than any roof; it conformed, more, to the sides of a French war-ship. Trees grew vertically from it, however, and a man burdened only with his rifle usually pulled himself wheezingly up in a sort of ladder-climbing process, grabbing the slim trunks above him. How the loaded carriers were to conquer it in a hurry, no one knew. Rodriguez shrugged his shoulders as one who would say with philosophy, smiles, tears, courage: "Isn't this a mess!"

At an order, the men scattered back for four hundred yards with the rapidity and mystery of a handful of pebbles flung in the night. They left one behind who cried out, but it was now a game in which some were sure to be left behind to cry out.

The Spaniards deployed on the road and for twenty minutes remained there pouring into the field such a fire from their magazines as was hardly heard at Gettysburg. As a matter of truth the insurgents were at this time doing very little shooting, being chary of ammunition. But it is possible for the soldier to confuse himself with his own noise and undoubtedly the Spanish troops thought throughout their din that they were being fiercely engaged. Moreover, a firing-line—particularly at night or when opposed to a hidden foe—is nothing less than an emotional chord, a chord of a harp that sings because a puff of air arrives or when a bit of down touches it. This is always true of new troops or stupid troops and these troops were rather stupid troops. But, the way in which they mowed the verdure in the distance was a sight for a farmer.

Presently the insurgents slunk back to another position where they fired enough shots to stir again the Spaniards into an opinion that they were in a heavy fight. But such a misconception could only endure for a number of minutes. Presently it was plain that the Spaniards were about to advance and, moreover, word was brought to Rodriguez that a small band of guerillas were already making an attempt to worm around the right flank. Rodriguez cursed despairingly; he sent both Bas and the young lieutenant to that end of the line to hold the men to their work as long as possible.

In reality the men barely needed the presence of their officers. The kind of fighting left practically everything to the discretion of the individual and they arrived at concert of action mainly because of the equality of experience, in the wisdoms of bushwhacking.

The yells of the guerillas could plainly be heard and the insurgents answered in kind. The young lieutenant found desperate work on the right flank. The men were raving mad with it, babbling, tearful, almost frothing at the mouth. Two terrible bloody creatures passed him, creeping on all fours, and one in a whimper was calling upon God, his mother, and a saint. The guerillas, as effectually concealed as the insurgents, were driving their bullets low through the smoke at sight of a flame, a movement of the grass or sight of a patch of dirty brown coat. They were no column-o'-four soldiers; they were as slinky and snaky and quick as so many Indians. They were, moreover, native Cubans and because of their treachery to the one-star flag, they never by any chance received quarter if they fell into the hands of the insurgents. Nor, if the case was reversed, did they ever give quarter. It was life and life, death and death; there was no middle ground, no compromise. If a man's crowd was rapidly retreating and he was tumbled over by a slight hit, he should curse the sacred graves that the wound was not through the precise centre of his heart. The machete is a fine broad blade but it is not so nice as a drilled hole in the chest; no man wants his death-bed to be a shambles. The men fighting on the insurgents' right knew that if they fell they were lost.

On the extreme right, the young lieutenant found five men in a little saucer-like hollow. Two were dead, one was wounded and staring blankly at the sky and two were emptying hot rifles furiously. Some of the guerillas had snaked into positions only a hundred yards away.

The young man rolled in among the men in the saucer. He could hear the barking of the guerillas and the screams of the two insurgents. The rifles were popping and spitting in his face, it seemed, while the whole land was alive with a noise of rolling and drumming. Men could have gone drunken in all this flashing and flying and snarling and din, but at this time he was very deliberate. He knew that he was thrusting himself into a trap whose door, once closed, opened only when the black hand knocked and every part of him seemed to be in panic-stricken revolt. But something controlled him; something moved him inexorably in one direction; he perfectly understood but he was only sad, sad with a serene dignity, with the countenance of a mournful young prince. He was of a kind—that seemed to be it—and the men of his kind, on peak or plain, from the dark northern ice-fields to the hot wet jungles, through all wine and want, through all lies and unfamiliar truth, dark or light, the men of his kind were governed by their gods, and each man knew the law and yet could not give tongue to it, but it was the law and if the spirits of the men of his kind were all sitting in critical judgment upon him even then in the sky, he could not have bettered his conduct; he needs must obey the law and always with the law there is only one way. But from peak and plain, from dark northern ice-fields and hot wet jungles, through wine and want, through all lies and unfamiliar truth, dark or light, he heard breathed to him the approval and the benediction of his brethren.

He stooped and gently took a dead man's rifle and some cartridges. The battle was hurrying, hurrying, hurrying, but he was in no haste. His glance caught the staring eye of the wounded soldier, and he smiled at him quietly. The man—simple doomed peasant—was not of his kind, but the law on fidelity was clear.

He thrust a cartridge into the Remington and crept up beside the two unhurt men. Even as he did so, three or four bullets cut so close to him that all his flesh tingled. He fired carefully into the smoke. The guerillas were certainly not now more than fifty yards away.

He raised him coolly for his second shot, and almost instantly it was as if some giant had struck him in the chest with a beam. It whirled him in a great spasm back into the saucer. As he put his two hands to his breast, he could hear the guerillas screeching exultantly, every throat vomiting forth all the infamy of a language prolific in the phrasing of infamy.

One of the other men came rolling slowly down the slope, while his rifle followed him, and, striking another rifle, clanged out. Almost immediately the survivor howled and fled wildly. A whole volley missed him and then one or more shots caught him as a bird is caught on the wing.

The young lieutenant's body seemed galvanised from head to foot. He concluded that he was not hurt very badly, but when he tried to move he found that he could not lift his hands from his breast. He had turned to lead. He had had a plan of taking a photograph from his pocket and looking at it.

There was a stir in the grass at the edge of the saucer, and a man appeared there, looking where lay the four insurgents. His negro face was not an eminently ferocious one in its lines, but now it was lit with an illimitable blood-greed. He and the young lieutenant exchanged a singular glance; then he came stepping eagerly down. The young lieutenant closed his eyes, for he did not want to see the flash of the machete.

VIII

The Spanish colonel was in a rage, and yet immensely proud; immensely proud, and yet in a rage of disappointment. There had been a fight and the insurgents had retreated leaving their dead, but still a valuable expedition had broken through his lines and escaped to the mountains. As a matter of truth, he was not sure whether to be wholly delighted or wholly angry, for well he knew that the importance lay not so much in the truthful account of the action as it did in the heroic prose of the official report, and in the fight itself lay material for a purple splendid poem. The insurgents had run away; no one could deny it; it was plain even to whatever privates had fired with their eyes shut. This was worth a loud blow and splutter. However, when all was said and done, he could not help but reflect that if he had captured this expedition, he would have been a brigadier-general, if not more.

He was a short, heavy man with a beard, who walked in a manner common to all elderly Spanish officers, and to many young ones; that is to say, he walked as if his spine was a stick and a little longer than his body; as if he suffered from some disease of the backbone, which allowed him but scant use of his legs. He toddled along the road, gesticulating disdainfully and muttering: "Ca! Ca! Ca!"

He berated some soldiers for an immaterial thing, and as he approached the men stepped precipitately back as if he were a fire-engine. They were most of them young fellows, who displayed, when under orders, the manner of so many faithful dogs. At present, they were black, tongue-hanging, thirsty boys, bathed in the nervous weariness of the after-battle time.

Whatever he may truly have been in character, the colonel closely resembled a gluttonous and libidinous old pig, filled from head to foot with the pollution of a sinful life. "Ca!" he snarled, as he toddled. "Ca! Ca!" The soldiers saluted as they backed to the side of the road. The air was full of the odour of burnt rags. Over on the prairie guerillas and regulars were rummaging the grass. A few unimportant shots sounded from near the base of the hills.

A guerilla, glad with plunder, came to a Spanish captain. He held in his hand a photograph. "Mira, señor. I took this from the body of an officer whom I killed machete to machete."

The captain shot from the corner of his eye a cynical glance at the guerilla, a glance which commented upon the last part of the statement. "M-m-m," he said. He took the photograph and gazed with a slow faint smile, the smile of a man who knows bloodshed and homes and love, at the face of a girl. He turned the photograph presently, and on the back of it was written: "One lesson in English I will give you—this: I love you, Margharita." The photograph had been taken in Tampa.

The officer was silent for a half-minute, while his face still wore the slow faint smile. "Pobrecetto," he murmured finally, with a philosophic sigh, which was brother to a shrug. Without deigning a word to the guerilla he thrust the photograph in his pocket and walked away.

High over the green earth, in the dizzy blue heights, some great birds were slowly circling with down-turned beaks.

IX

Margharita was in the gardens. The blue electric rays shone through the plumes of the palm and shivered in feathery images on the walk. In the little foolish fish-pond some stalwart fish was apparently bullying the others, for often there sounded a frantic splashing.

Her mother came to her rapidly. "Margharita! Mister Smith is here! Come!"

"Oh, is he?" cried the girl. She followed her mother to the house. She swept into the little parlor with a grand air, the egotism of a savage. Smith had heard the whirl of her skirts in the hall, and his heart, as usual, thumped hard enough to make him gasp. Every time he called, he would sit waiting with the dull fear in his breast that her mother would enter and indifferently announce that she had gone up to heaven or off to New York, with one of his dream-rivals, and he would never see her again in this wide world. And he would conjure up tricks to then escape from the house without any one observing his face break up into furrows. It was part of his love to believe in the absolute treachery of his adored one. So whenever he heard the whirl of her skirts in the hall he felt that he had again leased happiness from a dark fate.

She was rosily beaming and all in white. "Why, Mister Smith," she exclaimed, as if he was the last man in the world she expected to see.

"Good-evenin'," he said, shaking hands nervously. He was always awkward and unlike himself, at the beginning of one of these calls. It took him some time to get into form.

She posed her figure in operatic style on a chair before him, and immediately galloped off a mile of questions, information of herself, gossip and general outcries which left him no obligation, but to look beamingly intelligent and from time to time say: "Yes?" His personal joy, however, was to stare at her beauty.

When she stopped and wandered as if uncertain which way to talk, there was a minute of silence, which each of them had been educated to feel was very incorrect; very incorrect indeed. Polite people always babbled at each other like two brooks.

He knew that the responsibility was upon him, and, although his mind was mainly upon the form of the proposal of marriage which he intended to make later, it was necessary that he should maintain his reputation as a well-bred man by saying something at once. It flashed upon him to ask: "Won't you please play?" But the time for the piano ruse was not yet; it was too early. So he said the first thing that came into his head: "Too bad about young Manolo Prat being killed over there in Cuba, wasn't it?"

"Wasn't it a pity?" she answered.

"They say his mother is heart-broken," he continued. "They're afraid she's goin' to die."

"And wasn't it queer that we didn't hear about it for almost two months?"

"Well, it's no use tryin' to git quick news from there."

Presently they advanced to matters more personal, and she used upon him a series of star-like glances which rumpled him at once to squalid slavery. He gloated upon her, afraid, afraid, yet more avaricious than a thousand misers. She fully comprehended; she laughed and taunted him with her eyes. She impressed upon him that she was like a will-o'-the-wisp, beautiful beyond compare but impossible, almost impossible, at least very difficult; then again, suddenly, impossible—impossible—impossible. He was glum; he would never dare propose to this radiance; it was like asking to be pope.

A moment later, there chimed into the room something that he knew to be a more tender note. The girl became dreamy as she looked at him; her voice lowered to a delicious intimacy of tone. He leaned forward; he was about to outpour his bully-ragged soul in fine words, when—presto—she was the most casual person he had ever laid eyes upon, and was asking him about the route of the proposed trolley line.

But nothing short of a fire could stop him now. He grabbed her hand. "Margharita," he murmured gutturally, "I want you to marry me."

She glared at him in the most perfect lie of astonishment. "What do you say?"

He arose, and she thereupon arose also and fled back a step. He could only stammer out her name. And thus they stood, defying the principles of the dramatic art.

"I love you," he said at last.

"How—how do I know you really—truly love me?" she said, raising her eyes timorously to his face and this timorous glance, this one timorous glance, made him the superior person in an instant. He went forward as confident as a grenadier, and, taking both her hands, kissed her.

That night she took a stained photograph from her dressing-table and holding it over the candle burned it to nothing, her red lips meanwhile parted with the intentness of her occupation. On the back of the photograph was written: "One lesson in English I will give you—this: I love you."

For the word is clear only to the kind who on peak or plain, from dark northern ice-fields to the hot wet jungles, through all wine and want, through lies and unfamiliar truth, dark or light, are governed by the unknown gods, and though each man knows the law, no man may give tongue to it.

GOD REST YE, MERRY GENTLEMEN

Little Nell, sometimes called the Blessed Damosel, was a war correspondent for the New York Eclipse, and at sea on the despatch boats he wore pajamas, and on shore he wore whatever fate allowed him, which clothing was in the main unsuitable to the climate. He had been cruising in the Caribbean on a small tug, awash always, habitable never, wildly looking for Cervera's fleet; although what he was going to do with four armoured cruisers and two destroyers in the event of his really finding them had not been explained by the managing editor. The cable instructions read:—"Take tug; go find Cervera's fleet." If his unfortunate nine-knot craft should happen to find these great twenty-knot ships, with their two spiteful and faster attendants, Little Nell had wondered how he was going to lose them again. He had marvelled, both publicly and in secret, on the uncompromising asininity of managing editors at odd moments, but he had wasted little time. The Jefferson G. Johnson was already coaled, so he passed the word to his skipper, bought some tinned meats, cigars, and beer, and soon the Johnson sailed on her mission, tooting her whistle in graceful farewell to some friends of hers in the bay.

So the Johnson crawled giddily to one wave-height after another, and fell, aslant, into one valley after another for a longer period than was good for the hearts of the men, because the Johnson was merely a harbour-tug, with no architectural intention of parading the high-seas, and the crew had never seen the decks all white water like a mere sunken reef. As for the cook, he blasphemed hopelessly hour in and hour out, meanwhile pursuing the equipment of his trade frantically from side to side of the galley. Little Nell dealt with a great deal of grumbling, but he knew it was not the real evil grumbling. It was merely the unhappy words of men who wished expression of comradeship for their wet, forlorn, half-starved lives, to which, they explained, they were not accustomed, and for which, they explained, they were not properly paid. Little Nell condoled and condoled without difficulty. He laid words of gentle sympathy before them, and smothered his own misery behind the face of a reporter of the New York Eclipse. But they tossed themselves in their cockleshell even as far as Martinique; they knew many races and many flags, but they did not find Cervera's fleet. If they had found that elusive squadron this timid story would never have been written; there would probably have been a lyric. The Johnson limped one morning into the Mole St. Nicholas, and there Little Nell received this despatch:—"Can't understand your inaction. What are you doing with the boat? Report immediately. Fleet transports already left Tampa. Expected destination near Santiago. Proceed there immediately. Place yourself under orders.—Rogers, Eclipse."

One day, steaming along the high, luminous blue coast of Santiago province, they fetched into view the fleets, a knot of masts and funnels, looking incredibly inshore, as if they were glued to the mountains. Then mast left mast, and funnel left funnel, slowly, slowly, and the shore remained still, but the fleets seemed to move out toward the eager Johnson. At the speed of nine knots an hour the scene separated into its parts. On an easily rolling sea, under a crystal sky, black-hulled transports—erstwhile packets—lay waiting, while grey cruisers and gunboats lay near shore, shelling the beach and some woods. From their grey sides came thin red flashes, belches of white smoke, and then over the waters sounded boom—boom—boom-boom. The crew of the Jefferson G. Johnson forgave Little Nell all the suffering of a previous fortnight.

To the westward, about the mouth of Santiago harbour, sat a row of castellated grey battleships, their eyes turned another way, waiting.

The Johnson swung past a transport whose decks and rigging were aswarm with black figures, as if a tribe of bees had alighted upon a log. She swung past a cruiser indignant at being left out of the game, her deck thick with white-clothed tars watching the play of their luckier brethren. The cold blue, lifting seas tilted the big ships easily, slowly, and heaved the little ones in the usual sinful way, as if very little babes had surreptitiously mounted sixteen-hand trotting hunters. The Johnson leered and tumbled her way through a community of ships. The bombardment ceased, and some of the troopships edged in near the land. Soon boats black with men and towed by launches were almost lost to view in the scintillant mystery of light which appeared where the sea met the land. A disembarkation had begun. The Johnson sped on at her nine knots, and Little Nell chafed exceedingly, gloating upon the shore through his glasses, anon glancing irritably over the side to note the efforts of the excited tug. Then at last they were in a sort of a cove, with troopships, newspaper boats, and cruisers on all sides of them, and over the water came a great hum of human voices, punctuated frequently by the clang of engine-room gongs as the steamers manoeuvred to avoid jostling.

In reality it was the great moment—the moment for which men, ships, islands, and continents had been waiting for months; but somehow it did not look it. It was very calm; a certain strip of high, green, rocky shore was being rapidly populated from boat after boat; that was all. Like many preconceived moments, it refused to be supreme.

But nothing lessened Little Nell's frenzy. He knew that the army was landing—he could see it; and little did he care if the great moment did not look its part—it was his virtue as a correspondent to recognise the great moment in any disguise. The Johnson lowered a boat for him, and he dropped into it swiftly, forgetting everything. However, the mate, a bearded philanthropist, flung after him a mackintosh and a bottle of whisky. Little Nell's face was turned toward those other boats filled with men, all eyes upon the placid, gentle, noiseless shore. Little Nell saw many soldiers seated stiffly beside upright rifle barrels, their blue breasts crossed with white shelter tent and blanket-rolls. Launches screeched; jack-tars pushed or pulled with their boathooks; a beach was alive with working soldiers, some of them stark naked. Little Nell's boat touched the shore amid a babble of tongues, dominated at that time by a single stern voice, which was repeating, "Fall in, B Company!"

He took his mackintosh and his bottle of whisky and invaded Cuba. It was a trifle bewildering. Companies of those same men in blue and brown were being rapidly formed and marched off across a little open space—near a pool—near some palm trees—near a house—into the hills. At one side, a mulatto in dirty linen and an old straw hat was hospitably using a machete to cut open some green cocoanuts for a group of idle invaders. At the other side, up a bank, a blockhouse was burning furiously; while near it some railway sheds were smouldering, with a little Roger's engine standing amid the ruins, grey, almost white, with ashes until it resembled a ghost. Little Nell dodged the encrimsoned blockhouse, and proceeded where he saw a little village street lined with flimsy wooden cottages. Some ragged Cuban cavalrymen were tranquilly tending their horses in a shed which had not yet grown cold of the Spanish occupation. Three American soldiers were trying to explain to a Cuban that they wished to buy drinks. A native rode by, clubbing his pony, as always. The sky was blue; the sea talked with a gravelly accent at the feet of some rocks; upon its bosom the ships sat quiet as gulls. There was no mention, directly, of invasion—invasion for war—save in the roar of the flames at the blockhouse; but none even heeded this conflagration, excepting to note that it threw out a great heat. It was warm, very warm. It was really hard for Little Nell to keep from thinking of his own affairs: his debts, other misfortunes, loves, prospects of happiness. Nobody was in a flurry; the Cubans were not tearfully grateful; the American troops were visibly glad of being released from those ill transports, and the men often asked, with interest, "Where's the Spaniards?" And yet it must have been a great moment! It was a great moment!

It seemed made to prove that the emphatic time of history is not the emphatic time of the common man, who throughout the change of nations feels an itch on his shin, a pain in his head, hunger, thirst, a lack of sleep; the influence of his memory of past firesides, glasses of beer, girls, theatres, ideals, religions, parents, faces, hurts, joy.

Little Nell was hailed from a comfortable veranda, and, looking up, saw Walkley of the Eclipse, stretched in a yellow and green hammock, smoking his pipe with an air of having always lived in that house, in that village. "Oh, dear little Nell, how glad I am to see your angel face again! There! don't try to hide it; I can see it. Did you bring a corkscrew too? You're superseded as master of the slaves. Did you know it? And by Rogers, too! Rogers is a Sadducee, a cadaver and a pelican, appointed to the post of chief correspondent, no doubt, because of his rare gift of incapacity. Never mind."

"Where is he now?" asked Little Nell, taking seat on the steps.

"He is down interfering with the landing of the troops," answered

Walkley, swinging a leg. "I hope you have the Johnson well stocked with food as well as with cigars, cigarettes and tobaccos, ales, wines and liquors. We shall need them. There is already famine in the house of Walkley. I have discovered that the system of transportation for our gallant soldiery does not strike in me the admiration which I have often felt when viewing the management of an ordinary bun-shop. A hunger, stifling, jammed together amid odours, and everybody irritable—ye gods, how irritable! And so I—— Look! look!"

The Jefferson G. Johnson, well known to them at an incredible distance, could be seen striding the broad sea, the smoke belching from her funnel, headed for Jamaica. "The Army Lands in Cuba!" shrieked Walkley. "Shafter's Army Lands near Santiago! Special type! Half the front page! Oh, the Sadducee! The cadaver! The pelican!"

Little Nell was dumb with astonishment and fear. Walkley, however, was at least not dumb. "That's the pelican! That's Mr. Rogers making his first impression upon the situation. He has engraved himself upon us. We are tattooed with him. There will be a fight to-morrow, sure, and we will cover it even as you found Cervera's fleet. No food, no horses, no money. I am transport lame; you are sea-weak. We will never see our salaries again. Whereby Rogers is a fool."

"Anybody else here?" asked Little Nell wearily.

"Only young Point." Point was an artist on the Eclipse. "But he has nothing. Pity there wasn't an almshouse in this God-forsaken country. Here comes Point now." A sad-faced man came along carrying much luggage. "Hello, Point! lithographer and genius, have you food? Food. Well, then, you had better return yourself to Tampa by wire. You are no good here. Only one more little mouth to feed."

Point seated himself near Little Nell. "I haven't had anything to eat since daybreak," he said gloomily, "and I don't care much, for I am simply dog-tired."

"Don' tell me you are dog-tired, my talented friend," cried Walkley from his hammock. "Think of me. And now what's to be done?"

56

They stared for a time disconsolately at where, over the rim of the sea, trailed black smoke from the Johnson. From the landing-place below and to the right came the howls of a man who was superintending the disembarkation of some mules. The burning blockhouse still rendered its hollow roar. Suddenly the men-crowded landing set up its cheer, and the steamers all whistled long and raucously. Tiny black figures were raising an American flag over a blockhouse on the top of a great hill.

"That's mighty fine Sunday stuff," said Little Nell. "Well, I'll go and get the order in which the regiments landed, and who was first ashore, and all that. Then I'll go and try to find General Lawton's headquarters. His division has got the advance, I think."

"And, lo! I will write a burning description of the raising of the flag," said Walkley. "While the brilliant Point buskies for food—and makes damn sure he gets it," he added fiercely.

Little Nell thereupon wandered over the face of the earth, threading out the story of the landing of the regiments. He only found about fifty men who had been the first American soldier to set foot on Cuba, and of these he took the most probable. The army was going forward in detail, as soon as the pieces were landed. There was a house something like a crude country tavern—the soldiers in it were looking over their rifles and talking. There was a well of water quite hot—more palm trees—an inscrutable background.

When he arrived again at Walkley's mansion he found the verandah crowded with correspondents in khaki, duck, dungaree and flannel. They wore riding-breeches, but that was mainly forethought. They could see now that fate intended them to walk. Some were writing copy, while Walkley discoursed from his hammock. Rhodes—doomed to be shot in action some days later—was trying to borrow a canteen from men who had one, and from men who had none. Young Point, wan, utterly worn out, was asleep on the floor. Walkley pointed to him. "That is how he appears after his foraging journey, during which he ran all Cuba through a sieve. Oh, yes; a can of corn and a half-bottle of lime juice."

"Say, does anybody know, the name of the commander of the 26th

Infantry?"

"Who commands the first brigade of Kent's Division?"

"What was the name of the chap that raised the flag?"

"What time is it?"

And a woeful man was wandering here and there with a cold pipe, saying plaintively, "Who's got a match? Anybody here got a match?"

Little Nell's left boot hurt him at the heel, and so he removed it, taking great care and whistling through his teeth. The heated dust was upon them all, making everybody feel that bathing was unknown and shattering their tempers. Young Point developed a snore which brought grim sarcasm from all quarters. Always below, hummed the traffic of the landing-place.

When night came Little Nell thought best not to go to bed until late, because he recognised the mackintosh as but a feeble comfort. The evening was a glory. A breeze came from the sea, fanning spurts of flame out of the ashes and charred remains of the sheds, while overhead lay a splendid summer-night sky, aflash with great tranquil stars. In the streets of the village were two or three fires, frequently and suddenly reddening with their glare the figures of low-voiced men who moved here and there. The lights of the transports blinked on the murmuring plain in front of the village; and far to the westward Little Nell could sometimes note a subtle indication of a playing search-light, which alone marked the presence of the invisible battleships, half-mooned about the entrance of Santiago Harbour, waiting—waiting— waiting.

When Little Nell returned to the veranda he stumbled along a man-strewn place, until he came to the spot where he left his mackintosh; but he found it gone. His curses mingled then with those of the men upon whose bodies he had trodden. Two English correspondents, lying awake to smoke a last pipe, reared and looked at him lazily. "What's wrong, old chap?" murmured one. "Eh? Lost it, eh? Well, look here; come here and take a bit of my blanket. It's a jolly big one. Oh, no trouble at all, man. There you are. Got enough? Comfy? Good-night."

A sleepy voice arose in the darkness. "If this hammock breaks, I shall hit at least ten of those Indians down there. Never mind. This is war."

The men slept. Once the sound of three or four shots rang across the windy night, and one head uprose swiftly from the verandah, two eyes looked dazedly at nothing, and the head as swiftly sank. Again a sleepy voice was heard. "Usual thing! Nervous sentries!" The men slept. Before dawn a pulseless, penetrating chill came into the air, and the correspondents awakened, shivering, into a blue world. Some of the fires still smouldered. Walkley and Little Nell kicked vigorously into Point's framework. "Come on, brilliance! Wake up, talent! Don't be sodgering. It's too cold to sleep, but it's not too cold to hustle." Point sat up dolefully. Upon his face was a childish expression. "Where are we going to get breakfast?" he asked, sulking.

"There's no breakfast for you, you hound! Get up and hustle." Accordingly they hustled. With exceeding difficulty they learned that nothing emotional had happened during the night, save the killing of two Cubans who were so secure in ignorance that they could not understand the challenge of two American sentries. Then Walkley ran a gamut of commanding officers, and Little Nell pumped privates for their impressions of Cuba. When his indignation at the absence of breakfast allowed him, Point made sketches. At the full break of day the Adolphus, and Eclipse despatch boat, sent a boat ashore with Tailor and Shackles in it, and Walkley departed tearlessly for Jamaica, soon after he had bestowed upon his friends much tinned goods and blankets.

"Well, we've got our stuff off," said Little Nell. "Now Point and I must breakfast."

Shackles, for some reason, carried a great hunting-knife, and with it Little Nell opened a tin of beans.

"Fall to," he said amiably to Point.

There were some hard biscuits. Afterwards they—the four of them—marched off on the route of the troops. They were well loaded with luggage, particularly young Point, who had somehow made a great gathering of unnecessary things. Hills covered with verdure soon enclosed them. They heard that the army had advanced some nine miles with no fighting. Evidences of the rapid advance were here and there—coats, gauntlets, blanket rolls on the ground. Mule-trains came herding back along the narrow trail to the sound of a little tinkling bell. Cubans were appropriating the coats and blanket-rolls.

The four correspondents hurried onward. The surety of impending battle weighed upon them always, but there was a score of minor things more intimate. Little Nell's left heel had chafed until it must have been quite raw, and every moment he wished to take seat by the roadside and console himself from pain. Shackles and Point disliked each other extremely, and often they foolishly quarrelled over something, or nothing. The blanket-rolls and packages for the hand oppressed everybody. It was like being burned out of a boarding-house, and having to carry one's trunk eight miles to the nearest neighbour. Moreover, Point, since he had stupidly overloaded, with great wisdom placed various cameras and other trifles in the hands of his three less-burdened and more sensible friends. This made them fume and gnash, but in complete silence, since he was hideously youthful and innocent and unaware. They all wished to rebel, but none of them saw their way clear, because—they did not understand. But somehow it seemed a barbarous project—no one wanted to say anything—cursed him privately for a little ass, but—said nothing. For instance, Little Nell wished to remark, "Point, you are not a thoroughbred in a half of a way. You are an inconsiderate, thoughtless little swine." But, in truth, he said, "Point, when you started out you looked like a Christmas-tree. If we keep on robbing you of your bundles there soon won't be anything left for the children." Point asked dubiously, "What do you mean?" Little Nell merely laughed with deceptive good-nature.

They were always very thirsty. There was always a howl for the half-bottle of lime juice. Five or six drops from it were simply heavenly in the warm water from the canteens. Point seemed to try to keep the lime juice in his possession, in order that he might get more benefit of it. Before the war was ended the others found themselves declaring vehemently that they loathed Point, and yet when men asked them the reason they grew quite inarticulate. The reasons seemed then so small, so childish, as the reasons of a lot of women. And yet at the time his offences loomed enormous.

The surety of impending battle still weighed upon them. Then it came that Shackles turned seriously ill. Suddenly he dropped his own and much of Point's traps upon the trail, wriggled out of his blanket-roll, flung it away, and took seat heavily at the roadside. They saw with surprise that his face was pale as death, and yet streaming with sweat.

"Boys," he said in his ordinary voice, "I'm clean played out. I can't go another step. You fellows go on, and leave me to come as soon as I am able."

"Oh, no, that wouldn't do at all," said Little Nell and Tailor together.

Point moved over to a soft place, and dropped amid whatever traps he was himself carrying.

"Don't know whether it's ancestral or merely from the—sun—but I've got a stroke," said Shackles, and gently slumped over to a prostrate position before either Little Nell or Tailor could reach him.

Thereafter Shackles was parental; it was Little Nell and Tailor who were really suffering from a stroke, either ancestral or from the sun.

"Put my blanket-roll under my head, Nell, me son," he said gently. "There now! That is very nice. It is delicious. Why, I'm all right, only—only tired." He closed his eyes, and something like an easy slumber came over him. Once he opened his eyes. "Don't trouble about me," he remarked.

But the two fussed about him, nervous, worried, discussing this plan and that plan. It was Point who first made a business-like statement. Seated carelessly and indifferently upon his soft place, he finally blurted out:

"Say! Look here! Some of us have got to go on. We can't all stay here. Some of us have got to go on."

It was quite true; the Eclipse could take no account of strokes. In the end Point and Tailor went on, leaving Little Nell to bring on Shackles as soon as possible. The latter two spent many hours in the grass by the roadside. They made numerous abrupt acquaintances with passing staff officers, privates, muleteers, many stopping to inquire the wherefore of the death-faced figure on the ground. Favours were done often and often, by peer and peasant—small things, of no consequence, and yet warming.

It was dark when Shackles and Little Nell had come slowly to where they could hear the murmur of the army's bivouac.

"Shack," gasped Little Nell to the man leaning forlornly upon him, "I guess we'd better bunk down here where we stand."

"All right, old boy. Anything you say," replied Shackles, in the bass and hollow voice which arrives with such condition.

They crawled into some bushes, and distributed their belongings upon the ground. Little Nell spread out the blankets, and generally played housemaid. Then they lay down, supperless, being too weary to eat. The men slept.

At dawn Little Nell awakened and looked wildly for Shackles, whose empty blanket was pressed flat like a wet newspaper on the ground. But at nearly the same moment Shackles appeared, elate.

"Come on," he cried; "I've rustled an invitation for breakfast."

Little Nell came on with celerity.

"Where? Who?" he said.

"Oh! some officers," replied Shackles airily. If he had been ill the previous day, he showed it now only in some curious kind of deference he paid to Little Nell.

Shackles conducted his comrade, and soon they arrived at where a captain and his one subaltern arose courteously from where they were squatting near a fire of little sticks. They wore the wide white trouser-stripes of infantry officers, and upon the shoulders of their blue campaign shirts were the little marks of their rank; but otherwise there was little beyond their manners to render them different from the men who were busy with breakfast near them. The captain was old, grizzled—a common type of captain in the tiny American army—overjoyed at the active service, confident of his business, and yet breathing out in some way a note of pathos. The war was come too late. Age was grappling him, and honours were only for his widow and his children—merely a better life insurance policy. He had spent his life policing Indians with much labour, cold and heat, but with no glory for him nor his fellows. All he now could do was to die at the head of his men. If he had youthfully dreamed of a general's stars, they were now impossible to him, and he knew it. He was too old to leap so far; his sole honour was a new invitation to face death. And yet, with his ambitions lying half-strangled, he was going to take his men into any sort of holocaust, because his traditions were of gentlemen and soldiers, and because—he loved it for itself—the thing itself—the whirl, the unknown. If he had been degraded at that moment to be a pot-wrestler, no power could have starved him from going through the campaign as a spectator. Why, the army! It was in each drop of his blood.

The lieutenant was very young. Perhaps he had been hurried out of West Point at the last moment, upon a shortage of officers appearing. To him, all was opportunity. He was, in fact, in great luck. Instead of going off in 1898 to grill for an indefinite period on some God-forgotten heap of red-hot sand in New Mexico, he was here in Cuba, on real business, with his regiment. When the big engagement came he was sure to emerge from it either horizontally or at the head of a company, and what more could a boy ask? He was a very modest lad, and talked nothing of his frame of mind, but an expression of blissful contentment was ever upon his face. He really accounted himself the most fortunate boy of his time; and he felt almost certain that he would do well. It was necessary to do well. He would do well.

And yet in many ways these two were alike; the grizzled captain with his gently mournful countenance—"Too late"—and the elate young second lieutenant, his commission hardly dry. Here again it was the influence of the army. After all they were both children of the army.

It is possible to spring into the future here and chronicle what happened later. The captain, after thirty-five years of waiting for his chance, took his Mauser bullet through the brain at the foot of San Juan Hill in the very beginning of the battle, and the boy arrived on the crest panting, sweating, but unscratched, and not sure whether he commanded one company or a whole battalion. Thus fate dealt to the hosts of Shackles and Little Nell.

The breakfast was of canned tomatoes stewed with hard bread, more hard bread, and coffee. It was very good fare, almost royal. Shackles and Little Nell were absurdly grateful as they felt the hot bitter coffee tingle in them. But they departed joyfully before the sun was fairly up, and passed into Siboney. They never saw the captain again.

The beach at Siboney was furious with traffic, even as had been the beach at Daqueri. Launches shouted, jack-tars prodded with their boathooks, and load of men followed load of men. Straight, parade-like, on the shore stood a trumpeter playing familiar calls to the troop-horses who swam towards him eagerly through the salt seas. Crowding closely into the cove were transports of all sizes and ages. To the left and to the right of the little landing-beach green hills shot upward like the wings in a theatre. They were scarred here and there with blockhouses and rifle-pits. Up one hill a regiment was crawling, seemingly inch by inch. Shackles and Little Nell walked among palms and scrubby bushes, near pools, over spaces of sand holding little monuments of biscuit-boxes, ammunition-boxes, and supplies of all kinds. Some regiment was just collecting itself from the ships, and the men made great patches of blue on the brown sand.

Shackles asked a question of a man accidentally: "Where's that regiment going to?" He pointed to the force that was crawling up the hill. The man grinned, and said, "They're going to look for a fight!"

"Looking for a fight!" said Shackles and Little Nell together. They stared into each other's eyes. Then they set off for the foot of the hill. The hill was long and toilsome. Below them spread wider and wider a vista of ships quiet on a grey sea; a busy, black disembarkation-place; tall, still, green hills; a village of well separated cottages; palms; a bit of road; soldiers marching. They passed vacant Spanish trenches; little twelve-foot blockhouses. Soon they were on a fine upland near the sea. The path, under ordinary conditions, must have been a beautiful wooded way. It wound in the shade of thickets of fine trees, then through rank growths of bushes with revealed and fantastic roots, then through a grassy space which had all the beauty of a neglected orchard. But always from under their feet scuttled noisy land-crabs, demons to the nerves, which in some way possessed a semblance of moon-like faces upon their blue or red bodies, and these faces were turned with expressions of deepest horror upon Shackles and Little Nell as they sped to overtake the pugnacious regiment. The route was paved with coats, hats, tent and blanket rolls, ration-tins, haversacks—everything but ammunition belts, rifles and canteens.

They heard a dull noise of voices in front of them—men talking too loud for the etiquette of the forest—and presently they came upon two or three soldiers lying by the roadside, flame-faced, utterly spent from the hurried march in the heat. One man came limping back along the path. He looked to them anxiously for sympathy and comprehension. "Hurt m' knee. I swear I couldn't keep up with th' boys. I had to leave 'm. Wasn't that tough luck?" His collar rolled away from a red, muscular neck, and his bare forearms were better than stanchions. Yet he was almost babyishly tearful in his attempt to make the two correspondents feel that he had not turned back because he was afraid. They gave him scant courtesy, tinctured with one drop of sympathetic yet cynical understanding. Soon they overtook the hospital squad; men addressing chaste language to some pack-mules; a talkative sergeant; two amiable, cool-eyed young surgeons. Soon they were amid the rear troops of the dismounted volunteer cavalry regiment which was moving to attack. The men strode easily along, arguing one to another on ulterior matters. If they were going into battle, they either did not know it or they concealed it well. They were more like men going into a bar at one o'clock in the morning. Their laughter rang through the Cuban woods. And in the meantime, soft, mellow, sweet, sang the voice of the Cuban wood-dove, the Spanish guerilla calling to his mate—forest music; on the flanks, deep back on both flanks, the adorable wood-dove, singing only of love. Some of the advancing Americans said it was beautiful. It was beautiful. The Spanish guerilla calling to his mate. What could be more beautiful?

Shackles and Little Nell rushed precariously through waist-high bushes until they reached the centre of the single-filed regiment. The firing then broke out in front. All the woods set up a hot sputtering; the bullets sped along the path and across it from both sides. The thickets presented nothing but dense masses of light green foliage, out of which these swift steel things were born supernaturally.

It was a volunteer regiment going into its first action, against an enemy of unknown force, in a country where the vegetation was thicker than fur on a cat. There might have been a dreadful mess; but in military matters the only way to deal with a situation of this kind is to take it frankly by the throat and squeeze it to death. Shackles and Little Nell felt the thrill of the orders. "Come ahead, men! Keep right ahead, men! Come on!" The volunteer cavalry regiment, with all the willingness in the world, went ahead into the angle of V-shaped Spanish formation.

It seemed that every leaf had turned into a soda-bottle and was popping its cork. Some of the explosions seemed to be against the men's very faces, others against the backs of their necks. "Now, men! Keep goin' ahead. Keep on goin'." The forward troops were already engaged. They, at least, had something at which to shoot. "Now, captain, if you're ready." "Stop that swearing there." "Got a match?" "Steady, now, men."

A gate appeared in a barbed-wire fence. Within were billowy fields of long grass, dotted with palms and luxuriant mango trees. It was Elysian—a place for lovers, fair as Eden in its radiance of sun, under its blue sky. One might have expected to see white-robed figures walking slowly in the shadows. A dead man, with a bloody face, lay twisted in a curious contortion at the waist. Someone was shot in the leg, his pins knocked cleanly from under him.

"Keep goin', men." The air roared, and the ground fled reelingly under their feet. Light, shadow, trees, grass. Bullets spat from every side. Once they were in a thicket, and the men, blanched and bewildered, turned one way, and then another, not knowing which way to turn. "Keep goin', men." Soon they were in the sunlight again. They could see the long scant line, which was being drained man by man—one might say drop by drop. The musketry rolled forth in great full measure from the magazine carbines. "Keep goin', men." "Christ, I'm shot!" "They're flankin' us, sir." "We're bein' fired into by our own crowd, sir." "Keep goin', men." A low ridge before them was a bottling establishment blowing up in detail. From the right—it seemed at that time to be the far right—they could hear steady, crashing volleys—the United States regulars in action.

Then suddenly—to use a phrase of the street—the whole bottom of the thing fell out. It was suddenly and mysteriously ended. The Spaniards had run away, and some of the regulars were chasing them. It was a victory.

When the wounded men dropped in the tall grass they quite disappeared, as if they had sunk in water. Little Nell and Shackles were walking along through the fields, disputing.

"Well, damn it, man!" cried Shackles, "we must get a list of the killed and wounded."

"That is not nearly so important," quoth little Nell, academically, "as to get the first account to New York of the first action of the army in Cuba."

They came upon Tailor, lying with a bared torso and a small red hole through his left lung. He was calm, but evidently out of temper. "Good God, Tailor!" they cried, dropping to their knees like two pagans; "are you hurt, old boy?"

"Hurt?" he said gently. "No, 'tis not so deep as a well nor so wide as a church-door, but 'tis enough, d'you see? You understand, do you? Idiots!"

Then he became very official. "Shackles, feel and see what's under my leg. It's a small stone, or a burr, or something. Don't be clumsy now! Be careful! Be careful!" Then he said, angrily, "Oh, you didn't find it at all. Damn it!"

In reality there was nothing there, and so Shackles could not have removed it. "Sorry, old boy," he said, meekly.

"Well, you may observe that I can't stay here more than a year," said Tailor, with some oratory, "and the hospital people have their own work in hand. It behoves you, Nell, to fly to Siboney, arrest a despatch boat, get a cot and some other things, and some minions to carry me. If I get once down to the base I'm all right, but if I stay here I'm dead. Meantime Shackles can stay here and try to look as if he liked it."

There was no disobeying the man. Lying there with a little red hole in his left lung, he dominated them through his helplessness, and through their fear that if they angered him he would move and—bleed.

"Well?" said Little Nell.

"Yes," said Shackles, nodding.

Little Nell departed.

"That blanket you lent me," Tailor called after him, "is back there somewhere with Point."

Little Nell noted that many of the men who were wandering among the wounded seemed so spent with the toil and excitement of their first action that they could hardly drag one leg after the other. He found himself suddenly in the same condition, His face, his neck, even his mouth, felt dry as sun-baked bricks, and his legs were foreign to him. But he swung desperately into his five-mile task. On the way he passed many things: bleeding men carried by comrades; others making their way grimly, with encrimsoned arms; then the little settlement of the hospital squad; men on the ground everywhere, many in the path; one young captain dying, with great gasps, his body pale blue, and glistening, like the inside of a rabbit's skin. But the voice of the Cuban wood-dove, soft, mellow, sweet, singing only of love, was no longer heard from the wealth of foliage.

Presently the hurrying correspondent met another regiment coming to assist—a line of a thousand men in single file through the jungle. "Well, how is it going, old man?" "How is it coming on?" "Are we doin' 'em?" Then, after an interval, came other regiments, moving out. He had to take to the bush to let these long lines pass him, and he was delayed, and had to flounder amid brambles. But at last, like a successful pilgrim, he arrived at the brow of the great hill overlooking Siboney. His practised eye scanned the fine broad brow of the sea with its clustering ships, but he saw thereon no Eclipse despatch boats. He zigzagged heavily down the hill, and arrived finally amid the dust and outcries of the base. He seemed to ask a thousand men if they had seen an Eclipse boat on the water, or an Eclipse correspondent on the shore. They all answered, "No."

He was like a poverty-stricken and unknown suppliant at a foreign Court. Even his plea got only ill-hearings. He had expected the news of the serious wounding of Tailor to appal the other correspondents, but they took it quite calmly. It was as if their sense of an impending great battle between two large armies had quite got them out of focus for these minor tragedies. Tailor was hurt—yes? They looked at Little Nell, dazed. How curious that Tailor should be almost the first—how very curious—yes. But, as far as arousing them to any enthusiasm of active pity, it seemed impossible. He was lying up there in the grass, was he? Too bad, too bad, too bad!

Little Nell went alone and lay down in the sand with his back against a rock. Tailor was prostrate up there in the grass. Never mind. Nothing was to be done. The whole situation was too colossal. Then into his zone came Walkley the invincible.

"Walkley!" yelled Little Nell. Walkley came quickly, and Little Nell lay weakly against his rock and talked. In thirty seconds Walkley understood everything, had hurled a drink of whisky into Little Nell, had admonished him to lie quiet, and had gone to organise and manipulate. When he returned he was a trifle dubious and backward. Behind him was a singular squad of volunteers from the Adolphus, carrying among them a wire-woven bed.

"Look here, Nell!" said Walkley, in bashful accents; "I've collected a battalion here which is willing to go bring Tailor; but—they say—you—can't you show them where he is?"

"Yes," said Little Nell, arising.

When the party arrived at Siboney, and deposited Tailor in the best place, Walkley had found a house and stocked it with canned soups. Therein Shackles and Little Nell revelled for a time, and then rolled on the floor in their blankets. Little Nell tossed a great deal. "Oh, I'm so tired. Good God,

I'm tired. I'm—tired."

In the morning a voice aroused them. It was a swollen, important, circus voice saying, "Where is Mr. Nell? I wish to see him immediately."

"Here I am, Rogers," cried Little Nell.

"Oh, Nell," said Rogers, "here's a despatch to me which I thought you had better read."

Little Nell took the despatch. It was: "Tell Nell can't understand his inaction; tell him come home first steamer from Port Antonio, Jamaica."

THE REVENGE OF THE ADOLPHUS

I

"Stand by."

Shackles had come down from the bridge of the Adolphus and flung this command at three fellow-correspondents who in the galley were busy with pencils trying to write something exciting and interesting from four days quiet cruising. They looked up casually. "What for?" They did not intend to arouse for nothing. Ever since Shackles had heard the men of the navy directing each other to stand by for this thing and that thing, he had used the two words as his pet phrase and was continually telling his friends to stand by. Sometimes its portentous and emphatic reiteration became highly exasperating and men were apt to retort sharply. "Well, I am standing by, ain't I?" On this occasion they detected that he was serious. "Well, what for?" they repeated. In his answer Shackles was reproachful as well as impressive. "Stand by? Stand by for a Spanish gunboat. A Spanish gunboat in chase! Stand by for two Spanish gunboats—both of them in chase!"

The others looked at him for a brief space and were almost certain that they saw truth written upon his countenance. Whereupon they tumbled out of the galley and galloped up to the bridge. The cook with a mere inkling of tragedy was now out on deck bawling, "What's the matter? What's the matter? What's the matter?" Aft, the grimy head of a stoker was thrust suddenly up through the deck, so to speak. The eyes flashed in a quick look astern and then the head vanished. The correspondents were scrambling on the bridge. "Where's my glasses, damn it? Here—let me take a look. Are they Spaniards, Captain? Are you sure?"

The skipper of the Adolphus was at the wheel. The pilot-house was so arranged that he could not see astern without hanging forth from one of the side windows, but apparently he had made early investigation. He did not reply at once. At sea, he never replied at once to questions. At the very first, Shackles had discovered the merits of this deliberate manner and had taken delight in it. He invariably detailed his talk with the captain to the other correspondents. "Look here. I've just been to see the skipper. I said 'I would like to put into Cape Haytien.' Then he took a little think. Finally he said: 'All right.' Then I said: 'I suppose we'll need to take on more coal there?' He took another little think. I said: 'Ever ran into that port before?' He took another little think. Finally he said: 'Yes.' I said 'Have a cigar?' He took another little think. See? There's where I fooled 'im———"

While the correspondents spun the hurried questions at him, the captain of the Adolphus stood with his brown hands on the wheel and his cold glance aligned straight over the bow of his ship.

"Are they Spanish gunboats, Captain? Are they, Captain?"

After a profound pause, he said: "Yes." The four correspondents hastily and in perfect time presented their backs to him and fastened their gaze on the pursuing foe. They saw a dull grey curve of sea going to the feet of the high green and blue coast-line of north-eastern Cuba, and on this sea were two miniature ships with clouds of iron-coloured smoke pouring from their funnels.

One of the correspondents strolled elaborately to the pilot-house. "Aw—Captain," he drawled, "do you think they can catch us?"

The captain's glance was still aligned over the bow of his ship. Ultimately he answered: "I don't know."

From the top of the little Adolphus' stack, thick dark smoke swept level for a few yards and then went rolling to leeward in great hot obscuring clouds. From time to time the grimy head was thrust through the deck, the eyes took the quick look astern and then the head vanished. The cook was trying to get somebody to listen to him. "Well, you know, damn it all, it won't be no fun to be ketched by them Spaniards. Be-Gawd, it won't. Look here, what do you think they'll do to us, hey? Say, I don't like this, you know. I'm damned if I do." The sea, cut by the hurried bow of the Adolphus, flung its waters astern in the formation of a wide angle and the lines of the angle ruffled and hissed as they fled, while the thumping screw tormented the water at the stern.

The frame of the steamer underwent regular convulsions as in the strenuous sobbing of a child.

The mate was standing near the pilot-house. Without looking at him, the captain spoke his name. "Ed!"

"Yes, sir," cried the mate with alacrity.

The captain reflected for a moment. Then he said: "Are they gainin' on us?"

The mate took another anxious survey of the race. "No—o—yes, I think they are—a little."

After a pause the captain said: "Tell the chief to shake her up more."

The mate, glad of an occupation in these tense minutes, flew down to the engine-room door. "Skipper says shake 'er up more!" he bawled. The head of the chief engineer appeared, a grizzly head now wet with oil and sweat. "What?" he shouted angrily. It was as if he had been propelling the ship with his own arms. Now he was told that his best was not good enough. "What? shake 'er up more? Why she can't carry another pound, I tell you! Not another ounce! We——" Suddenly he ran forward and climbed to the bridge. "Captain," he cried in the loud harsh voice of one who lived usually amid the thunder of machinery, "she can't do it, sir! Be-Gawd, she can't! She's turning over now faster than she ever did in her life and we'll all blow to hell——"

The low-toned, impassive voice of the captain suddenly checked the chief's clamour. "I'll blow her up," he said, "but I won't git ketched if I kin help it." Even then the listening correspondents found a second in which to marvel that the captain had actually explained his point of view to another human being.

The engineer stood blank. Then suddenly he cried: "All right, sir!" He threw a hurried look of despair at the correspondents, the deck of the Adolphus, the pursuing enemy, Cuba, the sky and the sea; he vanished in the direction of his post.

A correspondent was suddenly regifted with the power of prolonged speech. "Well, you see, the game is up, damn it. See? We can't get out of it. The skipper will blow up the whole bunch before he'll let his ship be taken, and the Spaniards are gaining. Well, that's what comes from going to war in an eight-knot tub." He bitterly accused himself, the others, and the dark, sightless, indifferent world.

This certainty of coming evil affected each one differently. One was made garrulous; one kept absent-mindedly snapping his fingers and gazing at the sea; another stepped nervously to and fro, looking everywhere as if for employment for his mind. As for Shackles he was silent and smiling, but it was a new smile that caused the lines about his mouth to betray quivering weakness. And each man looked at the others to discover their degree of fear and did his best to conceal his own, holding his crackling nerves with all his strength.

As the Adolphus rushed on, the sun suddenly emerged from behind grey clouds and its rays dealt titanic blows so that in a few minutes the sea was a glowing blue plain with the golden shine dancing at the tips of the waves. The coast of Cuba glowed with light. The pursuers displayed detail after detail in the new atmosphere. The voice of the cook was heard in high vexation. "Am I to git dinner as usual? How do I know? Nobody tells me what to do? Am I to git dinner as usual?"

The mate answered ferociously. "Of course you are! What do you s'pose? Ain't you the cook, you damn fool?"

The cook retorted in a mutinous scream. "Well, how would I know? If this ship is goin' to blow up——"

II

The captain called from the pilot-house. "Mr. Shackles! Oh, Mr. Shackles!" The correspondent moved hastily to a window. "What is it, Captain?" The skipper of the Adolphus raised a battered finger and pointed over the bows. "See 'er?" he asked, laconic but quietly jubilant. Another steamer was smoking at full speed over the sun-lit seas. A great billow of pure white was on her bows. "Great Scott!" cried Shackles. "Another Spaniard?"

"No," said the captain, "that there is a United States cruiser!"

"What?" Shackles was dumfounded into muscular paralysis. "No! Are you sure?"

The captain nodded. "Sure, take the glass. See her ensign? Two funnels, two masts with fighting tops. She ought to be the Chancellorville."

Shackles choked. "Well, I'm blowed!"

"Ed!" said the captain.

"Yessir!"

"Tell the chief there is no hurry."

Shackles suddenly bethought him of his companions. He dashed to them and was full of quick scorn of their gloomy faces. "Hi, brace up there! Are you blind? Can't you see her?"

"See what?"

"Why, the Chancellorville, you blind mice!" roared Shackles. "See 'er? See 'er? See 'er?"

The others sprang, saw, and collapsed. Shackles was a madman for the purpose of distributing the news. "Cook!" he shrieked. "Don't you see 'er, cook? Good Gawd, man, don't you see 'er?" He ran to the lower deck and howled his information everywhere. Suddenly the whole ship smiled. Men clapped each other on the shoulder and joyously shouted. The captain thrust his head from the pilot-house to look back at the Spanish ships. Then he looked at the American cruiser. "Now, we'll see," he said grimly and vindictively to the mate. "Guess somebody else will do some running," the mate chuckled.

The two gunboats were still headed hard for the Adolphus and she kept on her way. The American cruiser was coming swiftly. "It's the Chancellorville!" cried Shackles. "I know her! We'll see a fight at sea, my boys! A fight at sea!" The enthusiastic correspondents pranced in Indian revels.

The Chancellorville—2000 tons—18.6 knots—10 five-inch guns— came on tempestuously, sheering the water high with her sharp bow. From her funnels the smoke raced away in driven sheets. She loomed with extraordinary rapidity like a ship bulging and growing out of the sea. She swept by the Adolphus so close that one could have thrown a walnut on board. She was a glistening grey apparition with a blood-red water-line, with brown gun-muzzles and white-clothed motionless jack-tars; and in her rush she was silent, deadly silent. Probably there entered the mind of every man on board the Adolphus a feeling of almost idolatry for this living thing, stern but, to their thought, incomparably beautiful. They would have cheered but that each man seemed to feel that a cheer would be too puny a tribute.

It was at first as if she did not see the Adolphus. She was going to pass without heeding this little vagabond of the high-seas. But suddenly a megaphone gaped over the rail of her bridge and a voice was heard measuredly, calmly intoning. "Hello—there! Keep—well—to— the—north'ard—and— out of my—way—and I'll—go—in—and—see— what—those—people— want——" Then nothing was heard but the swirl of water. In a moment the Adolphus was looking at a high grey stern. On the quarter-deck, sailors were poised about the breach of the after-pivot-gun.

The correspondents were revelling. "Captain," yelled Shackles, "we can't miss this! We must see it!" But the skipper had already flung over the wheel. "Sure," he answered almost at once. "We can't miss it."

The cook was arrogantly, grossly triumphant. His voice rang along the deck. "There, now! How will the Spinachers like that? Now, it's our turn! We've been doin' the runnin' away but now we'll do the chasin'!" Apparently feeling some twinge of nerves from the former strain, he suddenly demanded: "Say, who's got any whisky? I'm near dead for a drink."

When the Adolphus came about, she laid her course for a position to the northward of a coming battle, but the situation suddenly became complicated. When the Spanish ships discovered the identity of the ship that was steaming toward them, they did not hesitate over their plan of action. With one accord they turned and ran for port. Laughter arose from the Adolphus. The captain broke his orders, and, instead of keeping to the northward, he headed in the wake of the impetuous Chancellorville. The correspondents crowded on the bow.

The Spaniards when their broadsides became visible were seen to be ships of no importance, mere little gunboats for work in the shallows back of the reefs, and it was certainly discreet to refuse encounter with the five-inch guns of the Chancellorville. But the joyful Adolphus took no account of this discretion. The pursuit of the Spaniards had been so ferocious that the quick change to heels-overhead flight filled that corner of the mind which is devoted to the spirit of revenge. It was this that moved Shackles to yell taunts futilely at the far-away ships. "Well, how do you like it, eh? How do you like it?" The Adolphus was drinking compensation for her previous agony.

The mountains of the shore now shadowed high into the sky and the square white houses of a town could be seen near a vague cleft which seemed to mark the entrance to a port. The gunboats were now near to it.

Suddenly white smoke streamed from the bow of the Chancellorville and developed swiftly into a great bulb which drifted in fragments down the wind. Presently the deep-throated boom of the gun came to the ears on board the Adolphus. The shot kicked up a high jet of water into the air astern of the last gunboat. The black smoke from the funnels of the cruiser made her look like a collier on fire, and in her desperation she tried many more long shots, but presently the Adolphus, murmuring disappointment, saw the Chancellorville sheer from the chase.

In time they came up with her and she was an indignant ship. Gloom and wrath was on the forecastle and wrath and gloom was on the quarter-deck. A sad voice from the bridge said: "Just missed 'em." Shackles gained permission to board the cruiser, and in the cabin, he talked to Lieutenant-Commander Surrey, tall, bald-headed and angry. "Shoals," said the captain of the Chancellorville. "I can't go any nearer and those gunboats could steam along a stone sidewalk if only it was wet." Then his bright eyes became brighter. "I tell you what! The Chicken, the Holy Moses and the Mongolian are on station off Nuevitas. If you will do me a favour—why, to-morrow I will give those people a game!"

III

The Chancellorville lay all night watching off the port of the two gunboats and, soon after daylight, the lookout descried three smokes to the westward and they were later made out to be the Chicken, the Holy Moses and the Adolphus, the latter tagging hurriedly after the United States vessels.

The Chicken had been a harbour tug but she was now the U.S.S. Chicken, by your leave. She carried a six-pounder forward and a six-pounder aft and her main point was her conspicuous vulnerability. The Holy Moses had been the private yacht of a Philadelphia millionaire. She carried six six-pounders and her main point was the chaste beauty of the officer's quarters.

On the bridge of the Chancellorville, Lieutenant-Commander Surrey surveyed his squadron with considerable satisfaction. Presently he signalled to the lieutenant who commanded the Holy Moses and to the boatswain who commanded the Chicken to come aboard the flag-ship. This was all very well for the captain of the yacht, but it was not so easy for the captain of the tug-boat who had two heavy lifeboats swung fifteen feet above the water. He had been accustomed to talking with senior officers from his own pilot house through the intercession of the blessed megaphone. However he got a lifeboat overside and was pulled to the Chancellorville by three men—which cut his crew almost into halves.

In the cabin of the Chancellorville, Surrey disclosed to his two captains his desires concerning the Spanish gunboats and they were glad for being ordered down from the Nuevitas station where life was very dull. He also announced that there was a shore battery containing, he believed, four field guns—three-point-twos. His draught—he spoke of it as his draught—would enable him to go in close enough to engage the battery at moderate range, but he pointed out that the main parts of the attempt to destroy the Spanish gunboats must be left to the Holy Moses and the Chicken. His business, he thought, could only be to keep the air so singing about the ears of the battery that the men at the guns would be unable to take an interest in the dash of the smaller American craft into the bay.

The officers spoke in their turns. The captain of the Chicken announced that he saw no difficulties. The squadron would follow the senior officer in line ahead, the S. O. would engage the batteries as soon as possible, she would turn to starboard when the depth of water forced her to do so and the Holy Moses and the Chicken would run past her into the bay and fight the Spanish ships wherever they were to be found. The captain of the Holy Moses after some moments of dignified thought said that he had no suggestions to make that would better this plan.

Surrey pressed an electric bell; a marine orderly appeared; he was sent with a message. The message brought the navigating officer of the Chancellorville to the cabin and the four men nosed over a chart.

In the end Surrey declared that he had made up his mind and the juniors remained in expectant silence for three minutes while he stared at the bulkhead. Then he said that the plan of the Chicken's captain seemed to him correct in the main. He would make one change. It was that he should first steam in and engage the battery and the other vessels should remain in their present positions until he signalled them to run into the bay. If the squadron steamed ahead in line, the battery could, if it chose, divide its fire between the cruiser and the gunboats constituting the more important attack. He had no doubt, he said, that he could soon silence the battery by tumbling the earth-works on to the guns and driving away the men even if he did not succeed in hitting the pieces. Of course he had no doubt of being able to silence the battery in twenty minutes. Then he would signal for the Holy Moses and the Chicken to make their rush, and of course he would support them with his fire as much as conditions enabled him. He arose then indicating that the conference was at an end. In the few moments more that all four men remained in the cabin, the talk changed its character completely. It was now unofficial, and the sharp badinage concealed furtive affections, Academy friendships, the feelings of old-time ship-mates, hiding everything under a veil of jokes. "Well, good luck to you, old boy! Don't get that valuable packet of yours sunk under you. Think how it would weaken the navy. Would you mind buying me three pairs of pajamas in the town yonder? If your engines get disabled, tote her under your arm. You can do it. Good-bye, old man, don't forget to come out all right———"

When the captains of the Holy Moses and the Chicken emerged from the cabin, they strode the deck with a new step. They were proud men. The marine on duty above their boats looked at them curiously and with awe. He detected something which meant action, conflict, The boats' crews saw it also. As they pulled their steady stroke, they studied fleetingly the face of the officer in the stern sheets. In both cases they perceived a glad man and yet a man filled with a profound consideration of the future.

IV

A bird-like whistle stirred the decks of the Chancellorville. It was followed by the hoarse bellowing of the boatswain's mate. As the cruiser turned her bow toward the shore, she happened to steam near the Adolphus. The usual calm voice hailed the despatch boat. "Keep—that—gauze under-shirt of yours—well—out of the—line of fire."

"Ay, ay, sir!"

The cruiser then moved slowly toward the shore, watched by every eye in the smaller American vessels. She was deliberate and steady, and this was reasonable even to the impatience of the other craft because the wooded shore was likely to suddenly develop new factors. Slowly she swung to starboard; smoke belched over her and the roar of a gun came along the water.

The battery was indicated by a long thin streak of yellow earth. The first shot went high, ploughing the chaparral on the hillside. The Chancellorville wore an air for a moment of being deep in meditation. She flung another shell, which landed squarely on the earth-work, making a great dun cloud. Before the smoke had settled, there was a crimson flash from the battery. To the watchers at sea, it was smaller than a needle. The shot made a geyser of crystal water, four hundred yards from the Chancellorville.

The cruiser, having made up her mind, suddenly went at the battery, hammer and tongs. She moved to and fro casually, but the thunder of her guns was gruff and angry. Sometimes she was quite hidden in her own smoke, but with exceeding regularity the earth of the battery spurted into the air. The Spanish shells, for the most part, went high and wide of the cruiser, jetting the water far away.

Once a Spanish gunner took a festive side-show chance at the waiting group of the three nondescripts. It went like a flash over the Adolphus, singing a wistful metallic note. Whereupon the Adolphus broke hurriedly for the open sea, and men on the Holy Moses and the Chicken laughed hoarsely and cruelly. The correspondents had been standing excitedly on top of the pilot-house, but at the passing of the shell, they promptly eliminated themselves by dropping with a thud to the deck below. The cook again was giving tongue. "Oh, say, this won't do! I'm damned if it will! We ain't no armoured cruiser, you know. If one of them shells hits us—well, we finish right there. 'Tain't like as if it was our business, foolin' 'round within the range of them guns. There's no sense in it. Them other fellows don't seem to mind it, but it's their business. If it's your business, you go ahead and do it, but if it ain't, you—look at that, would you!"

The Chancellorville had sent up a spread of flags, and the Holy Moses and the Chicken were steaming in.

V

They, on the Chancellorville, sometimes could see into the bay, and they perceived the enemy's gunboats moving out as if to give battle. Surrey feared that this impulse would not endure or that it was some mere pretence for the edification of the town's people and the garrison, so he hastily signalled the Holy Moses and the Chicken to go in. Thankful for small favours, they came on like charging bantams. The battery had ceased firing. As the two auxiliaries passed under the stern of the cruiser, the megaphone hailed them. "You—will—see—the—en—em—y—soon—as—you—round—the—point. A—fine—chance. Good—luck."

As a matter of fact, the Spanish gunboats had not been informed of the presence of the Holy Moses and the Chicken off the bar, and they were just blustering down the bay over the protective shoals to make it appear that they scorned the Chancellorville. But suddenly, from around the point, there burst into view a steam yacht, closely followed by a harbour tug. The gunboats took one swift look at this horrible sight and fled screaming.

Lieutenant Reigate, commanding the Holy Moses, had under his feet a craft that was capable of some speed, although before a solemn tribunal, one would have to admit that she conscientiously belied almost everything that the contractors had said of her, originally. Boatswain Pent, commanding the

Chicken, was in possession of an utterly different kind. The Holy Moses was an antelope; the Chicken was a man who could carry a piano on his back. In this race Pent had the mortification of seeing his vessel outstripped badly.

The entrance of the two American craft had had a curious effect upon the shores of the bay. Apparently everyone had slept in the assurance that the Chancellorville could not cross the bar, and that the Chancellorville was the only hostile ship. Consequently, the appearance of the Holy Moses and the Chicken, created a curious and complete emotion. Reigate, on the bridge of the Holy Moses, laughed when he heard the bugles shrilling and saw through his glasses the wee figures of men running hither and thither on the shore. It was the panic of the china when the bull entered the shop. The whole bay was bright with sun. Every detail of the shore was plain. From a brown hut abeam of the Holy Moses, some little men ran out waving their arms and turning their tiny faces to look at the enemy. Directly ahead, some four miles, appeared the scattered white houses of a town with a wharf, and some schooners in front of it. The gunboats were making for the town. There was a stone fort on the hill overshadowing, but Reigate conjectured that there was no artillery in it.

There was a sense of something intimate and impudent in the minds of the Americans. It was like climbing over a wall and fighting a man in his own garden. It was not that they could be in any wise shaken in their resolve; it was simply that the overwhelmingly Spanish aspect of things made them feel like gruff intruders. Like many of the emotions of war-time, this emotion had nothing at all to do with war.

Reigate's only commissioned subordinate called up from the bow gun. "May I open fire, sir? I think I can fetch that last one."

"Yes." Immediately the six-pounder crashed, and in the air was the spinning-wire noise of the flying shot. It struck so close to the last gunboat that it appeared that the spray went aboard. The swift-handed men at the gun spoke of it. "Gave 'm a bath that time anyhow. First one they've ever had. Dry 'em off this time, Jim." The young ensign said: "Steady." And so the Holy Moses raced in, firing, until the whole town, fort, waterfront, and shipping were as plain as if they had been done on paper by a mechanical draftsman. The gunboats were trying to hide in the bosom of the town. One was frantically tying up to the wharf and the other was anchoring within a hundred yards of the shore. The Spanish infantry, of course, had dug trenches along the beach, and suddenly the air over the Holy Moses sung with bullets. The shore-line thrummed with musketry. Also some antique shells screamed.

VI

The Chicken was doing her best. Pent's posture at the wheel seemed to indicate that her best was about thirty-four knots. In his eagerness he was braced as if he alone was taking in a 10,000 ton battleship through Hell Gate.

But the Chicken was not too far in the rear and Pent could see clearly that he was to have no minor part to play. Some of the antique shells had struck the Holy Moses and he could see the escaped steam shooting up from her. She lay close inshore and was lashing out with four six-pounders as if this was the last opportunity she would have to fire them. She had made the Spanish gunboats very sick. A solitary gun on the one moored to the wharf was from time to time firing wildly; otherwise the gunboats were silent. But the beach in front of the town was a line of fire. The Chicken headed for the Holy Moses and, as soon as possible, the six-pounder in her bow began to crack at the gunboat moored to the wharf.

In the meantime, the Chancellorville prowled off the bar, listening to the firing, anxious, acutely anxious, and feeling her impotency in every inch of her smart steel frame. And in the meantime, the Adolphus squatted on the waves and brazenly waited for news. One could thoughtfully count the seconds and reckon that, in this second and that second, a man had died—if one chose. But no one did it. Undoubtedly, the spirit was that the flag should come away with honour, honour complete, perfect, leaving no loose unfinished end over which the Spaniards could erect a monument of satisfaction, glorification. The distant guns boomed to the ears of the silent blue-jackets at their stations on the cruiser.

The Chicken steamed up to the Holy Moses and took into her nostrils the odour of steam, gunpowder and burnt things. Rifle bullets simply steamed over them both. In the merest flash of time, Pent took into his remembrance the body of a dead quartermaster on the bridge of his consort. The two megaphones uplifted together, but Pent's eager voice cried out first. "Are you injured, sir?"

"No, not completely. My engines can get me out after—after we have sunk those gunboats." The voice had been utterly conventional but it changed to sharpness. "Go in and sink that gunboat at anchor."

As the Chicken rounded the Holy Moses and started inshore, a man called to him from the depths of finished disgust. "They're takin' to their boats, sir." Pent looked and saw the men of the anchored gunboat lower their boats and pull like mad for shore.

The Chicken, assisted by the Holy Moses, began a methodical killing of the anchored gunboat. The Spanish infantry on shore fired frenziedly at the Chicken. Pent, giving the wheel to a waiting sailor, stepped out to a point where he could see the men at the guns. One bullet spanged past him and into the pilot-house. He ducked his head into the window. "That hit you, Murry?" he inquired with interest.

"No, sir," cheerfully responded the man at the wheel.

Pent became very busy superintending the fire of his absurd battery. The anchored gunboat simply would not sink. It evinced that unnatural stubbornness which is sometimes displayed by inanimate objects. The gunboat at the wharf had sunk as if she had been scuttled but this riddled thing at anchor would not even take fire. Pent began to grow flurried—privately. He could not stay there for ever. Why didn't the damned gunboat admit its destruction. Why——

He was at the forward gun when one of his engine room force came to him and, after saluting, said serenely: "The men at the after-gun are all down, sir."

It was one of those curious lifts which an enlisted man, without in any way knowing it, can give his officer. The impudent tranquillity of the man at once set Pent to rights and the stoker departed admiring the extraordinary

84

coolness of his captain.

The next few moments contained little but heat, an odour, applied mechanics and an expectation of death. Pent developed a fervid and amazed appreciation of the men, his men, men he knew very well, but strange men. What explained them? He was doing his best because he was captain of the Chicken and he lived or died by the Chicken. But what could move these men to watch his eye in bright anticipation of his orders and then obey them with enthusiastic rapidity? What caused them to speak of the action as some kind of a joke—particularly when they knew he could overhear them? What manner of men? And he anointed them secretly with his fullest affection.

Perhaps Pent did not think all this during the battle. Perhaps he thought it so soon after the battle that his full mind became confused as to the time. At any rate, it stands as an expression of his feeling.

The enemy had gotten a field-gun down to the shore and with it they began to throw three-inch shells at the Chicken. In this war it was usual that the down-trodden Spaniards in their ignorance should use smokeless powder while the Americans, by the power of the consistent everlasting three-ply, wire-woven, double back-action imbecility of a hay-seed government, used powder which on sea and on land cried their position to heaven, and, accordingly, good men got killed without reason. At first, Pent could not locate the field-gun at all, but as soon as he found it, he ran aft with one man and brought the after six-pounder again into action. He paid little heed to the old gun crew. One was lying on his face apparently dead; another was prone with a wound in the chest, while the third sat with his back to the deck-house holding a smitten arm. This last one called out huskily, "Give'm hell, sir."

The minutes of the battle were either days, years, or they were flashes of a second. Once Pent looking up was astonished to see three shell holes in the Chicken's funnel—made surreptitiously, so to speak.... "If we don't silence that field-gun, she'll sink us, boys." ... The eyes of the man sitting with his back against the deck-house were looking from out his ghastly face at the new gun-crew. He spoke with the supreme laziness of a wounded man. "Give'm hell." ... Pent felt a sudden twist of his shoulder. He was wounded—slightly.... The anchored gunboat was in flames.

VII

Pent took his little blood-stained tow-boat out to the Holy Moses. The yacht was already under way for the bay entrance. As they were passing out of range the Spaniards heroically redoubled their fire—which is their custom. Pent, moving busily about the decks, stopped suddenly at the door of the engine-room. His face was set and his eyes were steely. He spoke to one of the engineers. "During the action I saw you firing at the enemy with a rifle. I told you once to stop, and then I saw you at it again. Pegging away with a rifle is no part of your business. I want you to understand that you are in trouble." The humbled man did not raise his eyes from the deck. Presently the Holy Moses displayed an anxiety for the Chicken's health.

"One killed and four wounded, sir."

"Have you enough men left to work your ship?"

After deliberation, Pent answered: "No, sir."

"Shall I send you assistance?"

"No, sir. I can get to sea all right."

As they neared the point they were edified by the sudden appearance of a serio-comic ally. The Chancellorville at last had been unable to stand the strain, and had sent in her launch with an ensign, five seamen and a number of marksmen marines. She swept hot-foot around the point, bent on terrible slaughter; the one-pounder of her bow presented a formidable appearance. The Holy Moses and the Chicken laughed until they brought indignation to the brow of the young ensign. But he forgot it when with some of his men he boarded the Chicken to do what was possible for the wounded. The nearest surgeon was aboard the Chancellorville. There was absolute silence on board the cruiser as the Holy Moses steamed up to report. The blue-jackets listened with all their ears. The commander of the yacht spoke slowly into his megaphone: "We have—destroyed—the two—gun-boats—sir." There was a burst of confused cheering on the forecastle of the Chancellorville, but an officer's cry quelled it.

"Very—good. Will—you—come aboard?"

Two correspondents were already on the deck of the cruiser. Before the last of the wounded were hoisted aboard the cruiser the Adolphus was on her way to Key West. When she arrived at that port of desolation Shackles fled to file the telegrams and the other correspondents fled to the hotel for clothes, good clothes, clean clothes; and food, good food, much food; and drink, much drink, any kind of drink.

Days afterward, when the officers of the noble squadron received the newspapers containing an account of their performance, they looked at each other somewhat dejectedly: "Heroic assault—grand daring of Boatswain Pent—superb accuracy of the Holy Moses' fire—gallant tars of the Chicken—their names should be remembered as long as America stands—terrible losses of the enemy——"

When the Secretary of the Navy ultimately read the report of Commander Surrey, S.O.P., he had to prick himself with a dagger in order to remember that anything at all out of the ordinary had occurred.

THE SERGEANT'S PRIVATE MADHOUSE

The moonlight was almost steady blue flame and all this radiance was lavished out upon a still lifeless wilderness of stunted trees and cactus plants. The shadows lay upon the ground, pools of black and sharply outlined, resembling substances, fabrics, and not shadows at all. From afar came the sound of the sea coughing among the hollows in the coral rock.

The land was very empty; one could easily imagine that Cuba was a simple vast solitude; one could wonder at the moon taking all the trouble of this splendid illumination. There was no wind; nothing seemed to live.

But in a particular large group of shadows lay an outpost of some forty United States marines. If it had been possible to approach them from any direction without encountering one of their sentries, one could have gone stumbling among sleeping men and men who sat waiting, their blankets tented over their heads; one would have been in among them before one's mind could have decided whether they were men or devils. If a marine moved, he took the care and the time of one who walks across a death-chamber. The lieutenant in command reached for his watch and the nickel chain gave forth the faintest tinkling sound. He could see the glistening five or six pairs of eyes that slowly turned to regard him. His sergeant lay near him and he bent his face down to whisper. "Who's on post behind the big cactus plant?"

"Dryden," rejoined the sergeant just over his breath.

After a pause the lieutenant murmured: "He's got too many nerves. I shouldn't have put him there." The sergeant asked if he should crawl down and look into affairs at Dryden's post. The young officer nodded assent and the sergeant, softly cocking his rifle, went away on his hands and knees. The lieutenant with his back to a dwarf tree, sat watching the sergeant's progress for the few moments that he could see him moving from one shadow to another. Afterward, the officer waited to hear Dryden's quick but low-voiced challenge, but time passed and no sound came from the direction of the post behind the cactus bush.

The sergeant, as he came nearer and nearer to this cactus bush—a number of peculiarly dignified columns throwing shadows of inky darkness—had slowed his pace, for he did not wish to trifle with the feelings of the sentry, and he was expecting the stern hail and was ready with the immediate answer which turns away wrath. He was not made anxious by the fact that he could not yet see Dryden, for he knew that the man would be hidden in a way practised by sentry marines since the time when two men had been killed by a disease of excessive confidence on picket. Indeed, as the sergeant went still nearer, he became more and more angry. Dryden was evidently a most proper sentry.

Finally he arrived at a point where he could see Dryden seated in the shadow, staring into the bushes ahead of him, his rifle ready on his knee. The sergeant in his rage longed for the peaceful precincts of the Washington Marine Barracks where there would have been no situation to prevent the most complete non-commissioned oratory. He felt indecent in his capacity of a man able to creep up to the back of a G Company member on guard duty. Never mind; in the morning back at camp——

But, suddenly, he felt afraid. There was something wrong with Dryden. He remembered old tales of comrades creeping out to find a picket seated against a tree perhaps, upright enough but stone dead. The sergeant paused and gave the inscrutable back of the sentry a long stare. Dubious he again moved forward. At three paces, he hissed like a little snake. Dryden did not show a sign of hearing. At last, the sergeant was in a position from which he was able to reach out and touch Dryden on the arm. Whereupon was turned to him the face of a man livid with mad fright. The sergeant grabbed him by the wrist and with discreet fury shook him. "Here! Pull yourself together!"

Dryden paid no heed but turned his wild face from the newcomer to the ground in front. "Don't you see 'em, sergeant? Don't you see 'em?"

"Where?" whispered the sergeant.

"Ahead, and a little on the right flank. A reg'lar skirmish line. Don't you see 'em?"

"Naw," whispered the sergeant. Dryden began to shake. He began

89

moving one hand from his head to his knee and from his knee to his head rapidly, in a way that is without explanation. "I don't dare fire," he wept. "If I do they'll see me, and oh, how they'll pepper me!"

The sergeant lying on his belly, understood one thing. Dryden had gone mad. Dryden was the March Hare. The old man gulped down his uproarious emotions as well as he was able and used the most simple device. "Go," he said, "and tell the lieutenant while I cover your post for you."

"No! They'd see me! They'd see me! And then they'd pepper me! O, how they'd pepper me!"

The sergeant was face to face with the biggest situation of his life. In the first place he knew that at night a large or small force of Spanish guerillas was never more than easy rifle range from any marine outpost, both sides maintaining a secrecy as absolute as possible in regard to their real position and strength. Everything was on a watch-spring foundation. A loud word might be paid for by a night-attack which would involve five hundred men who needed their earned sleep, not to speak of some of them who would need their lives. The slip of a foot and the rolling of a pint of gravel might go from consequence to consequence until various crews went to general quarters on their ships in the harbour, their batteries booming as the swift search-light flashes tore through the foliage. Men would get killed—notably the sergeant and Dryden—and outposts would be cut off and the whole night would be one pitiless turmoil. And so Sergeant George H. Peasley began to run his private madhouse behind the cactus-bush.

"Dryden," said the sergeant, "you do as I tell you and go tell the lieutenant."

"I don't dare move," shivered the man. "They'll see me if I move. They'll see me. They're almost up now. Let's hide——"

"Well, then you stay here a moment and I'll go and——"

Dryden turned upon him a look so tigerish that the old man felt his hair move. "Don't you stir," he hissed. "You want to give me away. You want them to see me. Don't you stir." The sergeant decided not to stir.

He became aware of the slow wheeling of eternity, its majestic incomprehensibility of movement. Seconds, minutes, were quaint little things, tangible as toys, and there were billions of them, all alike. "Dryden," he whispered at the end of a century in which, curiously, he had never joined the marine corps at all but had taken to another walk of life and prospered greatly in it. "Dryden, this is all foolishness." He thought of the expedient of smashing the man over the head with his rifle, but Dryden was so supernaturally alert that there surely would issue some small scuffle and there could be not even the fraction of a scuffle. The sergeant relapsed into the contemplation of another century.

His patient had one fine virtue. He was in such terror of the phantom skirmish line that his voice never went above a whisper, whereas his delusion might have expressed itself in hyena yells and shots from his rifle. The sergeant, shuddering, had visions of how it might have been—the mad private leaping into the air and howling and shooting at his friends and making them the centre of the enemy's eager attention. This, to his mind, would have been conventional conduct for a maniac. The trembling victim of an idea was somewhat puzzling. The sergeant decided that from time to time he would reason with his patient. "Look here, Dryden, you don't see any real Spaniards. You've been drinking or—something. Now——"

But Dryden only glared him into silence. Dryden was inspired with such a profound contempt of him that it was become hatred. "Don't you stir!" And it was clear that if the sergeant did stir, the mad private would introduce calamity. "Now," said Peasley to himself, "if those guerillas should take a crack at us to-night, they'd find a lunatic asylum right in the front and it would be astonishing."

The silence of the night was broken by the quick low voice of a sentry to the left some distance. The breathless stillness brought an effect to the words as if they had been spoken in one's ear.

"*Halt—who's there—halt or I'll fire!*" Bang!

At the moment of sudden attack particularly at night, it is improbable that a man registers much detail of either thought or action. He may afterward say: "I was here." He may say: "I was there." "I did this." "I did that." But there remains a great incoherency because of the tumultuous thought which seethes through the head. "Is this defeat?" At night in a wilderness and against skilful foes half-seen, one does not trouble to ask if it is also Death. Defeat is Death, then, save for the miraculous. But the exaggerating magnifying first thought subsides in the ordered mind of the soldier and he knows, soon, what he is doing and how much of it. The sergeant's immediate impulse had been to squeeze close to the ground and listen—listen—above all else, listen. But the next moment he grabbed his private asylum by the scruff of its neck, jerked it to its feet and started to retreat upon the main outpost.

To the left, rifle-flashes were bursting from the shadows. To the rear, the lieutenant was giving some hoarse order or admonition. Through the air swept some Spanish bullets, very high, as if they had been fired at a man in a tree. The private asylum came on so hastily that the sergeant found he could remove his grip, and soon they were in the midst of the men of the outpost. Here there was no occasion for enlightening the lieutenant. In the first place such surprises required statement, question and answer. It is impossible to get a grossly original and fantastic idea through a man's head in less than one minute of rapid talk, and the sergeant knew the lieutenant could not spare the minute. He himself had no minutes to devote to anything but the business of the outpost. And the madman disappeared from his pen and he forgot about him.

It was a long night and the little fight was as long as the night. It was a heart-breaking work. The forty marines lay in an irregular oval. From all sides, the Mauser bullets sang low and hard. Their occupation was to prevent a rush, and to this end they potted carefully at the flash of a Mauser—save when they got excited for a moment, in which case their magazines rattled like a great Waterbury watch. Then they settled again to a systematic potting.

The enemy were not of the regular Spanish forces. They were of a corps of guerillas, native-born Cubans, who preferred the flag of Spain. They were all men who knew the craft of the woods and were all recruited from the district. They fought more like red Indians than any people but the red Indians themselves. Each seemed to possess an individuality, a fighting individuality, which is only found in the highest order of irregular soldiers. Personally they were as distinct as possible, but through equality of knowledge and experience, they arrived at concert of action. So long as they operated in the wilderness, they were formidable troops. It mattered little whether it was daylight or dark; they were mainly invisible. They had schooled from the Cubans insurgent to Spain. As the Cubans fought the Spanish troops, so would these particular Spanish troops fight the Americans. It was wisdom.

The marines thoroughly understood the game. They must lie close and fight until daylight when the guerillas promptly would go away. They had withstood other nights of this kind, and now their principal emotion was probably a sort of frantic annoyance.

Back at the main camp, whenever the roaring volleys lulled, the men in the trenches could hear their comrades of the outpost, and the guerillas pattering away interminably. The moonlight faded and left an equal darkness upon the wilderness. A man could barely see the comrade at his side. Sometimes guerillas crept so close that the flame from their rifles seemed to scorch the faces of the marines, and the reports sounded as if from two or three inches of their very noses. If a pause came, one could hear the guerillas gabbling to each other in a kind of drunken delirium. The lieutenant was praying that the ammunition would last. Everybody was praying for daybreak.

A black hour came finally, when the men were not fit to have their troubles increased. The enemy made a wild attack on one portion of the oval, which was held by about fifteen men. The remainder of the force was busy enough, and the fifteen were naturally left to their devices. Amid the whirl of it, a loud voice suddenly broke out in song:

"When shepherds guard their flocks by night,

All seated on the ground,

An angel of the Lord came down

And glory shone around."

"Who the hell is that?" demanded the lieutenant from a throat full of smoke. There was almost a full stop of the firing. The Americans were somewhat puzzled. Practical ones muttered that the fool should have a bayonet-hilt shoved down his throat. Others felt a thrill at the strangeness of the thing. Perhaps it was a sign!

"The minstrel boy to the war has gone,

In the ranks of death you'll find him,

His father's sword he has girded on

And his wild harp slung behind him."

This croak was as lugubrious as a coffin. "Who is it? Who is it?" snapped the lieutenant. "Stop him, somebody."

"It's Dryden, sir," said old Sergeant Peasley, as he felt around in the darkness for his madhouse. "I can't find him—yet."

"Please, O, please, O, do not let me fall;

You're—gurgh—ugh——"

The sergeant had pounced upon him.

This singing had had an effect upon the Spaniards. At first they had fired frenziedly at the voice, but they soon ceased, perhaps from sheer amazement. Both sides took a spell of meditation.

The sergeant was having some difficulty with his charge. "Here, you, grab 'im. Take 'im by the throat. Be quiet, you devil."

One of the fifteen men, who had been hard-pressed, called out, "We've only got about one clip a-piece, Lieutenant. If they come again——"

The lieutenant crawled to and fro among his men, taking clips of cartridges from those who had many. He came upon the sergeant and his madhouse. He felt Dryden's belt and found it simply stuffed with ammunition. He examined Dryden's rifle and found in it a full clip. The madhouse had not fired a shot. The lieutenant distributed these valuable prizes among the fifteen men. As the men gratefully took them, one said: "If they had come again hard enough, they would have had us, sir,—maybe."

94

But the Spaniards did not come again. At the first indication of daybreak, they fired their customary good-bye volley. The marines lay tight while the slow dawn crept over the land. Finally the lieutenant arose among them, and he was a bewildered man, but very angry. "Now where is that idiot, Sergeant?"

"Here he is, sir," said the old man cheerfully. He was seated on the ground beside the recumbent Dryden who, with an innocent smile on his face, was sound asleep.

"Wake him up," said the lieutenant briefly.

The sergeant shook the sleeper. "Here, Minstrel Boy, turn out. The lieutenant wants you."

Dryden climbed to his feet and saluted the officer with a dazed and childish air. "Yes, sir."

The lieutenant was obviously having difficulty in governing his feelings, but he managed to say with calmness, "You seem to be fond of singing, Dryden? Sergeant, see if he has any whisky on him."

"Sir?" said the madhouse stupefied. "Singing—fond of singing?"

Here the sergeant interposed gently, and he and the lieutenant held palaver apart from the others. The marines, hitching more comfortably their almost empty belts, spoke with grins of the madhouse. "Well, the Minstrel Boy made 'em clear out. They couldn't stand it. But—I wouldn't want to be in his boots. He'll see fireworks when the old man interviews him on the uses of grand opera in modern warfare. How do you think he managed to smuggle a bottle along without us finding it out?"

When the weary outpost was relieved and marched back to camp, the men could not rest until they had told a tale of the voice in the wilderness. In the meantime the sergeant took Dryden aboard a ship, and to those who took charge of the man, he defined him as "the most useful —— —— crazy man in the service of the United States."

VIRTUE IN WAR

I

Gates had left the regular army in 1890, those parts of him which had not been frozen having been well fried. He took with him nothing but an oaken constitution and a knowledge of the plains and the best wishes of his fellow-officers. The Standard Oil Company differs from the United States Government in that it understands the value of the loyal and intelligent services of good men and is almost certain to reward them at the expense of incapable men. This curious practice emanates from no beneficent emotion of the Standard Oil Company, on whose feelings you could not make a scar with a hammer and chisel. It is simply that the Standard Oil Company knows more than the United States Government and makes use of virtue whenever virtue is to its advantage. In 1890 Gates really felt in his bones that, if he lived a rigorously correct life and several score of his class-mates and intimate friends died off, he would get command of a troop of horse by the time he was unfitted by age to be an active cavalry leader. He left the service of the United States and entered the service of the Standard Oil Company. In the course of time he knew that, if he lived a rigorously correct life, his position and income would develop strictly in parallel with the worth of his wisdom and experience, and he would not have to walk on the corpses of his friends.

But he was not happier. Part of his heart was in a barracks, and it was not enough to discourse of the old regiment over the port and cigars to ears which were polite enough to betray a languid ignorance. Finally came the year 1898, and Gates dropped the Standard Oil Company as if it were hot. He hit the steel trail to Washington and there fought the first serious action of the war. Like most Americans, he had a native State, and one morning he found himself major in a volunteer infantry regiment whose voice had a peculiar sharp twang to it which he could remember from childhood. The colonel welcomed the West Pointer with loud cries of joy; the lieutenant-colonel looked at him with the pebbly eye of distrust; and the senior major, having had up to this time the best battalion in the regiment, strongly disapproved of him. There were only two majors, so the lieutenant-colonel commanded the first battalion, which gave him an occupation. Lieutenant-colonels under the new rules do not always have occupations. Gates got the third battalion—four companies commanded by intelligent officers who could gauge the opinions of their men at two thousand yards and govern themselves accordingly. The battalion was immensely interested in the new major. It thought it ought to develop views about him. It thought it was its blankety-blank business to find out immediately if it liked him personally. In the company streets the talk was nothing else. Among the non-commissioned officers there were eleven old soldiers of the regular army, and they knew—and cared—that Gates had held commission in the "Sixteenth Cavalry"—as Harper's Weekly says. Over this fact they rejoiced and were glad, and they stood by to jump lively when he took command. He would know his work and he would know their work, and then in battle there would be killed only what men were absolutely necessary and the sick list would be comparatively free of fools.

The commander of the second battalion had been called by an Atlanta paper, "Major Rickets C. Carmony, the commander of the second battalion of the 307th ——, is when at home one of the biggest wholesale hardware dealers in his State. Last evening he had ice-cream, at his own expense, served out at the regular mess of the battalion, and after dinner the men gathered about his tent where three hearty cheers for the popular major were given." Carmony had bought twelve copies of this newspaper and mailed them home to his friends.

In Gates's battalion there were more kicks than ice-cream, and there was no ice-cream at all. Indignation ran high at the rapid manner in which he proceeded to make soldiers of them. Some of his officers hinted finally that the men wouldn't stand it. They were saying that they had enlisted to fight for their country—yes, but they weren't going to be bullied day in and day out by a perfect stranger. They were patriots, they were, and just as good men as ever stepped—just as good as Gates or anybody like him. But, gradually, despite itself, the battalion progressed. The men were not altogether conscious of it. They evolved rather blindly. Presently there were fights with Carmony's crowd as to which was the better battalion at drills, and at last there was no argument. It was generally admitted that Gates commanded the crack battalion. The men, believing that the beginning and the end of all soldiering was in these drills of precision, were somewhat reconciled to their major when they began to understand more of what he was trying to do for them, but they were still fiery untamed patriots of lofty pride and they resented his manner toward them. It was abrupt and sharp.

The time came when everybody knew that the Fifth Army Corps was the corps designated for the first active service in Cuba. The officers and men of the 307th observed with despair that their regiment was not in the Fifth Army Corps. The colonel was a strategist. He understood everything in a flash. Without a moment's hesitation he obtained leave and mounted the night express for Washington. There he drove Senators and Congressmen in span, tandem and four-in-hand. With the telegraph he stirred so deeply the governor, the people and the newspapers of his State that whenever on a quiet night the President put his head out of the White House he could hear the distant vast commonwealth humming with indignation. And as it is well known that the Chief Executive listens to the voice of the people, the 307th was transferred to the Fifth Army Corps. It was sent at once to Tampa, where it was brigaded with two dusty regiments of regulars, who looked at it calmly, and said nothing. The brigade commander happened to be no less a person than Gates's old colonel in the "Sixteenth Cavalry"—as Harper's Weekly says—and Gates was cheered. The old man's rather solemn look brightened when he saw Gates in the 307th. There was a great deal of battering and pounding and banging for the 307th at Tampa, but the men stood it more in wonder than in anger. The two regular regiments carried them along when they could, and when they couldn't waited impatiently for them to come up. Undoubtedly the regulars wished the volunteers were in garrison at Sitka, but they said practically nothing. They minded their own regiments. The colonel was an invaluable man in a telegraph office. When came the scramble for transports the colonel retired to a telegraph office and talked so ably to Washington that the authorities pushed a number of corps aside and made way for the 307th, as if on it depended everything. The regiment got one of the best transports, and after a series of delays and some starts, and an equal number of returns, they finally sailed for Cuba.

II

Now Gates had a singular adventure on the second morning after his arrival at Atlanta to take his post as a major in the 307th.

He was in his tent, writing, when suddenly the flap was flung away and a tall young private stepped inside.

"Well, Maje," said the newcomer, genially, "how goes it?"

The major's head flashed up, but he spoke without heat.

"Come to attention and salute."

"Huh!" said the private.

"Come to attention and salute."

The private looked at him in resentful amazement, and then inquired:

"Ye ain't mad, are ye? Ain't nothin' to get huffy about, is there?"

"I—— Come to attention and salute."

"Well," drawled the private, as he stared, "seein' as ye are so darn perticular, I don't care if I do—if it'll make yer meals set on yer stomick any better."

Drawing a long breath and grinning ironically, he lazily pulled his heels together and saluted with a flourish.

"There," he said, with a return to his earlier genial manner. "How's that suit ye, Maje?"

There was a silence which to an impartial observer would have seemed pregnant with dynamite and bloody death. Then the major cleared his throat and coldly said:

"And now, what is your business?"

"Who—me?" asked the private. "Oh, I just sorter dropped in." With a deeper meaning he added: "Sorter dropped in in a friendly way, thinkin' ye was mebbe a different kind of a feller from what ye be."

The inference was clearly marked.

It was now Gates's turn to stare, and stare he unfeignedly did.

"Go back to your quarters," he said at length.

The volunteer became very angry.

"Oh, ye needn't be so up-in-th'-air, need ye? Don't know's I'm dead anxious to inflict my company on yer since I've had a good look at ye. There may be men in this here battalion what's had just as much edjewcation as you have, and I'm damned if they ain't got better manners. Good-mornin'," he said, with dignity; and, passing out of the tent, he flung the flap back in place with an air of slamming it as if it had been a door. He made his way back to his company street, striding high. He was furious. He met a large crowd of his comrades.

"What's the matter, Lige?" asked one, who noted his temper.

"Oh, nothin'," answered Lige, with terrible feeling. "Nothin'. I jest been lookin' over the new major—that's all."

"What's he like?" asked another.

"Like?" cried Lige. "He's like nothin'. He ain't out'n the same kittle as us. No. Gawd made him all by himself—sep'rate. He's a speshul produc', he is, an' he won't have no truck with jest common—men, like you be."

He made a venomous gesture which included them all.

"Did he set on ye?" asked a soldier.

"Set on me? No," replied Lige, with contempt "I set on him. I sized 'im up in a minute. 'Oh, I don't know,' I says, as I was comin' out; 'guess you ain't the only man in the world,' I says."

For a time Lige Wigram was quite a hero. He endlessly repeated the tale of his adventure, and men admired him for so soon taking the conceit out of the new officer. Lige was proud to think of himself as a plain and simple patriot who had refused to endure any high-soaring nonsense.

But he came to believe that he had not disturbed the singular composure of the major, and this concreted his hatred. He hated Gates, not as a soldier sometimes hates an officer, a hatred half of fear. Lige hated as man to man. And he was enraged to see that so far from gaining any hatred in return, he seemed incapable of making Gates have any thought of him save as a unit in a body of three hundred men. Lige might just as well have gone and grimaced at the obelisk in Central Park.

When the battalion became the best in the regiment he had no part in the pride of the companies. He was sorry when men began to speak well of Gates. He was really a very consistent hater.

III

The transport occupied by the 307th was commanded by some sort of a Scandinavian, who was afraid of the shadows of his own topmasts. He would have run his steamer away from a floating Gainsborough hat, and, in fact, he ran her away from less on some occasions. The officers, wishing to arrive with the other transports, sometimes remonstrated, and to them he talked of his owners. Every officer in the convoying warships loathed him, for in case any hostile vessel should appear they did not see how they were going to protect this rabbit, who would probably manage during a fight to be in about a hundred places on the broad, broad sea, and all of them offensive to the navy's plan. When he was not talking of his owners he was remarking to the officers of the regiment that a steamer really was not like a valise, and that he was unable to take his ship under his arm and climb trees with it. He further said that "them naval fellows" were not near so smart as they thought they were.

From an indigo sea arose the lonely shore of Cuba. Ultimately, the fleet was near Santiago, and most of the transports were bidden to wait a minute while the leaders found out their minds. The skipper, to whom the 307th were prisoners, waited for thirty hours half way between Jamaica and Cuba. He explained that the Spanish fleet might emerge from Santiago Harbour at any time, and he did not propose to be caught. His owners—— Whereupon the colonel arose as one having nine hundred men at his back, and he passed up to the bridge and he spake with the captain. He explained indirectly that each individual of his nine hundred men had decided to be the first American soldier to land for this campaign, and that in order to accomplish the marvel it was necessary for the transport to be nearer than forty-five miles from the Cuban coast. If the skipper would only land the regiment the colonel would consent to his then taking his interesting old ship and going to h—— with it. And the skipper spake with the colonel. He pointed out that as far as he officially was concerned, the United States Government did not exist. He was responsible solely to his owners. The colonel pondered these sayings. He perceived that the skipper meant that he was running his ship as he deemed best, in consideration of the capital invested by his owners, and that he was not at all concerned with the feelings of a certain American military expedition to Cuba. He was a free son of the sea—he was a sovereign citizen of the republic of the waves. He was like Lige.

However, the skipper ultimately incurred the danger of taking his ship under the terrible guns of the New York, Iowa, Oregon, Massachusetts, Indiana, Brooklyn, Texas and a score of cruisers and gunboats. It was a brave act for the captain of a United States transport, and he was visibly nervous until he could again get to sea, where he offered praises that the accursed 307th was no longer sitting on his head. For almost a week he rambled at his cheerful will over the adjacent high seas, having in his hold a great quantity of military stores as successfully secreted as if they had been buried in a copper box in the cornerstone of a new public building in Boston. He had had his master's certificate for twenty-one years, and those people couldn't tell a marlin-spike from the starboard side of the ship.

The 307th was landed in Cuba, but to their disgust they found that about ten thousand regulars were ahead of them. They got immediate orders to move out from the base on the road to Santiago. Gates was interested to note that the only delay was caused by the fact that many men of the other battalions strayed off sight-seeing. In time the long regiment wound slowly among hills that shut them from sight of the sea.

For the men to admire, there were palm-trees, little brown huts, passive, uninterested Cuban soldiers much worn from carrying American rations inside and outside. The weather was not oppressively warm, and the journey was said to be only about seven miles. There were no rumours save that there had been one short fight and the army had advanced to within sight of Santiago. Having a peculiar faculty for the derision of the romantic, the 307th began to laugh. Actually there was not anything in the world which turned out to be as books describe it. Here they had landed from the transport expecting to be at once flung into line of battle and sent on some kind of furious charge, and now they were trudging along a quiet trail lined with somnolent trees and grass. The whole business so far struck them as being a highly tedious burlesque.

After a time they came to where the camps of regular regiments marked the sides of the road—little villages of tents no higher than a man's waist. The colonel found his brigade commander and the 307th was sent off into a field of long grass, where the men grew suddenly solemn with the importance of getting their supper.

In the early evening some regulars told one of Gates's companies that at daybreak this division would move to an attack upon something.

"How d'you know?" said the company, deeply awed.

"Heard it."

"Well, what are we to attack?"

"Dunno."

The 307th was not at all afraid, but each man began to imagine the morrow. The regulars seemed to have as much interest in the morrow as they did in the last Christmas. It was none of their affair, apparently.

"Look here," said Lige Wigram, to a man in the 17th Regular Infantry, "whereabouts are we goin' ter-morrow an' who do we run up against—do ye know?"

The 17th soldier replied, truculently: "If I ketch th' —— —— —— what stole my terbaccer, I'll whirl in an' break every —— —— bone in his body."

Gates's friends in the regular regiments asked him numerous questions as to the reliability of his organisation. Would the 307th stand the racket? They were certainly not contemptuous; they simply did not seem to consider it important whether the 307th would or whether it would not.

"Well," said Gates, "they won't run the length of a tent-peg if they can gain any idea of what they're fighting; they won't bunch if they've about six acres of open ground to move in; they won't get rattled at all if they see you fellows taking it easy, and they'll fight like the devil as long as they thoroughly, completely, absolutely, satisfactorily, exhaustively understand what the business is. They're lawyers. All excepting my battalion."

IV

Lige awakened into a world obscured by blue fog. Somebody was gently shaking him. "Git up; we're going to move." The regiment was buckling up itself. From the trail came the loud creak of a light battery moving ahead. The tones of all men were low; the faces of the officers were composed, serious. The regiment found itself moving along behind the battery before it had time to ask itself more than a hundred questions. The trail wound through a dense tall jungle, dark, heavy with dew.

The battle broke with a snap—far ahead. Presently Lige heard from the air above him a faint low note as if somebody were blowing softly in the mouth of a bottle. It was a stray bullet which had wandered a mile to tell him that war was before him. He nearly broke his neck looking upward. "Did ye hear that?" But the men were fretting to get out of this gloomy jungle. They wanted to see something. The faint rup-rup-rrrrup-rup on in the front told them that the fight had begun; death was abroad, and so the mystery of this wilderness excited them. This wilderness was portentously still and dark.

They passed the battery aligned on a hill above the trail, and they had not gone far when the gruff guns began to roar and they could hear the rocket-like swish of the flying shells. Presently everybody must have called out for the assistance of the 307th. Aides and couriers came flying back to them.

"Is this the 307th? Hurry up your men, please, Colonel. You're needed more every minute."

104

Oh, they were, were they? Then the regulars were not going to do all the fighting? The old 307th was bitterly proud or proudly bitter. They left their blanket rolls under the guard of God and pushed on, which is one of the reasons why the Cubans of that part of the country were, later, so well equipped. There began to appear fields, hot, golden-green in the sun. On some palm-dotted knolls before them they could see little lines of black dots—the American advance. A few men fell, struck down by other men who, perhaps half a mile away, were aiming at somebody else. The loss was wholly in Carmony's battalion, which immediately bunched and backed away, coming with a shock against Gates's advance company. This shock sent a tremor through all of Gates's battalion until men in the very last files cried out nervously, "Well, what in hell is up now?" There came an order to deploy and advance. An occasional hoarse yell from the regulars could be heard. The deploying made Gates's heart bleed for the colonel. The old man stood there directing the movement, straight, fearless, sombrely defiant of—everything. Carmony's four companies were like four herds. And all the time the bullets from no living man knows where kept pecking at them and pecking at them. Gates, the excellent Gates, the highly educated and strictly military Gates, grew rankly insubordinate. He knew that the regiment was suffering from nothing but the deadly range and oversweep of the modern rifle, of which many proud and confident nations know nothing save that they have killed savages with it, which is the least of all informations.

Gates rushed upon Carmony.

"―― ―― it, man, if you can't get your people to deploy, for ―― sake give me a chance! I'm stuck in the woods!"

Carmony gave nothing, but Gates took all he could get and his battalion deployed and advanced like men. The old colonel almost burst into tears, and he cast one quick glance of gratitude at Gates, which the younger officer wore on his heart like a secret decoration.

There was a wild scramble up hill, down dale, through thorny thickets. Death smote them with a kind of slow rhythm, leisurely taking a man now here, now there, but the cat-spit sound of the bullets was always. A large number of the men of Carmony's battalion came on with Gates. They were willing to do anything, anything. They had no real fault, unless it was that early conclusion that any brave high-minded youth was necessarily a good soldier immediately, from the beginning. In them had been born a swift feeling that the unpopular Gates knew everything, and they followed the trained soldier.

If they followed him, he certainly took them into it. As they swung heavily up one steep hill, like so many wind-blown horses, they came suddenly out into the real advance. Little blue groups of men were making frantic rushes forward and then flopping down on their bellies to fire volleys while other groups made rushes. Ahead they could see a heavy house-like fort which was inadequate to explain from whence came the myriad bullets. The remainder of the scene was landscape. Pale men, yellow men, blue men came out of this landscape quiet and sad-eyed with wounds. Often they were grimly facetious. There is nothing in the American regulars so amazing as his conduct when he is wounded—his apologetic limp, his deprecatory arm-sling, his embarrassed and ashamed shot-hole through the lungs. The men of the 307th looked at calm creatures who had divers punctures and they were made better. These men told them that it was only necessary to keep a-going. They of the 307th lay on their bellies, red, sweating and panting, and heeded the voice of the elder brother.

Gates walked back of his line, very white of face, but hard and stern past anything his men knew of him. After they had violently adjured him to lie down and he had given weak backs a cold, stiff touch, the 307th charged by rushes. The hatless colonel made frenzied speech, but the man of the time was Gates. The men seemed to feel that this was his business. Some of the regular officers said afterward that the advance of the 307th was very respectable indeed. They were rather surprised, they said. At least five of the crack regiments of the regular army were in this division, and the 307th could win no more than a feeling of kindly appreciation.

Yes, it was very good, very good indeed, but did you notice what was being done at the same moment by the 12th, the 17th, the 7th, the 8th, the 25th, the——

106

Gates felt that his charge was being a success. He was carrying out a successful function. Two captains fell bang on the grass and a lieutenant slumped quietly down with a death wound. Many men sprawled suddenly. Gates was keeping his men almost even with the regulars, who were charging on his flanks. Suddenly he thought that he must have come close to the fort and that a Spaniard had tumbled a great stone block down upon his leg. Twelve hands reached out to help him, but he cried:

"No—d—— your souls—go on—go on!"

He closed his eyes for a moment, and it really was only for a moment. When he opened them he found himself alone with Lige Wigram, who lay on the ground near him.

"Maje," said Lige, "yer a good man. I've been a-follerin' ye all day an' I want to say yer a good man."

The major turned a coldly scornful eye upon the private.

"Where are you wounded? Can you walk? Well, if you can, go to the rear and leave me alone. I'm bleeding to death, and you bother me."

Lige, despite the pain in his wounded shoulder, grew indignant.

"Well," he mumbled, "you and me have been on th' outs fer a long time, an' I only wanted to tell ye that what I seen of ye t'day has made me feel mighty different."

"Go to the rear—if you can walk," said the major.

"Now, Maje, look here. A little thing like that——"

"Go to the rear."

Lige gulped with sobs.

"Maje, I know I didn't understand ye at first, but ruther'n let a little thing like that come between us, I'd—I'd——"

"Go to the rear."

In this reiteration Lige discovered a resemblance to that first old offensive

107

phrase, "Come to attention and salute." He pondered over the resemblance and he saw that nothing had changed. The man bleeding to death was the same man to whom he had once paid a friendly visit with unfriendly results. He thought now that he perceived a certain hopeless gulf, a gulf which is real or unreal, according to circumstances. Sometimes all men are equal; occasionally they are not. If Gates had ever criticised Lige's manipulation of a hay fork on the farm at home, Lige would have furiously disdained his hate or blame. He saw now that he must not openly approve the major's conduct in war. The major's pride was in his business, and his, Lige's congratulations, were beyond all enduring.

The place where they were lying suddenly fell under a new heavy rain of bullets. They sputtered about the men, making the noise of large grasshoppers.

"Major!" cried Lige. "Major Gates! It won't do for ye to be left here, sir. Ye'll be killed."

"But you can't help it, lad. You take care of yourself."

"I'm damned if I do," said the private, vehemently. "If I can't git you out, I'll stay and wait."

The officer gazed at his man with that same icy, contemptuous gaze.

"I'm—I'm a dead man anyhow. You go to the rear, do you hear?"

"No."

The dying major drew his revolver, cocked it and aimed it unsteadily at Lige's head.

"Will you obey orders?"

"No."

"One?"

"No."

"Two?"

"No."

Gates weakly dropped his revolver.

"Go to the devil, then. You're no soldier, but——" He tried to add something, "But——"

He heaved a long moan. "But—you—you—oh, I'm so-o-o tired."

V

After the battle, three correspondents happened to meet on the trail. They were hot, dusty, weary, hungry and thirsty, and they repaired to the shade of a mango tree and sprawled luxuriously. Among them they mustered twoscore friends who on that day had gone to the far shore of the hereafter, but their senses were no longer resonant. Shackles was babbling plaintively about mint-juleps, and the others were bidding him to have done.

"By-the-way," said one, at last, "it's too bad about poor old Gates of the 307th. He bled to death. His men were crazy. They were blubbering and cursing around there like wild people. It seems that when they got back there to look for him they found him just about gone, and another wounded man was trying to stop the flow with his hat! His hat, mind you. Poor old Gatesie!"

"Oh, no, Shackles!" said the third man of the party. "Oh, no, you're wrong. The best mint-juleps in the world are made right in New York, Philadelphia or Boston. That Kentucky idea is only a tradition."

A wounded man approached them. He had been shot through the shoulder and his shirt had been diagonally cut away, leaving much bare skin. Over the bullet's point of entry there was a kind of a white spider, shaped from pieces of adhesive plaster. Over the point of departure there was a bloody bulb of cotton strapped to the flesh by other pieces of adhesive plaster. His eyes were dreamy, wistful, sad. "Say, gents, have any of ye got a bottle?" he asked.

A correspondent raised himself suddenly and looked with bright eyes at the soldier.

"Well, you have got a nerve," he said grinning. "Have we got a bottle, eh! Who in h—— do you think we are? If we had a bottle of good licker, do you suppose we could let the whole army drink out of it? You have too much faith in the generosity of men, my friend!"

The soldier stared, ox-like, and finally said, "Huh?"

"I say," continued the correspondent, somewhat more loudly, "that if we had had a bottle we would have probably finished it ourselves by this time."

"But," said the other, dazed, "I meant an empty bottle. I didn't mean no full bottle."

The correspondent was humorously irascible.

"An empty bottle! You must be crazy! Who ever heard of a man looking for an empty bottle? It isn't sense! I've seen a million men looking for full bottles, but you're the first man I ever saw who insisted on the bottle's being empty. What in the world do you want it for?"

"Well, ye see, mister," explained Lige, slowly, "our major he was killed this mornin' an' we're jes' goin' to bury him, an' I thought I'd jest take a look 'round an' see if I couldn't borry an empty bottle, an' then I'd take an' write his name an' reg'ment on a paper an' put it in th' bottle an' bury it with him, so's when they come fer to dig him up sometime an' take him home, there sure wouldn't be no mistake."

"Oh!"

MARINES SIGNALLING UNDER FIRE AT GUANTANAMO

They were four Guantanamo marines, officially known for the time as signalmen, and it was their duty to lie in the trenches of Camp McCalla, that faced the water, and, by day, signal the Marblehead with a flag and, by night, signal the Marblehead with lanterns. It was my good fortune—at that time I considered it my bad fortune, indeed—to be with them on two of the nights when a wild storm of fighting was pealing about the hill; and, of all the actions of the war, none were so hard on the nerves, none strained courage so near the panic point, as those swift nights in Camp McCalla. With a thousand rifles rattling; with the field-guns booming in your ears; with the diabolic Colt automatics clacking; with the roar of the Marblehead coming from the bay, and, last, with Mauser bullets sneering always in the air a few inches over one's head, and with this enduring from dusk to dawn, it is extremely doubtful if any one who was there will be able to forget it easily. The noise; the impenetrable darkness; the knowledge from the sound of the bullets that the enemy was on three sides of the camp; the infrequent bloody stumbling and death of some man with whom, perhaps, one had messed two hours previous; the weariness of the body, and the more terrible weariness of the mind, at the endlessness of the thing, made it wonderful that at least some of the men did not come out of it with their nerves hopelessly in shreds.

But, as this interesting ceremony proceeded in the darkness, it was necessary for the signal squad to coolly take and send messages. Captain McCalla always participated in the defence of the camp by raking the woods on two of its sides with the guns of the Marblehead. Moreover, he was the senior officer present, and he wanted to know what was happening. All night long the crews of the ships in the bay would stare sleeplessly into the blackness toward the roaring hill.

The signal squad had an old cracker-box placed on top of the trench. When not signalling they hid the lanterns in this-box; but as soon as an order to send a message was received, it became necessary for one of the men to stand up and expose the lights. And then—oh, my eye—how the guerillas hidden in the gulf of night would turn loose at those yellow gleams!

Signalling in this way is done by letting one lantern remain stationary—on top of the cracker-box, in this case—and moving the other over to the left and right and so on in the regular gestures of the wig-wagging code. It is a very simple system of night communication, but one can see that it presents rare possibilities when used in front of an enemy who, a few hundred yards away, is overjoyed at sighting so definite a mark.

How, in the name of wonders, those four men at Camp McCalla were not riddled from head to foot and sent home more as repositories of Spanish ammunition than as marines is beyond all comprehension. To make a confession—when one of these men stood up to wave his lantern, I, lying in the trench, invariably rolled a little to the right or left, in order that, when he was shot, he would not fall on me. But the squad came off scathless, despite the best efforts of the most formidable corps in the Spanish army—the Escuadra de Guantanamo. That it was the most formidable corps in the Spanish army of occupation has been told me by many Spanish officers and also by General Menocal and other insurgent officers. General Menocal was Garcia's chief-of-staff when the latter was operating busily in Santiago province. The regiment was composed solely of practicos, or guides, who knew every shrub and tree on the ground over which they moved.

Whenever the adjutant, Lieutenant Draper, came plunging along through the darkness with an order—such as: "Ask the Marblehead to please shell the woods to the left"—my heart would come into my mouth, for I knew then that one of my pals was going to stand up behind the lanterns and have all Spain shoot at him.

The answer was always upon the instant:

"Yes, sir." Then the bullets began to snap, snap, snap, at his head while all the woods began to crackle like burning straw. I could lie near and watch the face of the signalman, illumed as it was by the yellow shine of lantern light, and the absence of excitement, fright, or any emotion at all on his countenance, was something to astonish all theories out of one's mind. The face was in every instance merely that of a man intent upon his business, the business of wig-wagging into the gulf of night where a light on the Marblehead was seen to move slowly.

These times on the hill resembled, in some days, those terrible scenes on the stage—scenes of intense gloom, blinding lightning, with a cloaked devil or assassin or other appropriate character muttering deeply amid the awful roll of the thunder-drums. It was theatric beyond words: one felt like a leaf in this booming chaos, this prolonged tragedy of the night. Amid it all one could see from time to time the yellow light on the face of a preoccupied signalman.

Possibly no man who was there ever before understood the true eloquence of the breaking of the day. We would lie staring into the east, fairly ravenous for the dawn. Utterly worn to rags, with our nerves standing on end like so many bristles, we lay and watched the east—the unspeakably obdurate and slow east. It was a wonder that the eyes of some of us did not turn to glass balls from the fixity of our gaze.

Then there would come into the sky a patch of faint blue light. It was like a piece of moonshine. Some would say it was the beginning of daybreak; others would declare it was nothing of the kind. Men would get very disgusted with each other in these low-toned arguments held in the trenches. For my part, this development in the eastern sky destroyed many of my ideas and theories concerning the dawning of the day; but then I had never before had occasion to give it such solemn attention.

This patch widened and whitened in about the speed of a man's accomplishment if he should be in the way of painting Madison Square Garden with a camel's hair brush. The guerillas always set out to whoop it up about this time, because they knew the occasion was approaching when it would be expedient for them to elope. I, at least, always grew furious with this wretched sunrise. I thought I could have walked around the world in the time required for the old thing to get up above the horizon.

One midnight, when an important message was to be sent to the Marblehead, Colonel Huntington came himself to the signal place with

Adjutant Draper and Captain McCauley, the quartermaster. When the man stood up to signal, the colonel stood beside him. At sight of the lights, the Spaniards performed as usual. They drove enough bullets into that immediate vicinity to kill all the marines in the corps.

Lieutenant Draper was agitated for his chief. "Colonel, won't you step down, sir?"

"Why, I guess not," said the grey old veteran in his slow, sad, always-gentle way. "I am in no more danger than the man."

"But, sir——" began the adjutant.

"Oh, it's all right, Draper."

So the colonel and the private stood side to side and took the heavy fire without either moving a muscle.

Day was always obliged to come at last, punctuated by a final exchange of scattering shots. And the light shone on the marines, the dumb guns, the flag. Grimy yellow face looked into grimy yellow face, and grinned with weary satisfaction. Coffee!

Usually it was impossible for many of the men to sleep at once. It always took me, for instance, some hours to get my nerves combed down. But then it was great joy to lie in the trench with the four signalmen, and understand thoroughly that that night was fully over at last, and that, although the future might have in store other bad nights, that one could never escape from the prison-house which we call the past.

At the wild little fight at Cusco there were some splendid exhibitions of wig-wagging under fire. Action began when an advanced detachment of marines under Lieutenant Lucas with the Cuban guides had reached the summit of a ridge overlooking a small valley where there was a house, a well, and a thicket of some kind of shrub with great broad, oily leaves. This thicket, which was perhaps an acre in extent, contained the guerillas. The valley was open to the sea. The distance from the top of the ridge to the thicket was barely two hundred yards.

The Dolphin had sailed up the coast in line with the marine advance, ready with her guns to assist in any action. Captain Elliott, who commanded the two hundred marines in this fight, suddenly called out for a signalman. He wanted a man to tell the Dolphin to open fire on the house and the thicket. It was a blazing, bitter hot day on top of the ridge with its shrivelled chaparral and its straight, tall cactus plants. The sky was bare and blue, and hurt like brass. In two minutes the prostrate marines were red and sweating like so many hull-buried stokers in the tropics.

Captain Elliott called out:

"Where's a signalman? Who's a signalman here?"

A red-headed "mick"—I think his name was Clancy—at any rate, it will do to call him Clancy—twisted his head from where he lay on his stomach pumping his Lee, and, saluting, said that he was a signalman.

There was no regulation flag with the expedition, so Clancy was obliged to tie his blue polka-dot neckerchief on the end of his rifle. It did not make a very good flag. At first Clancy moved a ways down the safe side of the ridge and wigwagged there very busily. But what with the flag being so poor for the purpose, and the background of ridge being so dark, those on the Dolphin did not see it. So Clancy had to return to the top of the ridge and outline himself and his flag against the sky.

The usual thing happened. As soon as the Spaniards caught sight of this silhouette, they let go like mad at it. To make things more comfortable for Clancy, the situation demanded that he face the sea and turn his back to the Spanish bullets. This was a hard game, mark you—to stand with the small of your back to volley firing. Clancy thought so. Everybody thought so. We all cleared out of his neighbourhood. If he wanted sole possession of any particular spot on that hill, he could have it for all we would interfere with him.

It cannot be denied that Clancy was in a hurry. I watched him. He was so occupied with the bullets that snarled close to his ears that he was obliged to repeat the letters of his message softly to himself. It seemed an intolerable time before the Dolphin answered the little signal. Meanwhile, we gazed at him, marvelling every second that he had not yet pitched headlong. He swore at times.

Finally the Dolphin replied to his frantic gesticulation, and he delivered his message. As his part of the transaction was quite finished—whoop!—he dropped like a brick into the firing line and began to shoot; began to get "hunky" with all those people who had been plugging at him. The blue polka-dot neckerchief still fluttered from the barrel of his rifle. I am quite certain that he let it remain there until the end of the fight.

The shells of the Dolphin began to plough up the thicket, kicking the bushes, stones, and soil into the air as if somebody was blasting there.

Meanwhile, this force of two hundred marines and fifty Cubans and the force of—probably—six companies of Spanish guerillas were making such an awful din that the distant Camp McCalla was all alive with excitement. Colonel Huntington sent out strong parties to critical points on the road to facilitate, if necessary, a safe retreat, and also sent forty men under Lieutenant Magill to come up on the left flank of the two companies in action under Captain Elliott. Lieutenant Magill and his men had crowned a hill which covered entirely the flank of the fighting companies, but when the Dolphin opened fire, it happened that Magill was in the line of the shots. It became necessary to stop the Dolphin at once. Captain Elliott was not near Clancy at this time, and he called hurriedly for another signalman.

Sergeant Quick arose, and announced that he was a signalman. He produced from somewhere a blue polka-dot neckerchief as large as a quilt. He tied it on a long, crooked stick. Then he went to the top of the ridge, and turning his back to the Spanish fire, began to signal to the Dolphin. Again we gave a man sole possession of a particular part of the ridge. We didn't want it. He could have it and welcome. If the young sergeant had had the smallpox, the cholera, and the yellow fever, we could not have slid out with more celerity.

As men have said often, it seemed as if there was in this war a God of Battles who held His mighty hand before the Americans. As I looked at

Sergeant Quick wig-wagging there against the sky, I would not have given a tin tobacco-tag for his life. Escape for him seemed impossible. It seemed absurd to hope that he would not be hit; I only hoped that he would be hit just a little, in the arm, the shoulder, or the leg.

I watched his face, and it was as grave and serene as that of a man writing in his own library. He was the very embodiment of tranquillity in occupation. He stood there amid the animal-like babble of the Cubans, the crack of rifles, and the whistling snarl of the bullets, and wig-wagged whatever he had to wig-wag without heeding anything but his business. There was not a single trace of nervousness or haste.

To say the least, a fight at close range is absorbing as a spectacle. No man wants to take his eyes from it until that time comes when he makes up his mind to run away. To deliberately stand up and turn your back to a battle is in itself hard work. To deliberately stand up and turn your back to a battle and hear immediate evidences of the boundless enthusiasm with which a large company of the enemy shoot at you from an adjacent thicket is, to my mind at least, a very great feat. One need not dwell upon the detail of keeping the mind carefully upon a slow spelling of an important code message.

I saw Quick betray only one sign of emotion. As he swung his clumsy flag to and fro, an end of it once caught on a cactus pillar, and he looked sharply over his shoulder to see what had it. He gave the flag an impatient jerk. He looked annoyed.

THIS MAJESTIC LIE

I

In the twilight, a great crowd was streaming up the Prado in Havana. The people had been down to the shore to laugh and twiddle their fingers at the American blockading fleet—mere colourless shapes on the edge of the sea. Gorgeous challenges had been issued to the far-away ships by little children and women while the men laughed. Havana was happy, for it was known that the illustrious sailor Don Patricio de Montojo had with his fleet met the decaying ships of one Dewey and smitten them into stuffing for a baby's pillow. Of course the American sailors were drunk at the time, but the American sailors were always drunk. Newsboys galloped among the crowd crying La Lucha and La Marina. The papers said: "This is as we foretold. How could it be otherwise when the cowardly Yankees met our brave sailors?" But the tongues of the exuberant people ran more at large. One man said in a loud voice: "How unfortunate it is that we still have to buy meat in Havana when so much pork is floating in Manila Bay!" Amid the consequent laughter, another man retorted: "Oh, never mind! That pork in Manila is rotten. It always was rotten." Still another man said: "But, little friend, it would make good manure for our fields if only we had it." And still another man said: "Ah, wait until our soldiers get with the wives of the Americans and there will be many little Yankees to serve hot on our tables. The men of the Maine simply made our appetites good. Never mind the pork in Manila. There will be plenty." Women laughed; children laughed because their mothers laughed; everybody laughed. And—a word with you—these people were cackling and chuckling and insulting their own dead, their own dead men of Spain, for if the poor green corpses floated then in Manila Bay they were not American corpses.

The newsboys came charging with an extra. The inhabitants of Philadelphia had fled to the forests because of a Spanish bombardment and also Boston was besieged by the Apaches who had totally invested the town. The Apache artillery had proven singularly effective and an American garrison had been unable to face it. In Chicago millionaires were giving away their palaces for two or three loaves of bread. These despatches were from Madrid and every word was truth, but they added little to the enthusiasm because the crowd—God help mankind—was greatly occupied with visions of Yankee pork floating in Manila Bay. This will be thought to be embittered writing. Very well; the writer admits its untruthfulness in one particular. It is untruthful in that it fails to reproduce one-hundredth part of the grossness and indecency of popular expression in Havana up to the time when the people knew they were beaten.

There were no lights on the Prado or in other streets because of a military order. In the slow-moving crowd, there was a young man and an old woman. Suddenly the young man laughed a strange metallic laugh and spoke in English, not cautiously. "That's damned hard to listen to."

The woman spoke quickly. "Hush, you little idiot. Do you want to be walkin' across that grass-plot in Cabanas with your arms tied behind you?" Then she murmured sadly: "Johnnie, I wonder if that's true—what they say about Manila?"

"I don't know," said Johnnie, "but I think they're lying."

As they crossed the Plaza, they could see that the Café Tacon was crowded with Spanish officers in blue and white pajama uniforms. Wine and brandy was being wildly consumed in honour of the victory at Manila. "Let's hear what they say," said Johnnie to his companion, and they moved across the street and in under the portales. The owner of the Café Tacon was standing on a table making a speech amid cheers. He was advocating the crucifixion of such Americans as fell into Spanish hands and—it was all very sweet and white and tender, but above all, it was chivalrous, because it is well known that the Spaniards are a chivalrous people. It has been remarked both by the English newspapers and by the bulls that are bred for the red death. And secretly the corpses in Manila Bay mocked this jubilee; the mocking, mocking corpses in Manila Bay.

To be blunt, Johnnie was an American spy. Once he had been the manager of a sugar plantation in Pinar del Rio, and during the insurrection it had been his distinguished function to pay tribute of money, food and forage alike to Spanish columns and insurgent bands. He was performing this straddle with benefit to his crops and with mildew to his conscience when Spain and the United States agreed to skirmish, both in the name of honour. It then became a military necessity that he should change his base. Whatever of the province that was still alive was sorry to see him go for he had been a very dexterous man and food and wine had been in his house even when a man with a mango could gain the envy of an entire Spanish battalion. Without doubt he had been a mere trimmer, but it was because of his crop and he always wrote the word thus: C R O P. In those days a man of peace and commerce was in a position parallel to the watchmaker who essayed a task in the midst of a drunken brawl with oaths, bottles and bullets flying about his intent bowed head. So many of them—or all of them—were trimmers, and to any armed force they fervently said: "God assist you." And behold, the trimmers dwelt safely in a tumultuous land and without effort save that their little machines for trimming ran night and day. So many a plantation became covered with a maze of lies as if thick-webbing spiders had run from stalk to stalk in the cane. So sometimes a planter incurred an equal hatred from both sides and when in trouble there was no camp to which he could flee save, straight in air, the camp of the heavenly host.

If Johnnie had not had a crop, he would have been plainly on the side of the insurgents, but his crop staked him down to the soil at a point where the Spaniards could always be sure of finding him—him or his crop—it is the same thing. But when war came between Spain and the United States he could no longer be the cleverest trimmer in Pinar del Rio. And he retreated upon Key West losing much of his baggage train, not because of panic but because of wisdom. In Key West, he was no longer the manager of a big Cuban plantation; he was a little tan-faced refugee without much money. Mainly he listened; there was nought else to do. In the first place he was a young man of extremely slow speech and in the Key West Hotel tongues ran like pin-wheels. If he had projected his methodic way of thought and speech upon this hurricane, he would have been as effective as the man who tries to smoke against the gale. This truth did not impress him. Really, he was impressed with the fact that although he knew much of Cuba, he could not

120

talk so rapidly and wisely of it as many war-correspondents who had not yet seen the island. Usually he brooded in silence over a bottle of beer and the loss of his crop. He received no sympathy, although there was a plentitude of tender souls. War's first step is to make expectation so high that all present things are fogged and darkened in a tense wonder of the future. None cared about the collapse of Johnnie's plantation when all were thinking of the probable collapse of cities and fleets.

In the meantime, battle-ships, monitors, cruisers, gunboats and torpedo craft arrived, departed, arrived, departed. Rumours sang about the ears of warships hurriedly coaling. Rumours sang about the ears of warships leisurely coming to anchor. This happened and that happened and if the news arrived at Key West as a mouse, it was often enough cabled north as an elephant. The correspondents at Key West were perfectly capable of adjusting their perspective, but many of the editors in the United States were like deaf men at whom one has to roar. A few quiet words of information was not enough for them; one had to bawl into their ears a whirlwind tale of heroism, blood, death, victory—or defeat—at any rate, a tragedy. The papers should have sent playwrights to the first part of the war. Play-wrights are allowed to lower the curtain from time to time and say to the crowd: "Mark, ye, now! Three or four months are supposed to elapse. But the poor devils at Key West were obliged to keep the curtain up all the time." "This isn't a continuous performance." "Yes, it is; it's got to be a continuous performance. The welfare of the paper demands it. The people want news." Very well: continuous performance. It is strange how men of sense can go aslant at the bidding of other men of sense and combine to contribute to a general mess of exaggeration and bombast. But we did; and in the midst of the furor I remember the still figure of Johnnie, the planter, the ex-trimmer. He looked dazed.

This was in May.

We all liked him. From time to time some of us heard in his words the vibrant of a thoughtful experience. But it could not be well heard; it was only like the sound of a bell from under the floor. We were too busy with our own clatter. He was taciturn and competent while we solved the war in a babble of tongues. Soon we went about our peaceful paths saying ironically one to another: "War is hell." Meanwhile, managing editors fought us tooth and nail and we all were sent boxes of medals inscribed: "Incompetency." We became furious with ourselves. Why couldn't we send hair-raising despatches? Why couldn't we inflame the wires? All this we did. If a first-class armoured cruiser which had once been a tow-boat fired a six-pounder shot from her forward thirteen-inch gun turret, the world heard of it, you bet. We were not idle men. We had come to report the war and we did it. Our good names and our salaries depended upon it and we were urged by our managing-editors to remember that the American people were a collection of super-nervous idiots who would immediately have convulsions if we did not throw them some news—any news. It was not true, at all. The American people were anxious for things decisive to happen; they were not anxious to be lulled to satisfaction with a drug. But we lulled them. We told them this and we told them that, and I warrant you our screaming sounded like the noise of a lot of sea-birds settling for the night among the black crags.

In the meantime, Johnnie stared and meditated. In his unhurried, unstartled manner he was singularly like another man who was flying the pennant as commander-in-chief of the North Atlantic Squadron. Johnnie was a refugee; the admiral was an admiral. And yet they were much akin, these two. Their brother was the Strategy Board—the only capable political institution of the war. At Key West the naval officers spoke of their business and were devoted to it and were bound to succeed in it, but when the flagship was in port the only two people who were independent and sane were the admiral and Johnnie. The rest of us were lulling the public with drugs.

There was much discussion of the new batteries at Havana. Johnnie was a typical American. In Europe a typical American is a man with a hard eye, chin-whiskers and a habit of speaking through his nose. Johnnie was a young man of great energy, ready to accomplish a colossal thing for the basic reason that he was ignorant of its magnitude. In fact he attacked all obstacles in life in a spirit of contempt, seeing them smaller than they were until he had actually surmounted them—when he was likely to be immensely pleased with himself. Somewhere in him there was a sentimental tenderness, but it was like a light seen afar at night; it came, went, appeared again in a

122

new place, flickered, flared, went out, left you in a void and angry. And if his sentimental tenderness was a light, the darkness in which it puzzled you was his irony of soul. This irony was directed first at himself; then at you; then at the nation and the flag; then at God. It was a midnight in which you searched for the little elusive, ashamed spark of tender sentiment. Sometimes, you thought this was all pretext, the manner and the way of fear of the wit of others; sometimes you thought he was a hardened savage; usually you did not think but waited in the cheerful certainty that in time the little flare of light would appear in the gloom.

Johnnie decided that he would go and spy upon the fortifications of Havana. If any one wished to know of those batteries it was the admiral of the squadron, but the admiral of the squadron knew much. I feel sure that he knew the size and position of every gun. To be sure, new guns might be mounted at any time, but they would not be big guns, and doubtless he lacked in his cabin less information than would be worth a man's life. Still, Johnnie decided to be a spy. He would go and look. We of the newspapers pinned him fast to the tail of our kite and he was taken to see the admiral. I judge that the admiral did not display much interest in the plan. But at any rate it seems that he touched Johnnie smartly enough with a brush to make him, officially, a spy. Then Johnnie bowed and left the cabin. There was no other machinery. If Johnnie was to end his life and leave a little book about it, no one cared—least of all, Johnnie and the admiral. When he came aboard the tug, he displayed his usual stalwart and rather selfish zest for fried eggs. It was all some kind of an ordinary matter. It was done every day. It was the business of packing pork, sewing shoes, binding hay. It was commonplace. No one could adjust it, get it in proportion, until—afterwards. On a dark night, they heaved him into a small boat and rowed him to the beach.

And one day he appeared at the door of a little lodging-house in Havana kept by Martha Clancy, born in Ireland, bred in New York, fifteen years married to a Spanish captain, and now a widow, keeping Cuban lodgers who had no money with which to pay her. She opened the door only a little way and looked down over her spectacles at him.

"Good-mornin' Martha," he said.

She looked a moment in silence. Then she made an indescribable gesture of weariness. "Come in," she said. He stepped inside. "And in God's name couldn't you keep your neck out of this rope? And so you had to come here, did you—to Havana? Upon my soul, Johnnie, my son, you are the biggest fool on two legs."

He moved past her into the court-yard and took his old chair at the table—between the winding stairway and the door—near the orange tree. "Why am I?" he demanded stoutly. She made no reply until she had taken seat in her rocking-chair and puffed several times upon a cigarette. Then through the smoke she said meditatively: "Everybody knows ye are a damned little mambi." Sometimes she spoke with an Irish accent.

He laughed. "I'm no more of a mambi than you are, anyhow."

"I'm no mambi. But your name is poison to half the Spaniards in Havana. That you know. And if you were once safe in Cayo Hueso, 'tis nobody but a born fool who would come blunderin' into Havana again. Have ye had your dinner?"

"What have you got?" he asked before committing himself.

She arose and spoke without confidence as she moved toward the cupboard. "There's some codfish salad."

"What?" said he.

"Codfish salad."

"Codfish what?"

"Codfish salad. Ain't it good enough for ye? Maybe this is Delmonico's— no? Maybe ye never heard that the Yankees have us blockaded, hey? Maybe ye think food can be picked in the streets here now, hey? I'll tell ye one thing, my son, if you stay here long you'll see the want of it and so you had best not throw it over your shoulder."

The spy settled determinedly in his chair and delivered himself his final decision. "That may all be true, but I'm damned if I eat codfish salad."

Old Martha was a picture of quaint despair. "You'll not?"

"No!"

"Then," she sighed piously, "may the Lord have mercy on ye, Johnnie, for you'll never do here. 'Tis not the time for you. You're due after the blockade. Will you do me the favour of translating why you won't eat codfish salad, you skinny little insurrecto?"

"Cod-fish salad!" he said with a deep sneer. "Who ever heard of it!"

Outside, on the jumbled pavement of the street, an occasional two-wheel cart passed with deafening thunder, making one think of the overturning of houses. Down from the pale sky over the patio came a heavy odour of Havana itself, a smell of old straw. The wild cries of vendors could be heard at intervals.

"You'll not?"

"No."

"And why not?"

"Cod-fish salad? Not by a blame sight!"

"Well—all right then. You are more of a pig-headed young imbecile than even I thought from seeing you come into Havana here where half the town knows you and the poorest Spaniard would give a gold piece to see you go into Cabanas and forget to come out. Did I tell you, my son Alfred is sick? Yes, poor little fellow, he lies up in the room you used to have. The fever. And did you see Woodham in Key West? Heaven save us, what quick time he made in getting out. I hear Figtree and Button are working in the cable office over there—no? And when is the war going to end? Are the Yankees going to try to take Havana? It will be a hard job, Johnnie? The Spaniards say it is impossible. Everybody is laughing at the Yankees. I hate to go into the street and hear them. Is General Lee going to lead the army? What's become of Springer? I see you've got a new pair of shoes."

In the evening there was a sudden loud knock at the outer door. Martha

125

looked at Johnnie and Johnnie looked at Martha. He was still sitting in the patio, smoking. She took the lamp and set it on a table in the little parlour. This parlour connected the street-door with the patio, and so Johnnie would be protected from the sight of the people who knocked by the broad illuminated tract. Martha moved in pensive fashion upon the latch. "Who's there?" she asked casually.

"The police." There it was, an old melodramatic incident from the stage, from the romances. One could scarce believe it. It had all the dignity of a classic resurrection. "The police!" One sneers at its probability; it is too venerable. But so it happened.

"Who?" said Martha.

"The police!"

"What do you want here?"

"Open the door and we'll tell you."

Martha drew back the ordinary huge bolts of a Havana house and opened the door a trifle. "Tell me what you want and begone quickly," she said, "for my little boy is ill of the fever——"

She could see four or five dim figures, and now one of these suddenly placed a foot well within the door so that she might not close it. "We have come for Johnnie. We must search your house."

"Johnnie? Johnnie? Who is Johnnie?" said Martha in her best manner.

The police inspector grinned with the light upon his face. "Don't you know Señor Johnnie from Pinar del Rio?" he asked.

"Before the war—yes. But now—where is he—he must be in Key West?"

"He is in your house."

"He? In my house? Do me the favour to think that I have some intelligence. Would I be likely to be harbouring a Yankee in these times? You must think I have no more head than an Orden Publico. And I'll not have you search my house, for there is no one here save my son—who is maybe dying of the fever—and the doctor. The doctor is with him because now is the crisis, and any one little thing may kill or cure my boy, and you will do me the favour to consider what may happen if I allow five or six heavy-footed policemen to go tramping all over my house. You may think——"

"Stop it," said the chief police officer at last. He was laughing and weary and angry.

Martha checked her flow of Spanish. "There!" she thought, "I've done my best. He ought to fall in with it." But as the police entered she began on them again. "You will search the house whether I like it or no. Very well; but if anything happens to my boy? It is a nice way of conduct, anyhow—coming into the house of a widow at night and talking much about this Yankee and——"

"For God's sake, señora, hold your tongue. We——"

"Oh, yes, the señora can for God's sake very well hold her tongue, but that wouldn't assist you men into the street where you belong. Take care: if my sick boy suffers from this prowling! No, you'll find nothing in that wardrobe. And do you think he would be under the table? Don't overturn all that linen. Look you, when you go upstairs, tread lightly."

Leaving a man on guard at the street door and another in the patio, the chief policeman and the remainder of his men ascended to the gallery from which opened three sleeping-rooms. They were followed by Martha abjuring them to make no noise. The first room was empty; the second room was empty; as they approached the door of the third room, Martha whispered supplications. "Now, in the name of God, don't disturb my boy." The inspector motioned his men to pause and then he pushed open the door. Only one weak candle was burning in the room and its yellow light fell upon the bed whereon was stretched the figure of a little curly-headed boy in a white nightey. He was asleep, but his face was pink with fever and his lips were murmuring some half-coherent childish nonsense. At the head of the bed stood the motionless figure of a man. His back was to the door, but upon hearing a noise he held a solemn hand. There was an odour of medicine. Out

127

on the balcony, Martha apparently was weeping.

The inspector hesitated for a moment; then he noiselessly entered the room and with his yellow cane prodded under the bed, in the cupboard and behind the window-curtains. Nothing came of it. He shrugged his shoulders and went out to the balcony. He was smiling sheepishly. Evidently he knew that he had been beaten. "Very good, Señora," he said. "You are clever; some day I shall be clever, too." He shook his finger at her. He was threatening her but he affected to be playful. "Then—beware! Beware!"

Martha replied blandly, "My late husband, El Capitan Señor Don Patricio de Castellon y Valladolid was a cavalier of Spain and if he was alive to-night he would now be cutting the ears from the heads of you and your miserable men who smell frightfully of cognac."

"Por Dios!" muttered the inspector as followed by his band he made his way down the spiral staircase. "It is a tongue! One vast tongue!" At the street-door they made ironical bows; they departed; they were angry men.

Johnnie came down when he heard Martha bolting the door behind the police. She brought back the lamp to the table in the patio and stood beside it, thinking. Johnnie dropped into his old chair. The expression on the spy's face was curious; it pictured glee, anxiety, self-complacency; above all it pictured self-complacency. Martha said nothing; she was still by the lamp, musing.

The long silence was suddenly broken by a tremendous guffaw from Johnnie. "Did you ever see sich a lot of fools!" He leaned his head far back and roared victorious merriment.

Martha was almost dancing in her apprehension. "Hush! Be quiet, you little demon! Hush! Do me the favour to allow them to get to the corner before you bellow like a walrus. Be quiet."

The spy ceased his laughter and spoke in indignation. "Why?" he demanded. "Ain't I got a right to laugh?"

"Not with a noise like a cow fallin' into a cucumber-frame," she answered sharply. "Do me the favour———" Then she seemed overwhelmed with a sense of the general hopelessness of Johnnie's character. She began to wag her head. "Oh, but you are the boy for gettin' yourself into the tiger's cage without even so much as the thought of a pocket-knife in your thick head. You would be a genius of the first water if you only had a little sense. And now you're here, what are you going to do?"

He grinned at her. "I'm goin' to hold an inspection of the land and sea defences of the city of Havana."

Martha's spectacles dropped low on her nose and, looking over the rims of them in grave meditation, she said: "If you can't put up with codfish salad you had better make short work of your inspection of the land and sea defences of the city of Havana. You are likely to starve in the meantime. A man who is particular about his food has come to the wrong town if he is in Havana now."

"No, but———" asked Johnnie seriously. "Haven't you any bread?"

"Bread!"

"Well, coffee then? Coffee alone will do."

"Coffee!"

Johnnie arose deliberately and took his hat. Martha eyed him. "And where do you think you are goin'?" she asked cuttingly.

Still deliberate, Johnnie moved in the direction of the street-door. "I'm goin' where I can get something to eat."

Martha sank into a chair with a moan which was a finished opinion— almost a definition—of Johnnie's behaviour in life. "And where will you go?" she asked faintly.

"Oh, I don't know," he rejoined. "Some café. Guess I'll go to the Café Aguacate. They feed you well there. I remember———"

"You remember? They remember! They know you as well as if you were the sign over the door."

"Oh, they won't give me away," said Johnnie with stalwart confidence.

"Gi-give you away? Give you a-way?" stammered Martha.

The spy made no answer but went to the door, unbarred it and passed into the street. Martha caught her breath and ran after him and came face to face with him as he turned to shut the door. "Johnnie, if ye come back, bring a loaf of bread. I'm dyin' for one good honest bite in a slice of bread."

She heard his peculiar derisive laugh as she bolted the door. She returned to her chair in the patio. "Well, there," she said with affection, admiration and contempt. "There he goes! The most hard-headed little ignoramus in twenty nations! What does he care? Nothin'! And why is it? Pure bred-in-the-bone ignorance. Just because he can't stand codfish salad he goes out to a café! A café where they know him as if they had made him!... Well.... I won't see him again, probably.... But if he comes back, I hope he brings some bread. I'm near dead for it."

II

Johnnie strolled carelessly through dark narrow streets. Near every corner were two Orden Publicos—a kind of soldier-police—quiet in the shadow of some doorway, their Remingtons ready, their eyes shining. Johnnie walked past as if he owned them, and their eyes followed him with a sort of a lazy mechanical suspicion which was militant in none of its moods.

Johnnie was suffering from a desire to be splendidly imprudent. He wanted to make the situation gasp and thrill and tremble. From time to time he tried to conceive the idea of his being caught, but to save his eyes he could not imagine it. Such an event was impossible to his peculiar breed of fatalism which could not have conceded death until he had mouldered seven years.

He arrived at the Café Aguacate and found it much changed. The thick wooden shutters were up to keep light from shining into the street. Inside, there were only a few Spanish officers. Johnnie walked to the private rooms at the rear. He found an empty one and pressed the electric button. When he had passed through the main part of the café no one had noted him. The first to recognise him was the waiter who answered the bell. This worthy man turned to stone before the presence of Johnnie.

"Buenos noche, Francisco," said the spy, enjoying himself. "I have hunger. Bring me bread, butter, eggs and coffee." There was a silence; the waiter did not move; Johnnie smiled casually at him.

The man's throat moved; then like one suddenly re-endowed with life, he bolted from the room. After a long time, he returned with the proprietor of the place. In the wicked eye of the latter there gleamed the light of a plan. He did not respond to Johnnie's genial greeting, but at once proceeded to develop his position. "Johnnie," he said, "bread is very dear in Havana. It is very dear."

"Is it?" said Johnnie looking keenly at the speaker. He understood at once that here was some sort of an attack upon him.

"Yes," answered the proprietor of the Café Aguacate slowly and softly. "It is very dear. I think to-night one small bit of bread will cost you one centene—in advance." A centene approximates five dollars in gold.

The spy's face did not change. He appeared to reflect. "And how much for the butter?" he asked at last.

The proprietor gestured. "There is no butter. Do you think we can have everything with those Yankee pigs sitting out there on their ships?"

"And how much for the coffee?" asked Johnnie musingly.

Again the two men surveyed each other during a period of silence. Then the proprietor said gently, "I think your coffee will cost you about two centenes."

"And the eggs?"

"Eggs are very dear. I think eggs would cost you about three centenes for each one."

The new looked at the old; the North Atlantic looked at the Mediterranean; the wooden nutmeg looked at the olive. Johnnie slowly took six centenes from his pocket and laid them on the table. "That's for bread,

131

coffee, and one egg. I don't think I could eat more than one egg to-night. I'm not so hungry as I was."

The proprietor held a perpendicular finger and tapped the table with it. "Oh, señor," he said politely, "I think you would like two eggs."

Johnnie saw the finger. He understood it. "Ye-e-es," he drawled. "I would like two eggs." He placed three more centenes on the table.

"And a little thing for the waiter? I am sure his services will be excellent, invaluable."

"Ye-e-es, for the waiter." Another centene was laid on the table.

The proprietor bowed and preceded the waiter out of the room. There was a mirror on the wall and, springing to his feet, the spy thrust his face close to the honest glass. "Well, I'm damned!" he ejaculated. "Is this me or is this the Honourable D. Hayseed Whiskers of Kansas? Who am I, anyhow? Five dollars in gold!... Say, these people are clever. They know their business, they do. Bread, coffee and two eggs and not even sure of getting it! Fifty dol——— ... Never mind; wait until the war is over. Fifty dollars gold!" He sat for a long time; nothing happened. "Eh," he said at last, "that's the game." As the front door of the café closed upon him, he heard the proprietor and one of the waiters burst into derisive laughter.

Martha was waiting for him. "And here ye are, safe back," she said with delight as she let him enter. "And did ye bring the bread? Did ye bring the bread?"

But she saw that he was raging like a lunatic. His face was red and swollen with temper; his eyes shot forth gleams. Presently he stood before her in the patio where the light fell on him. "Don't speak to me," he choked out waving his arms. "Don't speak to me! Damn your bread! I went to the Café Aguacate! Oh, yes, I went there! Of course, I did! And do you know what they did to me? No! Oh, they didn't do anything to me at all! Not a thing! Fifty dollars! Ten gold pieces!"

"May the saints guard us," cried Martha. "And what was that for?"

"Because they wanted them more than I did," snarled Johnnie. "Don't you see the game. I go into the Café Aguacate. The owner of the place says to himself, 'Hello! Here's that Yankee what they call Johnnie. He's got no right here in Havana. Guess I'll peach on him to the police. They'll put him in Cabanas as a spy.' Then he does a little more thinking, and finally he says, 'No; I guess I won't peach on him just this minute. First, I'll take a small flyer myself.' So in he comes and looks me right in the eye and says, 'Excuse me but it will be a centene for the bread, a centene for the coffee, and eggs are at three centenes each. Besides there will be a small matter of another gold-piece for the waiter.' I think this over. I think it over hard…. He's clever anyhow…. When this cruel war is over, I'll be after him…. I'm a nice secret agent of the United States government, I am. I come here to be too clever for all the Spanish police, and the first thing I do is get buncoed by a rotten, little thimble-rigger in a café. Oh, yes, I'm all right."

"May the saints guard us!" cried Martha again. "I'm old enough to be your mother, or maybe, your grandmother, and I've seen a lot; but it's many a year since I laid eyes on such a ign'rant and wrong-headed little, red Indian as ye are! Why didn't ye take my advice and stay here in the house with decency and comfort. But he must be all for doing everything high and mighty. The Café Aguacate, if ye please. No plain food for his highness. He turns up his nose at cod-fish sal———"

"Thunder and lightnin', are you going to ram that thing down my throat every two minutes, are you?" And in truth she could see that one more reference to that illustrious viand would break the back of Johnnie's gentle disposition as one breaks a twig on the knee. She shifted with Celtic ease. "Did ye bring the bread?" she asked.

He gazed at her for a moment and suddenly laughed. "I forgot to mention," he informed her impressively, "that they did not take the trouble to give me either the bread, the coffee or the eggs."

"The powers!" cried Martha.

"But it's all right. I stopped at a shop." From his pockets, he brought a small loaf, some kind of German sausage and a flask of Jamaica rum. "About all I could get. And they didn't want to sell them either. They expect presently they can exchange a box of sardines for a grand piano."

"'We are not blockaded by the Yankee warships; we are blockaded by our grocers,'" said Martha, quoting the epidemic Havana saying. But she did not delay long from the little loaf. She cut a slice from it and sat eagerly munching. Johnnie seemed more interested in the Jamaica rum. He looked up from his second glass, however, because he heard a peculiar sound. The old woman was weeping. "Hey, what's this?" he demanded in distress, but with the manner of a man who thinks gruffness is the only thing that will make people feel better and cease. "What's this anyhow? What are you cryin' for?"

"It's the bread," sobbed Martha. "It's the—the br-e-a-ddd."

"Huh? What's the matter with it?"

"It's so good, so g-good." The rain of tears did not prevent her from continuing her unusual report. "Oh, it's so good! This is the first in weeks. I didn't know bread could be so l-like heaven."

"Here," said Johnnie seriously. "Take a little mouthful of this rum. It will do you good."

"No; I only want the bub-bub-bread."

"Well, take the bread, too…. There you are. Now you feel better…. By Jove, when I think of that Café Aguacate man! Fifty dollars gold! And then not to get anything either. Say, after the war, I'm going there, and I'm just going to raze that place to the ground. You see! I'll make him think he can charge ME fifteen dollars for an egg…. And then not give me the egg."

III

Johnnie's subsequent activity in Havana could truthfully be related in part to a certain temporary price of eggs. It is interesting to note how close that famous event got to his eye so that, according to the law of perspective, it was as big as the Capitol of Washington, where centres the spirit of his nation. Around him, he felt a similar and ferocious expression of life which informed him too plainly that if he was caught, he was doomed. Neither the garrison nor the citizens of Havana would tolerate any nonsense in regard to him if he was caught. He would have the steel screw against his neck in short order. And what was the main thing to bear him up against the desire to run away before his work was done? A certain temporary price of eggs! It not only hid the Capitol at Washington; it obscured the dangers in Havana.

Something was learned of the Santa Clara battery, because one morning an old lady in black accompanied by a young man—evidently her son— visited a house which was to rent on the height, in rear of the battery. The portero was too lazy and sleepy to show them over the premises, but he granted them permission to investigate for themselves. They spent most of their time on the flat parapeted roof of the house. At length they came down and said that the place did not suit them. The portero went to sleep again.

Johnnie was never discouraged by the thought that his operations would be of small benefit to the admiral commanding the fleet in adjacent waters, and to the general commanding the army which was not going to attack Havana from the land side. At that time it was all the world's opinion that the army from Tampa would presently appear on the Cuban beach at some convenient point to the east or west of Havana. It turned out, of course, that the condition of the defences of Havana was of not the slightest military importance to the United States since the city was never attacked either by land or sea. But Johnnie could not foresee this. He continued to take his fancy risk, continued his majestic lie, with satisfaction, sometimes with delight, and with pride. And in the psychologic distance was old Martha dancing with fear and shouting: "Oh, Johnnie, me son, what a born fool ye are!"

Sometimes she would address him thus: "And when ye learn all this, how are ye goin' to get out with it?" She was contemptuous.

He would reply, as serious as a Cossack in his fatalism. "Oh, I'll get out some way."

His manœuvres in the vicinity of Regla and Guanabacoa were of a brilliant character. He haunted the sunny long grass in the manner of a jack-rabbit. Sometimes he slept under a palm, dreaming of the American advance fighting its way along the military road to the foot of Spanish defences. Even when awake, he often dreamed it and thought of the all-day crash and hot roar of an assault. Without consulting Washington, he had decided that Havana should be attacked from the south-east. An advance from the west could be contested right up to the bar of the Hotel Inglaterra, but when the first ridge in the south-east would be taken, the whole city with most of its defences would lie under the American siege guns. And the approach to this position was as reasonable as is any approach toward the muzzles of magazine rifles. Johnnie viewed the grassy fields always as a prospective battle-ground, and one can see him lying there, filling the landscape with visions of slow-crawling black infantry columns, galloping batteries of artillery, streaks of faint blue smoke marking the modern firing lines, clouds of dust, a vision of ten thousand tragedies. And his ears heard the noises.

But he was no idle shepherd boy with a head haunted by sombre and glorious fancies. On the contrary, he was much occupied with practical matters. Some months after the close of the war, he asked me: "Were you ever fired at from very near?" I explained some experiences which I had stupidly esteemed as having been rather near. "But did you ever have'm fire a volley on you from close—very close—say, thirty feet?"

Highly scandalised I answered, "No; in that case, I would not be the crowning feature of the Smithsonian Institute."

"Well," he said, "it's a funny effect. You feel as every hair on your head had been snatched out by the roots." Questioned further he said, "I walked right up on a Spanish outpost at daybreak once, and about twenty men let go at me. Thought I was a Cuban army, I suppose."

"What did you do?"

"I run."

"Did they hit you, at all?"

"Naw."

It had been arranged that some light ship of the squadron should rendezvous with him at a certain lonely spot on the coast on a certain day and hour and pick him up. He was to wave something white. His shirt was not white, but he waved it whenever he could see the signal-tops of a warship. It was a very tattered banner. After a ten-mile scramble through almost pathless thickets, he had very little on him which respectable men would call a shirt, and the less one says about his trousers the better. This naked savage, then, walked all day up and down a small bit of beach waving a brown rag. At night, he slept in the sand. At full daybreak he began to wave his rag; at noon he was waving his rag; at night-fall he donned his rag and strove to think of it as a shirt. Thus passed two days, and nothing had happened. Then he retraced a twenty-five mile way to the house of old Martha. At first she took him to be one of Havana's terrible beggars and cried, "And do you come here for alms? Look out, that I do not beg of you." The one unchanged thing was his laugh of pure mockery. When she heard it, she dragged him through the door. He paid no heed to her ejaculations but went straight to where he had hidden some gold. As he was untying a bit of string from the neck of a small bag, he said, "How is little Alfred?" "Recovered, thank Heaven." He handed Martha a piece of gold. "Take this and buy what you can on the corner. I'm hungry." Martha departed with expedition. Upon her return, she was beaming. She had foraged a thin chicken, a bunch of radishes and two bottles of wine. Johnnie had finished the radishes and one bottle of wine when the chicken was still a long way from the table. He called stoutly for more, and so Martha passed again into the street with another gold piece. She bought more radishes, more wine and some cheese. They had a grand feast, with Johnnie audibly wondering until a late hour why he had waved his rag in vain.

There was no end to his suspense, no end to his work. He knew everything. He was an animate guide-book. After he knew a thing once, he verified it in several different ways in order to make sure. He fitted himself for a useful career, like a young man in a college—with the difference that the shadow of the garote fell ever upon his way, and that he was occasionally shot at, and that he could not get enough to eat, and that his existence was apparently forgotten, and that he contracted the fever. But——

One cannot think of the terms in which to describe a futility so vast, so colossal. He had built a little boat, and the sea had receded and left him and his boat a thousand miles inland on the top of a mountain. The war-fate had left Havana out of its plan and thus isolated Johnnie and his several pounds of useful information. The war-fate left Havana to become the somewhat indignant victim of a peaceful occupation at the close of the conflict, and Johnnie's data were worth as much as a carpenter's lien on the north pole. He had suffered and laboured for about as complete a bit of absolute nothing as one could invent. If the company which owned the sugar plantation had not generously continued his salary during the war, he would not have been able to pay his expenses on the amount allowed him by the government, which, by the way, was a more complete bit of absolute nothing than one could possibly invent.

IV

I met Johnnie in Havana in October, 1898. If I remember rightly the U.S.S. Resolute and the U.S.S. Scorpion were in the harbour, but beyond these two terrible engines of destruction there were not as yet any of the more stern signs of the American success. Many Americans were to be seen in the streets of Havana where they were not in any way molested. Among them was Johnnie in white duck and a straw hat, cool, complacent and with eyes rather more steady than ever. I addressed him upon the subject of his supreme failure, but I could not perturb his philosophy. In reply he simply asked me to dinner. "Come to the Café Aguacate at 7:30 to-night," he said. "I haven't been there in a long time. We shall see if they cook as well as ever." I turned up promptly and found Johnnie in a private room smoking a cigar in the presence of a waiter who was blue in the gills. "I've ordered the dinner," he said cheerfully. "Now I want to see if you won't be surprised how well they can do here in Havana." I was surprised. I was dumfounded. Rarely in the history of the world have two rational men sat down to such a dinner. It must have taxed the ability and endurance of the entire working force of the establishment to provide it. The variety of dishes was of course related to the markets of Havana, but the abundance and general profligacy was related only to Johnnie's imagination. Neither of us had an appetite. Our fancies fled in confusion before this puzzling luxury. I looked at Johnnie as if he were a native of Thibet. I had thought him to be a most simple man, and here I found him revelling in food like a fat, old senator of Rome's decadence. And if the dinner itself put me to open-eyed amazement, the names of the wines finished everything. Apparently Johnny had had but one standard, and that was the cost. If a wine had been very expensive, he had ordered it. I began to think him probably a maniac. At any rate, I was sure that we were both fools. Seeing my fixed stare, he spoke with affected languor: "I wish peacocks' brains and melted pearls were to be had here in Havana. We'd have 'em." Then he grinned. As a mere skirmisher I said, "In New York, we think we dine well; but really this, you know—well—Havana———"

Johnnie waved his hand pompously. "Oh, I know."

Directly after coffee, Johnnie excused himself for a moment and left the room. When he returned he said briskly, "Well, are you ready to go?" As soon as we were in a cab and safely out of hearing of the Café Aguacate, Johnnie lay back and laughed long and joyously.

But I was very serious. "Look here, Johnnie," I said to him solemnly, "when you invite me to dine with you, don't you ever do that again. And I'll tell you one thing—when you dine with me you will probably get the ordinary table d'hôte." I was an older man.

"Oh, that's all right," he cried. And then he too grew serious. "Well, as far as I am concerned—as far as I am concerned," he said, "the war is now over."

WAR MEMORIES

"But to get the real thing!" cried Vernall, the war-correspondent. "It seems impossible! It is because war is neither magnificent nor squalid; it is simply life, and an expression of life can always evade us. We can never tell life, one to another, although sometimes we think we can."

When I climbed aboard the despatch-boat at Key West, the mate told me irritably that as soon as we crossed the bar, we would find ourselves monkey-climbing over heavy seas. It wasn't my fault, but he seemed to insinuate that it was all a result of my incapacity. There were four correspondents in the party. The leader of us came aboard with a huge bunch of bananas, which he hung like a chandelier in the centre of the tiny cabin. We made acquaintance over, around, and under this bunch of bananas, which really occupied the cabin as a soldier occupies a sentry box. But the bunch did not become really aggressive until we were well at sea. Then it began to spar. With the first roll of the ship, it launched its honest pounds at McCurdy and knocked him wildly through the door to the deck-rail, where he hung cursing hysterically. Without a moment's pause, it made for me. I flung myself head-first into my bunk and watched the demon sweep Brownlow into a corner and wedge his knee behind a sea-chest. Kary gave a shrill cry and fled. The bunch of bananas swung to and fro, silent, determined, ferocious, looking for more men. It had cleared a space for itself. My comrades looked in at the door, calling upon me to grab the thing and hold it. I pointed out to them the security and comfort of my position. They were angry. Finally the mate came and lashed the thing so that it could not prowl about the cabin and assault innocent war-correspondents. You see? War! A bunch of bananas rampant because the ship rolled.

In that early period of the war we were forced to continue our dreams. And we were all dreamers, envisioning the seas with death grapples, ship and ship. Even the navy grew cynical. Officers on the bridge lifted their megaphones and told you in resigned voices that they were out of ice, onions, and eggs. At other times, they would shoot quite casually at us with six-pounders. This industry usually progressed in the night, but it sometimes happened in the day. There was never any resentment on our side, although at moments there was some nervousness. They were impressively quick with their lanyards; our means of replying to signals were correspondingly slow. They gave you opportunity to say, "Heaven guard me!" Then they shot. But we recognised the propriety of it. Everything was correct save the war, which lagged and lagged and lagged. It did not play; it was not a gory giant; it was a bunch of bananas swung in the middle of the cabin.

Once we had the honour of being rammed at midnight by the U.S.S. Machias. In fact the exceeding industry of the naval commanders of the Cuban blockading fleet caused a certain liveliness to at times penetrate our mediocre existence. We were all greatly entertained over an immediate prospect of being either killed by rapid fire guns, cut in half by the ram or merely drowned, but even our great longing for diversion could not cause us to ever again go near the Machias on a dark night. We had sailed from Key West on a mission that had nothing to do with the coast of Cuba, and steaming due east and some thirty-five miles from the Cuban land, we did not think we were liable to an affair with any of the fierce American cruisers. Suddenly a familiar signal of red and white lights flashed like a brooch of jewels on the pall that covered the sea. It was far away and tiny, but we knew all about it. It was the electric question of an American war-ship and it demanded a swift answer in kind. The man behind the gun! What about the man in front of the gun? The war-ship signals vanished and the sea presented nothing but a smoky black stretch lit with the hissing white tops of the flying waves. A thin line of flame swept from a gun.

Thereafter followed one of those silences which had become so peculiarly instructive to the blockade-runner. Somewhere in the darkness we knew that a slate-coloured cruiser, red below the water-line and with a gold scroll on her bows, was flying over the waves toward us, while upon the dark decks the men stood at general quarters in silence about the long thin guns, and it was the law of life and death that we should make true answer in about the twelfth part of a second. Now I shall with regret disclose a certain dreadful

141

secret of the despatch-boat service. Our signals, far from being electric, were two lanterns which we kept in a tub and covered with a tarpaulin. The tub was placed just forward of the pilot-house, and when we were accosted at night it was everybody's duty to scramble wildly for the tub and grab out the lanterns and wave them. It amounted to a slowness of speech. I remember a story of an army sentry who upon hearing a noise in his front one dark night called his usual sharp query. "Halt—who's there? Halt or I'll fire!" And getting no immediate response he fired even as he had said, killing a man with a hair-lip who unfortunately could not arrange his vocal machinery to reply in season. We were something like a boat with a hair-lip. And sometimes it was very trying to the nerves.... The pause was long. Then a voice spoke from the sea through a megaphone. It was faint but clear. "What ship is that?" No one hesitated over his answer in cases of this kind. Everybody was desirous of imparting fullest information. There was another pause. Then out of the darkness flew an American cruiser, silent as death, handled as ferociously as if the devil commanded her. Again the little voice hailed from the bridge. "What ship is that?" Evidently the reply to the first hail had been misunderstood or not heard. This time the voice rang with menace, menace of immediate and certain destruction, and the last word was intoned savagely and strangely across the windy darkness as if the officer would explain that the cruiser was after either fools or the common enemy. The yells in return did not stop her. She was hurling herself forward to ram us amidships, and the people on the little Three Friends looked at a tall swooping bow, and it was keener than any knife that has ever been made. As the cruiser lunged every man imagined the gallant and famous but frail Three Friends cut into two parts as neatly as if she had been cheese. But there was a sheer and a hard sheer to starboard, and down upon our quarter swung a monstrous thing larger than any ship in the world—the U.S.S. Machias. She had a freeboard of about three hundred feet and the top of her funnel was out of sight in the clouds like an Alp. I shouldn't wonder that at the top of that funnel there was a region of perpetual snow. And at a range which swiftly narrowed to nothing every gun in her port-battery swung deliberately into aim. It was closer, more deliciously intimate than a duel across a handkerchief. We all had an opportunity of looking miles down the muzzles of this festive artillery before came the collision. Then the Machias reeled her steel shoulder against the wooden side of the Three Friends and up went a roar as if a vast shingle roof had fallen. The poor little tug dipped as if she meant to pass under the war-ship, staggered and finally righted, trembling from head to foot. The cries of the splintered timbers ceased. The men on the tug gazed at each other with white faces shining faintly in the darkness. The Machias backed away even as the Three Friends drew slowly ahead, and again we were alone with the piping of the wind and the slash of the gale-driven water. Later, from some hidden part of the sea, the bullish eye of a searchlight looked at us and the widening white rays bathed us in the glare. There was another hail. "Hello there, Three Friends!" "Ay, ay, sir!" "Are you injured?" Our first mate had taken a lantern and was studying the side of the tug, and we held our breath for his answer. I was sure that he was going to say that we were sinking. Surely there could be no other ending to this terrific bloodthirsty assault. But the first mate said, "No, sir." Instantly the glare of the search-light was gone; the Machias was gone; the incident was closed.

I was dining once on board the flag-ship, the New York, armoured cruiser. It was the junior officers' mess, and when the coffee came, a young ensign went to the piano and began to bang out a popular tune. It was a cheerful scene, and it resembled only a cheerful scene. Suddenly we heard the whistle of the bos'n's mate, and directly above us, it seemed, a voice, hoarse as that of a sea-lion, bellowed a command: "Man the port battery." In a moment the table was vacant; the popular tune ceased in a jangle. On the quarter-deck assembled a group of officers—spectators. The quiet evening sea, lit with faint red lights, went peacefully to the feet of a verdant shore. One could hear the far-away measured tumbling of surf upon a reef. Only this sound pulsed in the air. The great grey cruiser was as still as the earth, the sea, and the sky. Then they let off a four-inch gun directly under my feet. I thought it turned me a back-somersault. That was the effect upon my mind. But it appears I did not move. The shell went carousing off to the Cuban shore, and from the vegetation there spirted a cloud of dust. Some of the officers on the quarter-deck laughed. Through their glasses they had seen a Spanish column of cavalry much agitated by the appearance of this shell among them. As far as I was concerned, there was nothing but the spirt of dust from the side of a long-suffering island. When I returned to my coffee I found that most of the young officers had also returned. Japanese boys were bringing liquors. The piano's clattering of the popular air was often interrupted by the boom of a four-inch gun. A bunch of bananas!

One day, our despatch-boat found the shores of Guantanamo Bay flowing past on either side. It was at nightfall and on the eastward point a small village was burning, and it happened that a fiery light was thrown upon some palm-trees so that it made them into enormous crimson feathers. The water was the colour of blue steel; the Cuban woods were sombre; high shivered the gory feathers. The last boatloads of the marine battalion were pulling for the beach. The marine officers gave me generous hospitality to the camp on the hill. That night there was an alarm and amid a stern calling of orders and a rushing of men, I wandered in search of some other man who had no occupation. It turned out to be the young assistant surgeon, Gibbs. We foregathered in the centre of a square of six companies of marines. There was no firing. We thought it rather comic. The next night there was an alarm; there was some firing; we lay on our bellies; it was no longer comic. On the third night the alarm came early; I went in search of Gibbs, but I soon gave over an active search for the more congenial occupation of lying flat and feeling the hot hiss of the bullets trying to cut my hair. For the moment I was no longer a cynic. I was a child who, in a fit of ignorance, had jumped into the vat of war. I heard somebody dying near me. He was dying hard. Hard. It took him a long time to die. He breathed as all noble machinery breathes when it is making its gallant strife against breaking, breaking. But he was going to break. He was going to break. It seemed to me, this breathing, the noise of a heroic pump which strives to subdue a mud which comes upon it in tons. The darkness was impenetrable. The man was lying in some depression within seven feet of me. Every wave, vibration, of his anguish beat upon my senses. He was long past groaning. There was only the bitter strife for air which pulsed out into the night in a clear penetrating whistle with intervals of terrible silence in which I held my own breath in the common unconscious aspiration to help. I thought this man would never die. I wanted him to die. Ultimately he died. At the moment the adjutant came bustling along erect amid the spitting bullets. I knew him by his voice. "Where's the doctor? There's some wounded men over there. Where's the doctor?" A man answered briskly: "Just died this minute, sir." It was as if he had said: "Just gone around the corner this minute, sir." Despite the horror of this night's business, the man's mind was somehow influenced by the coincidence of the adjutant's calling aloud for the doctor within a few seconds of the doctor's death. It—what shall I say? It interested him, this coincidence.

The day broke by inches, with an obvious and maddening reluctance. From some unfathomable source I procured an opinion that my friend was not dead at all—the wild and quivering darkness had caused me to misinterpret a few shouted words. At length the land brightened in a violent atmosphere, the perfect dawning of a tropic day, and in this light I saw a clump of men near me. At first I thought they were all dead. Then I thought they were all asleep. The truth was that a group of wan-faced, exhausted men had gone to sleep about Gibbs' body so closely and in such abandoned attitudes that one's eye could not pick the living from the dead until one saw that a certain head had beneath it a great dark pool.

In the afternoon a lot of men went bathing, and in the midst of this festivity firing was resumed. It was funny to see the men come scampering out of the water, grab at their rifles and go into action attired in nought but their cartridge-belts. The attack of the Spaniards had interrupted in some degree the services over the graves of Gibbs and some others. I remember Paine came ashore with a bottle of whisky which I took from him violently. My faithful shooting boots began to hurt me, and I went to the beach and poulticed my feet in wet clay, sitting on the little rickety pier near where the corrugated iron cable-station showed how the shells slivered through it. Some marines, desirous of mementoes, were poking with sticks in the smoking ruins of the hamlet. Down in the shallow water crabs were meandering among the weeds, and little fishes moved slowly in schools.

The next day we went shooting. It was exactly like quail shooting. I'll tell you. These guerillas who so cursed our lives had a well some five miles away, and it was the only water supply within about twelve miles of the marine camp. It was decided that it would be correct to go forth and destroy the well. Captain Elliott, of C company, was to take his men with Captain Spicer's company, D, out to the well, beat the enemy away and destroy everything. He was to start at the next daybreak. He asked me if I cared to go, and, of course, I accepted with glee; but all that night I was afraid. Bitterly afraid. The moon was very bright, shedding a magnificent radiance upon the trenches. I watched the men of C and D companies lying so tranquilly—some snoring, confound them—whereas I was certain that I could never sleep with the weight of a coming battle upon my mind, a battle in which the poor life of a war-correspondent might easily be taken by a careless enemy. But if I was frightened I was also very cold. It was a chill night and I wanted a heavy top-coat almost as much as I wanted a certificate of immunity from rifle bullets. These two feelings were of equal importance to my mind. They were twins. Elliott came and flung a tent-fly over Lieutenant Bannon and me as we lay on the ground back of the men. Then I was no longer cold, but I was still afraid, for tent-flies cannot mend a fear. In the morning I wished for some mild attack of disease, something that would incapacitate me for the business of going out gratuitously to be bombarded. But I was in an awkwardly healthy state, and so I must needs smile and look pleased with my prospects. We were to be guided by fifty Cubans, and I gave up all dreams of a postponement when I saw them shambling off in single file through the cactus. We followed presently. "Where you people goin' to?" "Don't know, Jim." "Well, good luck to you, boys." This was the world's lazy inquiry and conventional God-speed. Then the mysterious wilderness swallowed us.

The men were silent because they were ordered to be silent, but whatever faces I could observe were marked with a look of serious meditation. As they trudged slowly in single file they were reflecting upon—what? I don't know. But at length we came to ground more open. The sea appeared on our right, and we saw the gunboat Dolphin steaming along in a line parallel to ours. I was as glad to see her as if she had called out my name. The trail wound about the bases of some high bare spurs. If the Spaniards had occupied them I don't see how we could have gone further. But upon them were only the dove-voiced guerilla scouts calling back into the hills the news of our approach. The effect of sound is of course relative. I am sure I have never heard such a horrible sound as the beautiful cooing of the wood-dove when I was certain that it came from the yellow throat of a guerilla. Elliott sent

Lieutenant Lucas with his platoon to ascend the hills and cover our advance by the trail. We halted and watched them climb, a long black streak of men in the vivid sunshine of the hillside. We did not know how tall were these hills until we saw Lucas and his men on top, and they were no larger than specks. We marched on until, at last, we heard—it seemed in the sky—the sputter of firing. This devil's dance was begun. The proper strategic movement to cover the crisis seemed to me to be to run away home and swear I had never started on this expedition. But Elliott yelled: "Now, men; straight up this hill." The men charged up against the cactus, and, because I cared for the opinion of others, I found myself tagging along close at Elliott's heels. I don't know how I got up that hill, but I think it was because I was afraid to be left behind. The immediate rear did not look safe. The crowd of strong young marines afforded the only spectacle of provisional security. So I tagged along at Elliott's heels. The hill was as steep as a Swiss roof. From it sprang out great pillars of cactus, and the human instinct was to assist one's self in the ascent by grasping cactus with one's hands. I remember the watch I had to keep upon this human instinct even when the sound of the bullets was attracting my nervous attention. However, the attractive thing to my sense at the time was the fact that every man of the marines was also climbing away like mad. It was one thing for Elliott, Spicer, Neville, Shaw and Bannon; it was another thing for me; but—what in the devil was it to the men? Not the same thing surely. It was perfectly easy for any marine to get overcome by the burning heat and, lying down, bequeath the work and the danger to his comrades. The fine thing about "the men" is that you can't explain them. I mean when you take them collectively. They do a thing, and afterward you find that they have done it because they have done it. However, when Elliott arrived at the top of the ridge, myself and many other men were with him. But there was no battle scene. Off on another ridge we could see Lucas' men and the Cubans peppering away into a valley. The bullets about our ears were really intended to lodge in them. We went over there.

I walked along the firing line and looked at the men. I kept somewhat on what I shall call the lee side of the ridge. Why? Because I was afraid of being shot. No other reason. Most of the men as they lay flat, shooting, looked contented, almost happy. They were pleased, these men, at the situation. I don't know. I cannot imagine. But they were pleased, at any rate. I wasn't pleased. I was picturing defeat. I was saying to myself:—"Now if the enemy should suddenly do so-and-so, or so-and-so, why—what would become of me?" During these first few moments I did not see the Spanish position because—I was afraid to look at it. Bullets were hissing and spitting over the crest of the ridge in such showers as to make observation to be a task for a brave man. No, now, look here, why the deuce should I have stuck my head up, eh? Why? Well, at any rate, I didn't until it seemed to be a far less thing than most of the men were doing as if they liked it. Then I saw nothing. At least it was only the bottom of a small valley. In this valley there was a thicket—a big thicket—and this thicket seemed to be crowded with a mysterious class of persons who were evidently trying to kill us. Our enemies? Yes—perhaps—I suppose so. Leave that to the people in the streets at home. They know and cry against the public enemy, but when men go into actual battle not one in a thousand concerns himself with an animus against the men who face him. The great desire is to beat them—beat them whoever they are as a matter, first, of personal safety, second, of personal glory. It is always safest to make the other chap quickly run away. And as he runs away, one feels, as one tries to hit him in the back and knock him sprawling, that he must be a very good and sensible fellow. But these people apparently did not mean to run away. They clung to their thicket and, amid the roar of the firing, one could sometimes hear their wild yells of insult and defiance. They were actually the most obstinate, headstrong, mulish people that you could ever imagine. The Dolphin was throwing shells into their immediate vicinity and the fire from the marines and Cubans was very rapid and heavy, but still those incomprehensible mortals remained in their thicket. The scene on the top of the ridge was very wild, but there was only one truly romantic figure. This was a Cuban officer who held in one hand a great glittering machete and in the other a cocked revolver. He posed like a statue of victory. Afterwards he confessed to me that he alone had been responsible for the winning of the fight. But outside of this splendid person it was simply a picture of men at work, men terribly hard at work, red-faced, sweating, gasping toilers. A Cuban negro soldier was shot though the heart and one man took the body on his back and another took it by its feet and trundled away toward the rear looking precisely like a wheelbarrow. A man in C company was shot through the ankle and he sat behind the line nursing his wound. Apparently he was pleased with it. It seemed to suit him. I don't know why. But beside him sat a comrade with a face drawn, solemn and responsible like that of a New England spinster at the bedside of a sick child.

The fight banged away with a roar like a forest fire. Suddenly a marine wriggled out of the firing line and came frantically to me. "Say, young feller, I'll give you five dollars for a drink of whisky." He tried to force into my hand a gold piece. "Go to the devil," said I, deeply scandalised. "Besides, I haven't got any whisky," "No, but look here," he beseeched me. "If I don't get a drink I'll die. And I'll give you five dollars for it. Honest, I will." I finally tried to escape from him by walking away, but he followed at my heels, importuning me with all the exasperating persistence of a professional beggar and trying to force this ghastly gold piece into my hand. I could not shake him off, and amid that clatter of furious fighting I found myself intensely embarrassed, and glancing fearfully this way and that way to make sure that people did not see me, the villain and his gold. In vain I assured him that if I had any whisky I should place it at his disposal. He could not be turned away. I thought of the European expedient in such a crisis—to jump in a cab. But unfortunately—— In the meantime I had given up my occupation of tagging at Captain Elliott's heels, because his business required that he should go into places of great danger. But from time to time I was under his attention. Once he turned to me and said: "Mr. Vernall, will you go and satisfy yourself who those people are?" Some men had appeared on a hill about six hundred yards from our left flank. "Yes, sir," cried I with, I assure you, the finest alacrity and cheerfulness, and my tone proved to me that I had inherited histrionic abilities. This tone was of course a black lie, but I went off briskly and was as jaunty as a real soldier while all the time my heart was in my boots and I was cursing the day that saw me landed on the shores of the tragic isle. If the men on the distant hill had been guerillas, my future might have been seriously jeopardised, but I had not gone far toward them when I was able to recognise the uniforms of the marine corps. Whereupon I scampered back to the firing line and with the same alacrity and cheerfulness reported my information. I mention to you that I was afraid, because there were about me that day many men who did not seem to be afraid at all, men with quiet, composed faces who went about this business as if they proceeded from a sense of habit. They were not old soldiers; they were mainly recruits, but many of them betrayed all the emotion and merely the emotion that one sees in the face of a man earnestly at work.

I don't know how long the action lasted. I remember deciding in my own mind that the Spaniards stood forty minutes. This was a mere arbitrary decision based on nothing. But at any rate we finally arrived at the satisfactory moment when the enemy began to run away. I shall never forget how my courage increased. And then began the great bird shooting. From the far side of the thicket arose an easy slope covered with plum-coloured bush. The Spaniards broke in coveys of from six to fifteen men—or birds—and swarmed up this slope. The marines on our ridge then had some fine, open field shooting. No charge could be made because the shells from the Dolphin were helping the Spaniards to evacuate the thicket, so the marines had to be content with this extraordinary paraphrase of a kind of sport. It was strangely like the original. The shells from the Dolphin were the dogs; dogs who went in and stirred out the game. The marines were suddenly gentlemen in leggings, alive with the sharp instinct which marks the hunter. The Spaniards were the birds. Yes, they were the birds, but I doubt if they would sympathise with my metaphors.

We destroyed their camp, and when the tiled roof of a burning house fell with a crash it was so like the crash of a strong volley of musketry that we all turned with a start, fearing that we would have to fight again on that same day. And this struck me at least as being an impossible thing. They gave us water from the Dolphin and we filled our canteens. None of the men were particularly jubilant. They did not altogether appreciate their victory. They were occupied in being glad that the fight was over. I discovered to my amazement that we were on the summit of a hill so high that our released eyes seemed to sweep over half the world. The vast stretch of sea shimmering like fragile blue silk in the breeze, lost itself ultimately in an indefinite pink haze, while in the other direction, ridge after ridge, ridge after ridge, rolled brown and arid into the north. The battle had been fought high in the air—where the rain clouds might have been. That is why everybody's face was the colour of beetroot and men lay on the ground and only swore feebly when the cactus spurs sank into them.

Finally we started for camp. Leaving our wounded, our cactus pincushions, and our heat-prostrated men on board the Dolphin. I did not see that the men were elate or even grinning with satisfaction. They seemed only anxious to get to food and rest. And yet it was plain that Elliott and his men had performed a service that would prove invaluable to the security and comfort of the entire battalion. They had driven the guerillas to take a road along which they would have to proceed for fifteen miles before they could get as much water as would wet the point of a pin. And by the destruction of a well at the scene of the fight, Elliott made an arid zone almost twenty miles wide between the enemy and the base camp. In Cuba this is the best of protections. However, a cup of coffee! Time enough to think of a brilliant success after one had had a cup of coffee. The long line plodded wearily through the dusky jungle which was never again to be alive with ambushes.

It was dark when we stumbled into camp, and I was sad with an ungovernable sadness, because I was too tired to remember where I had left my kit. But some of my colleagues were waiting on the beach, and they put me on a despatch-boat to take my news to a Jamaica cable-station. The appearance of this despatch-boat struck me with wonder. It was reminiscent of something with which I had been familiar in early years. I looked with dull surprise at three men of the engine-room force, who sat aft on some bags of coal smoking their pipes and talking as if there had never been any battles fought anywhere. The sudden clang of the gong made me start and listen eagerly, as if I would be asking: "What was that?" The chunking of the screw affected me also, but I seemed to relate it to a former and pleasing experience. One of the correspondents on board immediately began to tell me of the chief engineer, who, he said, was a comic old character. I was taken to see this marvel, which presented itself as a gray-bearded man with an oil can, who had the cynical, malicious, egotistic eye of proclaimed and admired ignorance. I looked dazedly at the venerable impostor. What had he to do with battles—the humming click of the locks, the odour of burnt cotton, the bullets, the firing? My friend told the scoundrel that I was just returned from the afternoon's action. He said: "That so?" And looked at me with a smile, faintly, faintly derisive. You see? I had just come out of my life's most fiery time, and that old devil looked at me with that smile. What colossal conceit. The four-times-damned doddering old head-mechanic of a derelict junk shop. The whole trouble lay in the fact that I had not shouted out with mingled awe and joy as he stood there in his wisdom and experience, with all his ancient saws and home-made epigrams ready to fire.

My friend took me to the cabin. What a squalid hole! My heart sank. The reward after the labour should have been a great airy chamber, a gigantic four-poster, iced melons, grilled birds, wine, and the delighted attendance of my friends. When I had finished my cablegram, I retired to a little shelf of a berth, which reeked of oil, while the blankets had soaked recently with sea-water. The vessel heeled to leeward in spasmodic attempts to hurl me out, and I resisted with the last of my strength. The infamous pettiness of it all! I thought the night would never end. "But never mind," I said to myself at last, "to-morrow in Fort Antonio I shall have a great bath and fine raiment, and I shall dine grandly and there will be lager beer on ice. And there will be attendants to run when I touch a bell, and I shall catch every interested romantist in the town, and spin him the story of the fight at Cusco." We reached Fort Antonio and I fled from the cable office to the hotel. I procured the bath and, as I donned whatever fine raiment I had foraged, I called the boy and pompously told him of a dinner—a real dinner, with furbelows and complications, and yet with a basis of sincerity. He looked at me calf-like for a moment, and then he went away. After a long interval, the manager himself appeared and asked me some questions which led me to see that he thought I had attempted to undermine and disintegrate the intellect of the boy, by the elocution of Arabic incantations. Well, never mind. In the end, the manager of the hotel elicited from me that great cry, that cry which during the war, rang piteously from thousands of throats, that last grand cry of anguish and despair: "Well, then, in the name of God, can I have a cold bottle of beer?"

Well, you see to what war brings men? War is death, and a plague of the lack of small things, and toil. Nor did I catch my sentimentalists and pour forth my tale to them, and thrill, appal, and fascinate them. However, they did feel an interest in me, for I heard a lady at the hotel ask: "Who is that chap in the very dirty jack-boots?" So you see, that whereas you can be very much frightened upon going into action, you can also be greatly annoyed after you have come out.

Later, I fell into the hands of one of my closest friends, and he mercilessly outlined a scheme for landing to the west of Santiago and getting through the Spanish lines to some place from which we could view the Spanish squadron lying in the harbour. There was rumour that the Viscaya had escaped, he said, and it would be very nice to make sure of the truth. So we steamed to a point opposite a Cuban camp which my friend knew, and flung two crop-tailed Jamaica polo ponies into the sea. We followed in a small boat and were met on the beach by a small Cuban detachment who immediately caught our ponies and saddled them for us. I suppose we felt rather god-like. We were almost the first Americans they had seen and they looked at us with eyes of grateful affection. I don't suppose many men have the experience of being looked at with eyes of grateful affection. They guide us to a Cuban camp where, in a little palm-bark hut, a black-faced lieutenant-colonel was lolling in a hammock. I couldn't understand what was said, but at any rate he must have ordered his half-naked orderly to make coffee, for it was done. It was a dark syrup in smoky tin-cups, but it was better than the cold bottle of beer which I did not drink in Jamaica.

The Cuban camp was an expeditious affair of saplings and palm-bark tied with creepers. It could be burned to the ground in fifteen minutes and in ten reduplicated. The soldiers were in appearance an absolutely good-natured set of half-starved ragamuffins. Their breeches hung in threads about their black legs and their shirts were as nothing. They looked like a collection of real tropic savages at whom some philanthropist had flung a bundle of rags and some of the rags had stuck here and there. But their condition was now a habit. I doubt if they knew they were half-naked. Anyhow they didn't care. No more they should; the weather was warm. This lieutenant-colonel gave us an escort of five or six men and we went up into the mountains, lying flat on our Jamaica ponies while they went like rats up and down extraordinary trails. In the evening we reached the camp of a major who commanded the outposts. It was high, high in the hills. The stars were as big as cocoanuts. We lay in borrowed hammocks and watched the firelight gleam blood-red on the trees. I remember an utterly naked negro squatting, crimson, by the fire and cleaning an iron-pot. Some voices were singing an Afric wail of forsaken love and death. And at dawn we were to try to steal through the Spanish lines. I was very, very sorry.

In the cold dawn the situation was the same, but somehow courage seemed to be in the breaking day. I went off with the others quite cheerfully. We came to where the pickets stood behind bulwarks of stone in frameworks of saplings. They were peering across a narrow cloud-steeped gulch at a dull fire marking a Spanish post. There was some palaver and then, with fifteen men, we descended the side of this mountain, going down into the chill blue-and-grey clouds. We had left our horses with the Cuban pickets. We proceeded stealthily, for we were already within range of the Spanish pickets. At the bottom of the cañon it was still night. A brook, a regular salmon-stream, brawled over the rocks. There were grassy banks and most delightful trees. The whole valley was a sylvan fragrance. But—the guide waved his arm and scowled warningly, and in a moment we were off, threading thickets, climbing hills, crawling through fields on our hands and knees, sometimes sweeping like seventeen phantoms across a Spanish road. I was in a dream, but I kept my eye on the guide and halted to listen when he halted to listen and ambled onward when he ambled onward. Sometimes he turned and pantomimed as ably and fiercely as a man being stung by a thousand hornets. Then we knew that the situation was extremely delicate. We were now of course well inside the Spanish lines and we ascended a great hill which overlooked the harbour of Santiago. There, tranquilly at anchor, lay the Oquendo, the Maria Theresa, the Christobal Colon, the Viscaya, the Pluton, the Furor. The bay was white in the sun and the great blacked-hull armoured cruisers were impressive in a dignity massive yet graceful. We did not know that they were all doomed ships, soon to go out to a swift death. My friend drew maps and things while I devoted myself to complete rest, blinking lazily at the Spanish squadron. We did not know that we were the last Americans to view them alive and unhurt and at peace. Then we retraced our way, at the same noiseless canter. I did not understand my condition until I considered that we were well through the Spanish lines and practically out of danger. Then I discovered that I was a dead man. The nervous force having evaporated I was a mere corpse. My limbs were of dough and my spinal cord burned within me as if it were red-hot wire. But just at this time we were discovered by a Spanish patrol, and I ascertained that I was not dead at all. We ultimately reached the foot of the mother-mountain on whose shoulders were the Cuban pickets, and here I was so sure of safety that I could not resist the temptation to die again. I think I passed into eleven distinct stupors during the ascent of that mountain while the escort stood leaning on their Remingtons. We had done twenty-five miles at a sort of a man-gallop, never once using a beaten track, but always going promiscuously through the jungle and over the rocks. And many of the miles stood straight on end so that it was as hard to come down as it was to go up. But during my stupors, the escort stood, mind you, and chatted in low voices. For all the signs they showed, we might have been starting. And they had had nothing to eat but mangoes for over eight days. Previous to the eight days they had been living on mangoes and the carcase of a small lean pony. They were, in fact, of the stuff of Fenimore Cooper's Indians, only they made no preposterous orations. At the major's camp, my friend and I agreed that if our worthy escort would send down a representative with us to the coast, we would send back to them whatever we could spare from the stores of our despatch-boat. With one voice the escort answered that they themselves would go the additional four leagues, as in these starving times they did not care to trust a representative, thank you. "They can't do it; they'll peg out; there must be a limit," I said. "No," answered my friend. "They're all right; they'd run three times around the whole island for a mouthful of beer." So we saddled up and put off with our fifteen Cuban infantrymen wagging along tirelessly behind us. Sometimes, at the foot of a precipitous hill, a man asked permission to cling to my horse's tail, and then the Jamaica pony would snake him to the summit so swiftly that only his toes seemed to touch the rocks. And for this assistance the man was grateful. When we crowned the last great ridge we saw our squadron to the eastward spread in its patient semicircular about the mouth of the harbour. But as we wound towards the beach we saw a more dramatic thing—our own despatch-boat leaving the rendezvous and

155

putting off to sea. Evidently we were late. Behind me were fifteen stomachs, empty. It was a frightful situation. My friend and I charged for the beach and those fifteen fools began to run.

It was no use. The despatch-boat went gaily away trailing black smoke behind her. We turned in distress wondering what we could say to that abused escort. If they massacred us, I felt that it would be merely a virtuous reply to fate and they should in no ways be blamed. There are some things which a man's feelings will not allow him to endure after a diet of mangoes and pony. However, we perceived to our amazement that they were not indignant at all. They simply smiled and made a gesture which expressed an habitual pessimism. It was a philosophy which denied the existence of everything but mangoes and pony. It was the Americans who refused to be comforted. I made a deep vow with myself that I would come as soon as possible and play a regular Santa Claus to that splendid escort. But—we put to sea in a dug-out with two black boys. The escort waved us a hearty good-bye from the shore and I never saw them again. I hope they are all on the police-force in the new Santiago.

In time we were rescued from the dug-out by our despatch-boat, and we relieved our feelings by over-rewarding the two black boys. In fact they reaped a harvest because of our emotion over our failure to fill the gallant stomachs of the escort. They were two rascals. We steamed to the flagship and were given permission to board her. Admiral Sampson is to me the most interesting personality of the war. I would not know how to sketch him for you even if I could pretend to sufficient material. Anyhow, imagine, first of all, a marble block of impassivity out of which is carved the figure of an old man. Endow this with life, and you've just begun. Then you must discard all your pictures of bluff, red-faced old gentlemen who roar against the gale, and understand that the quiet old man is a sailor and an admiral. This will be difficult; if I told you he was anything else it would be easy. He resembles other types; it is his distinction not to resemble the preconceived type of his standing. When first I met him I was impressed that he was immensely bored by the war and with the command of the North Atlantic Squadron. I perceived a manner where I thought I perceived a mood, a point of view. Later, he seemed so indifferent to small things which bore upon large things that I bowed to his apathy as a thing unprecedented, marvellous. Still I mistook a manner for a mood. Still I could not understand that this was the way of the man. I am not to blame, for my communication was slight and depended upon sufferance—upon, in fact, the traditional courtesy of the navy. But finally I saw that it was all manner, that hidden in his indifferent, even apathetic, manner, there was the alert, sure, fine mind of the best sea-captain that America has produced since—since Farragut? I don't know. I think—since Hull.

Men follow heartily when they are well led. They balk at trifles when a blockhead cries go on. For my part, an impressive thing of the war is the absolute devotion to Admiral Sampson's person—no, to his judgment and wisdom—which was paid by his ship-commanders—Evans of the Iowa, Taylor of the Oregon, Higginson of the Massachusetts, Phillips of the Texas, and all the other captains—barring one. Once, afterward, they called upon him to avenge himself upon a rival—they were there and they would have to say—but he said no-o-o, he guessed it—wouldn't do—any—g-o-oo-o-d—to the—service.

Men feared him, but he never made threats; men tumbled heels over head to obey him, but he never gave a sharp order; men loved him, but he said no word, kindly or unkindly; men cheered for him and he said: "Who are they yelling for?" Men behaved badly to him and he said nothing. Men thought of glory and he considered the management of ships. All without a sound. A noiseless campaign—on his part. No bunting, no arches, no fireworks; nothing but the perfect management of a big fleet. That is a record for you. No trumpets, no cheers of the populace. Just plain, pure, unsauced accomplishment. But ultimately he will reap his reward in—in what? In text-books on sea-campaigns. No more. The people choose their own and they choose the kind they like. Who has a better right? Anyhow he is a great man. And when you are once started you can continue to be a great man without the help of bouquets and banquets. He don't need them—bless your heart.

The flag-ship's battle-hatches were down, and between decks it was insufferable despite the electric fans. I made my way somewhat forwards, past the smart orderly, past the companion, on to the den of the junior mess. Even there they were playing cards in somebody's cabin. "Hello, old man. Been ashore? How'd it look? It's your deal, Chick." There was nothing but steamy wet heat and the decent suppression of the consequent ill-tempers. The junior officers' quarters were no more comfortable than the admiral's cabin. I had expected it to be so because of my remembrance of their gay spirits. But they were not gay. They were sweltering. Hello, old man, had I been ashore? I fled to the deck, where other officers not on duty were smoking quiet cigars. The hospitality of the officers of the flag-ship is another charming memory of the war.

I rolled into my berth on the despatch-boat that night feeling a perfect wonder of the day. Was the figure that leaned over the card-game on the flag-ship, the figure with a whisky and soda in its hand and a cigar in its teeth—was it identical with the figure scrambling, afraid of its life, through Cuban jungle? Was it the figure of the situation of the fifteen pathetic hungry men? It was the same and it went to sleep, hard sleep. I don't know where we voyaged. I think it was Jamaica. But, at any rate, upon the morning of our return to the Cuban coast, we found the sea alive with transports—United States transports from Tampa, containing the Fifth Army Corps under Major-General Shafter. The rigging and the decks of these ships were black with men and everybody wanted to land first. I landed, ultimately, and immediately began to look for an acquaintance. The boats were banged by the waves against a little flimsy dock. I fell ashore somehow, but I did not at once find an acquaintance. I talked to a private in the 2d Massachusetts Volunteers who told me that he was going to write war correspondence for a Boston newspaper. This statement did not surprise me.

There was a straggly village, but I followed the troops who at this time seemed to be moving out by companies. I found three other correspondents and it was luncheon time. Somebody had two bottles of Bass, but it was so warm that it squirted out in foam. There was no firing; no noise of any kind. An old shed was full of soldiers loafing pleasantly in the shade. It was a hot, dusty, sleepy afternoon; bees hummed. We saw Major-General Lawton standing with his staff under a tree. He was smiling as if he would say: "Well, this will be better than chasing Apaches." His division had the advance, and so he had the right to be happy. A tall man with a grey moustache, light but very strong, an ideal cavalryman. He appealed to one all the more because of the vague rumours that his superiors—some of them—were going to take mighty good care that he shouldn't get much to do. It was rather sickening to hear such talk, but later we knew that most of it must have been mere lies.

Down by the landing-place a band of correspondents were making a sort of permanent camp. They worked like Trojans, carrying wall-tents, cots, and boxes of provisions. They asked me to join them, but I looked shrewdly at the sweat on their faces and backed away. The next day the army left this permanent camp eight miles to the rear. The day became tedious. I was glad when evening came. I sat by a camp-fire and listened to a soldier of the 8th Infantry who told me that he was the first enlisted man to land. I lay pretending to appreciate him, but in fact I considered him a great shameless liar. Less than a month ago, I learned that every word he said was gospel truth. I was much surprised. We went for breakfast to the camp of the 20th Infantry, where Captain Greene and his subaltern, Exton, gave us tomatoes stewed with hard bread and coffee. Later, I discovered Greene and Exton down at the beach good-naturedly dodging the waves which seemed to be trying to prevent them from washing the breakfast dishes. I felt tremendously ashamed because my cup and my plate were there, you know, and—— Fate provides some men greased opportunities for making dizzy jackasses of themselves and I fell a victim to my flurry on this occasion. I was a blockhead. I walked away blushing. What? The battles? Yes, I saw something of all of them. I made up my mind that the next time I met Greene and Exton I'd say: "Look here; why didn't you tell me you had to wash your own dishes that morning so that I could have helped? I felt beastly when I saw you scrubbing there. And me walking around idly." But I never saw Captain Greene again. I think he is in the Philippines now fighting the Tagals. The next time I saw Exton—what? Yes, La Guasimas. That was the "rough rider fight." However, the next time I saw Exton I—what do you think? I forgot to speak about it. But if ever I meet Greene or Exton again—even if it should be twenty years—I am going to say, first thing: "Why——" What? Yes. Roosevelt's regiment and the First and Tenth Regular Cavalry. I'll say, first thing: "Say, why didn't you tell me you had to wash your own dishes, that morning, so that I could have helped?" My stupidity will be on my conscience until I die, if, before that, I do not meet either Greene or Exton. Oh, yes, you are howling for blood, but I tell you it is more emphatic that I lost my tooth-brush. Did I tell you that? Well, I lost it, you see, and I thought of it for ten hours at a stretch. Oh, yes—he? He was shot through the heart. But, look here, I contend that the French cable company buncoed us throughout the war. What? Him? My tooth-brush I never found, but he died of his wound in time. Most of the regular soldiers carried their tooth-brushes stuck in the bands of their hats. It made a quaint military decoration. I have had a line of a thousand men pass me in the jungle and not a hat lacking the simple emblem.

The first of July? All right. My Jamaica polo-pony was not present. He was still in the hills to the westward of Santiago, but the Cubans had promised to fetch him to me. But my kit was easy to carry. It had nothing superfluous in it but a pair of spurs which made me indignant every time I looked at them. Oh, but I must tell you about a man I met directly after the La Guasimas fight. Edward Marshall, a correspondent whom I had known with a degree of intimacy for seven years, was terribly hit in that fight and asked me if I would not go to Siboney—the base—and convey the news to his colleagues of the New York Journal and round up some assistance. I went to Siboney, and there was not a Journal man to be seen, although usually you judged from appearances that the Journal staff was about as large as the army. Presently I met two correspondents, strangers to me, but I questioned them, saying that Marshall was badly shot and wished for such succour as Journal men could bring from their despatch-boat. And one of these correspondents replied. He is the man I wanted to describe. I love him as a brother. He said: "Marshall? Marshall? Why, Marshall isn't in Cuba at all. He left for New York just before the expedition sailed from Tampa." I said: "Beg pardon, but I remarked that Marshall was shot in the fight this morning, and have you seen any Journal people?" After a pause, he said: "I am sure Marshall is not down here at all. He's in New York." I said: "Pardon me, but I remarked that Marshall was shot in the fight this morning, and have you seen any Journal people?" He said: "No; now look here, you must have gotten two chaps mixed somehow. Marshall isn't in Cuba at all. How could he be shot?" I said: "Pardon me, but I remarked that Marshall was shot in the fight this morning, and have you seen any Journal people?" He said: "But it can't really be Marshall, you know, for the simple reason that he's not down here." I clasped my hands to my temples, gave one piercing cry to heaven and fled from his presence. I couldn't go on with him. He excelled me at all points. I have faced death by bullets, fire, water, and disease, but to die thus—to wilfully batter myself against the ironclad opinion of this mummy—no, no, not that. In the meantime, it was admitted that a correspondent was shot, be his name Marshall, Bismarck, or Louis XIV. Now, supposing the name of this wounded correspondent had been Bishop Potter? Or Jane Austen? Or Bernhardt? Or Henri Georges Stephane Adolphe Opper de Blowitz? What effect—never mind.

We will proceed to July 1st. On that morning I marched with my kit—having everything essential save a tooth-brush—the entire army put me to shame, since there must have been at least fifteen thousand tooth-brushes in the invading force—I marched with my kit on the road to Santiago. It was a fine morning and everybody—the doomed and the immunes—how could we tell one from the other—everybody was in the highest spirits. We were enveloped in forest, but we could hear, from ahead, everybody peppering away at everybody. It was like the roll of many drums. This was Lawton over at El Caney. I reflected with complacency that Lawton's division did not concern me in a professional way. That was the affair of another man. My business was with Kent's division and Wheeler's division. We came to El Poso—a hill at nice artillery range from the Spanish defences. Here Grimes's battery was shooting a duel with one of the enemy's batteries. Scovel had established a little camp in the rear of the guns and a servant had made coffee. I invited Whigham to have coffee, and the servant added some hard biscuit and tinned tongue. I noted that Whigham was staring fixedly over my shoulder, and that he waved away the tinned tongue with some bitterness. It was a horse, a dead horse. Then a mule, which had been shot through the nose, wandered up and looked at Whigham. We ran away.

On top of the hill one had a fine view of the Spanish lines. We stared across almost a mile of jungle to ash-coloured trenches on the military crest of the ridge. A goodly distance back of this position were white buildings, all flying great red-cross flags. The jungle beneath us rattled with firing and the Spanish trenches crackled out regular volleys, but all this time there was nothing to indicate a tangible enemy. In truth, there was a man in a Panama hat strolling to and fro behind one of the Spanish trenches, gesticulating at times with a walking stick. A man in a Panama hat, walking with a stick! That was the strangest sight of my life—that symbol, that quaint figure of Mars. The battle, the thunderous row, was his possession. He was the master. He mystified us all with his infernal Panama hat and his wretched walking-stick. From near his feet came volleys and from near his side came roaring shells, but he stood there alone, visible, the one tangible thing. He was a Colossus, and he was half as high as a pin, this being. Always somebody would be saying: "Who can that fellow be?"

Later, the American guns shelled the trenches and a blockhouse near them, and Mars had vanished. It could not have been death. One cannot kill Mars. But there was one other figure, which arose to symbolic dignity. The balloon of our signal corps had swung over the tops of the jungle's trees toward the Spanish trenches. Whereat the balloon and the man in the Panama hat and with a walking stick—whereat these two waged tremendous battle.

Suddenly the conflict became a human thing. A little group of blue figures appeared on the green of the terrible hillside. It was some of our infantry. The attaché of a great empire was at my shoulder, and he turned to me and spoke with incredulity and scorn. "Why, they're trying to take the position," he cried, and I admitted meekly that I thought they were. "But they can't do it, you know," he protested vehemently. "It's impossible." And— good fellow that he was—he began to grieve and wail over a useless sacrifice of gallant men. "It's plucky, you know! By Gawd, it's plucky! But they can't do it!" He was profoundly moved; his voice was quite broken. "It will simply be a hell of a slaughter with no good coming out of it."

The trail was already crowded with stretcher-bearers and with wounded men who could walk. One had to stem a tide of mute agony. But I don't know that it was mute agony. I only know that it was mute. It was something in which the silence or, more likely, the reticence was an appalling and inexplicable fact. One's senses seemed to demand that these men should cry out. But you could really find wounded men who exhibited all the signs of a pleased and contented mood. When thinking of it now it seems strange beyond words. But at the time—I don't know—it did not attract one's wonder. A man with a hole in his arm or his shoulder, or even in the leg below the knee, was often whimsical, comic. "Well, this ain't exactly what I enlisted for, boys. If I'd been told about this in Tampa, I'd have resigned from th' army. Oh, yes, you can get the same thing if you keep on going. But I think the Spaniards may run out of ammunition in the course of a week or ten days." Then suddenly one would be confronted by the awful majesty of a man shot in the face. Particularly I remember one. He had a great dragoon moustache, and the blood streamed down his face to meet this moustache even as a torrent goes to meet the jammed log, and then swarmed out to the tips and fell in big slow drops. He looked steadily into my eyes; I was ashamed to return his glance. You understand? It is very curious—all that.

The two lines of battle were royally whacking away at each other, and there was no rest or peace in all that region. The modern bullet is a far-flying bird. It rakes the air with its hot spitting song at distances which, as a usual thing, place the whole landscape in the danger-zone. There was no direction from which they did not come. A chart of their courses over one's head would have resembled a spider's web. My friend Jimmie, the photographer, mounted to the firing line with me and we gallivanted as much as we dared. The "sense of the meeting" was curious. Most of the men seemed to have no idea of a grand historic performance, but they were grimly satisfied with themselves. "Well, begawd, we done it." Then they wanted to know about other parts of the line. "How are things looking, old man? Everything all right?" "Yes, everything is all right if you can hold this ridge." "Aw, hell," said the men, "we'll hold the ridge. Don't you worry about that, son."

It was Jimmie's first action, and, as we cautiously were making our way to the right of our lines, the crash of the Spanish fire became uproarious, and the air simply whistled. I heard a quavering voice near my shoulder, and, turning, I beheld Jimmie—Jimmie—with a face bloodless, white as paper. He looked at me with eyes opened extremely wide. "Say," he said, "this is pretty hot, ain't it?" I was delighted. I knew exactly what he meant. He wanted to have the situation defined. If I had told him that this was the occasion of some mere idle desultory firing and recommended that he wait until the real battle began, I think he would have gone in a bee-line for the rear. But I told him the truth. "Yes, Jimmie," I replied earnestly. "You can take it from me that this is patent, double-extra-what-for." And immediately he nodded. "All right." If this was a big action, then he was willing to pay in his fright as a rational price for the privilege of being present. But if this was only a penny affray, he considered the price exorbitant, and he would go away. He accepted my assurance with simple faith, and deported himself with kindly dignity as one moving amid great things. His face was still as pale as paper, but that counted for nothing. The main point was his perfect willingness to be frightened for reasons. I wonder where is Jimmie? I lent him the Jamaica polo-pony one day and it ran away with him and flung him off in the middle of a ford. He appeared to me afterward and made bitter speech concerning this horse which I had assured him was a gentle and pious animal. Then I never saw Jimmie again.

Then came the night of the first of July. A group of correspondents limped back to El Poso. It had been a day so long that the morning seemed as remote as a morning in the previous year. But I have forgotten to tell you about Reuben McNab. Many years ago, I went to school at a place called Claverack, in New York State, where there was a semi-military institution. Contemporaneous with me, as a student, was Reuben McNab, a long, lank boy, freckled, sandy-haired—an extraordinary boy in no way, and yet, I wager, a boy clearly marked in every recollection. Perhaps there is a good deal in that name. Reuben McNab. You can't fling that name carelessly over your shoulder and lose it. It follows you like the haunting memory of a sin. At any rate, Reuben McNab was identified intimately in my thought with the sunny irresponsible days at Claverack, when all the earth was a green field and all the sky was a rainless blue. Then I looked down into a miserable huddle at Bloody Bend, a huddle of hurt men, dying men, dead men. And there I saw Reuben McNab, a corporal in the 71st New York Volunteers, and with a hole through his lung. Also, several holes through his clothing. "Well, they got me," he said in greeting. Usually they said that. There were no long speeches. "Well, they got me." That was sufficient. The duty of the upright, unhurt, man is then difficult. I doubt if many of us learned how to speak to our own wounded. In the first place, one had to play that the wound was nothing; oh, a mere nothing; a casual interference with movement, perhaps, but nothing more; oh, really nothing more. In the second place, one had to show a comrade's appreciation of this sad plight. As a result I think most of us bungled and stammered in the presence of our wounded friends. That's curious, eh? "Well, they got me," said Reuben McNab. I had looked upon five hundred wounded men with stolidity, or with a conscious indifference which filled me with amazement. But the apparition of Reuben McNab, the schoolmate, lying there in the mud, with a hole through his lung, awed me into stutterings, set me trembling with a sense of terrible intimacy with this war which theretofore I could have believed was a dream—almost. Twenty shot men rolled their eyes and looked at me. Only one man paid no heed. He was dying; he had no time. The bullets hummed low over them all. Death, having already struck, still insisted upon raising a venomous crest. "If you're goin' by the hospital, step in and see me," said Reuben McNab. That was all.

At the correspondents' camp, at El Poso, there was hot coffee. It was very good. I have a vague sense of being very selfish over my blanket and rubber coat. I have a vague sense of spasmodic firing during my sleep; it rained, and then I awoke to hear that steady drumming of an infantry fire— something which was never to cease, it seemed. They were at it again. The trail from El Poso to the positions along San Juan ridge had become an exciting thoroughfare. Shots from large-bore rifles dropped in from almost every side. At this time the safest place was the extreme front. I remember in particular the one outcry I heard. A private in the 71st, without his rifle, had gone to a stream for some water, and was returning, being but a little in rear of me. Suddenly I heard this cry—"Oh, my God, come quick"—and I was conscious then to having heard the hateful zip of a close shot. He lay on the ground, wriggling. He was hit in the hip. Two men came quickly. Presently everybody seemed to be getting knocked down. They went over like men of wet felt, quietly, calmly, with no more complaint than so many automatons. It was only that lad—"Oh, my God, come quick." Otherwise, men seemed to consider that their hurts were not worthy of particular attention. A number of people got killed very courteously, tacitly absolving the rest of us from any care in the matter. A man fell; he turned blue; his face took on an expression of deep sorrow; and then his immediate friends worried about him, if he had friends. This was July 1. I crave the permission to leap back again to that date.

On the morning of July 2, I sat on San Juan hill and watched Lawton's division come up. I was absolutely sheltered, but still where I could look into the faces of men who were trotting up under fire. There wasn't a high heroic face among them. They were all men intent on business. That was all. It may seem to you that I am trying to make everything a squalor. That would be wrong. I feel that things were often sublime. But they were differently sublime. They were not of our shallow and preposterous fictions. They stood out in a simple, majestic commonplace. It was the behaviour of men on the street. It was the behaviour of men. In one way, each man was just pegging along at the heels of the man before him, who was pegging along at the heels of still another man, who was pegging along at the heels of still another man who—— It was that in the flat and obvious way. In another way it was pageantry, the pageantry of the accomplishment of naked duty. One cannot speak of it—the spectacle of the common man serenely doing his work, his appointed work. It is the one thing in the universe which makes one fling expression to the winds and be satisfied to simply feel. Thus they moved at San Juan—the soldiers of the United States Regular Army. One pays them the tribute of the toast of silence.

Lying near one of the enemy's trenches was a red-headed Spanish corpse. I wonder how many hundreds were cognisant of this red-headed Spanish corpse? It arose to the dignity of a landmark. There were many corpses but only one with a red head. This red-head. He was always there. Each time I approached that part of the field I prayed that I might find that he had been buried. But he was always there—red-headed. His strong simple countenance was a malignant sneer at the system which was forever killing the credulous peasants in a sort of black night of politics, where the peasants merely followed whatever somebody had told them was lofty and good. But, nevertheless, the red-headed Spaniard was dead. He was irrevocably dead. And to what purpose? The honour of Spain? Surely the honour of Spain could have existed without the violent death of this poor red-headed peasant? Ah well, he was buried when the heavy firing ceased and men had time for such small things as funerals. The trench was turned over on top of him. It was a fine, honourable, soldierly fate—to be buried in a trench, the trench of the fight and the death. Sleep well, red-headed peasant. You came to another hemisphere to fight because—because you were told to, I suppose. Well, there you are, buried in your trench on San Juan hill. That is the end of it, your life has been taken—that is a flat, frank fact. And foreigners buried you expeditiously while speaking a strange tongue. Sleep well, red-headed mystery.

On the day before the destruction of Cervera's fleet, I steamed past our own squadron, doggedly lying in its usual semicircle, every nose pointing at the mouth of the harbour. I went to Jamaica, and on the placid evening of the next day I was again steaming past our own squadron, doggedly lying in its usual semicircle, every nose pointing at the mouth of the harbour. A megaphone-hail from the bridge of one of the yacht-gunboats came casually over the water. "Hello! hear the news?" "No; what was it?" "The Spanish fleet came out this morning." "Oh, of course, it did." "Honest, I mean." "Yes, I know; well, where are they now?" "Sunk." Was there ever such a preposterous statement? I was humiliated that my friend, the lieutenant on the yacht-gunboat, should have measured me as one likely to swallow this bad joke.

But it was all true; every word. I glanced back at our squadron, lying in its usual semicircle, every nose pointing at the mouth of the harbour. It would have been absurd to think that anything had happened. The squadron hadn't changed a button. There it sat without even a smile on the face of the tiger. And it had eaten four armoured cruisers and two torpedo-boat-destroyers while my back was turned for a moment. Courteously, but clearly, we announced across the waters that until despatch-boats came to be manned from the ranks of the celebrated horse-marines, the lieutenant's statement would probably remain unappreciated. He made a gesture, abandoning us to our scepticism. It infuriates an honourable and serious man to be taken for a liar or a joker at a time when he is supremely honourable and serious. However, when we went ashore, we found Siboney ringing with the news. It was true, then; that mishandled collection of sick ships had come out and taken the deadly thrashing which was rightfully the due of—I don't know—somebody in Spain—or perhaps nobody anywhere. One likes to wallop incapacity, but one has mingled emotions over the incapacity which is not so much personal as it is the development of centuries. This kind of incapacity cannot be centralised. You cannot hit the head which contains it all. This is the idea, I imagine, which moved the officers and men of our fleet. Almost immediately they began to speak of the Spanish Admiral as "poor old boy" with a lucid suggestion in their tones that his fate appealed to them as being undue hard, undue cruel. And yet the Spanish guns hit nothing. If a man shoots, he should hit something occasionally, and men say that from the time the Spanish ships broke clear of the harbour entrance until they were one by one overpowered, they were each a band of flame. Well, one can only mumble out that when a man shoots he should be required to hit something occasionally.

In truth, the greatest fact of the whole campaign on land and sea seems to be the fact that the Spaniards could only hit by chance, by a fluke. If he had been an able marksman, no man of our two unsupported divisions would have set foot on San Juan hill on July 1. They should have been blown to smithereens. The Spaniards had no immediate lack of ammunition, for they fired enough to kill the population of four big cities. I admit neither Velasquez nor Cervantes into this discussion, although they have appeared by authority as reasons for something which I do not clearly understand. Well, anyhow they couldn't hit anything. Velasquez? Yes. Cervantes? Yes. But the Spanish troops seemed only to try to make a very rapid fire. Thus we lost many men. We lost them because of the simple fury of the fire; never because the fire was well-directed, intelligent. But the Americans were called upon to be whipped because of Cervantes and Velasquez. It was impossible.

Out on the slopes of San Juan the dog-tents shone white. Some kind of negotiations were going forward, and men sat on their trousers and waited. It was all rather a blur of talks with officers, and a craving for good food and good water. Once Leighton and I decided to ride over to El Caney, into which town the civilian refugees from Santiago were pouring. The road from the beleaguered city to the out-lying village was a spectacle to make one moan.

There were delicate gentle families on foot, the silly French boots of the girls twisting and turning in a sort of absolute paper futility; there were sons and grandsons carrying the venerable patriarch in his own armchair; there were exhausted mothers with babes who wailed; there were young dandies with their toilettes in decay; there were puzzled, guideless women who didn't know what had happened. The first sentence one heard was the murmurous "What a damn shame." We saw a godless young trooper of the Second Cavalry sharply halt a waggon. "Hold on a minute. You must carry this woman. She's fainted twice already." The virtuous driver of the U.S. Army waggon mildly answered: "But I'm full-up now." "You can make room for her," said the private of the Second Cavalry. A young, young man with a straight mouth. It was merely a plain bit of nothing—at—all but, thank God, thank God, he seemed to have not the slightest sense of excellence. He said: "If you've got any man in there who can walk at all, you put him out and let this woman get in." "But," answered the teamster, "I'm filled up with a lot of cripples and grandmothers." Thereupon they discussed the point fairly, and ultimately the woman was lifted into the waggon.

The vivid thing was the fact that these people did not visibly suffer. Somehow they were numb. There was not a tear. There was rarely a countenance which was not wondrously casual. There was no sign of fatalistic theory. It was simply that what was happening to-day had happened yesterday, as near as one could judge. I could fancy that these people had been thrown out of their homes every day. It was utterly, utterly casual. And they accepted the ministrations of our men in the same fashion. Everything was a matter of course. I had a filled canteen. I was frightfully conscious of this fact because a filled canteen was a pearl of price; it was a great thing. It was an enormous accident which led one to offer praises that he was luckier than ten thousand better men.

As Leighton and I rode along, we came to a tree under which a refugee family had halted. They were a man, his wife, two handsome daughters and a pimply son. It was plain that they were superior people, because the girls had dressed for the exodus and wore corsets which captivated their forms with a steel-ribbed vehemence only proper for wear on a sun-blistered road to a distant town. They asked us for water. Water was the gold of the moment. Leighton was almost maudlin in his generosity. I remember being angry with him. He lavished upon them his whole canteen and he received in return not even a glance of—what? Acknowledgment? No, they didn't even admit anything. Leighton wasn't a human being; he was some sort of a mountain spring. They accepted him on a basis of pure natural phenomena. His canteen was purely an occurrence. In the meantime the pimple-faced approached me. He asked for water and held out a pint cup. My response was immediate. I tilted my canteen and poured into his cup almost a pint of my treasure. He glanced into the cup and apparently he beheld there some innocent sediment for which he alone or his people were responsible. In the American camps the men were accustomed to a sediment. Well, he glanced at my poor cupful and then negligently poured it out on the ground and held up his cup for more. I gave him more; I gave him his cup full again, but there was something within me which made me swear him out completely. But he didn't understand a word. Afterward I watched if they were capable of being moved to help on their less able fellows on this miserable journey. Not they! Nor yet anybody else. Nobody cared for anybody save my young friend of the Second Cavalry, who rode seriously to and fro doing his best for people, who took him as a result of a strange upheaval.

The fight at El Caney had been furious. General Vera del Rey with somewhat less than 1000 men—the Spanish accounts say 520—had there made such a stand that only about 80 battered soldiers ever emerged from it. The attack cost Lawton about 400 men. The magazine rifle! But the town was now a vast parrot-cage of chattering refugees. If, on the road, they were silent, stolid and serene, in the town they found their tongues and set up such a cackle as one may seldom hear. Notably the women; it is they who invariably confuse the definition of situations, and one could wonder in amaze if this crowd of irresponsible, gabbling hens had already forgotten that this town was the deathbed, so to speak, of scores of gallant men whose blood was not yet dry; whose hands, of the hue of pale amber, stuck from the soil of the hasty burial. On the way to El Caney I had conjured a picture of the women of Santiago, proud in their pain, their despair, dealing glances of defiance, contempt, hatred at the invader; fiery ferocious ladies, so true to their vanquished and to their dead that they spurned the very existence of the low-bred churls who lacked both Velasquez and Cervantes. And instead, there was this mere noise, which reminded one alternately of a tea-party in Ireland, a village fête in the south of France, and the vacuous morning screech of a swarm of sea-gulls. "Good. There is Donna Maria. This will lower her high head. This will teach her better manners to her neighbours. She wasn't too grand to send her rascal of a servant to borrow a trifle of coffee of me in the morning, and then when I met her on the calle—por Dios, she was too blind to see me. But we are all equal here. No? Little Juan has a sore toe. Yes, Donna Maria; many thanks, many thanks. Juan, do me the favour to be quiet while Donna Maria is asking about your toe. Oh, Donna Maria, we were always poor, always. But you. My heart bleeds when I see how hard this is for you. The old cat! She gives me a head-shake."

Pushing through the throng in the plaza we came in sight of the door of the church, and here was a strange scene. The church had been turned into a hospital for Spanish wounded who had fallen into American hands. The interior of the church was too cave-like in its gloom for the eyes of the operating surgeons, so they had had the altar table carried to the doorway, where there was a bright light. Framed then in the black archway was the altar table with the figure of a man upon it. He was naked save for a breech-clout and so close, so clear was the ecclesiastic suggestion, that one's mind leaped to a phantasy that this thin, pale figure had just been torn down from a cross. The flash of the impression was like light, and for this instant it illumined all the dark recesses of one's remotest idea of sacrilege, ghastly and wanton. I bring this to you merely as an effect, an effect of mental light and shade, if you like; something done in thought similar to that which the French impressionists do in colour; something meaningless and at the same time overwhelming, crushing, monstrous. "Poor devil; I wonder if he'll pull through," said Leighton. An American surgeon and his assistants were intent over the prone figure. They wore white aprons. Something small and silvery flashed in the surgeon's hand. An assistant held the merciful sponge close to the man's nostrils, but he was writhing and moaning in some horrible dream of this artificial sleep. As the surgeon's instrument played, I fancied that the man dreamed that he was being gored by a bull. In his pleading, delirious

171

babble occurred constantly the name of the Virgin, the Holy Mother. "Good morning," said the surgeon. He changed his knife to his left hand and gave me a wet palm. The tips of his fingers were wrinkled, shrunken, like those of a boy who has been in swimming too long. Now, in front of the door, there were three American sentries, and it was their business to—to do what? To keep this Spanish crowd from swarming over the operating table! It was perforce a public clinic. They would not be denied. The weaker women and the children jostled according to their might in the rear, while the stronger people, gaping in the front rank, cried out impatiently when the pushing disturbed their long stares. One burned with a sudden gift of public oratory. One wanted to say: "Oh, go away, go away, go away. Leave the man decently alone with his pain, you gogglers. This is not the national sport."

But within the church there was an audience of another kind. This was of the other wounded men awaiting their turn. They lay on their brown blankets in rows along the stone floor. Their eyes, too, were fastened upon the operating-table, but—that was different. Meek-eyed little yellow men lying on the floor awaiting their turns.

One afternoon I was seated with a correspondent friend, on the porch of one of the houses at Siboney. A vast man on horseback came riding along at a foot pace. When he perceived my friend, he pulled up sharply. "Whoa! Where's that mule I lent you?" My friend arose and saluted. "I've got him all right, General, thank you," said my friend. The vast man shook his finger. "Don't you lose him now." "No, sir, I won't; thank you, sir." The vast man rode away. "Who the devil is that?" said I. My friend laughed. "That's General Shafter," said he.

I gave five dollars for the Bos'n—small, black, spry imp of Jamaica sin. When I first saw him he was the property of a fireman on the Criton. The fireman had found him—a little wharf rat—in Port Antonio. It was not the purchase of a slave; it was that the fireman believed that he had spent about five dollars on a lot of comic supplies for the Bos'n, including a little suit of sailor clothes. The Bos'n was an adroit and fantastic black gamin. His eyes were like white lights, and his teeth were a row of little piano keys; otherwise he was black. He had both been a jockey and a cabin-boy, and he had the manners of a gentleman. After he entered my service I don't think there was ever an occasion upon which he was useful, save when he told me quaint stories of Guatemala, in which country he seemed to have lived some portion of his infantile existence. Usually he ran funny errands like little foot-races, each about fifteen yards in length. At Siboney he slept under my hammock like a poodle, and I always expected that, through the breaking of a rope, I would some night descend and obliterate him. His incompetence was spectacular. When I wanted him to do a thing, the agony of supervision was worse than the agony of personal performance. It would have been easier to have gotten my own spurs or boots or blanket than to have the bother of this little incapable's service. But the good aspect was the humorous view. He was like a boy, a mouse, a scoundrel, and a devoted servitor. He was immensely popular. His name of Bos'n became a Siboney stock-word. Everybody knew it. It was a name like President McKinley, Admiral Sampson, General Shafter. The Bos'n became a figure. One day he approached me with four one-dollar notes in United States currency. He besought me to preserve them for him, and I pompously tucked them away in my riding breeches, with an air which meant that his funds were now as safe as if they were in a national bank. Still, I asked with some surprise, where he had reaped all this money. He frankly admitted at once that it had been given to him by the enthusiastic soldiery as a tribute to his charm of person and manner. This was not astonishing for Siboney, where money was meaningless. Money was not worth carrying— "packing." However, a soldier came to our house one morning, and asked, "Got any more tobacco to sell?" As befitted men in virtuous poverty, we replied with indignation. "What tobacco?" "Why, that tobacco what the little nigger is sellin' round."

I said, "Bos'n!" He said, "Yes, mawstah." Wounded men on bloody stretchers were being carried into the hospital next door. "Bos'n, you've been stealing my tobacco." His defence was as glorious as the defence of that forlorn hope in romantic history, which drew itself up and mutely died. He lied as desperately, as savagely, as hopelessly as ever man fought.

One day a delegation from the 33d Michigan came to me and said: "Are you the proprietor of the Bos'n?" I said: "Yes." And they said: "Well, would you please be so kind as to be so good as to give him to us?" A big battle was expected for the next day. "Why," I answered, "if you want him you can have him. But he's a thief, and I won't let him go save on his personal announcement." The big battle occurred the next day, and the Bos'n did not disappear in it; but he disappeared in my interest in the battle, even as a waif might disappear in a fog. My interest in the battle made the Bos'n dissolve before my eyes. Poor little rascal! I gave him up with pain. He was such an innocent villain. He knew no more of thievery than the whole of it. Anyhow one was fond of him. He was a natural scoundrel. He was not an educated scoundrel. One cannot bear the educated scoundrel. He was ingenuous, simple, honest, abashed ruffianism.

I hope the 33d Michigan did not arrive home naked. I hope the Bos'n did not succeed in getting everything. If the Bos'n builds a palace in Detroit, I shall know where he got the money. He got it from the 33d Michigan. Poor little man. He was only eleven years old. He vanished. I had thought to preserve him as a relic, even as one preserves forgotten bayonets and fragments of shell. And now as to the pocket of my riding-breeches. It contained four dollars in United States currency. Bos'n! Hey, Bos'n, where are you? The morning was the morning of battle.

I was on San Juan Hill when Lieutenant Hobson and the men of the Merrimac were exchanged and brought into the American lines. Many of us knew that the exchange was about to be made, and gathered to see the famous party. Some of our Staff officers rode out with three Spanish officers —prisoners—these latter being blindfolded before they were taken through the American position. The army was majestically minding its business in the long line of trenches when its eye caught sight of this little procession. "What's that? What they goin' to do?" "They're goin' to exchange Hobson." Wherefore every man who was foot-free staked out a claim where he could get a good view of the liberated heroes, and two bands prepared to collaborate on "The Star Spangled Banner." There was a very long wait through the sunshiny afternoon. In our impatience, we imagined them—the Americans and Spaniards—dickering away out there under the big tree like so many peddlers. Once the massed bands, misled by a rumour, stiffened themselves into that dramatic and breathless moment when each man is ready to blow. But the rumour was exploded in the nick of time. We made ill jokes, saying one to another that the negotiations had found diplomacy to be a failure, and were playing freeze-out poker for the whole batch of prisoners.

But suddenly the moment came. Along the cut roadway, toward the crowded soldiers, rode three men, and it could be seen that the central one wore the undress uniform of an officer of the United States navy. Most of the soldiers were sprawled out on the grass, bored and wearied in the sunshine. However, they aroused at the old circus-parade, torch-light procession cry, "Here they come." Then the men of the regular army did a thing. They arose en masse and came to "Attention." Then the men of the regular army did another thing. They slowly lifted every weather-beaten hat and drooped it until it touched the knee. Then there was a magnificent silence, broken only by the measured hoof-beats of the little company's horses as they rode through the gap. It was solemn, funereal, this splendid silent welcome of a brave man by men who stood on a hill which they had earned out of blood and death— simply, honestly, with no sense of excellence, earned out of blood and death.

Then suddenly the whole scene went to rubbish. Before he reached the bottom of the hill, Hobson was bowing to right and left like another Boulanger, and, above the thunder of the massed bands, one could hear the venerable outbreak, "Mr. Hobson, I'd like to shake the hand of the man who——" But the real welcome was that welcome of silence. However, one could thrill again when the tail of the procession appeared—an army waggon containing the blue-jackets of the Merrimac adventure. I remember grinning heads stuck out from under the canvas cover of the waggon. And the army spoke to the navy. "Well, Jackie, how does it feel?" And the navy up and answered: "Great! Much obliged to you fellers for comin' here." "Say, Jackie, what did they arrest ye for anyhow? Stealin' a dawg?" The navy still grinned. Here was no rubbish. Here was the mere exchange of language between men.

Some of us fell in behind this small but royal procession and followed it to General Shafter's headquarters, some miles on the road to Siboney. I have a vague impression that I watched the meeting between Shafter and Hobson, but the impression ends there. However, I remember hearing a talk between them as to Hobson's men, and then the blue-jackets were called up to hear the congratulatory remarks of the general in command of the Fifth Army Corps. It was a scene in the fine shade of thickly-leaved trees. The general sat in his chair, his belly sticking ridiculously out before him as if he had adopted some form of artificial inflation. He looked like a joss. If the seamen had suddenly begun to burn a few sticks, most of the spectators would have exhibited no surprise. But the words he spoke were proper, clear, quiet, soldierly, the words of one man to others. The Jackies were comic. At the bidding of their officer they aligned themselves before the general, grinned with embarrassment one to the other, made funny attempts to correct the alignment, and—looked sheepish. They looked sheepish. They looked like bad little boys flagrantly caught. They had no sense of excellence. Here was no rubbish.

Very soon after this the end of the campaign came for me. I caught a fever. I am not sure to this day what kind of a fever it was. It was defined variously. I know, at any rate, that I first developed a languorous indifference to everything in the world. Then I developed a tendency to ride a horse even as a man lies on a cot. Then I—I am not sure—I think I grovelled and groaned about Siboney for several days. My colleagues, Scovel and George Rhea, found me and gave me of their best, but I didn't know whether London Bridge was falling down or whether there was a war with Spain. It was all the same. What of it? Nothing of it. Everything had happened, perhaps. But I cared not a jot. Life, death, dishonour—all were nothing to me. All I cared for was pickles. Pickles at any price! Pickles!!

If I had been the father of a hundred suffering daughters, I should have waved them all aside and remarked that they could be damned for all I cared. It was not a mood. One can defeat a mood. It was a physical situation. Sometimes one cannot defeat a physical situation. I heard the talk of Siboney and sometimes I answered, but I was as indifferent as the star-fish flung to die on the sands. The only fact in the universe was that my veins burned and boiled. Rhea finally staggered me down to the army-surgeon who had charge of the proceedings, and the army-surgeon looked me over with a keen healthy eye. Then he gave a permit that I should be sent home. The manipulation from the shore to the transport was something which was Rhea's affair. I am not sure whether we went in a boat or a balloon. I think it was a boat. Rhea pushed me on board and I swayed meekly and unsteadily toward the captain of the ship, a corpulent, well-conditioned, impickled person pacing noisily on the spar-deck. "Ahem, yes; well; all right. Have you got your own food? I hope, for Christ's sake, you don't expect us to feed you, do you?" Whereupon I went to the rail and weakly yelled at Rhea, but he was already afar. The captain was, meantime, remarking in bellows that, for Christ's sake, I couldn't expect him to feed me. I didn't expect to be fed. I didn't care to be fed. I wished for nothing on earth but some form of painless pause, oblivion. The insults of this old pie-stuffed scoundrel did not affect me then; they affect me now. I would like to tell him that, although I like collies, fox-terriers, and even screw-curled poodles, I do not like him. He was free to call me superfluous and throw me overboard, but he was not free to coarsely speak to a somewhat sick man. I—in fact I hate him—it is all wrong—I lose whatever ethics I possessed—but—I hate him, and I demand that you should imagine a milch cow endowed with a knowledge of navigation and in command of a ship—and perfectly capable of commanding a ship—oh, well, never mind.

I was crawling along the deck when somebody pounced violently upon me and thundered: "Who in hell are you, sir?" I said I was a correspondent. He asked me did I know that I had yellow fever. I said No. He yelled, "Well, by Gawd, you isolate yourself, sir." I said; "Where?" At this question he almost frothed at the mouth. I thought he was going to strike me. "Where?" he roared. "How in hell do I know, sir? I know as much about this ship as you do, sir. But you isolate yourself, sir." My clouded brain tried to comprehend these orders. This man was a doctor in the regular army, and it was necessary to obey him, so I bestirred myself to learn what he meant by these gorilla outcries. "All right, doctor; I'll isolate myself, but I wish you'd tell me where to go." And then he passed into such volcanic humour that I clung to the rail and gasped. "Isolate yourself, sir. Isolate yourself. That's all I've got to say, sir. I don't give a God damn where you go, but when you get there, stay there, sir." So I wandered away and ended up on the deck aft, with my head against the flagstaff and my limp body stretched on a little rug. I was not at all sorry for myself. I didn't care a tent-peg. And yet, as I look back upon it now, the situation was fairly exciting—a voyage of four or five days before me—no food—no friends—above all else, no friends—isolated on deck, and rather ill.

When I returned to the United States, I was able to move my feminine friends to tears by an account of this voyage, but, after all, it wasn't so bad. They kept me on my small reservation aft, but plenty of kindness loomed soon enough. At mess-time, they slid me a tin plate of something, usually stewed tomatoes and bread. Men are always good men. And, at any rate, most of the people were in worse condition than I—poor bandaged chaps looking sadly down at the waves. In a way, I knew the kind. First lieutenants at forty years of age, captains at fifty, majors at 102, lieutenant-colonels at 620, full colonels at 1000, and brigadiers at 9,768,295 plus. A man had to live two billion years to gain eminent rank in the regular army at that time. And, of course, they all had trembling wives at remote western posts waiting to hear the worst, the best, or the middle.

In rough weather, the officers made a sort of a common pool of all the sound legs and arms, and by dint of hanging hard to each other they managed to move from their deck chairs to their cabins and from their cabins again to their deck chairs. Thus they lived until the ship reached Hampton Roads. We slowed down opposite the curiously mingled hotels and batteries at Old Point Comfort, and at our mast-head we flew the yellow-flag, the grim ensign of the plague. Then we witnessed something which informed us that with all this ship-load of wounds and fevers and starvations we had forgotten the fourth element of war. We were flying the yellow flag, but a launch came and circled swiftly about us. There was a little woman in the launch, and she kept looking and looking and looking. Our ship was so high that she could see only those who rung at the rail, but she kept looking and looking and looking. It was plain enough—it was all plain enough—but my heart sank with the fear that she was not going to find him. But presently there was a commotion among some black dough-boys of the 24th Infantry, and two of them ran aft to Colonel Liscum, its gallant commander. Their faces were wreathed in darkey grins of delight. "Kunnel, ain't dat Mis' Liscum, Kunnel?" "What?" said the old man. He got up quickly and appeared at the rail, his arm in a sling. He cried, "Alice!" The little woman saw him, and instantly she covered up her face with her hands as if blinded with a flash of white fire. She made no outcry; it was all in this simply swift gesture, but we—we knew them. It told us. It told us the other part. And in a vision we all saw our own harbour-lights. That is to say those of us who had harbour-lights.

I was almost well, and had defeated the yellow-fever charge which had been brought against me, and so I was allowed ashore among the first. And now happened a strange thing. A hard campaign, full of wants and lacks and absences, brings a man speedily back to an appreciation of things long disregarded or forgotten. In camp, somewhere in the woods between Siboney and Santiago, I happened to think of ice-cream-soda. I had done very well without it for many years; in fact I think I loathe it; but I got to dreaming of ice-cream-soda, and I came near dying of longing for it. I couldn't get it out of my mind, try as I would to concentrate my thoughts upon the land crabs and mud with which I was surrounded. It certainly had been an institution of my childhood, but to have a ravenous longing for it in the year 1898 was about as illogical as to have a ravenous longing for kerosene. All I could do was to swear to myself that if I reached the United States again, I would immediately go to the nearest soda-water fountain and make it look like Spanish Fours. In a loud, firm voice, I would say, "Orange, please." And here is the strange thing: as soon as I was ashore I went to the nearest soda-water fountain, and in a loud, firm voice I said, "Orange, please." I remember one man who went mad that way over tinned peaches, and who wandered over the face of the earth saying plaintively, "Have you any peaches?"

Most of the wounded and sick had to be tabulated and marshalled in sections and thoroughly officialised, so that I was in time to take a position on the verandah of Chamberlain's Hotel and see my late shipmates taken to the hospital. The verandah was crowded with women in light, charming summer dresses, and with spruce officers from the Fortress. It was like a bank of flowers. It filled me with awe. All this luxury and refinement and gentle care and fragrance and colour seemed absolutely new. Then across the narrow street on the verandah of the hotel there was a similar bank of flowers. Two companies of volunteers dug a lane through the great crowd in the street and kept the way, and then through this lane there passed a curious procession. I had never known that they looked like that. Such a gang of dirty, ragged, emaciated, half-starved, bandaged cripples I had never seen. Naturally there were many men who couldn't walk, and some of these were loaded upon a big flat car which was in tow of a trolley-car. Then there were many stretchers, slow-moving. When that crowd began to pass the hotel the banks of flowers made a noise which could make one tremble. Perhaps it was a moan, perhaps it was a sob—but no, it was something beyond either a moan or a sob. Anyhow, the sound of women weeping was in it.—The sound of women weeping.

And how did these men of famous deeds appear when received thus by the people? Did they smirk and look as if they were bursting with the desire to tell everything which had happened? No they hung their heads like so many jail-birds. Most of them seemed to be suffering from something which was like stage-fright during the ordeal of this chance but supremely eloquent reception. No sense of excellence—that was it. Evidently they were willing to leave the clacking to all those natural born major-generals who after the war talked enough to make a great fall in the price of that commodity all over the world.

The episode was closed. And you can depend upon it that I have told you nothing at all, nothing at all, nothing at all.

THE SECOND GENERATION

I

Caspar Cadogan resolved to go to the tropic wars and do something. The air was blue and gold with the pomp of soldiering, and in every ear rang the music of military glory. Caspar's father was a United States Senator from the great State of Skowmulligan, where the war fever ran very high. Chill is the blood of many of the sons of millionaires, but Caspar took the fever and posted to Washington. His father had never denied him anything, and this time all that Caspar wanted was a little Captaincy in the Army—just a simple little Captaincy.

The old man had been entertaining a delegation of respectable bunco-steerers from Skowmulligan who had come to him on a matter which is none of the public's business.

Bottles of whisky and boxes of cigars were still on the table in the sumptuous private parlour. The Senator had said, "Well, gentlemen, I'll do what I can for you." By this sentence he meant whatever he meant.

Then he turned to his eager son. "Well, Caspar?" The youth poured out his modest desires. It was not altogether his fault. Life had taught him a generous faith in his own abilities. If any one had told him that he was simply an ordinary d—d fool he would have opened his eyes wide at the person's lack of judgment. All his life people had admired him.

The Skowmulligan war-horse looked with quick disapproval into the eyes of his son. "Well, Caspar," he said slowly, "I am of the opinion that they've got all the golf experts and tennis champions and cotillion leaders and piano tuners and billiard markers that they really need as officers. Now, if you were a soldier——"

"I know," said the young man with a gesture, "but I'm not exactly a fool, I hope, and I think if I get a chance I can do something. I'd like to try. I would, indeed."

The Senator lit a cigar. He assumed an attitude of ponderous reflection. "Y—yes, but this country is full of young men who are not fools. Full of 'em."

Caspar fidgeted in the desire to answer that while he admitted the profusion of young men who were not fools, he felt that he himself possessed interesting and peculiar qualifications which would allow him to make his mark in any field of effort which he seriously challenged. But he did not make this graceful statement, for he sometimes detected something ironic in his father's temperament. The Skowmulligan war-horse had not thought of expressing an opinion of his own ability since the year 1865, when he was young, like Caspar.

"Well, well," said the Senator finally. "I'll see about it. I'll see about it." The young man was obliged to await the end of his father's characteristic method of thought. The war-horse never gave a quick answer, and if people tried to hurry him they seemed able to arouse only a feeling of irritation against making a decision at all. His mind moved like the wind, but practice had placed a Mexican bit in the mouth of his judgment. This old man of light quick thought had taught himself to move like an ox cart. Caspar said, "Yes, sir." He withdrew to his club, where, to the affectionate inquiries of some envious friends, he replied, "The old man is letting the idea soak."

The mind of the war-horse was decided far sooner than Caspar expected. In Washington a large number of well-bred handsome young men were receiving appointments as Lieutenants, as Captains, and occasionally as Majors. They were a strong, healthy, clean-eyed educated collection. They were a prime lot. A German Field-Marshal would have beamed with joy if he could have had them—to send to school. Anywhere in the world they would have made a grand show as material, but, intrinsically they were not Lieutenants, Captains and Majors. They were fine men, though manhood is only an essential part of a Lieutenant, a Captain or a Major. But at any rate, this arrangement had all the logic of going to sea in a bathing-machine.

The Senator found himself reasoning that Caspar was as good as any of them, and better than many. Presently he was bleating here and there that his boy should have a chance. "The boy's all right, I tell you, Henry. He's wild to go, and I don't see why they shouldn't give him a show. He's got plenty of nerve, and he's keen as a whiplash. I'm going to get him an appointment, and if you can do anything to help it along I wish you would."

Then he betook himself to the White House and the War Department and made a stir. People think that Administrations are always slavishly, abominably anxious to please the Machine. They are not; they wish the Machine sunk in red fire, for by the power of ten thousand past words, looks, gestures, writings, the Machine comes along and takes the Administration by the nose and twists it, and the Administration dare not even yell. The huge force which carries an election to success looks reproachfully at the Administration and says, "Give me a bun." That is a very small thing with which to reward a Colossus.

The Skowmulligan war-horse got his bun and took it to his hotel where Caspar was moodily reading war rumours. "Well, my boy, here you are." Caspar was a Captain and Commissary on the staff of Brigadier-General Reilly, commander of the Second Brigade of the First Division of the Thirtieth Army Corps.

"I had to work for it," said the Senator grimly. "They talked to me as if they thought you were some sort of empty-headed idiot. None of 'em seemed to know you personally. They just sort of took it for granted. Finally I got pretty hot in the collar." He paused a moment; his heavy, grooved face set hard; his blue eyes shone. He clapped a hand down upon the handle of his chair.

"Caspar, I've got you into this thing, and I believe you'll do all right, and I'm not saying this because I distrust either your sense or your grit. But I want you to understand you've got to make a go of it. I'm not going to talk any twaddle about your country and your country's flag. You understand all about that. But now you're a soldier, and there'll be this to do and that to do, and fighting to do, and you've got to do every d———d one of 'em right up to the handle. I don't know how much of a shindy this thing is going to be, but any shindy is enough to show how much there is in a man. You've got your appointment, and that's all I can do for you; but I'll thrash you with my own hands if, when the Army gets back, the other fellows say my son is 'nothing but a good-looking dude.'"

He ceased, breathing heavily. Caspar looked bravely and frankly at his father, and answered in a voice which was not very tremulous. "I'll do my best. This is my chance. I'll do my best with it."

The Senator had a marvellous ability of transition from one manner to another. Suddenly he seemed very kind. "Well, that's all right, then. I guess you'll get along all right with Reilly. I know him well, and he'll see you through. I helped him along once. And now about this commissary business. As I understand it, a Commissary is a sort of caterer in a big way—that is, he looks out for a good many more things than a caterer has to bother his head about. Reilly's brigade has probably from two to three thousand men in it, and in regard to certain things you've got to look out for every man of 'em every day. I know perfectly well you couldn't successfully run a boarding-house in Ocean Grove. How are you going to manage for all these soldiers, hey? Thought about it?"

"No," said Caspar, injured. "I didn't want to be a Commissary. I wanted to be a Captain in the line."

"They wouldn't hear of it. They said you would have to take a staff appointment where people could look after you."

"Well, let them look after me," cried Caspar resentfully; "but when there's any fighting to be done I guess I won't necessarily be the last man."

"That's it," responded the Senator. "That's the spirit." They both thought that the problem of war would eliminate to an equation of actual battle.

Ultimately Caspar departed into the South to an encampment in salty grass under pine trees. Here lay an Army corps twenty thousand strong. Caspar passed into the dusty sunshine of it, and for many weeks he was lost to view.

II

"Of course I don't know a blamed thing about it," said Caspar frankly and modestly to a circle of his fellow staff officers. He was referring to the duties of his office.

Their faces became expressionless; they looked at him with eyes in which

184

he could fathom nothing. After a pause one politely said, "Don't you?" It was the inevitable two words of convention.

"Why," cried Caspar, "I didn't know what a commissary officer was until I was one. My old Guv'nor told me. He'd looked it up in a book somewhere, I suppose; but I didn't know."

"Didn't you?"

The young man's face glowed with sudden humour. "Do you know, the word was intimately associated in my mind with camels. Funny, eh? I think it came from reading that rhyme of Kipling's about the commissariat camel."

"Did it?"

"Yes. Funny, isn't it? Camels!"

The brigade was ultimately landed at Siboney as part of an army to attack Santiago. The scene at the landing sometimes resembled the inspiriting daily drama at the approach to the Brooklyn Bridge. There was a great bustle, during which the wise man kept his property gripped in his hands lest it might march off into the wilderness in the pocket of one of the striding regiments. Truthfully, Caspar should have had frantic occupation, but men saw him wandering bootlessly here and there crying, "Has any one seen my saddlebags? Why, if I lose them I'm ruined. I've got everything packed away in 'em. Everything!"

They looked at him gloomily and without attention. "No," they said. It was to intimate that they would not give a rip if he had lost his nose, his teeth and his self-respect. Reilly's brigade collected itself from the boats and went off, each regiment's soul burning with anger because some other regiment was in advance of it. Moving along through the scrub and under the palms, men talked mostly of things that did not pertain to the business in hand.

General Reilly finally planted his headquarters in some tall grass under a mango tree. "Where's Cadogan?" he said suddenly as he took off his hat and smoothed the wet grey hair from his brow. Nobody knew. "I saw him looking for his saddle-bags down at the landing," said an officer dubiously. "Bother him," said the General contemptuously. "Let him stay there."

Three venerable regimental commanders came, saluted stiffly and sat in the grass. There was a pow-wow, during which Reilly explained much that the Division Commander had told him. The venerable Colonels nodded; they understood. Everything was smooth and clear to their minds. But still, the Colonel of the Forty-fourth Regular Infantry murmured about the commissariat. His men—and then he launched forth in a sentiment concerning the privations of his men in which you were confronted with his feeling that his men—his men were the only creatures of importance in the universe, which feeling was entirely correct for him. Reilly grunted. He did what most commanders did. He set the competent line to doing the work of the incompetent part of the staff.

In time Caspar came trudging along the road merrily swinging his saddle-bags. "Well, General," he cried as he saluted, "I found 'em."

"Did you?" said Reilly. Later an officer rushed to him tragically: "General, Cadogan is off there in the bushes eatin' potted ham and crackers all by himself." The officer was sent back into the bushes for Caspar, and the General sent Caspar with an order. Then Reilly and the three venerable Colonels, grinning, partook of potted ham and crackers. "Tashe a' right," said Reilly, with his mouth full. "Dorsey, see if 'e got some'n else."

"Mush be selfish young pig," said one of the Colonels, with his mouth full. "Who's he, General?"

"Son—Sen'tor Cad'gan—ol' frien' mine—dash 'im."

Caspar wrote a letter:

"Dear Father: I am sitting under a tree using the flattest part of my canteen for a desk. Even as I write the division ahead of us is moving forward and we don't know what moment the storm of battle may break out. I don't know what the plans are. General Reilly knows, but he is so good as to give me very little of his confidence. In fact, I might be part of a forlorn hope from all to the contrary I've heard from him. I understood you to say in Washington that you at one time had been of some service to him, but if that is true I can assure you he has completely forgotten it. At times his manner to me is little short of being offensive, but of course I understand that it is only the way of a crusty old soldier who has been made boorish and bearish by a long life among the Indians. I dare say I shall manage it all right without a row.

"When you hear that we have captured Santiago, please send me by first steamer a box of provisions and clothing, particularly sardines, pickles, and light-weight underwear. The other men on the staff are nice quiet chaps, but they seem a bit crude. There has been no fighting yet save the skirmish by Young's brigade. Reilly was furious because we couldn't get in it. I met General Peel yesterday. He was very nice. He said he knew you well when he was in Congress. Young Jack May is on Peel's staff. I knew him well in college. We spent an hour talking over old times. Give my love to all at home."

The march was leisurely. Reilly and his staff strolled out to the head of the long, sinuous column and entered the sultry gloom of the forest. Some less fortunate regiments had to wait among the trees at the side of the trail, and as Reilly's brigade passed them, officer called to officer, classmate to classmate, and in these greetings rang a note of everything, from West Point to Alaska. They were going into an action in which they, the officers, would lose over a hundred in killed and wounded—officers alone—and these greetings, in which many nicknames occurred, were in many cases farewells such as one pictures being given with ostentation, solemnity, fervour. "There goes Gory Widgeon! Hello, Gory! Where you starting for? Hey, Gory!"

Caspar communed with himself and decided that he was not frightened. He was eager and alert; he thought that now his obligation to his country, or himself, was to be faced, and he was mad to prove to old Reilly and the others that after all he was a very capable soldier.

III

Old Reilly was stumping along the line of his brigade and mumbling like a man with a mouthful of grass. The fire from the enemy's position was incredible in its swift fury, and Reilly's brigade was getting its share of a very bad ordeal. The old man's face was of the colour of a tomato, and in his rage he mouthed and sputtered strangely. As he pranced along his thin line, scornfully erect, voices arose from the grass beseeching him to take care of himself. At his heels scrambled a bugler with pallid skin and clenched teeth, a chalky, trembling youth, who kept his eye on old Reilly's back and followed it.

The old gentleman was quite mad. Apparently he thought the whole thing a dreadful mess, but now that his brigade was irrevocably in it he was full-tilting here and everywhere to establish some irreproachable, immaculate kind of behaviour on the part of every man jack in his brigade. The intentions of the three venerable Colonels were the same. They stood behind their lines, quiet, stern, courteous old fellows, admonishing their regiments to be very pretty in the face of such a hail of magazine-rifle and machine-gun fire as has never in this world been confronted save by beardless savages when the white man has found occasion to take his burden to some new place.

And the regiments were pretty. The men lay on their little stomachs and got peppered according to the law and said nothing, as the good blood pumped out into the grass, and even if a solitary rookie tried to get a decent reason to move to some haven of rational men, the cold voice of an officer made him look criminal with a shame that was a credit to his regimental education. Behind Reilly's command was a bullet-torn jungle through which it could not move as a brigade; ahead of it were Spanish trenches on hills. Reilly considered that he was in a fix no doubt, but he said this only to himself. Suddenly he saw on the right a little point of blue-shirted men already halfway up the hill. It was some pathetic fragment of the Sixth United States Infantry. Chagrined, shocked, horrified, Reilly bellowed to his bugler, and the chalked-faced youth unlocked his teeth and sounded the charge by rushes.

The men formed hastily and grimly, and rushed. Apparently there awaited them only the fate of respectable soldiers. But they went because—of the opinions of others, perhaps. They went because—no loud-mouthed lot of jail-birds such as the Twenty-Seventh Infantry could do anything that they could not do better. They went because Reilly ordered it. They went because they went.

And yet not a man of them to this day has made a public speech explaining precisely how he did the whole thing and detailing with what initiative and ability he comprehended and defeated a situation which he did not comprehend at all.

Reilly never saw the top of the hill. He was heroically striving to keep up with his men when a bullet ripped quietly through his left lung, and he fell back into the arms of the bugler, who received him as he would have received a Christmas present. The three venerable Colonels inherited the brigade in swift succession. The senior commanded for about fifty seconds, at the end of which he was mortally shot. Before they could get the news to the next in rank he, too, was shot. The junior Colonel ultimately arrived with a lean and puffing little brigade at the top of the hill. The men lay down and fired volleys at whatever was practicable.

In and out of the ditch-like trenches lay the Spanish dead, lemon-faced corpses dressed in shabby blue and white ticking. Some were huddled down comfortably like sleeping children; one had died in the attitude of a man flung back in a dentist's chair; one sat in the trench with his chin sunk despondently to his breast; few preserved a record of the agitation of battle. With the greater number it was as if death had touched them so gently, so lightly, that they had not known of it. Death had come to them rather in the form of an opiate than of a bloody blow.

But the arrived men in the blue shirts had no thought of the sallow corpses. They were eagerly exchanging a hail of shots with the Spanish second line, whose ash-coloured entrenchments barred the way to a city white amid trees. In the pauses the men talked.

"We done the best. Old E Company got there. Why, one time the hull of B Company was behind us."

"Jones, he was the first man up. I saw 'im."

"Which Jones?"

"Did you see ol' Two-bars runnin' like a land-crab? Made good time, too. He hit only in the high places. He's all right."

"The Lootenant s all right, too. He was a good ten yards ahead of the best of us. I hated him at the post, but for this here active service there's none of 'em can touch him."

"This is mighty different from being at the post."

"Well, we done it, an' it wasn't b'cause I thought it could be done. When we started, I ses to m'self: 'Well, here goes a lot o' d——d fools.'"

"'Tain't over yet."

"Oh, they'll never git us back from here. If they start to chase us back from here we'll pile 'em up so high the last ones can't climb over. We've come this far, an' we'll stay here. I ain't done pantin'."

"Anything is better than packin' through that jungle an' gettin' blistered from front, rear, an' both flanks. I'd rather tackle another hill than go trailin' in them woods, so thick you can't tell whether you are one man or a division of cav'lry."

"Where's that young kitchen-soldier, Cadogan, or whatever his name is. Ain't seen him to-day."

"Well, I seen him. He was right in with it. He got shot, too, about half up the hill, in the leg. I seen it. He's all right. Don't worry about him. He's all right."

"I seen 'im, too. He done his stunt. As soon as I can git this piece of barbed-wire entanglement out o' me throat I'll give 'm a cheer."

"He ain't shot at all b'cause there he stands, there. See 'im?"

Rearward, the grassy slope was populous with little groups of men searching for the wounded. Reilly's brigade began to dig with its bayonets and shovel with its meat-ration cans.

IV

Senator Cadogan paced to and fro in his private parlour and smoked small, brown weak cigars. These little wisps seemed utterly inadequate to console such a ponderous satrap.

It was the evening of the 1st of July, 1898, and the Senator was immensely excited, as could be seen from the superlatively calm way in which he called out to his private secretary, who was in an adjoining room. The voice was serene, gentle, affectionate, low.

"Baker, I wish you'd go over again to the War Department and see if they've heard anything about Caspar."

A very bright-eyed, hatchet-faced young man appeared in a doorway, pen still in hand. He was hiding a nettle-like irritation behind all the finished audacity of a smirk, sharp, lying, trustworthy young politician. "I've just got back from there, sir," he suggested.

The Skowmulligan war-horse lifted his eyes and looked for a short second into the eyes of his private secretary. It was not a glare or an eagle glance; it was something beyond the practice of an actor; it was simply meaning. The clever private secretary grabbed his hat and was at once enthusiastically away. "All right, sir," he cried. "I'll find out."

The War Department was ablaze with light, and messengers were running. With the assurance of a retainer of an old house Baker made his way through much small-calibre vociferation. There was rumour of a big victory; there was rumour of a big defeat. In the corridors various watchdogs arose from their armchairs and asked him of his business in tones of uncertainty which in no wise compared with their previous habitual deference to the private secretary of the war-horse of Skowmulligan.

Ultimately Baker arrived in a room where some kind of head clerk sat writing feverishly at a roll-top desk. Baker asked a question, and the head clerk mumbled profanely without lifting his head. Apparently he said: "How in the blankety-blank blazes do I know?"

The private secretary let his jaw fall. Surely some new spirit had come suddenly upon the heart of Washington—a spirit which Baker understood to be almost defiantly indifferent to the wishes of Senator Cadogan, a spirit which was not courteously oily. What could it mean? Baker's fox-like mind sprang wildly to a conception of overturned factions, changed friends, new combinations. The assurance which had come from experience of a broad political situation suddenly left him, and he would not have been amazed if some one had told him that Senator Cadogan now controlled only six votes in the State of Skowmulligan. "Well," he stammered in his bewilderment, "well—there isn't any news of the old man's son, hey?" Again the head clerk replied blasphemously.

Eventually Baker retreated in disorder from the presence of this head clerk, having learned that the latter did not give a —— if Caspar Cadogan were sailing through Hades on an ice yacht.

Baker stormed other and more formidable officials. In fact, he struck as high as he dared. They one and all flung him short, hard words, even as men pelt an annoying cur with pebbles. He emerged from the brilliant light, from the groups of men with anxious, puzzled faces, and as he walked back to the hotel he did not know if his name were Baker or Cholmondeley.

However, as he walked up the stairs to the Senator's rooms he contrived to concentrate his intellect upon a manner of speaking.

The war-horse was still pacing his parlour and smoking. He paused at Baker's entrance. "Well?"

"Mr. Cadogan," said the private secretary coolly, "they told me at the Department that they did not give a cuss whether your son was alive or dead."

The Senator looked at Baker and smiled gently. "What's that, my boy?" he asked in a soft and considerate voice.

"They said——" gulped Baker, with a certain tenacity. "They said that they didn't give a cuss whether your son was alive or dead."

There was a silence for the space of three seconds. Baker stood like an image; he had no machinery for balancing the issues of this kind of a situation, and he seemed to feel that if he stood as still as a stone frog he would escape the ravages of a terrible Senatorial wrath which was about to break forth in a hurricane speech which would snap off trees and sweep away barns.

"Well," drawled the Senator lazily, "who did you see, Baker?"

The private secretary resumed a certain usual manner of breathing. He told the names of the men whom he had seen.

"Ye—e—es," remarked the Senator. He took another little brown cigar and held it with a thumb and first finger, staring at it with the calm and steady scrutiny of a scientist investigating a new thing. "So they don't care whether Caspar is alive or dead, eh? Well … maybe they don't…. That's all right…. However … I think I'll just look in on 'em and state my views."

When the Senator had gone, the private secretary ran to the window and leaned afar out. Pennsylvania Avenue was gleaming silver blue in the light of many arc-lamps; the cable trains groaned along to the clangour of gongs; from the window, the walks presented a hardly diversified aspect of shirt-waists and straw hats. Sometimes a newsboy screeched.

Baker watched the tall, heavy figure of the Senator moving out to intercept a cable train. "Great Scott!" cried the private secretary to himself, "there'll be three distinct kinds of grand, plain practical fireworks. The old man is going for 'em. I wouldn't be in Lascum's boots. Ye gods, what a row there'll be."

In due time the Senator was closeted with some kind of deputy third-assistant battery-horse in the offices of the War Department. The official obviously had been told off to make a supreme effort to pacify Cadogan, and he certainly was acting according to his instructions. He was almost in tears; he spread out his hands in supplication, and his voice whined and wheedled.

"Why, really, you know, Senator, we can only beg you to look at the circumstances. Two scant divisions at the top of that hill; over a thousand men killed and wounded; the line so thin that any strong attack would smash our Army to flinders. The Spaniards have probably received reenforcements under Pando; Shafter seems to be too ill to be actively in command of our troops; Lawton can't get up with his division before to-morrow. We are actually expecting … no, I won't say expecting … but we would not be surprised … nobody in the department would be surprised if before daybreak we were compelled to give to the country the news of a disaster which would be the worst blow the National pride has ever suffered. Don't you see? Can't you see our position, Senator?"

The Senator, with a pale but composed face, contemplated the official with eyes that gleamed in a way not usual with the big, self-controlled politician.

"I'll tell you frankly, sir," continued the other. "I'll tell you frankly, that at this moment we don't know whether we are a-foot or a-horseback. Everything is in the air. We don't know whether we have won a glorious victory or simply got ourselves in a deuce of a fix."

The Senator coughed. "I suppose my boy is with the two divisions at the top of that hill? He's with Reilly."

"Yes; Reilly's brigade is up there."

"And when do you suppose the War Department can tell me if he is all right. I want to know."

"My dear Senator, frankly, I don't know. Again I beg you to think of our position. The Army is in a muddle; it's a General thinking that he must fall back, and yet not sure that he can fall back without losing the Army. Why, we're worrying about the lives of sixteen thousand men and the self-respect of the nation, Senator."

"I see," observed the Senator, nodding his head slowly. "And naturally the welfare of one man's son doesn't—how do they say it—doesn't cut any ice."

V

And in Cuba it rained. In a few days Reilly's brigade discovered that by their successful charge they had gained the inestimable privilege of sitting in a wet trench and slowly but surely starving to death. Men's tempers crumbled like dry bread. The soldiers who so cheerfully, quietly and decently had captured positions which the foreign experts had said were impregnable, now in turn underwent an attack which was furious as well as insidious. The heat of the sun alternated with rains which boomed and roared in their falling like mountain cataracts. It seemed as if men took the fever through sheer lack of other occupation. During the days of battle none had had time to get even a tropic headache, but no sooner was that brisk period over than men began to shiver and shudder by squads and platoons. Rations were scarce enough to make a little fat strip of bacon seem of the size of a corner lot, and coffee grains were pearls. There would have been godless quarreling over fragments if it were not that with these fevers came a great listlessness, so that men were almost content to die, if death required no exertion.

It was an occasion which distinctly separated the sheep from the goats. The goats were few enough, but their qualities glared out like crimson spots.

One morning Jameson and Ripley, two Captains in the Forty-fourth Foot, lay under a flimsy shelter of sticks and palm branches. Their dreamy, dull eyes contemplated the men in the trench which went to left and right. To them came Caspar Cadogan, moaning. "By Jove," he said, as he flung himself wearily on the ground, "I can't stand much more of this, you know. It's killing me." A bristly beard sprouted through the grime on his face; his eyelids were crimson; an indescribably dirty shirt fell away from his roughened neck; and at the same time various lines of evil and greed were deepened on his face, until he practically stood forth as a revelation, a confession. "I can't stand it. By Jove, I can't."

Stanford, a Lieutenant under Jameson, came stumbling along toward them. He was a lad of the class of '98 at West Point. It could be seen that he was flaming with fever. He rolled a calm eye at them. "Have you any water, sir?" he said to his Captain. Jameson got upon his feet and helped Stanford to lay his shaking length under the shelter. "No, boy," he answered gloomily. "Not a drop. You got any, Rip?"

"No," answered Ripley, looking with anxiety upon the young officer. "Not a drop."

"You, Cadogan?"

Here Caspar hesitated oddly for a second, and then in a tone of deep regret made answer, "No, Captain; not a mouthful."

Jameson moved off weakly. "You lay quietly, Stanford, and I'll see what

I can rustle."

Presently Caspar felt that Ripley was steadily regarding him. He returned the look with one of half-guilty questioning.

"God forgive you, Cadogan," said Ripley, "but you are a damned beast. Your canteen is full of water."

Even then the apathy in their veins prevented the scene from becoming as sharp as the words sounded. Caspar sputtered like a child, and at length merely said: "No, it isn't." Stanford lifted his head to shoot a keen, proud glance at Caspar, and then turned away his face.

"You lie," said Ripley. "I can tell the sound of a full canteen as far as I can hear it."

"Well, if it is, I—I must have forgotten it."

"You lie; no man in this Army just now forgets whether his canteen is full or empty. Hand it over."

Fever is the physical counterpart of shame, and when a man has the one he accepts the other with an ease which would revolt his healthy self. However, Caspar made a desperate struggle to preserve the forms. He arose and taking the string from his shoulder, passed the canteen to Ripley. But after all there was a whine in his voice, and the assumption of dignity was really a farce. "I think I had better go, Captain. You can have the water if you want it, I'm sure. But—but I fail to see—I fail to see what reason you have for insulting me."

"Do you?" said Ripley stolidly. "That's all right."

Caspar stood for a terrible moment. He simply did not have the strength to turn his back on this—this affair. It seemed to him that he must stand forever and face it. But when he found the audacity to look again at Ripley he saw the latter was not at all concerned with the situation. Ripley, too, had the fever. The fever changes all laws of proportion. Caspar went away.

"Here, youngster; here is your drink."

Stanford made a weak gesture. "I wouldn't touch a drop from his blamed canteen if it was the last water in the world," he murmured in his high, boyish voice.

"Don't you be a young jackass," quoth Ripley tenderly.

The boy stole a glance at the canteen. He felt the propriety of arising and hurling it after Caspar, but—he, too, had the fever.

"Don't you be a young jackass," said Ripley again.

VI

Senator Cadogan was happy. His son had returned from Cuba, and the 8:30 train that evening would bring him to the station nearest to the stone and red shingle villa which the Senator and his family occupied on the shores of Long Island Sound. The Senator's steam yacht lay some hundred yards from the beach. She had just returned from a trip to Montauk Point where the Senator had made a gallant attempt to gain his son from the transport on which he was coming from Cuba. He had fought a brave sea-fight with sundry petty little doctors and ship's officers who had raked him with broadsides, describing the laws of quarantine and had used inelegant speech to a United States Senator as he stood on the bridge of his own steam yacht. These men had grimly asked him to tell exactly how much better was Caspar than any other returning soldier.

But the Senator had not given them a long fight. In fact, the truth came to him quickly, and with almost a blush he had ordered the yacht back to her anchorage off the villa. As a matter of fact, the trip to Montauk Point had been undertaken largely from impulse. Long ago the Senator had decided that when his boy returned the greeting should have something Spartan in it. He would make a welcome such as most soldiers get. There should be no flowers and carriages when the other poor fellows got none. He should consider Caspar as a soldier. That was the way to treat a man. But in the end a sharp acid of anxiety had worked upon the iron old man, until he had ordered the yacht to take him out and make a fool of him. The result filled him with a chagrin which caused him to delegate to the mother and sisters the entire business of succouring Caspar at Montauk Point Camp. He had remained at home conducting the huge correspondence of an active National politician and waiting for this son whom he so loved and whom he so wished to be a man of a certain strong, taciturn, shrewd ideal. The recent yacht voyage he now looked upon as a kind of confession of his weakness, and he was resolved that no more signs should escape him.

But yet his boy had been down there against the enemy and among the fevers. There had been grave perils, and his boy must have faced them. And he could not prevent himself from dreaming through the poetry of fine actions in which visions his son's face shone out manly and generous. During these periods the people about him, accustomed as they were to his silence and calm in time of stress, considered that affairs in Skowmulligan might be most critical. In no other way could they account for this exaggerated phlegm.

On the night of Caspar's return he did not go to dinner, but had a tray sent to his library, where he remained writing. At last he heard the spin of the dog-cart's wheels on the gravel of the drive, and a moment later there penetrated to him the sound of joyful feminine cries. He lit another cigar; he knew that it was now his part to bide with dignity the moment when his son should shake off that other welcome and come to him. He could still hear them; in their exuberance they seemed to be capering like schoolchildren. He was impatient, but this impatience took the form of a polar stolidity.

Presently there were quick steps and a jubilant knock at his door. "Come in," he said.

In came Caspar, thin, yellow, and in soiled khaki. "They almost tore me to pieces," he cried, laughing. "They danced around like wild things." Then as they shook hands he dutifully said "How are you, sir?"

"How are you, my boy?" answered the Senator casually but kindly.

"Better than I might expect, sir," cried Caspar cheerfully. "We had a pretty hard time, you know."

"You look as if they'd given you a hard run," observed the father in a tone of slight interest.

Caspar was eager to tell. "Yes, sir," he said rapidly. "We did, indeed.

Why, it was awful. We—any of us—were lucky to get out of it alive. It wasn't so much the Spaniards, you know. The Army took care of them all right. It was the fever and the—you know, we couldn't get anything to eat. And the mismanagement. Why, it was frightful."

"Yes, I've heard," said the Senator. A certain wistful look came into his eyes, but he did not allow it to become prominent. Indeed, he suppressed it. "And you, Caspar? I suppose you did your duty?"

Caspar answered with becoming modesty. "Well, I didn't do more than anybody else, I don't suppose, but—well, I got along all right, I guess."

"And this great charge up San Juan Hill?" asked, the father slowly. "Were you in that?"

"Well—yes; I was in it," replied the son.

The Senator brightened a trifle. "You were, eh? In the front of it? or just sort of going along?"

"Well—I don't know. I couldn't tell exactly. Sometimes I was in front of a lot of them, and sometimes I was—just sort of going along."

This time the Senator emphatically brightened. "That's all right, then. And of course—of course you performed your commissary duties correctly?"

The question seemed to make Caspar uncommunicative and sulky. "I did when there was anything to do," he answered. "But the whole thing was on the most unbusiness-like basis you can imagine. And they wouldn't tell you anything. Nobody would take time to instruct you in your duties, and of course if you didn't know a thing your superior officer would swoop down on you and ask you why in the deuce such and such a thing wasn't done in such and such a way. Of course I did the best I could."

The Senator's countenance had again become sombrely indifferent. "I see. But you weren't directly rebuked for incapacity, were you? No; of course you weren't. But—I mean—did any of your superior officers suggest that you were 'no good,' or anything of that sort? I mean—did you come off with a clean slate?"

Caspar took a small time to digest his father's meaning. "Oh, yes, sir," he cried at the end of his reflection. "The Commissary was in such a hopeless mess anyhow that nobody thought of doing anything but curse Washington."

"Of course," rejoined the Senator harshly. "But supposing that you had been a competent and well-trained commissary officer. What then?"

Again the son took time for consideration, and in the end deliberately replied "Well, if I had been a competent and well-trained Commissary I would have sat there and eaten up my heart and cursed Washington."

"Well, then, that's all right. And now about this charge up San Juan? Did any of the Generals speak to you afterward and say that you had done well? Didn't any of them see you?"

"Why, n—n—no, I don't suppose they did ... any more than I did them. You see, this charge was a big thing and covered lots of ground, and I hardly saw anybody excepting a lot of the men."

"Well, but didn't any of the men see you? Weren't you ahead some of the time leading them on and waving your sword?"

Caspar burst into laughter. "Why, no. I had all I could do to scramble along and try to keep up. And I didn't want to go up at all."

"Why?" demanded the Senator.

"Because—because the Spaniards were shooting so much. And you could see men falling, and the bullets rushed around you in—by the bushel. And then at last it seemed that if we once drove them away from the top of the hill there would be less danger. So we all went up."

The Senator chuckled over this description. "And you didn't flinch at all?"

"Well," rejoined Caspar humorously, "I won't say I wasn't frightened."

"No, of course not. But then you did not let anybody know it?"

"Of course not."

"You understand, naturally, that I am bothering you with all these questions because I desire to hear how my only son behaved in the crisis. I don't want to worry you with it. But if you went through the San Juan charge with credit I'll have you made a Major."

"Well," said Caspar, "I wouldn't say I went through that charge with credit. I went through it all good enough, but the enlisted men around went through in the same way."

"But weren't you encouraging them and leading them on by your example?"

Caspar smirked. He began to see a point. "Well, sir," he said with a charming hesitation. "Aw—er—I—well, I dare say I was doing my share of it."

The perfect form of the reply delighted the father. He could not endure blatancy; his admiration was to be won only by a bashful hero. Now he beat his hand impulsively down upon the table. "That's what I wanted to know. That's it exactly. I'll have you made a Major next week. You've found your proper field at last. You stick to the Army, Caspar, and I'll back you up. That's the thing. In a few years it will be a great career. The United States is pretty sure to have an Army of about a hundred and fifty thousand men. And starting in when you did and with me to back you up—why, we'll make you a General in seven or eight years. That's the ticket. You stay in the Army." The Senator's cheek was flushed with enthusiasm, and he looked eagerly and confidently at his son.

But Caspar had pulled a long face. "The Army?" he said. "Stay in the Army?"

The Senator continued to outline quite rapturously his idea of the future. "The Army, evidently, is just the place for you. You know as well as I do that you have not been a howling success, exactly, in anything else which you have tried. But now the Army just suits you. It is the kind of career which especially suits you. Well, then, go in, and go at it hard. Go in to win. Go at it."

"But—" began Caspar.

The Senator interrupted swiftly. "Oh, don't worry about that part of it. I'll take care of all that. You won't get jailed in some Arizona adobe for the rest of your natural life. There won't be much more of that, anyhow; and besides, as I say, I'll look after all that end of it. The chance is splendid. A young, healthy and intelligent man, with the start you've already got, and with my backing, can do anything—anything! There will be a lot of active service— oh, yes, I'm sure of it—and everybody who——"

"But," said Caspar, wan, desperate, heroic, "father, I don't care to stay in the Army."

The Senator lifted his eyes and darkened. "What?" he said. "What's that?" He looked at Caspar.

The son became tightened and wizened like an old miser trying to withhold gold. He replied with a sort of idiot obstinacy, "I don't care to stay in the Army."

The Senator's jaw clinched down, and he was dangerous. But, after all, there was something mournful somewhere. "Why, what do you mean?" he asked gruffly.

"Why, I couldn't get along, you know. The—the——"

"The what?" demanded the father, suddenly uplifted with thunderous anger. "The what?"

Caspar's pain found a sort of outlet in mere irresponsible talk. "Well, you know—the other men, you know. I couldn't get along with them, you know. They're peculiar, somehow; odd; I didn't understand them, and they didn't understand me. We—we didn't hitch, somehow. They're a queer lot. They've got funny ideas. I don't know how to explain it exactly, but—somehow—I don't like 'em. That's all there is to it. They're good fellows enough, I know, but——"

"Oh, well, Caspar," interrupted the Senator. Then he seemed to weigh a great fact in his mind. "I guess——" He paused again in profound consideration. "I guess——" He lit a small, brown cigar. "I guess you are no damn good."

THE END.

THE OPEN BOAT AND OTHER STORIES

Part I. Minor Conflicts

THE OPEN BOAT

A Tale intended to be after the Fact. Being the Experience of Four Men
from the Sunk Steamer 'Commodore'

I

None of them knew the colour of the sky. Their eyes glanced level, and
were fastened upon the waves that swept toward them. These waves were of
the hue of slate, save for the tops, which were of foaming white, and all of the
men knew the colours of the sea. The horizon narrowed and widened, and
dipped and rose, and at all times its edge was jagged with waves that seemed
thrust up in points like rocks.

Many a man ought to have a bath-tub larger than the boat which here
rode upon the sea. These waves were most wrongfully and barbarously abrupt
and tall, and each froth-top was a problem in small boat navigation.

The cook squatted in the bottom and looked with both eyes at the six
inches of gunwale which separated him from the ocean. His sleeves were
rolled over his fat forearms, and the two flaps of his unbuttoned vest dangled
as he bent to bail out the boat. Often he said: "Gawd! That was a narrow clip."
As he remarked it he invariably gazed eastward over the broken sea.

The oiler, steering with one of the two oars in the boat, sometimes raised
himself suddenly to keep clear of water that swirled in over the stern. It was a
thin little oar and it seemed often ready to snap.

The correspondent, pulling at the other oar, watched the waves and wondered why he was there.

The injured captain, lying in the bow, was at this time buried in that profound dejection and indifference which comes, temporarily at least, to even the bravest and most enduring when, willy nilly, the firm fails, the army loses, the ship goes down. The mind of the master of a vessel is rooted deep in the timbers of her, though he commanded for a day or a decade, and this captain had on him the stern impression of a scene in the greys of dawn of seven turned faces, and later a stump of a top-mast with a white ball on it that slashed to and fro at the waves, went low and lower, and down. Thereafter there was something strange in his voice. Although steady, it was deep with mourning, and of a quality beyond oration or tears.

"Keep 'er a little more south, Billie," said he.

"'A little more south,' sir," said the oiler in the stern.

A seat in this boat was not unlike a seat upon a bucking broncho, and, by the same token, a broncho is not much smaller. The craft pranced and reared, and plunged like an animal. As each wave came, and she rose for it, she seemed like a horse making at a fence outrageously high. The manner of her scramble over these walls of water is a mystic thing, and, moreover, at the top of them were ordinarily these problems in white water, the foam racing down from the summit of each wave, requiring a new leap, and a leap from the air. Then, after scornfully bumping a crest, she would slide, and race, and splash down a long incline, and arrive bobbing and nodding in front of the next menace.

A singular disadvantage of the sea lies in the fact that after successfully surmounting one wave you discover that there is another behind it just as important and just as nervously anxious to do something effective in the way of swamping boats. In a ten-foot dingey one can get an idea of the resources of the sea in the line of waves that is not probable to the average experience which is never at sea in a dingey. As each slaty wall of water approached, it shut all else from the view of the men in the boat, and it was not difficult to imagine that this particular wave was the final outburst of the ocean, the last effort of the grim water. There was a terrible grace in the move of the waves, and they came in silence, save for the snarling of the crests.

206

In the wan light, the faces of the men must have been grey. Their eyes must have glinted in strange ways as they gazed steadily astern. Viewed from a balcony, the whole thing would doubtlessly have been weirdly picturesque. But the men in the boat had no time to see it, and if they had had leisure there were other things to occupy their minds. The sun swung steadily up the sky, and they knew it was broad day because the colour of the sea changed from slate to emerald-green, streaked with amber lights, and the foam was like tumbling snow. The process of the breaking day was unknown to them. They were aware only of this effect upon the colour of the waves that rolled toward them.

In disjointed sentences the cook and the correspondent argued as to the difference between a life-saving station and a house of refuge. The cook had said: "There's a house of refuge just north of the Mosquito Inlet Light, and as soon as they see us, they'll come off in their boat and pick us up."

"As soon as who see us?" said the correspondent.

"The crew," said the cook.

"Houses of refuge don't have crews," said the correspondent. "As I understand them, they are only places where clothes and grub are stored for the benefit of shipwrecked people. They don't carry crews."

"Oh, yes, they do," said the cook.

"No, they don't," said the correspondent.

"Well, we're not there yet, anyhow," said the oiler, in the stern.

"Well," said the cook, "perhaps it's not a house of refuge that I'm thinking of as being near Mosquito Inlet Light. Perhaps it's a life-saving station."

"We're not there yet," said the oiler, in the stern.

II

As the boat bounced from the top of each wave, the wind tore through the hair of the hatless men, and as the craft plopped her stern down again the spray slashed past them. The crest of each of these waves was a hill, from the top of which the men surveyed, for a moment, a broad tumultuous expanse, shining and wind-riven. It was probably splendid. It was probably glorious, this play of the free sea, wild with lights of emerald and white and amber.

"Bully good thing it's an on-shore wind," said the cook. "If not, where would we be? Wouldn't have a show."

"That's right," said the correspondent.

The busy oiler nodded his assent.

Then the captain, in the bow, chuckled in a way that expressed humour, contempt, tragedy, all in one. "Do you think we've got much of a show now, boys?" said he.

Whereupon the three were silent, save for a trifle of hemming and hawing. To express any particular optimism at this time they felt to be childish and stupid, but they all doubtless possessed this sense of the situation in their mind. A young man thinks doggedly at such times. On the other hand, the ethics of their condition was decidedly against any open suggestion of hopelessness. So they were silent.

"Oh, well," said the captain, soothing his children, "we'll get ashore all right."

But there was that in his tone which made them think, so the oiler quoth: "Yes! If this wind holds!"

The cook was bailing: "Yes! If we don't catch hell in the surf."

Canton flannel gulls flew near and far. Sometimes they sat down on the sea, near patches of brown sea-weed that rolled over the waves with a movement like carpets on a line in a gale. The birds sat comfortably in groups, and they were envied by some in the dingey, for the wrath of the sea was no more to them than it was to a covey of prairie chickens a thousand miles inland. Often they came very close and stared at the men with black bead-like eyes. At these times they were uncanny and sinister in their unblinking scrutiny, and the men hooted angrily at them, telling them to be gone. One came, and evidently decided to alight on the top of the captain's head. The bird flew parallel to the boat and did not circle, but made short sidelong jumps in the air in chicken-fashion. His black eyes were wistfully fixed upon the captain's head. "Ugly brute," said the oiler to the bird. "You look as if you were made with a jack-knife." The cook and the correspondent swore darkly at the creature. The captain naturally wished to knock it away with the end of the heavy painter; but he did not dare do it, because anything resembling an emphatic gesture would have capsized this freighted boat, and so with his open hand, the captain gently and carefully waved the gull away. After it had been discouraged from the pursuit the captain breathed easier on account of his hair, and others breathed easier because the bird struck their minds at this time as being somehow grewsome and ominous.

In the meantime the oiler and the correspondent rowed. And also they rowed.

They sat together in the same seat, and each rowed an oar. Then the oiler took both oars; then the correspondent took both oars; then the oiler; then the correspondent. They rowed and they rowed. The very ticklish part of the business was when the time came for the reclining one in the stern to take his turn at the oars. By the very last star of truth, it is easier to steal eggs from under a hen than it was to change seats in the dingey. First the man in the stern slid his hand along the thwart and moved with care, as if he were of Sèvres. Then the man in the rowing seat slid his hand along the other thwart. It was all done with the most extraordinary care. As the two sidled past each other, the whole party kept watchful eyes on the coming wave, and the captain cried: "Look out now! Steady there!"

The brown mats of sea-weed that appeared from time to time were like islands, bits of earth. They were travelling, apparently, neither one way nor the other. They were, to all intents, stationary. They informed the men in the boat that it was making progress slowly toward the land.

The captain, rearing cautiously in the bow, after the dingey soared on a great swell, said that he had seen the lighthouse at Mosquito Inlet. Presently the cook remarked that he had seen it. The correspondent was at the oars then, and for some reason he too wished to look at the lighthouse, but his back was toward the far shore and the waves were important, and for some time he could not seize an opportunity to turn his head. But at last there came a wave more gentle than the others, and when at the crest of it he swiftly scoured the western horizon.

"See it?" said the captain.

"No," said the correspondent slowly, "I didn't see anything."

"Look again," said the captain. He pointed. "It's exactly in that direction."

At the top of another wave, the correspondent did as he was bid, and this time his eyes chanced on a small still thing on the edge of the swaying horizon. It was precisely like the point of a pin. It took an anxious eye to find a lighthouse so tiny.

"Think we'll make it, captain?"

"If this wind holds and the boat don't swamp, we can't do much else," said the captain.

The little boat, lifted by each towering sea, and splashed viciously by the crests, made progress that in the absence of sea-weed was not apparent to those in her. She seemed just a wee thing wallowing, miraculously top-up, at the mercy of five oceans. Occasionally, a great spread of water, like white flames, swarmed into her.

"Bail her, cook," said the captain serenely.

"All right, captain," said the cheerful cook.

III

It would be difficult to describe the subtle brotherhood of men that was here established on the seas. No one said that it was so. No one mentioned it. But it dwelt in the boat, and each man felt it warm him. They were a captain, an oiler, a cook, and a correspondent, and they were friends, friends in a more curiously iron-bound degree than may be common. The hurt captain, lying against the water-jar in the bow, spoke always in a low voice and calmly, but he could never command a more ready and swiftly obedient crew than the motley three of the dingey. It was more than a mere recognition of what was best for the common safety. There was surely in it a quality that was personal and heartfelt. And after this devotion to the commander of the boat there was this comradeship that the correspondent, for instance, who had been taught to be cynical of men, knew even at the time was the best experience of his life. But no one said that it was so. No one mentioned it.

"I wish we had a sail," remarked the captain. "We might try my overcoat on the end of an oar and give you two boys a chance to rest." So the cook and the correspondent held the mast and spread wide the overcoat. The oiler steered, and the little boat made good way with her new rig. Sometimes the oiler had to scull sharply to keep a sea from breaking into the boat, but otherwise sailing was a success.

Meanwhile the lighthouse had been growing slowly larger. It had now almost assumed colour, and appeared like a little grey shadow on the sky. The man at the oars could not be prevented from turning his head rather often to try for a glimpse of this little grey shadow.

At last, from the top of each wave the men in the tossing boat could see land. Even as the lighthouse was an upright shadow on the sky, this land seemed but a long black shadow on the sea. It certainly was thinner than paper. "We must be about opposite New Smyrna," said the cook, who had coasted this shore often in schooners. "Captain, by the way, I believe they abandoned that life-saving station there about a year ago."

"Did they?" said the captain.

The wind slowly died away. The cook and the correspondent were not now obliged to slave in order to hold high the oar. But the waves continued their old impetuous swooping at the dingey, and the little craft, no longer under way, struggled woundily over them. The oiler or the correspondent took the oars again.

Shipwrecks are à propos of nothing. If men could only train for them and have them occur when the men had reached pink condition, there would be less drowning at sea. Of the four in the dingey none had slept any time worth mentioning for two days and two nights previous to embarking in the dingey, and in the excitement of clambering about the deck of a foundering ship they had also forgotten to eat heartily.

For these reasons, and for others, neither the oiler nor the correspondent was fond of rowing at this time. The correspondent wondered ingenuously how in the name of all that was sane could there be people who thought it amusing to row a boat. It was not an amusement; it was a diabolical punishment, and even a genius of mental aberrations could never conclude that it was anything but a horror to the muscles and a crime against the back. He mentioned to the boat in general how the amusement of rowing struck him, and the weary-faced oiler smiled in full sympathy. Previously to the foundering, by the way, the oiler had worked double-watch in the engine-room of the ship.

"Take her easy, now, boys," said the captain. "Don't spend yourselves. If we have to run a surf you'll need all your strength, because we'll sure have to swim for it. Take your time."

Slowly the land arose from the sea. From a black line it became a line of black and a line of white, trees and sand. Finally, the captain said that he could make out a house on the shore. "That's the house of refuge, sure," said the cook. "They'll see us before long, and come out after us."

The distant lighthouse reared high. "The keeper ought to be able to make us out now, if he's looking through a glass," said the captain. "He'll notify the life-saving people."

"None of those other boats could have got ashore to give word of the wreck," said the oiler, in a low voice. "Else the life-boat would be out hunting us."

Slowly and beautifully the land loomed out of the sea. The wind came again. It had veered from the north-east to the south-east. Finally, a new sound struck the ears of the men in the boat. It was the low thunder of the surf on the shore. "We'll never be able to make the lighthouse now," said the captain. "Swing her head a little more north, Billie," said he.

"'A little more north,' sir," said the oiler.

Whereupon the little boat turned her nose once more down the wind, and all but the oarsman watched the shore grow. Under the influence of this expansion doubt and direful apprehension was leaving the minds of the men. The management of the boat was still most absorbing, but it could not prevent a quiet cheerfulness. In an hour, perhaps, they would be ashore.

Their backbones had become thoroughly used to balancing in the boat, and they now rode this wild colt of a dingey like circus men. The correspondent thought that he had been drenched to the skin, but happening to feel in the top pocket of his coat, he found therein eight cigars. Four of them were soaked with sea-water; four were perfectly scatheless. After a search, somebody produced three dry matches, and thereupon the four waifs rode impudently in their little boat, and with an assurance of an impending rescue shining in their eyes, puffed at the big cigars and judged well and ill of all men. Everybody took a drink of water.

IV

"Cook," remarked the captain, "there don't seem to be any signs of life about your house of refuge."

"No," replied the cook. "Funny they don't see us!"

A broad stretch of lowly coast lay before the eyes of the men. It was of dunes topped with dark vegetation. The roar of the surf was plain, and sometimes they could see the white lip of a wave as it spun up the beach. A tiny house was blocked out black upon the sky. Southward, the slim lighthouse lifted its little grey length.

Tide, wind, and waves were swinging the dingey northward. "Funny they don't see us," said the men.

The surf's roar was here dulled, but its tone was, nevertheless, thunderous and mighty. As the boat swam over the great rollers, the men sat listening to this roar. "We'll swamp sure," said everybody.

It is fair to say here that there was not a life-saving station within twenty miles in either direction, but the men did not know this fact, and in consequence they made dark and opprobrious remarks concerning the eyesight of the nation's life-savers. Four scowling men sat in the dingey and surpassed records in the invention of epithets.

"Funny they don't see us."

The light-heartedness of a former time had completely faded. To their sharpened minds it was easy to conjure pictures of all kinds of incompetency and blindness and, indeed, cowardice. There was the shore of the populous land, and it was bitter and bitter to them that from it came no sign.

"Well," said the captain, ultimately, "I suppose we'll have to make a try for ourselves. If we stay out here too long, we'll none of us have strength left to swim after the boat swamps."

And so the oiler, who was at the oars, turned the boat straight for the shore. There was a sudden tightening of muscles. There was some thinking.

"If we don't all get ashore—" said the captain. "If we don't all get ashore, I suppose you fellows know where to send news of my finish?"

They then briefly exchanged some addresses and admonitions. As for the reflections of the men, there was a great deal of rage in them. Perchance they might be formulated thus: "If I am going to be drowned—if I am going to be drowned—if I am going to be drowned, why, in the name of the seven mad gods who rule the sea, was I allowed to come thus far and contemplate sand and trees? Was I brought here merely to have my nose dragged away as I was about to nibble the sacred cheese of life? It is preposterous. If this old ninny-woman, Fate, cannot do better than this, she should be deprived of the management of men's fortunes. She is an old hen who knows not her intention. If she has decided to drown me, why did she not do it in the beginning and save me all this trouble? The whole affair is absurd.... But no, she cannot mean to drown me. She dare not drown me. She cannot drown me. Not after all this work." Afterward the man might have had an impulse to shake his fist at the clouds: "Just you drown me, now, and then hear what I call you!"

The billows that came at this time were more formidable. They seemed always just about to break and roll over the little boat in a turmoil of foam. There was a preparatory and long growl in the speech of them. No mind unused to the sea would have concluded that the dingey could ascend these sheer heights in time. The shore was still afar. The oiler was a wily surfman. "Boys," he said swiftly, "she won't live three minutes more, and we're too far out to swim. Shall I take her to sea again, captain?"

"Yes! Go ahead!" said the captain.

This oiler, by a series of quick miracles, and fast and steady oarsmanship, turned the boat in the middle of the surf and took her safely to sea again.

There was a considerable silence as the boat bumped over the furrowed sea to deeper water. Then somebody in gloom spoke. "Well, anyhow, they must have seen us from the shore by now."

The gulls went in slanting flight up the wind toward the grey desolate east. A squall, marked by dingy clouds, and clouds brick-red, like smoke from a burning building, appeared from the south-east.

"What do you think of those life-saving people? Ain't they peaches?"

"Funny they haven't seen us."

"Maybe they think we're out here for sport! Maybe they think we're fishin'. Maybe they think we're damned fools."

It was a long afternoon. A changed tide tried to force them southward, but wind and wave said northward. Far ahead, where coast-line, sea, and sky formed their mighty angle, there were little dots which seemed to indicate a city on the shore.

"St. Augustine?"

The captain shook his head. "Too near Mosquito Inlet."

And the oiler rowed, and then the correspondent rowed. Then the oiler rowed. It was a weary business. The human back can become the seat of more aches and pains than are registered in books for the composite anatomy of a regiment. It is a limited area, but it can become the theatre of innumerable muscular conflicts, tangles, wrenches, knots, and other comforts.

"Did you ever like to row, Billie?" asked the correspondent.

215

"No," said the oiler. "Hang it."

When one exchanged the rowing-seat for a place in the bottom of the boat, he suffered a bodily depression that caused him to be careless of everything save an obligation to wiggle one finger. There was cold sea-water swashing to and fro in the boat, and he lay in it. His head, pillowed on a thwart, was within an inch of the swirl of a wave crest, and sometimes a particularly obstreperous sea came in-board and drenched him once more. But these matters did not annoy him. It is almost certain that if the boat had capsized he would have tumbled comfortably out upon the ocean as if he felt sure that it was a great soft mattress.

"Look! There's a man on the shore!"

"Where?"

"There! See 'im? See 'im?"

"Yes, sure! He's walking along."

"Now he's stopped. Look! He's facing us!"

"He's waving at us!"

"So he is! By thunder!"

"Ah, now we're all right! Now we're all right! There'll be a boat out here for us in half-an-hour."

"He's going on. He's running. He's going up to that house there."

The remote beach seemed lower than the sea, and it required a searching glance to discern the little black figure. The captain saw a floating stick and they rowed to it. A bath-towel was by some weird chance in the boat, and, tying this on the stick, the captain waved it. The oarsman did not dare turn his head, so he was obliged to ask questions.

"What's he doing now?"

"He's standing still again. He's looking, I think.... There he goes again. Towards the house.... Now he's stopped again."

216

"Is he waving at us?"

"No, not now! he was, though."

"Look! There comes another man!"

"He's running."

"Look at him go, would you."

"Why, he's on a bicycle. Now he's met the other man. They're both waving at us. Look!"

"There comes something up the beach."

"What the devil is that thing?"

"Why, it looks like a boat."

"Why, certainly it's a boat."

"No, it's on wheels."

"Yes, so it is. Well, that must be the life-boat. They drag them along shore on a wagon."

"That's the life-boat, sure."

"No, by ——, it's—it's an omnibus."

"I tell you it's a life-boat."

"It is not! It's an omnibus. I can see it plain. See? One of these big hotel omnibuses."

"By thunder, you're right. It's an omnibus, sure as fate. What do you suppose they are doing with an omnibus? Maybe they are going around collecting the life-crew, hey?"

"That's it, likely. Look! There's a fellow waving a little black flag. He's standing on the steps of the omnibus. There come those other two fellows. Now they're all talking together. Look at the fellow with the flag. Maybe he ain't waving it."

217

"That ain't a flag, is it? That's his coat. Why certainly, that's his coat."

"So it is. It's his coat. He's taken it off and is waving it around his head. But would you look at him swing it."

"Oh, say, there isn't any life-saving station there. That's just a winter resort hotel omnibus that has brought over some of the boarders to see us drown."

"What's that idiot with the coat mean? What's he signaling, anyhow?"

"It looks as if he were trying to tell us to go north. There must be a life-saving station up there."

"No! He thinks we're fishing. Just giving us a merry hand. See? Ah, there, Willie."

"Well, I wish I could make something out of those signals. What do you suppose he means?"

"He don't mean anything. He's just playing."

"Well, if he'd just signal us to try the surf again, or to go to sea and wait, or go north, or go south, or go to hell—there would be some reason in it. But look at him. He just stands there and keeps his coat revolving like a wheel. The ass!"

"There come more people."

"Now there's quite a mob. Look! Isn't that a boat?"

"Where? Oh, I see where you mean. No, that's no boat."

"That fellow is still waving his coat."

"He must think we like to see him do that. Why don't he quit it? It don't mean anything."

"I don't know. I think he is trying to make us go north. It must be that there's a life-saving station there somewhere."

"Say, he ain't tired yet. Look at 'im wave."

"Wonder how long he can keep that up. He's been revolving his coat ever since he caught sight of us. He's an idiot. Why aren't they getting men to bring a boat out? A fishing boat—one of those big yawls—could come out here all right. Why don't he do something?"

"Oh, it's all right, now."

"They'll have a boat out here for us in less than no time, now that they've seen us."

A faint yellow tone came into the sky over the low land. The shadows on the sea slowly deepened. The wind bore coldness with it, and the men began to shiver.

"Holy smoke!" said one, allowing his voice to express his impious mood, "if we keep on monkeying out here! If we've got to flounder out here all night!"

"Oh, we'll never have to stay here all night! Don't you worry. They've seen us now, and it won't be long before they'll come chasing out after us."

The shore grew dusky. The man waving a coat blended gradually into this gloom, and it swallowed in the same manner the omnibus and the group of people. The spray, when it dashed uproariously over the side, made the voyagers shrink and swear like men who were being branded.

"I'd like to catch the chump who waved the coat. I feel like soaking him one, just for luck."

"Why? What did he do?"

"Oh, nothing, but then he seemed so damned cheerful."

In the meantime the oiler rowed, and then the correspondent rowed, and then the oiler rowed. Grey-faced and bowed forward, they mechanically, turn by turn, plied the leaden oars. The form of the lighthouse had vanished from the southern horizon, but finally a pale star appeared, just lifting from the sea. The streaked saffron in the west passed before the all-merging darkness, and the sea to the east was black. The land had vanished, and was expressed only by the low and drear thunder of the surf.

"If I am going to be drowned—if I am going to be drowned—if I am going to be drowned, why, in the name of the seven mad gods who rule the sea, was I allowed to come thus far and contemplate sand and trees? Was I brought here merely to have my nose dragged away as I was about to nibble the sacred cheese of life?"

The patient captain, drooped over the water-jar, was sometimes obliged to speak to the oarsman.

"Keep her head up! Keep her head up!"

"'Keep her head up,' sir." The voices were weary and low.

This was surely a quiet evening. All save the oarsman lay heavily and listlessly in the boat's bottom. As for him, his eyes were just capable of noting the tall black waves that swept forward in a most sinister silence, save for an occasional subdued growl of a crest.

The cook's head was on a thwart, and he looked without interest at the water under his nose. He was deep in other scenes. Finally he spoke. "Billie," he murmured, dreamfully, "what kind of pie do you like best?"

V

"Pie," said the oiler and the correspondent, agitatedly. "Don't talk about those things, blast you!"

"Well," said the cook, "I was just thinking about ham sandwiches, and——"

A night on the sea in an open boat is a long night. As darkness settled finally, the shine of the light, lifting from the sea in the south, changed to full gold. On the northern horizon a new light appeared, a small bluish gleam on the edge of the waters. These two lights were the furniture of the world. Otherwise there was nothing but waves.

Two men huddled in the stern, and distances were so magnificent in the dingey that the rower was enabled to keep his feet partly warmed by thrusting them under his companions. Their legs indeed extended far under the rowing-seat until they touched the feet of the captain forward. Sometimes, despite the efforts of the tired oarsman, a wave came piling into the boat, an icy wave of the night, and the chilling water soaked them anew. They would twist their bodies for a moment and groan, and sleep the dead sleep once more, while the water in the boat gurgled about them as the craft rocked.

The plan of the oiler and the correspondent was for one to row until he lost the ability, and then arouse the other from his sea-water couch in the bottom of the boat.

The oiler plied the oars until his head drooped forward, and the overpowering sleep blinded him. And he rowed yet afterward. Then he touched a man in the bottom of the boat, and called his name. "Will you spell me for a little while?" he said, meekly.

"Sure, Billie," said the correspondent, awakening and dragging himself to a sitting position. They exchanged places carefully, and the oiler, cuddling down in the sea-water at the cook's side, seemed to go to sleep instantly.

The particular violence of the sea had ceased. The waves came without snarling. The obligation of the man at the oars was to keep the boat headed so that the tilt of the rollers would not capsize her, and to preserve her from filling when the crests rushed past. The black waves were silent and hard to be seen in the darkness. Often one was almost upon the boat before the oarsman was aware.

In a low voice the correspondent addressed the captain. He was not sure that the captain was awake, although this iron man seemed to be always awake. "Captain, shall I keep her making for that light north, sir?"

The same steady voice answered him. "Yes. Keep it about two points off the port bow."

The cook had tied a life-belt around himself in order to get even the warmth which this clumsy cork contrivance could donate, and he seemed almost stove-like when a rower, whose teeth invariably chattered wildly as soon as he ceased his labour, dropped down to sleep.

The correspondent, as he rowed, looked down at the two men sleeping under-foot. The cook's arm was around the oiler's shoulders, and, with their fragmentary clothing and haggard faces, they were the babes of the sea, a grotesque rendering of the old babes in the wood.

Later he must have grown stupid at his work, for suddenly there was a growling of water, and a crest came with a roar and a swash into the boat, and it was a wonder that it did not set the cook afloat in his life-belt. The cook continued to sleep, but the oiler sat up, blinking his eyes and shaking with the new cold.

"Oh, I'm awful sorry, Billie," said the correspondent contritely.

"That's all right, old boy," said the oiler, and lay down again and was asleep.

Presently it seemed that even the captain dozed, and the correspondent thought that he was the one man afloat on all the oceans. The wind had a voice as it came over the waves, and it was sadder than the end.

There was a long, loud swishing astern of the boat, and a gleaming trail of phosphorescence, like blue flame, was furrowed on the black waters. It might have been made by a monstrous knife.

Then there came a stillness, while the correspondent breathed with the open mouth and looked at the sea.

Suddenly there was another swish and another long flash of bluish light, and this time it was alongside the boat, and might almost have been reached with an oar. The correspondent saw an enormous fin speed like a shadow through the water, hurling the crystalline spray and leaving the long glowing trail.

The correspondent looked over his shoulder at the captain. His face was hidden, and he seemed to be asleep. He looked at the babes of the sea. They certainly were asleep. So, being bereft of sympathy, he leaned a little way to one side and swore softly into the sea.

But the thing did not then leave the vicinity of the boat. Ahead or astern, on one side or the other, at intervals long or short, fled the long sparkling streak, and there was to be heard the whiroo of the dark fin. The speed and power of the thing was greatly to be admired. It cut the water like a gigantic and keen projectile.

The presence of this biding thing did not affect the man with the same horror that it would if he had been a picnicker. He simply looked at the sea dully and swore in an undertone.

Nevertheless, it is true that he did not wish to be alone. He wished one of his companions to awaken by chance and keep him company with it. But the captain hung motionless over the water-jar, and the oiler and the cook in the bottom of the boat were plunged in slumber.

VI

"If I am going to be drowned—if I am going to be drowned—if I am going to be drowned, why, in the name of the seven mad gods who rule the sea, was I allowed to come thus far and contemplate sand and trees?"

During this dismal night, it may be remarked that a man would conclude that it was really the intention of the seven mad gods to drown him, despite the abominable injustice of it. For it was certainly an abominable injustice to drown a man who had worked so hard, so hard. The man felt it would be a crime most unnatural. Other people had drowned at sea since galleys swarmed with painted sails, but still——

When it occurs to a man that nature does not regard him as important, and that she feels she would not maim the universe by disposing of him, he at first wishes to throw bricks at the temple, and he hates deeply the fact that there are no bricks and no temples. Any visible expression of nature would surely be pelleted with his jeers.

Then, if there be no tangible thing to hoot he feels, perhaps, the desire to confront a personification and indulge in pleas, bowed to one knee, and with hands supplicant, saying: "Yes, but I love myself."

A high cold star on a winter's night is the word he feels that she says to him. Thereafter he knows the pathos of his situation.

The men in the dingey had not discussed these matters, but each had, no doubt, reflected upon them in silence and according to his mind. There was seldom any expression upon their faces save the general one of complete weariness. Speech was devoted to the business of the boat.

To chime the notes of his emotion, a verse mysteriously entered the correspondent's head. He had even forgotten that he had forgotten this verse, but it suddenly was in his mind.

"A soldier of the Legion lay dying in Algiers,

There was lack of woman's nursing, there was dearth of woman's tears;

But a comrade stood beside him, and he took that comrade's hand,

And he said: 'I shall never see my own, my native land.'"

In his childhood, the correspondent had been made acquainted with the fact that a soldier of the Legion lay dying in Algiers, but he had never regarded the fact as important. Myriads of his school-fellows had informed him of the soldier's plight, but the dinning had naturally ended by making him perfectly indifferent. He had never considered it his affair that a soldier of the Legion lay dying in Algiers, nor had it appeared to him as a matter for sorrow. It was less to him than the breaking of a pencil's point.

Now, however, it quaintly came to him as a human, living thing. It was no longer merely a picture of a few throes in the breast of a poet, meanwhile drinking tea and warming his feet at the grate; it was an actuality—stern, mournful, and fine.

The correspondent plainly saw the soldier. He lay on the sand with his feet out straight and still. While his pale left hand was upon his chest in an attempt to thwart the going of his life, the blood came between his fingers. In the far Algerian distance, a city of low square forms was set against a sky that was faint with the last sunset hues. The correspondent, plying the oars and dreaming of the slow and slower movements of the lips of the soldier, was moved by a profound and perfectly impersonal comprehension. He was sorry for the soldier of the Legion who lay dying in Algiers.

The thing which had followed the boat and waited, had evidently grown bored at the delay. There was no longer to be heard the slash of the cut-water, and there was no longer the flame of the long trail. The light in the north still glimmered, but it was apparently no nearer to the boat. Sometimes the boom of the surf rang in the correspondent's ears, and he turned the craft seaward then and rowed harder. Southward, some one had evidently built a watch-fire on the beach. It was too low and too far to be seen, but it made a shimmering, roseate reflection upon the bluff back of it, and this could be discerned from the boat. The wind came stronger, and sometimes a wave suddenly raged out like a mountain-cat, and there was to be seen the sheen and sparkle of a broken crest.

The captain, in the bow, moved on his water-jar and sat erect. "Pretty long night," he observed to the correspondent. He looked at the shore. "Those life-saving people take their time."

"Did you see that shark playing around?"

"Yes, I saw him. He was a big fellow, all right."

"Wish I had known you were awake."

Later the correspondent spoke into the bottom of the boat.

"Billie!" There was a slow and gradual disentanglement. "Billie, will you spell me?"

"Sure," said the oiler.

As soon as the correspondent touched the cold comfortable sea-water in the bottom of the boat, and had huddled close to the cook's life-belt he was deep in sleep, despite the fact that his teeth played all the popular airs. This sleep was so good to him that it was but a moment before he heard a voice call his name in a tone that demonstrated the last stages of exhaustion. "Will you spell me?"

"Sure, Billie."

The light in the north had mysteriously vanished, but the correspondent took his course from the wide-awake captain.

Later in the night they took the boat farther out to sea, and the captain directed the cook to take one oar at the stern and keep the boat facing the seas. He was to call out if he should hear the thunder of the surf. This plan enabled the oiler and the correspondent to get respite together. "We'll give those boys a chance to get into shape again," said the captain. They curled down and, after a few preliminary chatterings and trembles, slept once more the dead sleep. Neither knew they had bequeathed to the cook the company of another shark, or perhaps the same shark.

As the boat caroused on the waves, spray occasionally bumped over the side and gave them a fresh soaking, but this had no power to break their repose. The ominous slash of the wind and the water affected them as it would have affected mummies.

"Boys," said the cook, with the notes of every reluctance in his voice, "she's drifted in pretty close. I guess one of you had better take her to sea again." The correspondent, aroused, heard the crash of the toppled crests.

As he was rowing, the captain gave him some whisky-and-water, and this steadied the chills out of him. "If I ever get ashore and anybody shows me even a photograph of an oar——"

At last there was a short conversation.

"Billie.... Billie, will you spell me?"

"Sure," said the oiler.

VII

When the correspondent again opened his eyes, the sea and the sky were each of the grey hue of the dawning. Later, carmine and gold was painted upon the waters. The morning appeared finally, in its splendour, with a sky of pure blue, and the sunlight flamed on the tips of the waves.

On the distant dunes were set many little black cottages, and a tall white windmill reared above them. No man, nor dog, nor bicycle appeared on the beach. The cottages might have formed a deserted village.

The voyagers scanned the shore. A conference was held in the boat. "Well," said the captain, "if no help is coming we might better try a run through the surf right away. If we stay out here much longer we will be too weak to do anything for ourselves at all." The others silently acquiesced in this reasoning. The boat was headed for the beach. The correspondent wondered if none ever ascended the tall wind-tower, and if then they never looked seaward. This tower was a giant, standing with its back to the plight of the ants. It represented in a degree, to the correspondent, the serenity of nature amid the struggles of the individual—nature in the wind, and nature in the vision of men. She did not seem cruel to him then, nor beneficent, nor treacherous, nor wise. But she was indifferent, flatly indifferent. It is, perhaps, plausible that a man in this situation, impressed with the unconcern of the universe, should see the innumerable flaws of his life, and have them taste wickedly in his mind and wish for another chance. A distinction between right and wrong seems absurdly clear to him, then, in this new ignorance of the grave-edge, and he understands that if he were given another opportunity he would mend his conduct and his words, and be better and brighter during an introduction or at a tea.

"Now, boys," said the captain, "she is going to swamp, sure. All we can do is to work her in as far as possible, and then when she swamps, pile out and scramble for the beach. Keep cool now, and don't jump until she swamps sure."

The oiler took the oars. Over his shoulders he scanned the surf. "Captain," he said, "I think I'd better bring her about, and keep her head-on to the seas and back her in."

"All right, Billie," said the captain. "Back her in." The oiler swung the boat then and, seated in the stern, the cook and the correspondent were obliged to look over their shoulders to contemplate the lonely and indifferent shore.

The monstrous in-shore rollers heaved the boat high until the men were again enabled to see the white sheets of water scudding up the slanted beach. "We won't get in very close," said the captain. Each time a man could wrest his attention from the rollers, he turned his glance toward the shore, and in the expression of the eyes during this contemplation there was a singular quality. The correspondent, observing the others, knew that they were not afraid, but the full meaning of their glances was shrouded.

As for himself, he was too tired to grapple fundamentally with the fact. He tried to coerce his mind into thinking of it, but the mind was dominated at this time by the muscles, and the muscles said they did not care. It merely occurred to him that if he should drown it would be a shame.

There were no hurried words, no pallor, no plain agitation. The men simply looked at the shore. "Now, remember to get well clear of the boat when you jump," said the captain.

Seaward the crest of a roller suddenly fell with a thunderous crash, and the long white comber came roaring down upon the boat.

"Steady now," said the captain. The men were silent. They turned their eyes from the shore to the comber and waited. The boat slid up the incline, leaped at the furious top, bounced over it, and swung down the long back of the wave. Some water had been shipped and the cook bailed it out.

But the next crest crashed also. The tumbling boiling flood of white water caught the boat and whirled it almost perpendicular. Water swarmed in from all sides. The correspondent had his hands on the gunwale at this time, and when the water entered at that place he swiftly withdrew his fingers, as if he objected to wetting them.

The little boat, drunken with this weight of water, reeled and snuggled deeper into the sea.

"Bail her out, cook! Bail her out," said the captain.

"All right, captain," said the cook.

"Now, boys, the next one will do for us, sure," said the oiler. "Mind to jump clear of the boat."

The third wave moved forward, huge, furious, implacable. It fairly swallowed the dingey, and almost simultaneously the men tumbled into the sea. A piece of life-belt had lain in the bottom of the boat, and as the correspondent went overboard he held this to his chest with his left hand.

The January water was icy, and he reflected immediately that it was colder than he had expected to find it off the coast of Florida. This appeared to his dazed mind as a fact important enough to be noted at the time. The coldness of the water was sad; it was tragic. This fact was somehow so mixed and confused with his opinion of his own situation that it seemed almost a proper reason for tears. The water was cold.

When he came to the surface he was conscious of little but the noisy water. Afterward he saw his companions in the sea. The oiler was ahead in the race. He was swimming strongly and rapidly. Off to the correspondent's left, the cook's great white and corked back bulged out of the water, and in the rear the captain was hanging with his one good hand to the keel of the overturned dingey.

There is a certain immovable quality to a shore, and the correspondent wondered at it amid the confusion of the sea.

It seemed also very attractive, but the correspondent knew that it was a long journey, and he paddled leisurely. The piece of life-preserver lay under him, and sometimes he whirled down the incline of a wave as if he were on a hand-sled.

But finally he arrived at a place in the sea where travel was beset with difficulty. He did not pause swimming to inquire what manner of current had caught him, but there his progress ceased. The shore was set before him like a bit of scenery on a stage, and he looked at it and understood with his eyes each detail of it.

As the cook passed, much farther to the left, the captain was calling to him, "Turn over on your back, cook! Turn over on your back and use the oar."

"All right, sir." The cook turned on his back, and, paddling with an oar, went ahead as if he were a canoe.

Presently the boat also passed to the left of the correspondent with the captain clinging with one hand to the keel. He would have appeared like a man raising himself to look over a board fence, if it were not for the extraordinary gymnastics of the boat. The correspondent marvelled that the captain could still hold to it.

They passed on, nearer to shore—the oiler, the cook, the captain—and following them went the water-jar, bouncing gaily over the seas.

The correspondent remained in the grip of this strange new enemy—a current. The shore, with its white slope of sand and its green bluff, topped with little silent cottages, was spread like a picture before him. It was very near to him then, but he was impressed as one who in a gallery looks at a scene from Brittany or Holland.

He thought: "I am going to drown? Can it be possible? Can it be possible? Can it be possible?" Perhaps an individual must consider his own death to be the final phenomenon of nature.

But later a wave perhaps whirled him out of this small deadly current, for he found suddenly that he could again make progress toward the shore. Later still, he was aware that the captain, clinging with one hand to the keel of the dingey, had his face turned away from the shore and toward him, and was calling his name. "Come to the boat! Come to the boat!"

In his struggle to reach the captain and the boat, he reflected that when one gets properly wearied, drowning must really be a comfortable arrangement, a cessation of hostilities accompanied by a large degree of relief, and he was glad of it, for the main thing in his mind for some moments had been horror of the temporary agony. He did not wish to be hurt.

Presently he saw a man running along the shore. He was undressing with most remarkable speed. Coat, trousers, shirt, everything flew magically off him.

"Come to the boat," called the captain.

"All right, captain." As the correspondent paddled, he saw the captain let himself down to bottom and leave the boat. Then the correspondent performed his one little marvel of the voyage. A large wave caught him and flung him with ease and supreme speed completely over the boat and far beyond it. It struck him even then as an event in gymnastics, and a true miracle of the sea. An overturned boat in the surf is not a plaything to a swimming man.

The correspondent arrived in water that reached only to his waist, but his condition did not enable him to stand for more than a moment. Each wave knocked him into a heap, and the under-tow pulled at him.

Then he saw the man who had been running and undressing, and undressing and running, come bounding into the water. He dragged ashore the cook, and then waded towards the captain, but the captain waved him away, and sent him to the correspondent. He was naked, naked as a tree in winter, but a halo was about his head, and he shone like a saint. He gave a strong pull, and a long drag, and a bully heave at the correspondent's hand. The correspondent, schooled in the minor formulæ, said: "Thanks, old man." But suddenly the man cried: "What's that?" He pointed a swift finger. The correspondent said: "Go."

In the shallows, face downward, lay the oiler. His forehead touched sand that was periodically, between each wave, clear of the sea.

The correspondent did not know all that transpired afterward. When he achieved safe ground he fell, striking the sand with each particular part of his body. It was as if he had dropped from a roof, but the thud was grateful to him.

It seems that instantly the beach was populated with men with blankets, clothes, and flasks, and women with coffee-pots and all the remedies sacred to their minds. The welcome of the land to the men from the sea was warm and generous, but a still and dripping shape was carried slowly up the beach, and the land's welcome for it could only be the different and sinister hospitality of the grave.

When it came night, the white waves paced to and fro in the moonlight, and the wind brought the sound of the great sea's voice to the men on shore, and they felt that they could then be interpreters.\

231

A MAN AND SOME OTHERS

I

Dark mesquit spread from horizon to horizon. There was no house or horseman from which a mind could evolve a city or a crowd. The world was declared to be a desert and unpeopled. Sometimes, however, on days when no heat-mist arose, a blue shape, dim, of the substance of a spectre's veil, appeared in the south-west, and a pondering sheep-herder might remember that there were mountains.

In the silence of these plains the sudden and childish banging of a tin pan could have made an iron-nerved man leap into the air. The sky was ever flawless; the manoeuvring of clouds was an unknown pageant; but at times a sheep-herder could see, miles away, the long, white streamers of dust rising from the feet of another's flock, and the interest became intense.

Bill was arduously cooking his dinner, bending over the fire, and toiling like a blacksmith. A movement, a flash of strange colour, perhaps, off in the bushes, caused him suddenly to turn his head. Presently he arose, and, shading his eyes with his hand, stood motionless and gazing. He perceived at last a Mexican sheep-herder winding through the brush toward his camp.

"Hello!" shouted Bill.

The Mexican made no answer, but came steadily forward until he was within some twenty yards. There he paused, and, folding his arms, drew himself up in the manner affected by the villain in the play. His serape muffled the lower part of his face, and his great sombrero shaded his brow. Being unexpected and also silent, he had something of the quality of an apparition; moreover, it was clearly his intention to be mysterious and devilish.

The American's pipe, sticking carelessly in the corner of his mouth, was twisted until the wrong side was uppermost, and he held his frying-pan poised in the air. He surveyed with evident surprise this apparition in the mesquit. "Hello, José!" he said; "what's the matter?"

The Mexican spoke with the solemnity of funeral tollings: "Beel, you mus' geet off range. We want you geet off range. We no like. Un'erstan'? We no like."

"What you talking about?" said Bill. "No like what?"

"We no like you here. Un'erstan'? Too mooch. You mus' geet out. We no like. Un'erstan'?"

"Understand? No; I don't know what the blazes you're gittin' at." Bill's eyes wavered in bewilderment, and his jaw fell. "I must git out? I must git off the range? What you givin' us?"

The Mexican unfolded his serape with his small yellow hand. Upon his face was then to be seen a smile that was gently, almost caressingly murderous. "Beel," he said, "geet out!"

Bill's arm dropped until the frying-pan was at his knee. Finally he turned again toward the fire. "Go on, you dog-gone little yaller rat!" he said over his shoulder. "You fellers can't chase me off this range. I got as much right here as anybody."

"Beel," answered the other in a vibrant tone, thrusting his head forward and moving one foot, "you geet out or we keel you."

"Who will?" said Bill.

"I—and the others." The Mexican tapped his breast gracefully.

Bill reflected for a time, and then he said: "You ain't got no manner of license to warn me off'n this range, and I won't move a rod. Understand? I've got rights, and I suppose if I don't see 'em through, no one is likely to give me a good hand and help me lick you fellers, since I'm the only white man in half a day's ride. Now, look; if you fellers try to rush this camp, I'm goin' to plug about fifty per cent. of the gentlemen present, sure. I'm goin' in for trouble, an' I'll git a lot of you. 'Nuther thing: if I was a fine valuable caballero like you, I'd stay in the rear till the shootin' was done, because I'm goin' to make a particular p'int of shootin' you through the chest." He grinned affably, and made a gesture of dismissal.

As for the Mexican, he waved his hands in a consummate expression of indifference. "Oh, all right," he said. Then, in a tone of deep menace and glee, he added: "We will keel you eef you no geet. They have decide'."

"They have, have they?" said Bill. "Well, you tell them to go to the devil!"

II

Bill had been a mine-owner in Wyoming, a great man, an aristocrat, one who possessed unlimited credit in the saloons down the gulch. He had the social weight that could interrupt a lynching or advise a bad man of the particular merits of a remote geographical point. However, the fates exploded the toy balloon with which they had amused Bill, and on the evening of the same day he was a professional gambler with ill-fortune dealing him unspeakable irritation in the shape of three big cards whenever another fellow stood pat. It is well here to inform the world that Bill considered his calamities of life all dwarfs in comparison with the excitement of one particular evening, when three kings came to him with criminal regularity against a man who always filled a straight. Later he became a cow-boy, more weirdly abandoned than if he had never been an aristocrat. By this time all that remained of his former splendour was his pride, or his vanity, which was one thing which need not have remained. He killed the foreman of the ranch over an inconsequent matter as to which of them was a liar, and the midnight train carried him eastward. He became a brakeman on the Union Pacific, and really gained high honours in the hobo war that for many years has devastated the beautiful railroads of our country. A creature of ill-fortune himself, he practised all the ordinary cruelties upon these other creatures of ill-fortune. He was of so fierce a mien that tramps usually surrendered at once whatever coin or tobacco they had in their possession; and if afterward he kicked them from the train, it was only because this was a recognized treachery of the war upon the hoboes. In a famous battle fought in Nebraska in 1879, he would have achieved a lasting distinction if it had not been for a deserter from the United States army. He was at the head of a heroic and sweeping charge, which really broke the power of the hoboes in that country for three months; he had already worsted four tramps with his own coupling-stick, when a stone thrown by the ex-third baseman of F Troop's nine laid him flat on the prairie, and later enforced a stay in the hospital in Omaha. After his recovery he engaged with other railroads, and shuffled cars in countless yards. An order to strike came upon him in Michigan, and afterward the vengeance of the railroad pursued him until he assumed a name. This mask is like the darkness in which the burglar chooses to move. It destroys many of the healthy fears. It is a small thing, but it eats that which we call our conscience. The conductor of No. 419 stood in the caboose within two feet of Bill's nose, and called him a liar. Bill requested him to use a milder term. He had not bored the foreman of Tin Can Ranch with any such request, but had killed him with expedition. The conductor seemed to insist, and so Bill let the matter drop.

He became the bouncer of a saloon on the Bowery in New York. Here most of his fights were as successful as had been his brushes with the hoboes in the West. He gained the complete admiration of the four clean bar-tenders who stood behind the great and glittering bar. He was an honoured man. He nearly killed Bad Hennessy, who, as a matter of fact, had more reputation than ability, and his fame moved up the Bowery and down the Bowery.

But let a man adopt fighting as his business, and the thought grows constantly within him that it is his business to fight. These phrases became mixed in Bill's mind precisely as they are here mixed; and let a man get this idea in his mind, and defeat begins to move toward him over the unknown ways of circumstances. One summer night three sailors from the U.S.S. Seattle sat in the saloon drinking and attending to other people's affairs in an amiable fashion. Bill was a proud man since he had thrashed so many citizens, and it suddenly occurred to him that the loud talk of the sailors was very offensive. So he swaggered upon their attention, and warned them that the saloon was the flowery abode of peace and gentle silence. They glanced at him in surprise, and without a moment's pause consigned him to a worse place than any stoker of them knew. Whereupon he flung one of them through the side door before the others could prevent it. On the sidewalk there was a short struggle, with many hoarse epithets in the air, and then Bill slid into the saloon again. A frown of false rage was upon his brow, and he strutted like a savage king. He took a long yellow night-stick from behind the lunch-counter, and started importantly toward the main doors to see that the incensed seamen did not again enter.

The ways of sailormen are without speech, and, together in the street, the three sailors exchanged no word, but they moved at once. Landsmen would have required two years of discussion to gain such unanimity. In silence, and immediately, they seized a long piece of scantling that lay handily. With one forward to guide the battering-ram, and with two behind him to furnish the power, they made a beautiful curve, and came down like the Assyrians on the front door of that saloon.

Mystic and still mystic are the laws of fate. Bill, with his kingly frown and his long night-stick, appeared at precisely that moment in the doorway. He stood like a statue of victory; his pride was at its zenith; and in the same second this atrocious piece of scantling punched him in the bulwarks of his stomach, and he vanished like a mist. Opinions differed as to where the end of the scantling landed him, but it was ultimately clear that it landed him in south-western Texas, where he became a sheep-herder.

The sailors charged three times upon the plate-glass front of the saloon, and when they had finished, it looked as if it had been the victim of a rural fire company's success in saving it from the flames. As the proprietor of the place surveyed the ruins, he remarked that Bill was a very zealous guardian of property. As the ambulance surgeon surveyed Bill, he remarked that the wound was really an excavation.

III

As his Mexican friend tripped blithely away, Bill turned with a thoughtful face to his frying-pan and his fire. After dinner he drew his revolver from its scarred old holster, and examined every part of it. It was the revolver that had dealt death to the foreman, and it had also been in free fights in which it had dealt death to several or none. Bill loved it because its allegiance was more than that of man, horse, or dog. It questioned neither social nor moral position; it obeyed alike the saint and the assassin. It was the claw of the eagle, the tooth of the lion, the poison of the snake; and when he swept it from its holster, this minion smote where he listed, even to the battering of a far penny. Wherefore it was his dearest possession, and was not to be exchanged in south-western Texas for a handful of rubies, nor even the shame and homage of the conductor of No. 419.

During the afternoon he moved through his monotony of work and leisure with the same air of deep meditation. The smoke of his supper-time fire was curling across the shadowy sea of mesquit when the instinct of the plainsman warned him that the stillness, the desolation, was again invaded. He saw a motionless horseman in black outline against the pallid sky. The silhouette displayed serape and sombrero, and even the Mexican spurs as large as pies. When this black figure began to move toward the camp, Bill's hand dropped to his revolver.

The horseman approached until Bill was enabled to see pronounced American features, and a skin too red to grow on a Mexican face. Bill released his grip on his revolver.

"Hello!" called the horseman.

"Hello!" answered Bill.

The horseman cantered forward. "Good evening," he said, as he again drew rein.

"Good evenin'," answered Bill, without committing himself by too much courtesy.

For a moment the two men scanned each other in a way that is not ill-mannered on the plains, where one is in danger of meeting horse-thieves or tourists.

Bill saw a type which did not belong in the mesquit. The young fellow had invested in some Mexican trappings of an expensive kind. Bill's eyes searched the outfit for some sign of craft, but there was none. Even with his local regalia, it was clear that the young man was of a far, black Northern city. He had discarded the enormous stirrups of his Mexican saddle; he used the small English stirrup, and his feet were thrust forward until the steel tightly gripped his ankles. As Bill's eyes travelled over the stranger, they lighted suddenly upon the stirrups and the thrust feet, and immediately he smiled in a friendly way. No dark purpose could dwell in the innocent heart of a man who rode thus on the plains.

As for the stranger, he saw a tattered individual with a tangle of hair and beard, and with a complexion turned brick-colour from the sun and whisky. He saw a pair of eyes that at first looked at him as the wolf looks at the wolf, and then became childlike, almost timid, in their glance. Here was evidently a man who had often stormed the iron walls of the city of success, and who now sometimes valued himself as the rabbit values his prowess.

The stranger smiled genially, and sprang from his horse. "Well, sir, I suppose you will let me camp here with you to-night?"

"Eh?" said Bill.

"I suppose you will let me camp here with you to-night?"

Bill for a time seemed too astonished for words. "Well,"—he answered, scowling in inhospitable annoyance—"well, I don't believe this here is a good place to camp to-night, mister."

The stranger turned quickly from his saddle-girth.

"What?" he said in surprise. "You don't want me here? You don't want me to camp here?"

Bill's feet scuffled awkwardly, and he looked steadily at a cactus plant. "Well, you see, mister," he said, "I'd like your company well enough, but— you see, some of these here greasers are goin' to chase me off the range to-night; and while I might like a man's company all right, I couldn't let him in for no such game when he ain't got nothin' to do with the trouble."

"Going to chase you off the range?" cried the stranger.

"Well, they said they were goin' to do it," said Bill.

"And—great heavens! will they kill you, do you think?"

"Don't know. Can't tell till afterwards. You see, they take some feller that's alone like me, and then they rush his camp when he ain't quite ready for 'em, and ginerally plug 'im with a sawed-off shot-gun load before he has a chance to git at 'em. They lay around and wait for their chance, and it comes soon enough. Of course a feller alone like me has got to let up watching some time. Maybe they ketch 'im asleep. Maybe the feller gits tired waiting, and goes out in broad day, and kills two or three just to make the whole crowd pile on him and settle the thing. I heard of a case like that once. It's awful hard on a man's mind—to git a gang after him."

"And so they're going to rush your camp to-night?" cried the stranger. "How do you know? Who told you?"

"Feller come and told me."

"And what are you going to do? Fight?"

"Don't see nothin' else to do," answered Bill gloomily, still staring at the cactus plant.

There was a silence. Finally the stranger burst out in an amazed cry. "Well, I never heard of such a thing in my life! How many of them are there?"

"Eight," answered Bill. "And now look-a-here; you ain't got no manner of business foolin' around here just now, and you might better lope off before dark. I don't ask no help in this here row. I know your happening along here just now don't give me no call on you, and you better hit the trail."

"Well, why in the name of wonder don't you go get the sheriff?" cried the stranger.

"Oh, h——!" said Bill.

IV

Long, smoldering clouds spread in the western sky, and to the east silver mists lay on the purple gloom of the wilderness.

Finally, when the great moon climbed the heavens and cast its ghastly radiance upon the bushes, it made a new and more brilliant crimson of the campfire, where the flames capered merrily through its mesquit branches, filling the silence with the fire chorus, an ancient melody which surely bears a message of the inconsequence of individual tragedy—a message that is in the boom of the sea, the sliver of the wind through the grass-blades, the silken clash of hemlock boughs.

No figures moved in the rosy space of the camp, and the search of the moonbeams failed to disclose a living thing in the bushes. There was no owl-faced clock to chant the weariness of the long silence that brooded upon the plain.

The dew gave the darkness under the mesquit a velvet quality that made air seem nearer to water, and no eye could have seen through it the black things that moved like monster lizards toward the camp. The branches, the leaves, that are fain to cry out when death approaches in the wilds, were frustrated by these uncanny bodies gliding with the finesse of the escaping serpent. They crept forward to the last point where assuredly no frantic attempt of the fire could discover them, and there they paused to locate the prey. A romance relates the tale of the black cell hidden deep in the earth, where, upon entering, one sees only the little eyes of snakes fixing him in menaces. If a man could have approached a certain spot in the bushes, he would not have found it romantically necessary to have his hair rise. There would have been a sufficient expression of horror in the feeling of the death-hand at the nape of his neck and in his rubber knee-joints.

Two of these bodies finally moved toward each other until for each there grew out of the darkness a face placidly smiling with tender dreams of assassination. "The fool is asleep by the fire, God be praised!" The lips of the other widened in a grin of affectionate appreciation of the fool and his plight. There was some signaling in the gloom, and then began a series of subtle rustlings, interjected often with pauses, during which no sound arose but the sound of faint breathing.

A bush stood like a rock in the stream of firelight, sending its long shadow backward. With painful caution the little company travelled along this shadow, and finally arrived at the rear of the bush. Through its branches they surveyed for a moment of comfortable satisfaction a form in a grey blanket extended on the ground near the fire. The smile of joyful anticipation fled quickly, to give place to a quiet air of business. Two men lifted shot-guns with much of the barrels gone, and sighting these weapons through the branches, pulled trigger together.

The noise of the explosions roared over the lonely mesquit as if these guns wished to inform the entire world; and as the grey smoke fled, the dodging company back of the bush saw the blanketed form twitching; whereupon they burst out in chorus in a laugh, and arose as merry as a lot of banqueters. They gleefully gestured congratulations, and strode bravely into the light of the fire.

Then suddenly a new laugh rang from some unknown spot in the darkness. It was a fearsome laugh of ridicule, hatred, ferocity. It might have been demoniac. It smote them motionless in their gleeful prowl, as the stern voice from the sky smites the legendary malefactor. They might have been a weird group in wax, the light of the dying fire on their yellow faces, and shining athwart their eyes turned toward the darkness whence might come the unknown and the terrible.

The thing in the grey blanket no longer twitched; but if the knives in their hands had been thrust toward it, each knife was now drawn back, and its owner's elbow was thrown upward, as if he expected death from the clouds.

This laugh had so chained their reason that for a moment they had no wit to flee. They were prisoners to their terror. Then suddenly the belated decision arrived, and with bubbling cries they turned to run; but at that instant there was a long flash of red in the darkness, and with the report one of the men shouted a bitter shout, spun once, and tumbled headlong. The thick bushes failed to impede the route of the others.

The silence returned to the wilderness. The tired flames faintly illumined the blanketed thing and the flung corpse of the marauder, and sang the fire chorus, the ancient melody which bears the message of the inconsequence of human tragedy.

V

"Now you are worse off than ever," said the young man, dry-voiced and awed.

"No, I ain't," said Bill rebelliously. "I'm one ahead."

After reflection, the stranger remarked, "Well, there's seven more."

They were cautiously and slowly approaching the camp. The sun was flaring its first warming rays over the grey wilderness. Upreared twigs, prominent branches, shone with golden light, while the shadows under the mesquit were heavily blue.

Suddenly the stranger uttered a frightened cry. He had arrived at a point whence he had, through openings in the thicket, a clear view of a dead face.

"Gosh!" said Bill, who at the next instant had seen the thing; "I thought at first it was that there José. That would have been queer, after what I told 'im yesterday."

They continued their way, the stranger wincing in his walk, and Bill exhibiting considerable curiosity.

The yellow beams of the new sun were touching the grim hues of the dead Mexican's face, and creating there an inhuman effect, which made his countenance more like a mask of dulled brass. One hand, grown curiously thinner, had been flung out regardlessly to a cactus bush.

Bill walked forward and stood looking respectfully at the body. "I know that feller; his name is Miguel. He———"

The stranger's nerves might have been in that condition when there is no backbone to the body, only a long groove. "Good heavens!" he exclaimed, much agitated; "don't speak that way!"

"What way?" said Bill. "I only said his name was Miguel."

After a pause the stranger said:

"Oh, I know; but———" He waved his hand. "Lower your voice, or something. I don't know. This part of the business rattles me, don't you see?"

"Oh, all right," replied Bill, bowing to the other's mysterious mood. But in a moment he burst out violently and loud in the most extraordinary profanity, the oaths winging from him as the sparks go from the funnel.

He had been examining the contents of the bundled grey blanket, and he had brought forth, among other things, his frying-pan. It was now only a rim with a handle; the Mexican volley had centered upon it. A Mexican shot-gun of the abbreviated description is ordinarily loaded with flat-irons, stove-lids, lead pipe, old horseshoes, sections of chain, window weights, railroad sleepers and spikes, dumb-bells, and any other junk which may be at hand. When one of these loads encounters a man vitally, it is likely to make an impression upon him, and a cooking-utensil may be supposed to subside before such an assault of curiosities.

Bill held high his desecrated frying-pan, turning it this way and that way. He swore until he happened to note the absence of the stranger. A moment later he saw him leading his horse from the bushes. In silence and sullenly the young man went about saddling the animal. Bill said, "Well, goin' to pull out?"

The stranger's hands fumbled uncertainly at the throat-latch. Once he exclaimed irritably, blaming the buckle for the trembling of his fingers. Once he turned to look at the dead face with the light of the morning sun upon it. At last he cried, "Oh, I know the whole thing was all square enough— couldn't be squarer—but—somehow or other, that man there takes the heart out of me." He turned his troubled face for another look. "He seems to be all the time calling me a—he makes me feel like a murderer."

"But," said Bill, puzzling, "you didn't shoot him, mister; I shot him."

"I know; but I feel that way, somehow. I can't get rid of it."

Bill considered for a time; then he said diffidently, "Mister, you're a eddycated man, ain't you?"

"What?"

"You're what they call a—a eddycated man, ain't you?"

The young man, perplexed, evidently had a question upon his lips, when there was a roar of guns, bright flashes, and in the air such hooting and whistling as would come from a swift flock of steam-boilers. The stranger's horse gave a mighty, convulsive spring, snorting wildly in its sudden anguish, fell upon its knees, scrambled afoot again, and was away in the uncanny death run known to men who have seen the finish of brave horses.

"This comes from discussin' things," cried Bill angrily.

He had thrown himself flat on the ground facing the thicket whence had come the firing. He could see the smoke winding over the bush-tops. He lifted his revolver, and the weapon came slowly up from the ground and poised like the glittering crest of a snake. Somewhere on his face there was a kind of smile, cynical, wicked, deadly, of a ferocity which at the same time had brought a deep flush to his face, and had caused two upright lines to glow in his eyes.

"Hello, José!" he called, amiable for satire's sake. "Got your old blunderbusses loaded up again yet?"

The stillness had returned to the plain. The sun's brilliant rays swept over the sea of mesquit, painting the far mists of the west with faint rosy light, and high in the air some great bird fled toward the south.

"You come out here," called Bill, again addressing the landscape, "and I'll give you some shootin' lessons. That ain't the way to shoot." Receiving no reply, he began to invent epithets and yell them at the thicket. He was something of a master of insult, and, moreover, he dived into his memory to bring forth imprecations tarnished with age, unused since fluent Bowery days. The occupation amused him, and sometimes he laughed so that it was uncomfortable for his chest to be against the ground.

Finally the stranger, prostrate near him, said wearily, "Oh, they've gone."

"Don't you believe it," replied Bill, sobering swiftly. "They're there yet—every man of 'em."

"How do you know?"

"Because I do. They won't shake us so soon. Don't put your head up, or they'll get you, sure."

Bill's eyes, meanwhile, had not wavered from their scrutiny of the thicket in front. "They're there all right; don't you forget it. Now you listen." So he called out: "José! Ojo, José! Speak up, hombre! I want have talk. Speak up, you yaller cuss, you!"

Whereupon a mocking voice from off in the bushes said, "Señor?"

"There," said Bill to his ally; "didn't I tell you? The whole batch." Again he lifted his voice. "José—look—ain't you gittin' kinder tired? You better go home, you fellers, and git some rest."

The answer was a sudden furious chatter of Spanish, eloquent with hatred, calling down upon Bill all the calamities which life holds. It was as if some one had suddenly enraged a cageful of wild cats. The spirits of all the revenges which they had imagined were loosened at this time, and filled the air.

"They're in a holler," said Bill, chuckling, "or there'd be shootin'."

Presently he began to grow angry. His hidden enemies called him nine kinds of coward, a man who could fight only in the dark, a baby who would run from the shadows of such noble Mexican gentlemen, a dog that sneaked. They described the affair of the previous night, and informed him of the base advantage he had taken of their friend. In fact, they in all sincerity endowed him with every quality which he no less earnestly believed them to possess. One could have seen the phrases bite him as he lay there on the ground fingering his revolver.

VI

It is sometimes taught that men do the furious and desperate thing from an emotion that is as even and placid as the thoughts of a village clergyman on Sunday afternoon. Usually, however, it is to be believed that a panther is at the time born in the heart, and that the subject does not resemble a man picking mulberries.

"B' G——!" said Bill, speaking as from a throat filled with dust, "I'll go after 'em in a minute."

"Don't you budge an inch!" cried the stranger, sternly. "Don't you budge!"

"Well," said Bill, glaring at the bushes—"well—"

"Put your head down!" suddenly screamed the stranger, in white alarm. As the guns roared, Bill uttered a loud grunt, and for a moment leaned panting on his elbow, while his arm shook like a twig. Then he upreared like a great and bloody spirit of vengeance, his face lighted with the blaze of his last passion. The Mexicans came swiftly and in silence.

The lightning action of the next few moments was of the fabric of dreams to the stranger. The muscular struggle may not be real to the drowning man. His mind may be fixed on the far, straight shadows back of the stars, and the terror of them. And so the fight, and his part in it, had to the stranger only the quality of a picture half drawn. The rush of feet, the spatter of shots, the cries, the swollen faces seen like masks on the smoke, resembled a happening of the night.

And yet afterward certain lines, forms, lived out so strongly from the incoherence that they were always in his memory.

He killed a man, and the thought went swiftly by him, like the feather on the gale, that it was easy to kill a man.

Moreover, he suddenly felt for Bill, this grimy sheep-herder, some deep form of idolatry. Bill was dying, and the dignity of last defeat, the superiority of him who stands in his grave, was in the pose of the lost sheep-herder.

The stranger sat on the ground idly mopping the sweat and powder-stain from his brow. He wore the gentle idiot smile of an aged beggar as he watched three Mexicans limping and staggering in the distance. He noted at this time that one who still possessed a serape had from it none of the grandeur of the cloaked Spaniard, but that against the sky the silhouette resembled a cornucopia of childhood's Christmas.

They turned to look at him, and he lifted his weary arm to menace them with his revolver. They stood for a moment banded together, and hooted curses at him.

Finally he arose, and, walking some paces, stooped to loosen Bill's grey hands from a throat. Swaying as if slightly drunk, he stood looking down into the still face.

Struck suddenly with a thought, he went about with dulled eyes on the ground, until he plucked his gaudy blanket from where it lay dirty from trampling feet. He dusted it carefully, and then returned and laid it over Bill's form. There he again stood motionless, his mouth just agape and the same stupid glance in his eyes, when all at once he made a gesture of fright and looked wildly about him.

He had almost reached the thicket when he stopped, smitten with alarm. A body contorted, with one arm stiff in the air, lay in his path. Slowly and warily he moved around it, and in a moment the bushes, nodding and whispering, their leaf-faces turned toward the scene behind him, swung and swung again into stillness and the peace of the wilderness.

THE BRIDE COMES TO YELLOW SKY

I

The great Pullman was whirling onward with such dignity of motion that a glance from the window seemed simply to prove that the plains of Texas were pouring eastward. Vast flats of green grass, dull-hued spaces of mesquit and cactus, little groups of frame houses, woods of light and tender trees, all were sweeping into the east, sweeping over the horizon, a precipice.

A newly-married pair had boarded this train at San Antonio. The man's face was reddened from many days in the wind and sun, and a direct result of his new black clothes was that his brick-coloured hands were constantly performing in a most conscious fashion. From time to time he looked down respectfully at his attire. He sat with a hand on each knee, like a man waiting in a barber's shop. The glances he devoted to other passengers were furtive and shy.

The bride was not pretty, nor was she very young. She wore a dress of blue cashmere, with small reservations of velvet here and there, and with steel buttons abounding. She continually twisted her head to regard her puff-sleeves, very stiff, straight, and high. They embarrassed her. It was quite apparent that she had cooked, and that she expected to cook, dutifully. The blushes caused by the careless scrutiny of some passengers as she had entered the car were strange to see upon this plain, under-class countenance, which was drawn in placid, almost emotionless lines.

They were evidently very happy. "Ever been in a parlour-car before?" he asked, smiling with delight.

"No," she answered; "I never was. It's fine, ain't it?"

"Great. And then, after a while, we'll go forward to the diner, and get a big lay-out. Finest meal in the world. Charge, a dollar."

"Oh, do they?" cried the bride. "Charge a dollar? Why, that's too much—for us—ain't it, Jack?"

"Not this trip, anyhow," he answered bravely. "We're going to go the whole thing."

Later, he explained to her about the train. "You see, it's a thousand miles from one end of Texas to the other, and this train runs right across it, and never stops but four times."

He had the pride of an owner. He pointed out to her the dazzling fittings of the coach, and, in truth, her eyes opened wider as she contemplated the sea-green figured velvet, the shining brass, silver, and glass, the wood that gleamed as darkly brilliant as the surface of a pool of oil. At one end a bronze figure sturdily held a support for a separated chamber, and at convenient places on the ceiling were frescoes in olive and silver.

To the minds of the pair, their surroundings reflected the glory of their marriage that morning in San Antonio. This was the environment of their new estate, and the man's face, in particular, beamed with an elation that made him appear ridiculous to the negro porter. This individual at times surveyed them from afar with an amused and superior grin. On other occasions he bullied them with skill in ways that did not make it exactly plain to them that they were being bullied. He subtly used all the manners of the most unconquerable kind of snobbery. He oppressed them, but of this oppression they had small knowledge, and they speedily forgot that unfrequently a number of travellers covered them with stares of derisive enjoyment. Historically there was supposed to be something infinitely humorous in their situation.

"We are due in Yellow Sky at 3.42," he said, looking tenderly into her eyes.

"Oh, are we?" she said, as if she had not been aware of it.

To evince surprise at her husband's statement was part of her wifely amiability. She took from a pocket a little silver watch, and as she held it before her, and stared at it with a frown of attention, the new husband's face shone.

"I bought it in San Anton' from a friend of mine," he told her gleefully.

249

"It's seventeen minutes past twelve," she said, looking up at him with a kind of shy and clumsy coquetry.

A passenger, noting this play, grew excessively sardonic, and winked at himself in one of the numerous mirrors.

At last they went to the dining-car. Two rows of negro waiters in dazzling white suits surveyed their entrance with the interest, and also the equanimity, of men who had been forewarned. The pair fell to the lot of a waiter who happened to feel pleasure in steering them through their meal. He viewed them with the manner of a fatherly pilot, his countenance radiant with benevolence. The patronage entwined with the ordinary deference was not palpable to them. And yet as they returned to their coach they showed in their faces a sense of escape.

To the left, miles down a long purple slope, was a little ribbon of mist, where moved the keening Rio Grande. The train was approaching it at an angle, and the apex was Yellow Sky. Presently it was apparent that as the distance from Yellow Sky grew shorter, the husband became commensurately restless. His brick-red hands were more insistent in their prominence. Occasionally he was even rather absent-minded and far away when the bride leaned forward and addressed him.

As a matter of truth, Jack Potter was beginning to find the shadow of a deed weigh upon him like a leaden slab. He, the town-marshal of Yellow Sky, a man known, liked, and feared in his corner, a prominent person, had gone to San Antonio to meet a girl he believed he loved, and there, after the usual prayers, had actually induced her to marry him without consulting Yellow Sky for any part of the transaction. He was now bringing his bride before an innocent and unsuspecting community.

Of course, people in Yellow Sky married as it pleased them in accordance with a general custom, but such was Potter's thought of his duty to his friends, or of their idea of his duty, or of an unspoken form which does not control men in these matters, that he felt he was heinous. He had committed an extraordinary crime. Face to face with this girl in San Antonio, and spurred by his sharp impulse, he had gone headlong over all the social hedges. At San

250

Antonio he was like a man hidden in the dark. A knife to sever any friendly duty, any form, was easy to his hand in that remote city. But the hour of Yellow Sky, the hour of daylight, was approaching.

He knew full well that his marriage was an important thing to his town. It could only be exceeded by the burning of the new hotel. His friends would not forgive him. Frequently he had reflected upon the advisability of telling them by telegraph, but a new cowardice had been upon him. He feared to do it. And now the train was hurrying him toward a scene of amazement, glee, reproach. He glanced out of the window at the line of haze swinging slowly in toward the train.

Yellow Sky had a kind of brass band which played painfully to the delight of the populace. He laughed without heart as he thought of it. If the citizens could dream of his prospective arrival with his bride, they would parade the band at the station, and escort them, amid cheers and laughing congratulations, to his adobe home.

He resolved that he would use all the devices of speed and plainscraft in making the journey from the station to his house. Once within that safe citadel, he could issue some sort of a vocal bulletin, and then not go among the citizens until they had time to wear off a little of their enthusiasm.

The bride looked anxiously at him. "What's worrying you, Jack?"

He laughed again. "I'm not worrying, girl. I'm only thinking of Yellow Sky."

She flushed in comprehension.

A sense of mutual guilt invaded their minds, and developed a finer tenderness. They looked at each other with eyes softly aglow. But Potter often laughed the same nervous laugh. The flush upon the bride's face seemed quite permanent.

The traitor to the feelings of Yellow Sky narrowly watched the speeding landscape.

"We're nearly there," he said.

251

Presently the porter came and announced the proximity of Potter's home. He held a brush in his hand, and, with all his airy superiority gone, he brushed Potter's new clothes, as the latter slowly turned this way and that way. Potter fumbled out a coin, and gave it to the porter as he had seen others do. It was a heavy and muscle-bound business, as that of a man shoeing his first horse.

The porter took their bag, and, as the train began to slow, they moved forward to the hooded platform of the car. Presently the two engines and their long string of coaches rushed into the station of Yellow Sky.

"They have to take water here," said Potter, from a constricted throat, and in mournful cadence as one announcing death. Before the train stopped his eye had swept the length of the platform, and he was glad and astonished to see there was no one upon it but the station-agent, who, with a slightly hurried and anxious air, was walking toward the water-tanks. When the train had halted, the porter alighted first and placed in position a little temporary step.

"Come on, girl," said Potter, hoarsely.

As he helped her down, they each laughed on a false note. He took the bag from the negro, and bade his wife cling to his arm. As they slunk rapidly away, his hang-dog glance perceived that they were unloading the two trunks, and also that the station-agent, far ahead, near the baggage-car, had turned, and was running toward him, making gestures. He laughed, and groaned as he laughed, when he noted the first effect of his marital bliss upon Yellow Sky. He gripped his wife's arm firmly to his side, and they fled. Behind them the porter stood chuckling fatuously.

II

The California Express on the Southron Railway was due at Yellow Sky in twenty-one minutes. There were six men at the bar of the Weary Gentleman saloon. One was a drummer, who talked a great deal and rapidly; three were Texans, who did not care to talk at that time; and two were Mexican sheep-herders, who did not talk as a general practice in the Weary Gentleman saloon. The bar-keeper's dog lay on the board-walk that crossed in front of the door. His head was on his paws, and he glanced drowsily here and there with the constant vigilance of a dog that is kicked on occasion. Across the sandy street were some vivid green grass plots, so wonderful in appearance amid the sands that burned near them in a blazing sun, that they caused a doubt in the mind. They exactly resembled the grass-mats used to represent lawns on the stage. At the cooler end of the railway-station a man without a coat sat in a tilted chair and smoked his pipe. The fresh-cut bank of the Rio Grande circled near the town, and there could be seen beyond it a great plum-coloured plain of mesquit.

Save for the busy drummer and his companions in the saloon, Yellow Sky was dozing. The new-comer leaned gracefully upon the bar, and recited many tales with the confidence of a bard who has come upon a new field.

"And at the moment that the old man fell down-stairs, with the bureau in his arms, the old woman was coming up with two scuttles of coal, and, of course——"

The drummer's tale was interrupted by a young man who suddenly appeared in the open door. He cried—

"Scratchy Wilson's drunk, and has turned loose with both hands."

The two Mexicans at once set down their glasses, and faded out of the rear entrance of the saloon.

The drummer, innocent and jocular, answered—

"All right, old man. S'pose he has. Come and have a drink, anyhow."

But the information had made such an obvious cleft in every skull in the room, that the drummer was obliged to see its importance. All had become instantly morose.

"Say," said he, mystified, "what is this?"

His three companions made the introductory gesture of eloquent speech, but the young man at the door forestalled them.

"It means, my friend," he answered, as he came into the saloon, "that for the next two hours this town won't be a health resort."

The bar-keeper went to the door, and locked and barred it. Reaching out of the window, he pulled in heavy wooden shutters and barred them. Immediately a solemn, chapel-like gloom was upon the place. The drummer was looking from one to another.

"But say," he cried, "what is this, anyhow? You don't mean there is going to be a gun-fight?"

"Don't know whether there'll be a fight or not," answered one man grimly. "But there'll be some shootin'—some good shootin'."

The young man who had warned them waved his hand. "Oh, there'll be a fight, fast enough, if any one wants it. Anybody can get a fight out there in the street. There's a fight just waiting."

The drummer seemed to be swayed between the interest of a foreigner, and a perception of personal danger.

"What did you say his name was?" he asked.

"Scratchy Wilson," they answered in chorus.

"And will he kill anybody? What are you going to do? Does this happen often? Does he rampage round like this once a week or so? Can he break in that door?"

"No, he can't break down that door," replied the bar-keeper. "He's tried it three times. But when he comes you'd better lay down on the floor, stranger. He's dead sure to shoot at it, and a bullet may come through."

Thereafter the drummer kept a strict eye on the door. The time had not yet been called for him to hug the floor, but as a minor precaution he sidled near to the wall.

"Will he kill anybody?" he said again.

The men laughed low and scornfully at the question.

"He's out to shoot, and he's out for trouble. Don't see any good in experimentin' with him."

"But what do you do in a case like this? What do you do?"

A man responded—"Why, he and Jack Potter——"

But, in chorus, the other men interrupted—"Jack Potter's in San Anton'."

"Well, who is he? What's he got to do with it?"

"Oh, he's the town-marshal. He goes out and fights Scratchy when he gets on one of these tears."

"Whow!" said the drummer, mopping his brow. "Nice job he's got."

The voices had toned away to mere whisperings. The drummer wished to ask further questions, which were born of an increasing anxiety and bewilderment, but when he attempted them, the men merely looked at him in irritation, and motioned him to remain silent. A tense waiting hush was upon them. In the deep shadows of the room their eyes shone as they listened for sounds from the street. One man made three gestures at the bar-keeper, and the latter, moving like a ghost, handed him a glass and a bottle. The man poured a full glass of whisky, and set down the bottle noiselessly. He gulped the whisky in a swallow, and turned again toward the door in immovable silence. The drummer saw that the bar-keeper, without a sound, had taken a Winchester from beneath the bar. Later, he saw this individual beckoning to him, so he tip-toed across the room.

"You better come with me back of the bar."

"No, thanks," said the drummer, perspiring. "I'd rather be where I can make a break for the back-door."

Whereupon the man of bottles made a kindly but peremptory gesture. The drummer obeyed it, and finding himself seated on a box, with his head below the level of the bar, balm was laid upon his soul at sight of various zinc and copper fittings that bore a resemblance to plate armour. The bar-keeper took a seat comfortably upon an adjacent box.

"You see," he whispered, "this here Scratchy Wilson is a wonder with a gun—a perfect wonder—and when he goes on the war-trail, we hunt our holes—naturally. He's about the last one of the old gang that used to hang out along the river here. He's a terror when he's drunk. When he's sober he's all right—kind of simple—wouldn't hurt a fly—nicest fellow in town. But when he's drunk—whoo!"

There were periods of stillness.

"I wish Jack Potter was back from San Anton'," said the bar-keeper. "He shot Wilson up once—in the leg—and he would sail in and pull out the kinks in this thing."

Presently they heard from a distance the sound of a shot, followed by three wild yells. It instantly removed a bond from the men in the darkened saloon. There was a shuffling of feet. They looked at each other.

"Here he comes," they said.

III

A man in a maroon-coloured flannel shirt, which had been purchased for purposes of decoration, and made, principally, by some Jewish women on the east side of New York, rounded a corner and walked into the middle of the main street of Yellow Sky. In either hand the man held a long, heavy blue-black revolver. Often he yelled, and these cries rang through a semblance of a deserted village, shrilly flying over the roofs in a volume that seemed to have no relation to the ordinary vocal strength of a man. It was as if the surrounding stillness formed the arch of a tomb over him. These cries of ferocious challenge rang against walls of silence. And his boots had red tops with gilded imprints, of the kind beloved in winter by little sledging boys on the hillsides of New England.

The man's face flamed in a rage begot of whisky. His eyes, rolling and yet keen for ambush, hunted the still door-ways and windows. He walked with the creeping movement of the midnight cat. As it occurred to him, he roared menacing information. The long revolvers in his hands were as easy as straws; they were moved with an electric swiftness. The little fingers of each hand played sometimes in a musician's way. Plain from the low collar of the shirt, the cords of his neck straightened and sank as passion moved him. The only sounds were his terrible invitations. The calm adobes preserved their demeanour at the passing of this small thing in the middle of the street.

There was no offer of fight—no offer of fight. The man called to the sky. There were no attractions. He bellowed and fumed and swayed his revolver here and everywhere.

The dog of the bar-keeper of the Weary Gentleman saloon had not appreciated the advance of events. He yet lay dozing in front of his master's door. At sight of the dog, the man paused and raised his revolver humorously. At sight of the man, the dog sprang up and walked diagonally away, with a sullen head and growling. The man yelled, and the dog broke into a gallop. As it was about to enter an alley, there was a loud noise, a whistling, and something spat the ground directly before it. The dog screamed, and, wheeling in terror, galloped headlong in a new direction. Again there was a noise, a whistling, and sand was kicked viciously before it. Fear-stricken, the dog turned and flurried like an animal in a pen. The man stood laughing, his weapons at his hips.

Ultimately the man was attracted by the closed door of the Weary Gentleman saloon. He went to it, and, hammering with a revolver, demanded drink.

The door remaining imperturbable, he picked a bit of paper from the walk, and nailed it to the framework with a knife. He then turned his back contemptuously upon this popular resort, and, walking to the opposite side of the street and spinning there on his heel quickly and lithely, fired at the bit of paper. He missed it by a half-inch. He swore at himself, and went away. Later, he comfortably fusiladed the windows of his most intimate friend. The man was playing with this town. It was a toy for him.

But still there was no offer of fight. The name of Jack Potter, his ancient antagonist, entered his mind, and he concluded that it would be a glad thing if he should go to Potter's house, and, by bombardment, induce him to come out and fight. He moved in the direction of his desire, chanting Apache scalp music.

When he arrived at it, Potter's house presented the same still, calm front as had the other adobes. Taking up a strategic position, the man howled a challenge. But this house regarded him as might a great stone god. It gave no sign. After a decent wait, the man howled further challenges, mingling with them wonderful epithets.

Presently there came the spectacle of a man churning himself into deepest rage over the immobility of a house. He fumed at it as the winter wind attacks a prairie cabin in the north. To the distance there should have gone the sound of a tumult like the fighting of two hundred Mexicans. As necessity bade him, he paused for breath or to reload his revolvers.

IV

Potter and his bride walked sheepishly and with speed. Sometimes they laughed together shamefacedly and low.

"Next corner, dear," he said finally.

They put forth the efforts of a pair walking bowed against a strong wind. Potter was about to raise a finger to point the first appearance of the new home, when, as they circled the corner, they came face to face with a man in a maroon-coloured shirt, who was feverishly pushing cartridges into a large revolver. Upon the instant the man dropped this revolver to the ground, and, like lightning, whipped another from its holster. The second weapon was aimed at the bridegroom's chest.

There was a silence. Potter's mouth seemed to be merely a grave for his tongue. He exhibited an instinct to at once loosen his arm from the woman's grip, and he dropped the bag to the sand. As for the bride, her face had gone as yellow as old cloth. She was a slave to hideous rites, gazing at the apparitional snake.

The two men faced each other at a distance of three paces. He of the revolver smiled with a new and quiet ferocity. "Tried to sneak up on me!" he said. "Tried to sneak up on me!" His eyes grew more baleful. As Potter made a slight movement, the man thrust his revolver venomously forward. "No;

don't you do it, Jack Potter. Don't you move a finger towards a gun just yet. Don't you move an eyelash. The time has come for me to settle with you, and I'm going to do it my own way, and loaf along with no interferin'. So if you don't want a gun bent on you, just mind what I tell you."

Potter looked at his enemy. "I ain't got a gun on me, Scratchy," he said. "Honest, I ain't." He was stiffening and steadying, but yet somewhere at the back of his mind a vision of the Pullman floated—the sea-green figured velvet, the shining brass, silver, and glass, the wood that gleamed as darkly brilliant as the surface of a pool of oil—all the glory of their marriage, the environment of the new estate.

"You know I fight when it comes to fighting, Scratchy Wilson, but I ain't got a gun on me. You'll have to do all the shootin' yourself."

His enemy's face went livid. He stepped forward, and lashed his weapon to and fro before Potter's chest.

"Don't you tell me you ain't got no gun on you, you whelp. Don't tell me no lie like that. There ain't a man in Texas ever seen you without no gun. Don't take me for no kid."

His eyes blazed with light and his throat worked like a pump.

"I ain't takin' you for no kid," answered Potter. His heels had not moved an inch backward. "I'm takin' you for a —— fool. I tell you I ain't got a gun, and I ain't. If you're goin' to shoot me up, you'd better begin now. You'll never get a chance like this again."

So much enforced reasoning had told on Wilson's rage. He was calmer.

"If you ain't got a gun, why ain't you got a gun?" he sneered. "Been to Sunday school?"

"I ain't got a gun because I've just come from San Anton' with my wife. I'm married," said Potter. "And if I'd thought there was going to be any galoots like you prowling around when I brought my wife home, I'd had a gun, and don't you forget it."

"Married!" said Scratchy, not at all comprehending.

"Yes, married! I'm married," said Potter, distinctly.

"Married!" said Scratchy; seeming for the first time he saw the drooping drowning woman at the other man's side. "No!" he said. He was like a creature allowed a glimpse of another world. He moved a pace backward, and his arm with the revolver dropped to his side. "Is this—is this the lady?" he asked.

"Yes, this is the lady," answered Potter.

There was another period of silence.

"Well," said Wilson at last, slowly, "I s'pose it's all off now?"

"It's all off if you say so, Scratchy. You know I didn't make the trouble."

Potter lifted his valise.

"Well, I 'low it's off, Jack," said Wilson. He was looking at the ground. "Married!" He was not a student of chivalry; it was merely that in the presence of this foreign condition he was a simple child of the earlier plains. He picked up his starboard revolver, and placing both weapons in their holsters, he went away. His feet made funnel-shaped tracks in the heavy sand.

THE WISE MEN

They were youths of subtle mind. They were very wicked according to report, and yet they managed to have it reflect great credit upon them. They often had the well-informed and the great talkers of the American colony engaged in reciting their misdeeds, and facts relating to their sins were usually told with a flourish of awe and fine admiration.

One was from San Francisco and one was from New York, but they resembled each other in appearance. This is an idiosyncrasy of geography.

They were never apart in the City of Mexico, at any rate, excepting perhaps when one had retired to his hotel for a respite, and then the other was usually camped down at the office sending up servants with clamorous messages. "Oh, get up and come on down."

They were two lads—they were called the kids—and far from their mothers. Occasionally some wise man pitied them, but he usually was alone in his wisdom. The other folk frankly were transfixed at the splendour of the audacity and endurance of these kids.

"When do those boys ever sleep?" murmured a man as he viewed them entering a café about eight o'clock one morning. Their smooth infantile faces looked bright and fresh enough, at any rate. "Jim told me he saw them still at it about 4.30 this morning."

"Sleep!" ejaculated a companion in a glowing voice. "They never sleep! They go to bed once in every two weeks." His boast of it seemed almost a personal pride.

"They'll end with a crash, though, if they keep it up at this pace," said a gloomy voice from behind a newspaper.

The Café Colorado has a front of white and gold, in which is set larger plate-glass windows than are commonly to be found in Mexico. Two little wings of willow flip-flapping incessantly serve as doors. Under them small stray dogs go furtively into the café, and are shied into the street again by the waiters. On the side-walk there is always a decorative effect of loungers, ranging from the newly-arrived and superior tourist to the old veteran of the silver mines bronzed by violent suns. They contemplate with various shades of interest the show of the street—the red, purple, dusty white, glaring forth against the walls in the furious sunshine.

One afternoon the kids strolled into the Café Colorado. A half-dozen of the men who sat smoking and reading with a sort of Parisian effect at the little tables which lined two sides of the room, looked up and bowed smiling, and although this coming of the kids was anything but an unusual event, at least a dozen men wheeled in their chairs to stare after them. Three waiters polished tables, and moved chairs noisily, and appeared to be eager. Distinctly these kids were of importance.

Behind the distant bar, the tall form of old Pop himself awaited them smiling with broad geniality. "Well, my boys, how are you?" he cried in a voice of profound solicitude. He allowed five or six of his customers to languish in the care of Mexican bartenders, while he himself gave his eloquent attention to the kids, lending all the dignity of a great event to their arrival. "How are the boys to-day, eh?"

"You're a smooth old guy," said one, eying him. "Are you giving us this welcome so we won't notice it when you push your worst whisky at us?"

Pop turned in appeal from one kid to the other kid. "There, now, hear that, will you?" He assumed an oratorical pose. "Why, my boys, you always get the best that this house has got."

"Yes, we do!" The kids laughed. "Well, bring it out, anyhow, and if it's the same you sold us last night, we'll grab your cash register and run."

Pop whirled a bottle along the bar and then gazed at it with a rapt expression. "Fine as silk," he murmured. "Now just taste that, and if it isn't the best whisky you ever put in your face, why I'm a liar, that's all."

The kids surveyed him with scorn, and poured their allowances. Then they stood for a time insulting Pop about his whisky. "Usually it tastes exactly

262

like new parlour furniture," said the San Francisco kid. "Well, here goes, and you want to look out for your cash register."

"Your health, gentlemen," said Pop with a grand air, and as he wiped his bristling grey moustaches he wagged his head with reference to the cash register question. "I could catch you before you got very far."

"Why, are you a runner?" said one derisively.

"You just bank on me, my boy," said Pop, with deep emphasis. "I'm a flier."

The kids sat down their glasses suddenly and looked at him. "You must be," they said. Pop was tall and graceful and magnificent in manner, but he did not display those qualities of form which mean speed in the animal. His hair was grey; his face was round and fat from much living. The buttons of his glittering white waistcoat formed a fine curve, so that if the concave surface of a piece of barrel-hoop had been laid against Pop it would have touched every button. "You must be," observed the kids again.

"Well, you can laugh all you like, but—no jolly now, boys, I tell you I'm a winner. Why, I bet you I can skin anything in this town on a square go. When I kept my place in Eagle Pass there wasn't anybody who could touch me. One of these sure things came down from San Anton'. Oh, he was a runner he was. One of these people with wings. Well, I skinned 'im. What? Certainly I did. Never touched me."

The kids had been regarding him in grave silence, but at this moment they grinned, and said quite in chorus, "Oh, you old liar!"

Pop's voice took on a whining tone of earnestness. "Boys, I'm telling it to you straight. I'm a flier."

One of the kids had had a dreamy cloud in his eye and he cried out suddenly—"Say, what a joke to play this on Freddie."

The other jumped ecstatically. "Oh, wouldn't it though. Say he wouldn't do a thing but howl! He'd go crazy."

They looked at Pop as if they longed to be certain that he was, after all, a runner. "Now, Pop, on the level," said one of them wistfully, "can you run?"

"Boys," swore Pop, "I'm a peach! On the dead level, I'm a peach."

"By golly, I believe the old Indian can run," said one to the other, as if they were alone in confidence.

"That's what I can," cried Pop.

The kids said—"Well, so long, old man." They went to a table and sat down. They ordered a salad. They were always ordering salads. This was because one kid had a wild passion for salads, and the other didn't care. So at any hour of the day they might be seen ordering a salad. When this one came they went into a sort of executive session. It was a very long consultation. Men noted it. Occasionally the kids laughed in supreme enjoyment of something unknown. The low rumble of wheels came from the street. Often could be heard the parrot-like cries of distant vendors. The sunlight streamed through the green curtains, and made little amber-coloured flitterings on the marble floor. High up among the severe decorations of the ceiling—reminiscent of the days when the great building was a palace—a small white butterfly was wending through the cool air spaces. The long billiard hall led back to a vague gloom. The balls were always clicking, and one could see countless crooked elbows. Beggars slunk through the wicker doors, and were ejected by the nearest waiter. At last the kids called Pop to them.

"Sit down, Pop. Have a drink." They scanned him carefully. "Say now, Pop, on your solemn oath, can you run?"

"Boys," said Pop piously, and raising his hand, "I can run like a rabbit."

"On your oath?"

"On my oath."

"Can you beat Freddie?"

Pop appeared to look at the matter from all sides. "Well, boys, I'll tell you. No man is ever cock-sure of anything in this world, and I don't want to say that I can best any man, but I've seen Freddie run, and I'm ready to swear I can beat him. In a hundred yards I'd just about skin 'im neat—you understand, just about neat. Freddie is a good average runner, but I—you understand—I'm just—a little—bit—better." The kids had been listening with the utmost attention. Pop spoke the latter part slowly and meanfully. They thought he intended them to see his great confidence.

One said—"Pop, if you throw us in this thing, we'll come here and drink for two weeks without paying. We'll back you and work a josh on Freddie! But O!—if you throw us!"

To this menace Pop cried—"Boys, I'll make the run of my life! On my oath!"

The salad having vanished, the kids arose. "All right, now," they warned him. "If you play us for duffers, we'll get square. Don't you forget it."

"Boys, I'll give you a race for your money. Book on that. I may lose—understand, I may lose—no man can help meeting a better man. But I think I can skin him, and I'll give you a run for your money, you bet."

"All right, then. But, look here," they told him, "you keep your face closed. Nobody gets in on this but us. Understand?"

"Not a soul," Pop declared. They left him, gesturing a last warning from the wicker doors.

In the street they saw Benson, his cane gripped in the middle, strolling through the white-clothed jabbering natives on the shady side. They semaphored to him eagerly. He came across cautiously, like a man who ventures into dangerous company.

"We're going to get up a race. Pop and Fred. Pop swears he can skin 'im. This is a tip. Keep it dark. Say, won't Freddie be hot?"

Benson looked as if he had been compelled to endure these exhibitions of insanity for a century. "Oh, you fellows are off. Pop can't beat Freddie. He's an old bat. Why, it's impossible. Pop can't beat Freddie."

"Can't he? Want to bet he can't?" said the kids. "There now, let's see—

you're talking so large."

"Well, you——"

"Oh, bet. Bet or else close your trap. That's the way."

"How do you know you can pull off the race? Seen Freddie?"

"No, but——"

"Well, see him then. Can't bet with no race arranged. I'll bet with you all right—all right. I'll give you fellows a tip though—you're a pair of asses. Pop can't run any faster than a brick school-house."

The kids scowled at him and defiantly said—"Can't he?" They left him and went to the Casa Verde. Freddie, beautiful in his white jacket, was holding one of his innumerable conversations across the bar. He smiled when he saw them. "Where you boys been?" he demanded, in a paternal tone. Almost all the proprietors of American cafés in the city used to adopt a paternal tone when they spoke to the kids.

"Oh, been 'round,'" they replied.

"Have a drink?" said the proprietor of the Casa Verde, forgetting his other social obligations. During the course of this ceremony one of the kids remarked—

"Freddie, Pop says he can beat you running."

"Does he?" observed Freddie without excitement. He was used to various snares of the kids.

"That's what. He says he can leave you at the wire and not see you again."

"Well, he lies," replied Freddie placidly.

"And I'll bet you a bottle of wine that he can do it, too."

"Rats!" said Freddie.

"Oh, that's all right," pursued a kid. "You can throw bluffs all you like, but he can lose you in a hundred yards' dash, you bet."

266

Freddie drank his whisky, and then settled his elbows on the bar.

"Say, now, what do you boys keep coming in here with some pipe-story all the time for? You can't josh me. Do you think you can scare me about Pop? Why, I know I can beat him. He can't run with me. Certainly not. Why, you fellows are just jollying me."

"Are we though!" said the kids. "You daren't bet the bottle of wine."

"Oh, of course I can bet you a bottle of wine," said Freddie disdainfully. "Nobody cares about a bottle of wine, but——"

"Well, make it five then," advised one of the kids.

Freddie hunched his shoulders. "Why, certainly I will. Make it ten if you like, but——"

"We do," they said.

"Ten, is it? All right; that goes." A look of weariness came over Freddie's face. "But you boys are foolish. I tell you Pop is an old man. How can you expect him to run? Of course, I'm no great runner, but then I'm young and healthy and—and a pretty smooth runner too. Pop is old and fat, and then he doesn't do a thing but tank all day. It's a cinch."

The kids looked at him and laughed rapturously. They waved their fingers at him. "Ah, there!" they cried. They meant that they had made a victim of him.

But Freddie continued to expostulate. "I tell you he couldn't win—an old man like him. You're crazy. Of course, I know you don't care about ten bottles of wine, but, then—to make such bets as that. You're twisted."

"Are we, though?" cried the kids in mockery. They had precipitated Freddie into a long and thoughtful treatise on every possible chance of the thing as he saw it. They disputed with him from time to time, and jeered at him. He laboured on through his argument. Their childish faces were bright with glee.

In the midst of it Wilburson entered. Wilburson worked; not too much, though. He had hold of the Mexican end of a great importing house of New York, and as he was a junior partner, he worked. But not too much, though. "What's the howl?" he said.

The kids giggled. "We've got Freddie rattled."

"Why," said Freddie, turning to him, "these two Indians are trying to tell me that Pop can beat me running."

"Like the devil," said Wilburson, incredulously.

"Well, can't he?" demanded a kid.

"Why, certainly not," said Wilburson, dismissing every possibility of it with a gesture. "That old bat? Certainly not. I'll bet fifty dollars that Freddie——"

"Take you," said a kid.

"What?" said Wilburson, "that Freddie won't beat Pop?"

The kid that had spoken now nodded his head.

"That Freddie won't beat Pop?" repeated Wilburson.

"Yes. It's a go?"

"Why, certainly," retorted Wilburson. "Fifty? All right."

"Bet you five bottles on the side," ventured the other kid.

"Why, certainly," exploded Wilburson wrathfully. "You fellows must take me for something easy. I'll take all those kinds of bets I can get. Cer—tain—ly."

They settled the details. The course was to be paced off on the asphalt of one of the adjacent side-streets, and then, at about eleven o'clock in the evening, the match would be run. Usually in Mexico the streets of a city grow lonely and dark but a little after nine o'clock. There are occasional lurking figures, perhaps, but no crowds, lights and noise. The course would doubtless be undisturbed. As for the policeman in the vicinity, they—well, they were conditionally amiable.

The kids went to see Pop; they told him of the arrangement, and then in deep tones they said, "Oh, Pop, if you throw us!"

Pop appeared to be a trifle shaken by the weight of responsibility thrust upon him, but he spoke out bravely. "Boys, I'll pinch that race. Now you watch me. I'll pinch it."

The kids went then on some business of their own, for they were not seen again till evening. When they returned to the neighbourhood of the Café Colorado the usual stream of carriages was whirling along the calle. The wheels hummed on the asphalt, and the coachmen towered in their great sombreros. On the sidewalk a gazing crowd sauntered, the better class self-satisfied and proud, in their Derby hats and cut-away coats, the lower classes muffling their dark faces in their blankets, slipping along in leather sandals. An electric light sputtered and fumed over the throng. The afternoon shower had left the pave wet and glittering. The air was still laden with the odour of rain on flowers, grass, leaves.

In the Café Colorado a cosmopolitan crowd ate, drank, played billiards, gossiped, or read in the glaring yellow light. When the kids entered a large circle of men that had been gesticulating near the bar greeted them with a roar.

"Here they are now!"

"Oh, you pair of peaches!"

"Say, got any more money to bet with?" Colonel Hammigan, grinning, pushed his way to them. "Say, boys, we'll all have a drink on you now because you won't have any money after eleven o'clock. You'll be going down the back stairs in your stocking feet."

Although the kids remained unnaturally serene and quiet, argument in the Café Colorado became tumultuous. Here and there a man who did not intend to bet ventured meekly that perchance Pop might win, and the others swarmed upon him in a whirlwind of angry denial and ridicule.

Pop, enthroned behind the bar, looked over at this storm with a shadow of anxiety upon his face. This widespread flouting affected him, but the kids looked blissfully satisfied with the tumult they had stirred.

Blanco, honest man, ever worrying for his friends, came to them. "Say, you fellows, you aren't betting too much? This thing looks kind of shaky, don't it?"

The faces of the kids grew sober, and after consideration one said—"No, I guess we've got a good thing, Blanco. Pop is going to surprise them, I think."

"Well, don't——"

"All right, old boy. We'll watch out."

From time to time the kids had much business with certain orange, red, blue, purple, and green bills. They were making little memoranda on the back of visiting cards. Pop watched them closely, the shadow still upon his face. Once he called to them, and when they came he leaned over the bar and said intensely—"Say, boys, remember, now—I might lose this race. Nobody can ever say for sure, and if I do, why——"

"Oh, that's all right, Pop," said the kids, reassuringly. "Don't mind it. Do your derndest, and let it go at that."

When they had left him, however, they went to a corner to consult. "Say, this is getting interesting. Are you in deep?" asked one anxiously of his friend.

"Yes, pretty deep," said the other stolidly. "Are you?"

"Deep as the devil," replied the other in the same tone.

They looked at each other stonily and went back to the crowd. Benson had just entered the café. He approached them with a gloating smile of victory. "Well, where's all that money you were going to bet?"

"Right here," said the kids, thrusting into their waistcoat pockets.

At eleven o'clock a curious thing was learned. When Pop and Freddie, the kids and all, came to the little side street, it was thick with people. It seemed that the news of this race had spread like the wind among the Americans, and they had come to witness the event. In the darkness the crowd moved, mumbling in argument.

The principals—the kids and those with them—surveyed this scene with some dismay. "Say—here's a go." Even then a policeman might be seen approaching, the light from his little lantern flickering on his white cap, gloves, brass buttons, and on the butt of the old-fashioned Colt's revolver which hung at his belt. He addressed Freddie in swift Mexican. Freddie listened, nodding from time to time. Finally Freddie turned to the others to translate. "He says he'll get into trouble if he allows this race when all this crowd is here."

There was a murmur of discontent. The policeman looked at them with an expression of anxiety on his broad, brown face.

"Oh, come on. We'll go hold it on some other fellow's beat," said one of the kids. The group moved slowly away debating. Suddenly the other kid cried, "I know! The Paseo!"

"By jiminy," said Freddie, "just the thing. We'll get a cab and go out to the Paseo. S-s-h! Keep it quiet; we don't want all this mob."

Later they tumbled into a cab—Pop, Freddie, the kids, old Colonel Hammigan and Benson. They whispered to the men who had wagered, "The Paseo." The cab whirled away up the black street. There were occasional grunts and groans, cries of "Oh, get off me feet," and of "Quit! you're killing me." Six people do not have fun in one cab. The principals spoke to each other with the respect and friendliness which comes to good men at such times. Once a kid put his head out of the window and looked backward. He pulled it in again and cried, "Great Scott! Look at that, would you!"

The others struggled to do as they were bid, and afterwards shouted, "Holy smoke! Well, I'll be blowed! Thunder and turf!"

Galloping after them came innumerable cabs, their lights twinkling, streaming in a great procession through the night.

"The street is full of them," ejaculated the old colonel.

The Paseo de la Reforma is the famous drive of the city of Mexico, leading to the Castle of Chapultepec, which last ought to be well known in the United States.

It is a fine broad avenue of macadam with a much greater quality of dignity than anything of the kind we possess in our own land. It seems of the old world, where to the beauty of the thing itself is added the solemnity of tradition and history, the knowledge that feet in buskins trod the same stones, that cavalcades of steel thundered there before the coming of carriages.

When the Americans tumbled out of their cabs the giant bronzes of Aztec and Spaniard loomed dimly above them like towers. The four roads of poplar trees rustled weirdly off there in the darkness. Pop took out his watch and struck a match. "Well, hurry up this thing. It's almost midnight."

The other cabs came swarming, the drivers lashing their horses, for these Americans, who did all manner of strange things, nevertheless always paid well for it. There was a mighty hubbub then in the darkness. Five or six men began to pace the distance and quarrel. Others knotted their handkerchiefs together to make a tape. Men were swearing over bets, fussing and fuming about the odds. Benson came to the kids swaggering. "You're a pair of asses." The cabs waited in a solid block down the avenue. Above the crowd the tall statues hid their visages in the night.

At last a voice floated through the darkness. "Are you ready there?" Everybody yelled excitedly. The men at the tape pulled it out straight. "Hold it higher, Jim, you fool," and silence fell then upon the throng. Men bended down trying to pierce the deep gloom with their eyes. From out at the starting point came muffled voices. The crowd swayed and jostled.

The racers did not come. The crowd began to fret, its nerves burning. "Oh, hurry up," shrilled some one.

The voice called again—"Ready there?" Everybody replied—"Yes, all ready. Hurry up!"

There was a more muffled discussion at the starting point. In the crowd

272

a man began to make a proposition. "I'll bet twenty—" but the crowd interrupted with a howl. "Here they come!" The thickly-packed body of men swung as if the ground had moved. The men at the tape shouldered madly at their fellows, bawling, "Keep back! Keep back!"

From the distance came the noise of feet pattering furiously. Vague forms flashed into view for an instant. A hoarse roar broke from the crowd. Men bended and swayed and fought. The kids back near the tape exchanged another stolid look. A white form shone forth. It grew like a spectre. Always could be heard the wild patter. A scream broke from the crowd. "By Gawd, it's Pop! Pop! Pop's ahead!"

The old man spun towards the tape like a madman, his chin thrown back, his grey hair flying. His legs moved like oiled machinery. And as he shot forward a howl as from forty cages of wild animals went toward the imperturbable chieftains in bronze. The crowd flung themselves forward. "Oh, you old Indian! You savage! Did anybody ever see such running?"

"Ain't he a peach! Well!"

"Where's the kids? H-e-y, kids!"

"Look at him, would you? Did you ever think?" These cries flew in the air blended in a vast shout of astonishment and laughter.

For an instant the whole tragedy was in view. Freddie, desperate, his teeth shining, his face contorted, whirling along in deadly effort, was twenty feet behind the tall form of old Pop, who, dressed only in his—only in his underclothes—gained with each stride. One grand insane moment, and then Pop had hurled himself against the tape—victor!

Freddie, fallen into the arms of some men, struggled with his breath, and at last managed to stammer—

"Say, can't—can't—that old—old—man run!"

Pop, puffing and heaving, could only gasp—"Where's my shoes? Who's got my shoes?"

Later Freddie scrambled panting through the crowd, and held out his hand. "Good man, Pop!" And then he looked up and down the tall, stout form. "Hell! who would think you could run like that?"

The kids were surrounded by a crowd, laughing tempestuously.

"How did you know he could run?"

"Why didn't you give me a line on him?"

"Say—great snakes!—you fellows had a nerve to bet on Pop."

"Why, I was cock-sure he couldn't win."

"Oh, you fellows must have seen him run before."

"Who would ever think it?"

Benson came by, filling the midnight air with curses. They turned to jibe him.

"What's the matter, Benson?"

"Somebody pinched my handkerchief. I tied it up in that string. Damn it."

The kids laughed blithely. "Why, hello! Benson," they said.

There was a great rush for cabs. Shouting, laughing, wondering, the crowd hustled into their conveyances, and the drivers flogged their horses toward the city again.

"Won't Freddie be crazy! Say, he'll be guyed about this for years."

"But who would ever think that old tank could run so?"

One cab had to wait while Pop and Freddie resumed various parts of their clothing.

As they drove home, Freddie said—"Well, Pop, you beat me."

Pop said—"That's all right, old man."

The kids, grinning, said—"How much did you lose, Benson?"

Benson said defiantly—"Oh, not so much. How much did you win?"

"Oh, not so much."

Old Colonel Hammigan, squeezed down in a corner, had apparently been reviewing the event in his mind, for he suddenly remarked, "Well, I'm damned!"

They were late in reaching the Café Colorado, but when they did, the bottles were on the bar as thick as pickets on a fence.

THE FIVE WHITE MICE

Freddie was mixing a cock-tail. His hand with the long spoon was whirling swiftly, and the ice in the glass hummed and rattled like a cheap watch. Over by the window, a gambler, a millionaire, a railway conductor, and the agent of a vast American syndicate were playing seven-up. Freddie surveyed them with the ironical glance of a man who is mixing a cock-tail.

From time to time a swarthy Mexican waiter came with his tray from the rooms at the rear, and called his orders across the bar. The sounds of the indolent stir of the city, awakening from its siesta, floated over the screens which barred the sun and the inquisitive eye. From the far-away kitchen could be heard the roar of the old French chef, driving, herding, and abusing his Mexican helpers.

A string of men came suddenly in from the street. They stormed up to the bar. There were impatient shouts. "Come now, Freddie, don't stand there like a portrait of yourself. Wiggle!" Drinks of many kinds and colours, amber, green, mahogany, strong and mild, began to swarm upon the bar with all the attendants of lemon, sugar, mint and ice. Freddie, with Mexican support, worked like a sailor in the provision of them, sometimes talking with that scorn for drink and admiration for those who drink which is the attribute of a good bar-keeper.

At last a man was afflicted with a stroke of dice-shaking. A herculean discussion was waging, and he was deeply engaged in it, but at the same time he lazily flirted the dice. Occasionally he made great combinations. "Look at that, would you?" he cried proudly. The others paid little heed. Then violently the craving took them. It went along the line like an epidemic, and involved them all. In a moment they had arranged a carnival of dice-shaking with money penalties and liquid prizes. They clamorously made it a point of honour with Freddie that he should play and take his chance of sometimes providing this large group with free refreshment. With bended heads like football players, they surged over the tinkling dice, jostling, cheering, and bitterly arguing. One of the quiet company playing seven-up at the corner table said profanely that the row reminded him of a bowling contest at a picnic.

After the regular shower, many carriages rolled over the smooth calle, and sent a musical thunder through the Casa Verde. The shop-windows became aglow with light, and the walks were crowded with youths, callow and ogling, dressed vainly according to superstitious fashions. The policemen had muffled themselves in their gnome-like cloaks, and placed their lanterns as obstacles for the carriages in the middle of the street. The city of Mexico gave forth the deep organ-mellow tones of its evening resurrection.

But still the group at the bar of the Casa Verde were shaking dice. They had passed beyond shaking for drinks for the crowd, for Mexican dollars, for dinners, for the wine at dinner. They had even gone to the trouble of separating the cigars and cigarettes from the dinner's bill, and causing a distinct man to be responsible for them. Finally they were aghast. Nothing remained in sight of their minds which even remotely suggested further gambling. There was a pause for deep consideration.

"Well——"

"Well——"

A man called out in the exuberance of creation. "I know! Let's shake for a box to-night at the circus! A box at the circus!" The group was profoundly edified. "That's it! That's it! Come on now! Box at the circus!" A dominating voice cried—"Three dashes—high man out!" An American, tall, and with a face of copper red from the rays that flash among the Sierra Madres and burn on the cactus deserts, took the little leathern cup and spun the dice out upon the polished wood. A fascinated assemblage hung upon the bar-rail. Three kings turned their pink faces upward. The tall man flourished the cup, burlesquing, and flung the two other dice. From them he ultimately extracted one more pink king. "There," he said. "Now, let's see! Four kings!" He began to swagger in a sort of provisional way.

The next man took the cup, and blew softly in the top of it. Poising it in his hand, he then surveyed the company with a stony eye and paused. They knew perfectly well that he was applying the magic of deliberation and ostentatious indifference, but they could not wait in tranquillity during the performance of all these rites. They began to call out impatiently. "Come now—hurry up." At last the man, with a gesture that was singularly impressive, threw the dice. The others set up a howl of joy. "Not a pair!" There was another solemn pause. The men moved restlessly. "Come, now, go ahead!" In the end, the man, induced and abused, achieved something that was nothing in the presence of four kings. The tall man climbed on the foot-rail and leaned hazardously forward. "Four kings! My four kings are good to go out," he bellowed into the middle of the mob, and although in a moment he did pass into the radiant region of exemption, he continued to bawl advice and scorn.

The mirrors and oiled woods of the Casa Verde were now dancing with blue flashes from a great buzzing electric lamp. A host of quiet members of the Anglo-Saxon colony had come in for their pre-dinner cock-tails. An amiable person was exhibiting to some tourists this popular American saloon. It was a very sober and respectable time of day. Freddie reproved courageously the dice-shaking brawlers, and, in return, he received the choicest advice in a tumult of seven combined vocabularies. He laughed; he had been compelled to retire from the game, but he was keeping an interested, if furtive, eye upon it.

Down at the end of the line there was a youth at whom everybody railed for his flaming ill-luck. At each disaster, Freddie swore from behind the bar in a sort of affectionate contempt. "Why, this kid has had no luck for two days. Did you ever see such throwin'?"

The contest narrowed eventually to the New York kid and an individual who swung about placidly on legs that moved in nefarious circles. He had a grin that resembled a bit of carving. He was obliged to lean down and blink rapidly to ascertain the facts of his venture, but fate presented him with five queens. His smile did not change, but he puffed gently like a man who has been running.

The others, having emerged unscathed from this part of the conflict, waxed hilarious with the kid. They smote him on either shoulders. "We've got you stuck for it, kid! You can't beat that game! Five queens!"

Up to this time the kid had displayed only the temper of the gambler, but the cheerful hoots of the players, supplemented now by a ring of guying non-combatants, caused him to feel profoundly that it would be fine to beat the five queens. He addressed a gambler's slogan to the interior of the cup.

"Oh, five white mice of chance,

Shirts of wool and corduroy pants,

Gold and wine, women and sin,

All for you if you let me come in—

Into the house of chance."

Flashing the dice sardonically out upon the bar, he displayed three aces. From two dice in the next throw he achieved one more ace. For his last throw, he rattled the single dice for a long time. He already had four aces; if he accomplished another one, the five queens were vanquished and the box at the circus came from the drunken man's pocket. All the kid's movements were slow and elaborate. For the last throw he planted the cup bottom-down on the bar with the one dice hidden under it. Then he turned and faced the crowd with the air of a conjuror or a cheat.

"Oh, maybe it's an ace," he said in boastful calm. "Maybe it's an ace."

Instantly he was presiding over a little drama in which every man was absorbed. The kid leaned with his back against the bar-rail and with his elbows upon it.

"Maybe it's an ace," he repeated.

A jeering voice in the background said—"Yes, maybe it is, kid!"

The kid's eyes searched for a moment among the men. "I'll bet fifty dollars it is an ace," he said.

Another voice asked—"American money?"

"Yes," answered the kid.

"Oh!" There was a genial laugh at this discomfiture. However, no one came forward at the kid's challenge, and presently he turned to the cup. "Now, I'll show you." With the manner of a mayor unveiling a statue, he lifted the cup. There was revealed naught but a ten-spot. In the roar which arose could be heard each man ridiculing the cowardice of his neighbour, and above all the din rang the voice of Freddie be-rating every one. "Why, there isn't one liver to every five men in the outfit. That was the greatest cold bluff I ever saw worked. He wouldn't know how to cheat with dice if he wanted to. Don't know the first thing about it. I could hardly keep from laughin' when I seen him drillin' you around. Why, I tell you, I had that fifty dollars right in my pocket if I wanted to be a chump. You're an easy lot——"

Nevertheless the group who had won in the theatre-box game did not relinquish their triumph. They burst like a storm about the head of the kid, swinging at him with their fists. "'Five white mice'!" they quoted, choking. "'Five white mice'!"

"Oh, they are not so bad," said the kid.

Afterward it often occurred that a man would jeer a finger at the kid and derisively say—"'Five white mice.'"

On the route from the dinner to the circus, others of the party often asked the kid if he had really intended to make his appeal to mice. They suggested other animals—rabbits, dogs, hedgehogs, snakes, opossums. To this banter the kid replied with a serious expression of his belief in the fidelity and wisdom of the five white mice. He presented a most eloquent case, decorated with fine language and insults, in which he proved that if one was going to believe in anything at all, one might as well choose the five white mice. His companions, however, at once and unanimously pointed out to him that his recent exploit did not place him in the light of a convincing advocate.

The kid discerned two figures in the street. They were making imperious signs at him. He waited for them to approach, for he recognized one as the other kid—the Frisco kid: there were two kids. With the Frisco kid was

Benson. They arrived almost breathless. "Where you been?" cried the Frisco kid. It was an arrangement that upon a meeting the one that could first ask this question was entitled to use a tone of limitless injury. "What you been doing? Where you going? Come on with us. Benson and I have got a little scheme."

The New York kid pulled his arm from the grapple of the other. "I can't. I've got to take these sutlers to the circus. They stuck me for it shaking dice at Freddie's. I can't, I tell you."

The two did not at first attend to his remarks. "Come on! We've got a little scheme."

"I can't. They stuck me. I've got to take'm to the circus."

At this time it did not suit the men with the scheme to recognize these objections as important. "Oh, take'm some other time. Well, can't you take'm some other time? Let 'em go. Damn the circus. Get cold feet. What did you get stuck for? Get cold feet."

But despite their fighting, the New York kid broke away from them. "I can't, I tell you. They stuck me." As he left them, they yelled with rage. "Well, meet us, now, do you hear? In the Casa Verde as soon as the circus quits! Hear?" They threw maledictions after him.

In the city of Mexico, a man goes to the circus without descending in any way to infant amusements, because the Circo Teatro Orrin is one of the best in the world, and too easily surpasses anything of the kind in the United States, where it is merely a matter of a number of rings, if possible, and a great professional agreement to lie to the public. Moreover, the American clown, who in the Mexican arena prances and gabbles, is the clown to whom writers refer as the delight of their childhood, and lament that he is dead. At this circus the kid was not debased by the sight of mournful prisoner elephants and caged animals forlorn and sickly. He sat in his box until late, and laughed and swore when past laughing at the comic foolish-wise clown.

When he returned to the Casa Verde there was no display of the Frisco kid and Benson. Freddie was leaning on the bar listening to four men terribly discuss a question that was not plain. There was a card-game in the corner, of course. Sounds of revelry pealed from the rear rooms.

When the kid asked Freddie if he had seen his friend and Benson, Freddie looked bored. "Oh, yes, they were in here just a minute ago, but I don't know where they went. They've got their skates on. Where've they been? Came in here rolling across the floor like two little gilt gods. They wobbled around for a time, and then Frisco wanted me to send six bottles of wine around to Benson's rooms, but I didn't have anybody to send this time of night, and so they got mad and went out. Where did they get their loads?"

In the first deep gloom of the street the kid paused a moment debating. But presently he heard quavering voices. "Oh, kid! kid! Com'ere!" Peering, he recognized two vague figures against the opposite wall. He crossed the street, and they said—"Hello-kid."

"Say, where did you get it?" he demanded sternly. "You Indians better go home. What did you want to get scragged for?" His face was luminous with virtue.

As they swung to and fro, they made angry denials. "We ain' load'! We ain' load'. Big chump. Comonangetadrink."

The sober youth turned then to his friend. "Hadn't you better go home, kid? Come on, it's late. You'd better break away."

The Frisco kid wagged his head decisively. "Got take Benson home first. He'll be wallowing around in a minute. Don't mind me. I'm all right."

"Cerly, he's all right," said Benson, arousing from deep thought. "He's all right. But better take'm home, though. That's ri—right. He's load'. But he's all right. No need go home any more'n you. But better take'm home. He's load'." He looked at his companion with compassion. "Kid, you're load'."

The sober kid spoke abruptly to his friend from San Francisco. "Kid, pull yourself together, now. Don't fool. We've got to brace this ass of a Benson all the way home. Get hold of his other arm."

The Frisco kid immediately obeyed his comrade without a word or a glower. He seized Benson and came to attention like a soldier. Later, indeed, he meekly ventured—"Can't we take cab?" But when the New York kid snapped out that there were no convenient cabs he subsided to an impassive silence. He seemed to be reflecting upon his state, without astonishment, dismay, or any particular emotion. He submitted himself woodenly to the direction of his friend.

Benson had protested when they had grasped his arms. "Washa doing?" he said in a new and guttural voice. "Washa doing? I ain' load'. Comonangetadrink. I——"

"Oh, come along, you idiot," said the New York kid. The Frisco kid merely presented the mien of a stoic to the appeal of Benson, and in silence dragged away at one of his arms. Benson's feet came from that particular spot on the pavement with the reluctance of roots and also with the ultimate suddenness of roots. The three of them lurched out into the street in the abandon of tumbling chimneys. Benson was meanwhile noisily challenging the others to produce any reasons for his being taken home. His toes clashed into the kerb when they reached the other side of the calle, and for a moment the kids hauled him along with the points of his shoes scraping musically on the pavement. He balked formidably as they were about to pass the Casa Verde. "No! No! Leshavanothdrink! Anothdrink! Onemore!"

But the Frisco kid obeyed the voice of his partner in a manner that was blind but absolute, and they scummed Benson on past the door. Locked together the three swung into a dark street. The sober kid's flank was continually careering ahead of the other wing. He harshly admonished the Frisco child, and the latter promptly improved in the same manner of unthinking complete obedience. Benson began to recite the tale of a love affair, a tale that didn't even have a middle. Occasionally the New York kid swore. They toppled on their way like three comedians playing at it on the stage.

At midnight a little Mexican street burrowing among the walls of the city is as dark as a whale's throat at deep sea. Upon this occasion heavy clouds hung over the capital and the sky was a pall. The projecting balconies could make no shadows.

"Shay," said Benson, breaking away from his escort suddenly, "what want gome for? I ain't load'. You got reg'lar spool-fact'ry in your head—you N' York kid there. Thish oth' kid, he's mos' proper shober, mos' proper shober. He's drunk, but—but he's shober."

"Ah, shup up, Benson," said the New York kid. "Come along now. We can't stay here all night." Benson refused to be corralled, but spread his legs and twirled like a dervish, meanwhile under the evident impression that he was conducting himself most handsomely. It was not long before he gained the opinion that he was laughing at the others. "Eight purple dogsh—dogs! Eight purple dogs. Thas what kid'll see in the morn'. Look ou' for 'em. They—"

As Benson, describing the canine phenomena, swung wildly across the sidewalk, it chanced that three other pedestrians were passing in shadowy rank. Benson's shoulder jostled one of them.

A Mexican wheeled upon the instant. His hand flashed to his hip. There was a moment of silence, during which Benson's voice was not heard raised in apology. Then an indescribable comment, one burning word, came from between the Mexican's teeth.

Benson, rolling about in a semi-detached manner, stared vacantly at the Mexican, who thrust his lean face forward while his fingers played nervously at his hip. The New York kid could not follow Spanish well, but he understood when the Mexican breathed softly: "Does the señor want to fight?"

Benson simply gazed in gentle surprise. The woman next to him at dinner had said something inventive. His tailor had presented his bill. Something had occurred which was mildly out of the ordinary, and his surcharged brain refused to cope with it. He displayed only the agitation of a smoker temporarily without a light.

The New York kid had almost instantly grasped Benson's arm, and was about to jerk him away, when the other kid, who up to this time had been an automaton, suddenly projected himself forward, thrust the rubber Benson aside, and said—"Yes."

There was no sound nor light in the world. The wall at the left happened to be of the common prison-like construction—no door, no window, no opening at all. Humanity was enclosed and asleep. Into the mouth of the sober kid came a wretched bitter taste as if it had filled with blood. He was transfixed as if he was already seeing the lightning ripples on the knife-blade.

But the Mexican's hand did not move at that time. His face went still further forward and he whispered—"So?" The sober kid saw this face as if he and it were alone in space—a yellow mask smiling in eager cruelty, in satisfaction, and above all it was lit with sinister decision. As for the features, they were reminiscent of an unplaced, a forgotten type, which really resembled with precision those of a man who had shaved him three times in Boston in 1888. But the expression burned his mind as sealing-wax burns the palm, and fascinated, stupefied, he actually watched the progress of the man's thought toward the point where a knife would be wrenched from its sheath. The emotion, a sort of mechanical fury, a breeze made by electric fans, a rage made by vanity, smote the dark countenance in wave after wave.

Then the New York kid took a sudden step forward. His hand was at his hip. He was gripping there a revolver of robust size. He recalled that upon its black handle was stamped a hunting scene in which a sportsman in fine leggings and a peaked cap was taking aim at a stag less than one-eighth of an inch away.

His pace forward caused instant movement of the Mexicans. One immediately took two steps to face him squarely. There was a general adjustment, pair and pair. This opponent of the New York kid was a tall man and quite stout. His sombrero was drawn low over his eyes. His serape was flung on his left shoulder. His back was bent in the supposed manner of a Spanish grandee. This concave gentleman cut a fine and terrible figure. The lad, moved by the spirits of his modest and perpendicular ancestors, had time to feel his blood roar at sight of the pose.

He was aware that the third Mexican was over on the left fronting Benson, and he was aware that Benson was leaning against the wall sleepily and peacefully eying the convention. So it happened that these six men stood, side fronting side, five of them with their right hands at their hips and with their bodies lifted nervously, while the central pair exchanged a crescendo of provocations. The meaning of their words rose and rose. They were travelling in a straight line toward collision.

The New York kid contemplated his Spanish grandee. He drew his revolver upward until the hammer was surely free of the holster. He waited immovable and watchful while the garrulous Frisco kid expended two and a half lexicons on the middle Mexican.

The eastern lad suddenly decided that he was going to be killed. His mind leaped forward and studied the aftermath. The story would be a marvel of brevity when first it reached the far New York home, written in a careful hand on a bit of cheap paper, topped and footed and backed by the printed fortifications of the cable company. But they are often as stones flung into mirrors, these bits of paper upon which are laconically written all the most terrible chronicles of the times. He witnessed the uprising of his mother and sister, and the invincible calm of his hard-mouthed old father, who would probably shut himself in his library and smoke alone. Then his father would come, and they would bring him here and say—"This is the place." Then, very likely, each would remove his hat. They would stand quietly with their hats in their hands for a decent minute. He pitied his old financing father, unyielding and millioned, a man who commonly spoke twenty-two words a year to his beloved son. The kid understood it at this time. If his fate was not impregnable, he might have turned out to be a man and have been liked by his father.

The other kid would mourn his death. He would be preternaturally correct for some weeks, and recite the tale without swearing. But it would not bore him. For the sake of his dead comrade he would be glad to be preternaturally correct, and to recite the tale without swearing.

These views were perfectly stereopticon, flashing in and away from his thought with an inconceivable rapidity until after all they were simply one quick dismal impression. And now here is the unreal real: into this kid's nostrils, at the expectant moment of slaughter, had come the scent of new-mown hay, a fragrance from a field of prostrate grass, a fragrance which contained the sunshine, the bees, the peace of meadows, and the wonder of a distant crooning stream. It had no right to be supreme, but it was supreme, and he breathed it as he waited for pain and a sight of the unknown.

But in the same instant, it may be, his thought flew to the Frisco kid, and it came upon him like a flicker of lightning that the Frisco kid was not going to be there to perform, for instance, the extraordinary office of respectable mourner. The other kid's head was muddled, his hand was unsteady, his agility was gone. This other kid was facing the determined and most ferocious gentleman of the enemy. The New York kid became convinced that his friend was lost. There was going to be a screaming murder. He was so certain of it that he wanted to shield his eyes from sight of the leaping arm and the knife. It was sickening, utterly sickening. The New York kid might have been taking his first sea-voyage. A combination of honourable manhood and inability prevented him from running away.

He suddenly knew that it was possible to draw his own revolver, and by a swift manoeuvre face down all three Mexicans. If he was quick enough he would probably be victor. If any hitch occurred in the draw he would undoubtedly be dead with his friends. It was a new game; he had never been obliged to face a situation of this kind in the Beacon Club in New York. In this test, the lungs of the kid still continued to perform their duty.

"Oh, five white mice of chance,

Shirts of wool and corduroy pants,

Gold and wine, women and sin,

All for you if you let me come in—

Into the house of chance."

He thought of the weight and size of his revolver, and dismay pierced him. He feared that in his hands it would be as unwieldy as a sewing-machine for this quick work. He imagined, too, that some singular providence might cause him to lose his grip as he raised his weapon. Or it might get fatally entangled in the tails of his coat. Some of the eels of despair lay wet and cold against his back.

But at the supreme moment the revolver came forth as if it were greased and it arose like a feather. This somnolent machine, after months of repose, was finally looking at the breasts of men.

Perhaps in this one series of movements, the kid had unconsciously used nervous force sufficient to raise a bale of hay. Before he comprehended it he was standing behind his revolver glaring over the barrel at the Mexicans, menacing first one and then another. His finger was tremoring on the trigger. The revolver gleamed in the darkness with a fine silver light.

The fulsome grandee sprang backward with a low cry. The man who had been facing the Frisco kid took a quick step away. The beautiful array of Mexicans was suddenly disorganized.

The cry and the backward steps revealed something of great importance to the New York kid. He had never dreamed that he did not have a complete monopoly of all possible trepidations. The cry of the grandee was that of a man who suddenly sees a poisonous snake. Thus the kid was able to understand swiftly that they were all human beings. They were unanimous in not wishing for too bloody combat. There was a sudden expression of the equality. He had vaguely believed that they were not going to evince much consideration for his dramatic development as an active factor. They even might be exasperated into an onslaught by it. Instead, they had respected his movement with a respect as great even as an ejaculation of fear and backward steps. Upon the instant he pounced forward and began to swear, unreeling great English oaths as thick as ropes, and lashing the faces of the Mexicans with them. He was bursting with rage, because these men had not previously confided to him that they were vulnerable. The whole thing had been an absurd imposition. He had been seduced into respectful alarm by the concave attitude of the grandee. And after all there had been an equality of emotion, an equality: he was furious. He wanted to take the serape of the grandee and swaddle him in it.

The Mexicans slunk back, their eyes burning wistfully. The kid took aim first at one and then at another. After they had achieved a certain distance they paused and drew up in a rank. They then resumed some of their old splendour of manner. A voice hailed him in a tone of cynical bravado as if it had come from between lips of smiling mockery. "Well, señor, it is finished?"

The kid scowled into the darkness, his revolver drooping at his side. After a moment he answered—"I am willing." He found it strange that he should be able to speak after this silence of years.

"Good-night, señor."

"Good-night."

When he turned to look at the Frisco kid he found him in his original position, his hand upon his hip. He was blinking in perplexity at the point from whence the Mexicans had vanished.

"Well," said the sober kid crossly, "are you ready to go home now?"

The Frisco kid said—"Where they gone?" His voice was undisturbed but inquisitive.

Benson suddenly propelled himself from his dreamful position against the wall. "Frishco kid's all right. He's drunk's fool and he's all right. But you New York kid, you're shober." He passed into a state of profound investigation. "Kid shober 'cause didn't go with us. Didn't go with us 'cause went to damn circus. Went to damn circus 'cause lose shakin' dice. Lose shakin' dice 'cause—what make lose shakin' dice, kid?"

The New York kid eyed the senile youth. "I don't know. The five white mice, maybe."

Benson puzzled so over this reply that he had to be held erect by his friends. Finally the Frisco kid said—"Let's go home."

Nothing had happened.

FLANAGAN AND HIS SHORT FILIBUSTERING ADVENTURE

I

"I have got twenty men at me back who will fight to the death," said the warrior to the old filibuster.

"And they can be blowed for all me," replied the old filibuster. "Common as sparrows. Cheap as cigarettes. Show me twenty men with steel clamps on their mouths, with holes in their heads where memory ought to be, and I want 'em. But twenty brave men merely? I'd rather have twenty brave onions."

Thereupon the warrior removed sadly, feeling that no salaams were paid to valour in these days of mechanical excellence.

Valour, in truth, is no bad thing to have when filibustering; but many medals are to be won by the man who knows not the meaning of "pow-wow," before or afterwards. Twenty brave men with tongues hung lightly may make trouble rise from the ground like smoke from grass, because of their subsequent fiery pride; whereas twenty cow-eyed villains who accept unrighteous and far-compelling kicks as they do the rain from heaven may halo the ultimate history of an expedition with gold, and plentifully bedeck their names, winning forty years of gratitude from patriots, simply by remaining silent. As for the cause, it may be only that they have no friends or other credulous furniture.

If it were not for the curse of the swinging tongue, it is surely to be said that the filibustering industry, flourishing now in the United States, would be pie. Under correct conditions, it is merely a matter of dealing with some little detectives whose skill at search is rated by those who pay them at a value of twelve or twenty dollars each week. It is nearly axiomatic that normally a twelve dollar per week detective cannot defeat a one hundred thousand dollar filibustering excursion. Against the criminal, the detective represents the commonwealth, but in this other case he represents his desire to show cause why his salary should be paid. He represents himself merely, and he counts no more than a grocer's clerk.

But the pride of the successful filibuster often smites him and his cause like an axe, and men who have not confided in their mothers go prone with him. It can make the dome of the Capitol tremble and incite the Senators to over-turning benches. It can increase the salaries of detectives who could not detect the location of a pain in the chest. It is a wonderful thing, this pride.

Filibustering was once such a simple game. It was managed blandly by gentle captains and smooth and undisturbed gentlemen, who at other times dealt in law, soap, medicine, and bananas. It was a great pity that the little cote of doves in Washington were obliged to rustle officially, and naval men were kept from their berths at night, and sundry Custom House people got wiggings, all because the returned adventurer pow-wowed in his pride. A yellow and red banner would have been long since smothered in a shame of defeat if a contract to filibuster had been let to some admirable organization like one of our trusts.

And yet the game is not obsolete. It is still played by the wise and the silent men whose names are not display-typed and blathered from one end of the country to the other.

There is in mind now a man who knew one side of a fence from the other side when he looked sharply. They were hunting for captains then to command the first vessels of what has since become a famous little fleet. One was recommended to this man, and he said, "Send him down to my office and I'll look him over." He was an attorney, and he liked to lean back in his chair, twirl a paper-knife, and let the other fellow talk.

The sea-faring man came and stood and appeared confounded. The attorney asked the terrible first question of the filibuster to the applicant. He said, "Why do you want to go?"

The captain reflected, changed his attitude three times, and decided ultimately that he didn't know. He seemed greatly ashamed. The attorney, looking at him, saw that he had eyes that resembled a lambkin's eyes.

"Glory?" said the attorney at last.

"No-o," said the captain.

"Pay?"

"No-o. Not that so much."

"Think they'll give you a land grant when they win out?"

"No; never thought."

"No glory; no immense pay; no land grant. What are you going for, then?"

"Well, I don't know," said the captain, with his glance on the floor and shifting his position again. "I don't know. I guess it's just for fun mostly." The attorney asked him out to have a drink.

When he stood on the bridge of his out-going steamer, the attorney saw him again. His shore meekness and uncertainty were gone. He was clear-eyed and strong, aroused like a mastiff at night. He took his cigar out of his mouth and yelled some sudden language at the deck.

This steamer had about her a quality of unholy mediæval disrepair, which is usually accounted the principal prerogative of the United States Revenue Marine. There is many a seaworthy ice-house if she were a good ship. She swashed through the seas as genially as an old wooden clock, burying her head under waves that came only like children at play, and, on board, it cost a ducking to go from anywhere to anywhere.

The captain had commanded vessels that shore-people thought were liners; but when a man gets the ant of desire-to-see-what-it's-like stirring in his heart, he will wallow out to sea in a pail. The thing surpasses a man's love for his sweetheart. The great tank-steamer Thunder-Voice had long been Flanagan's sweetheart, but he was far happier off Hatteras watching this wretched little portmanteau boom down the slant of a wave.

The crew scraped acquaintance one with another gradually. Each man came ultimately to ask his neighbour what particular turn of ill-fortune or inherited deviltry caused him to try this voyage. When one frank, bold man saw another frank, bold man aboard, he smiled, and they became friends. There was not a mind on board the ship that was not fastened to the dangers of the coast of Cuba, and taking wonder at this prospect and delight in it. Still, in jovial moments they termed each other accursed idiots.

At first there was some trouble in the engine-room, where there were many steel animals, for the most part painted red and in other places very shiny—bewildering, complex, incomprehensible to any one who don't care, usually thumping, thumping, thumping with the monotony of a snore.

It seems that this engine was as whimsical as a gas-meter. The chief engineer was a fine old fellow with a grey moustache, but the engine told him that it didn't intend to budge until it felt better. He came to the bridge and said, "The blamed old thing has laid down on us, sir."

"Who was on duty?" roared the captain.

"The second, sir."

"Why didn't he call you?"

"Don't know, sir." Later the stokers had occasion to thank the stars that they were not second engineers.

The Foundling was soundly thrashed by the waves for loitering while the captain and the engineers fought the obstinate machinery. During this wait on the sea, the first gloom came to the faces of the company. The ocean is wide, and a ship is a small place for the feet, and an ill ship is worriment. Even when she was again under way, the gloom was still upon the crew. From time to time men went to the engine-room doors, and looking down, wanted to ask questions of the chief engineer, who slowly prowled to and fro, and watched with careful eye his red-painted mysteries. No man wished to have a companion know that he was anxious, and so questions were caught at the lips. Perhaps none commented save the first mate, who remarked to the captain, "Wonder what the bally old thing will do, sir, when we're chased by a Spanish cruiser?"

The captain merely grinned. Later he looked over the side and said to himself with scorn, "Sixteen knots! sixteen knots! Sixteen hinges on the inner gates of Hades! Sixteen knots! Seven is her gait, and nine if you crack her up to it."

There may never be a captain whose crew can't sniff his misgivings. They scent it as a herd scents the menace far through the trees and over the ridges. A captain that does not know that he is on a foundering ship sometimes can take his men to tea and buttered toast twelve minutes before the disaster, but let him fret for a moment in the loneliness of his cabin, and in no time it affects the liver of a distant and sensitive seaman. Even as Flanagan reflected on the Foundling, viewing her as a filibuster, word arrived that a winter of discontent had come to the stoke-room.

The captain knew that it requires sky to give a man courage. He sent for a stoker and talked to him on the bridge. The man, standing under the sky, instantly and shamefacedly denied all knowledge of the business; nevertheless, a jaw had presently to be broken by a fist because the Foundling could only steam nine knots, and because the stoke-room has no sky, no wind, no bright horizon.

When the Foundling was somewhere off Savannah a blow came from the north-east, and the steamer, headed south-east, rolled like a boiling potato. The first mate was a fine officer, and so a wave crashed him into the deck-house and broke his arm. The cook was a good cook, and so the heave of the ship flung him heels over head with a pot of boiling water, and caused him to lose interest in everything save his legs. "By the piper," said Flanagan to himself, "this filibustering is no trick with cards."

Later there was more trouble in the stoke-room. All the stokers participated save the one with a broken jaw, who had become discouraged. The captain had an excellent chest development. When he went aft, roaring, it was plain that a man could beat carpets with a voice like that one.

II

One night the Foundling was off the southern coast of Florida, and running at half-speed towards the shore. The captain was on the bridge. "Four flashes at intervals of one minute," he said to himself, gazing steadfastly towards the beach. Suddenly a yellow eye opened in the black face of the night, and looked at the Foundling and closed again. The captain studied his watch and the shore. Three times more the eye opened and looked at the Foundling and closed again. The captain called to the vague figures on the deck below him. "Answer it." The flash of a light from the bow of the steamer displayed for a moment in golden colour the crests of the inriding waves.

The Foundling lay to and waited. The long swells rolled her gracefully, and her two stub masts reaching into the darkness swung with the solemnity of batons timing a dirge. When the ship had left Boston she had been as encrusted with ice as a Dakota stage-driver's beard, but now the gentle wind of Florida softly swayed the lock on the forehead of the coatless Flanagan, and he lit a new cigar without troubling to make a shield of his hands.

Finally a dark boat came plashing over the waves. As it came very near, the captain leaned forward and perceived that the men in her rowed like seamstresses, and at the same time a voice hailed him in bad English. "It's a dead sure connection," said he to himself.

At sea, to load two hundred thousand rounds of rifle ammunition, seven hundred and fifty rifles, two rapid-fire field guns with a hundred shells, forty bundles of machetes, and a hundred pounds of dynamite, from yawls, and by men who are not born stevedores, and in a heavy ground swell, and with the searchlight of a United States cruiser sometimes flashing like lightning in the sky to the southward, is no business for a Sunday-school class. When at last the Foundling was steaming for the open over the grey sea at dawn, there was not a man of the forty come aboard from the Florida shore, nor of the fifteen sailed from Boston, who was not glad, standing with his hair matted to his forehead with sweat, smiling at the broad wake of the Foundling and the dim streak on the horizon which was Florida.

But there is a point of the compass in these waters men call the north-east. When the strong winds come from that direction they kick up a turmoil that is not good for a Foundling stuffed with coals and war-stores. In the gale which came, this ship was no more than a drunken soldier.

The Cuban leader, standing on the bridge with the captain, was presently informed that of his men, thirty-nine out of a possible thirty-nine were sea-sick. And in truth they were sea-sick. There are degrees in this complaint, but that matter was waived between them. They were all sick to the limits. They strewed the deck in every posture of human anguish, and when the Foundling ducked and water came sluicing down from the bows, they let it sluice. They were satisfied if they could keep their heads clear of the wash; and if they could not keep their heads clear of the wash, they didn't care. Presently the Foundling swung her course to the south-east, and the waves pounded her broadside. The patriots were all ordered below decks, and there they howled and measured their misery one against another. All day the Foundling plopped and floundered over a blazing bright meadow of an ocean whereon the white foam was like flowers.

The captain on the bridge mused and studied the bare horizon. "Hell!" said he to himself, and the word was more in amazement than in indignation or sorrow. "Thirty-nine sea-sick passengers, the mate with a broken arm, a stoker with a broken jaw, the cook with a pair of scalded legs, and an engine likely to be taken with all these diseases, if not more! If I get back to a home port with a spoke of the wheel gripped in my hands, it'll be fair luck!"

There is a kind of corn-whisky bred in Florida which the natives declare is potent in the proportion of seven fights to a drink. Some of the Cuban volunteers had had the forethought to bring a small quantity of this whisky aboard with them, and being now in the fire-room and sea-sick, feeling that they would not care to drink liquor for two or three years to come, they gracefully tendered their portions to the stokers. The stokers accepted these gifts without avidity, but with a certain earnestness of manner.

As they were stokers, and toiling, the whirl of emotion was delayed, but it arrived ultimately, and with emphasis. One stoker called another stoker a weird name, and the latter, righteously inflamed at it, smote his mate with an iron shovel, and the man fell headlong over a heap of coal, which crashed gently while piece after piece rattled down upon the deck.

A third stoker was providently enraged at the scene, and assailed the second stoker. They fought for some moments, while the sea-sick Cubans sprawled on the deck watched with languid rolling glances the ferocity of this scuffle. One was so indifferent to the strategic importance of the space he occupied that he was kicked on the shins.

When the second engineer came to separating the combatants, he was sincere in his efforts, and he came near to disabling them for life.

The captain said, "I'll go down there and——" But the leader of the Cubans restrained him. "No, no," he cried, "you must not. We must treat them like children, very gently, all the time, you see, or else when we get back to a United States port they will—what you call? Spring? Yes, spring the whole business. We must—jolly them, you see?"

"You mean," said the captain thoughtfully, "they are likely to get mad, and give the expedition dead away when we reach port again unless we blarney them now?"

"Yes, yes," cried the Cuban leader, "unless we are so very gentle with them they will make many troubles afterwards for us in the newspapers and then in court."

"Well, but I won't have my crew——" began the captain.

"But you must," interrupted the Cuban, "you must. It is the only thing. You are like the captain of a pirate ship. You see? Only you can't throw them overboard like him. You see?"

"Hum," said the captain, "this here filibustering business has got a lot to it when you come to look it over."

He called the fighting stokers to the bridge, and the three came, meek and considerably battered. He was lecturing them soundly but sensibly, when he suddenly tripped a sentence and cried—"Here! Where's that other fellow? How does it come he wasn't in the fight?"

The row of stokers cried at once eagerly, "He's hurt, sir. He's got a broken jaw, sir."

"So he has; so he has," murmured the captain, much embarrassed.

And because of all these affairs, the Foundling steamed toward Cuba with its crew in a sling, if one may be allowed to speak in that way.

III

At night the Foundling approached the coast like a thief. Her lights were muffled, so that from the deck the sea shone with its own radiance, like the faint shimmer of some kinds of silk. The men on deck spoke in whispers, and even down in the fire-room the hidden stokers working before the blood-red furnace doors used no words and walked on tip-toe. The stars were out in the blue-velvet sky, and their light with the soft shine of the sea caused the coast to appear black as the side of a coffin. The surf boomed in low thunder on the distant beach.

The Foundling's engines ceased their thumping for a time. She glided quietly forward until a bell chimed faintly in the engine-room. Then she paused with a flourish of phosphorescent waters.

"Give the signal," said the captain. Three times a flash of light went from the bow. There was a moment of waiting. Then an eye like the one on the coast of Florida opened and closed, opened and closed, opened and closed. The Cubans, grouped in a great shadow on deck, burst into a low chatter of delight. A hiss from their leader silenced them.

"Well?" said the captain.

"All right," said the leader.

At the giving of the word it was not apparent that any one on board of the Foundling had ever been sea-sick. The boats were lowered swiftly— too swiftly. Boxes of cartridges were dragged from the hold and passed over the side with a rapidity that made men in the boats exclaim against it. They were being bombarded. When a boat headed for shore its rowers pulled like madmen. The captain paced slowly to and fro on the bridge. In the engine-room the engineers stood at their station, and in the stoke-hold the firemen fidgeted silently around the furnace doors.

On the bridge Flanagan reflected. "Oh, I don't know!" he observed. "This filibustering business isn't so bad. Pretty soon it'll be off to sea again with nothing to do but some big lying when I get into port."

In one of the boats returning from shore came twelve Cuban officers, the greater number of them convalescing from wounds, while two or three of them had been ordered to America on commissions from the insurgents. The captain welcomed them, and assured them of a speedy and safe voyage.

Presently he went again to the bridge and scanned the horizon. The sea was lonely like the spaces amid the suns. The captain grinned and softly smote his chest. "It's dead easy," he said.

It was near the end of the cargo, and the men were breathing like spent horses, although their elation grew with each moment, when suddenly a voice spoke from the sky. It was not a loud voice, but the quality of it brought every man on deck to full stop and motionless, as if they had all been changed to wax. "Captain," said the man at the masthead, "there's a light to the west'ard, sir. Think it's a steamer, sir."

There was a still moment until the captain called, "Well, keep your eye on it now." Speaking to the deck, he said, "Go ahead with your unloading."

The second engineer went to the galley to borrow a tin cup. "Hear the news, second?" asked the cook. "Steamer coming up from the west'ard."

"Gee!" said the second engineer. In the engine-room he said to the chief, "Steamer coming up from the west'ard, sir." The chief engineer began to test various little machines with which his domain was decorated. Finally he addressed the stoke-room. "Boys, I want you to look sharp now. There's a steamer coming up to the west'ard."

"All right, sir," said the stoke-room.

From time to time the captain hailed the masthead. "How is she now?"

"Seems to be coming down on us pretty fast, sir."

The Cuban leader came anxiously to the captain. "Do you think we can save all the cargo? It is rather delicate business. No?"

"Go ahead," said Flanagan. "Fire away! I'll wait."

There continued the hurried shuffling of feet on deck, and the low cries of the men unloading the cargo. In the engine-room the chief and his assistant were staring at the gong. In the stoke-room the firemen breathed through their teeth. A shovel slipped from where it leaned against the side and banged on the floor. The stokers started and looked around quickly.

Climbing to the rail and holding on to a stay, the captain gazed westward. A light had raised out of the deep. After watching this light for a time he called to the Cuban leader. "Well, as soon as you're ready now, we might as well be skipping out."

Finally, the Cuban leader told him, "Well, this is the last load. As soon as the boats come back you can be off."

"Shan't wait for all the boats," said the captain. "That fellow is too close." As the second boat came aboard, the Foundling turned, and like a black shadow stole seaward to cross the bows of the oncoming steamer. "Waited about ten minutes too long," said the captain to himself.

Suddenly the light in the west vanished. "Hum!" said Flanagan, "he's up to some meanness." Every one outside of the engine-rooms was set on watch. The Foundling, going at full speed into the north-east, slashed a wonderful trail of blue silver on the dark bosom of the sea.

A man on deck cried out hurriedly, "There she is, sir." Many eyes searched the western gloom, and one after another the glances of the men found a tiny shadow on the deep with a line of white beneath it. "He couldn't be heading better if he had a line to us," said Flanagan.

There was a thin flash of red in the darkness. It was long and keen like a crimson rapier. A short, sharp report sounded, and then a shot whined swiftly in the air and blipped into the sea. The captain had been about to take a bite of plug tobacco at the beginning of this incident, and his arm was raised. He remained like a frozen figure while the shot whined, and then, as it blipped into the sea, his hand went to his mouth and he bit the plug. He looked wide-eyed at the shadow with its line of white.

The senior Cuban officer came hurriedly to the bridge. "It is no good to surrender," he cried. "They would only shoot or hang all of us."

There was another thin red flash and a report. A loud whirring noise passed over the ship.

"I'm not going to surrender," said the captain, hanging with both hands to the rail. He appeared like a man whose traditions of peace are clinched in his heart. He was as astonished as if his hat had turned into a dog. Presently he wheeled quickly and said—"What kind of a gun is that?"

"It is a one-pounder," cried the Cuban officer. "The boat is one of those little gunboats made from a yacht. You see?"

"Well, if it's only a yawl, he'll sink us in five more minutes," said Flanagan. For a moment he looked helplessly off at the horizon. His under-jaw hung low. But a moment later, something touched him, like a stiletto point of inspiration. He leaped to the pilothouse and roared at the man at the wheel. The Foundling sheered suddenly to starboard, made a clumsy turn, and Flanagan was bellowing through the tube to the engine-room before everybody discovered that the old basket was heading straight for the Spanish gun-boat. The ship lunged forward like a draught-horse on the gallop.

This strange manoeuvre by the Foundling first dealt consternation on board of the Foundling. Men instinctively crouched on the instant, and then swore their supreme oath, which was unheard by their own ears.

Later the manoeuvre of the Foundling dealt consternation on board of the gunboat. She had been going victoriously forward dim-eyed from the fury of her pursuit. Then this tall threatening shape had suddenly loomed over her like a giant apparition.

The people on board the Foundling heard panic shouts, hoarse orders. The little gunboat was paralyzed with astonishment.

Suddenly Flanagan yelled with rage and sprang for the wheel. The helmsman had turned his eyes away. As the captain whirled the wheel far to starboard he heard a crunch as the Foundling, lifted on a wave, smashed her shoulder against the gunboat, and he saw shooting past a little launch sort of a thing with men on her that ran this way and that way. The Cuban officers, joined by the cook and a seaman, emptied their revolvers into the surprised terror of the seas.

There was naturally no pursuit. Under comfortable speed the Foundling stood to the northwards.

The captain went to his berth chuckling. "There, by God!" he said. "There now!"

IV

When Flanagan came again on deck, the first mate, his arm in a sling, walked the bridge. Flanagan was smiling a wide smile. The bridge of the Foundling was dipping afar and then afar. With each lunge of the little steamer the water seethed and boomed alongside, and the spray dashed high and swiftly.

"Well," said Flanagan, inflating himself, "we've had a great deal of a time, and we've come through it all right, and thank Heaven it is all over."

The sky in the north-east was of a dull brick-red in tone, shaded here and there by black masses that billowed out in some fashion from the flat heavens.

"Look there," said the mate.

"Hum!" said the captain. "Looks like a blow, don't it?"

Later the surface of the water rippled and flickered in the preliminary wind. The sea had become the colour of lead. The swashing sound of the waves on the sides of the Foundling was now provided with some manner of ominous significance. The men's shouts were hoarse.

A squall struck the Foundling on her starboard quarter, and she leaned under the force of it as if she were never to return to the even keel. "I'll be glad when we get in," said the mate. "I'm going to quit then. I've got enough."

"Hell!" said the beaming Flanagan.

The steamer crawled on into the north-west. The white water, sweeping out from her, deadened the chug-chug-chug of the tired old engines.

Once, when the boat careened, she laid her shoulder flat on the sea and rested in that manner. The mate, looking down the bridge, which slanted more than a coal-shute, whistled softly to himself. Slowly, heavily, the Foundling arose to meet another sea.

At night waves thundered mightily on the bows of the steamer, and water lit with the beautiful phosphorescent glamour went boiling and howling along deck.

By good fortune the chief engineer crawled safely, but utterly drenched, to the galley for coffee. "Well, how goes it, chief?" said the cook, standing with his fat arms folded in order to prove that he could balance himself under any conditions.

The engineer shook his head dejectedly. "This old biscuit-box will never see port again. Why, she'll fall to pieces."

Finally at night the captain said, "Launch the boats." The Cubans hovered about him. "Is the ship going to sink?" The captain addressed them politely. "Gentlemen, we are in trouble, but all I ask of you is that you just do what I tell you, and no harm will come to anybody."

The mate directed the lowering of the first boat, and the men performed this task with all decency, like people at the side of a grave.

A young oiler came to the captain. "The chief sends word, sir, that the water is almost up to the fires."

"Keep at it as long as you can."

"Keep at it as long as we can, sir?"

Flanagan took the senior Cuban officer to the rail, and, as the steamer sheered high on a great sea, showed him a yellow dot on the horizon. It was smaller than a needle when its point is towards you.

"There," said the captain. The wind-driven spray was lashing his face. "That's Jupiter Light on the Florida coast. Put your men in the boat we've just launched, and the mate will take you to that light."

Afterwards Flanagan turned to the chief engineer. "We can never beach," said the old man. "The stokers have got to quit in a minute." Tears were in his eyes.

The Foundling was a wounded thing. She lay on the water with gasping engines, and each wave resembled her death-blow.

Now the way of a good ship on the sea is finer than sword-play. But this is when she is alive. If a time comes that the ship dies, then her way is the way of a floating old glove, and she has that much vim, spirit, buoyancy. At this time many men on the Foundling suddenly came to know that they were clinging to a corpse.

The captain went to the stoke-room, and what he saw as he swung down the companion suddenly turned him hesitant and dumb. Water was swirling to and fro with the roll of the ship, fuming greasily around half-strangled machinery that still attempted to perform its duty. Steam arose from the water, and through its clouds shone the red glare of the dying fires. As for the stokers, death might have been with silence in this room. One lay in his berth, his hands under his head, staring moodily at the wall. One sat near the foot of the companion, his face hidden in his arms. One leaned against the side and gazed at the snarling water as it rose, and its mad eddies among the machinery. In the unholy red light and grey mist of this stifling dim Inferno they were strange figures with their silence and their immobility. The wretched Foundling groaned deeply as she lifted, and groaned deeply as she sank into the trough, while hurried waves then thundered over her with the noise of landslides. The terrified machinery was making gestures.

But Flanagan took control of himself suddenly. Then he stirred the fire-room. The stillness had been so unearthly that he was not altogether inapprehensive of strange and grim deeds when he charged into them; but precisely as they had submitted to the sea so they submitted to Flanagan. For a moment they rolled their eyes like hurt cows, but they obeyed the Voice. The situation simply required a Voice.

When the captain returned to the deck the hue of this fire-room was in his mind, and then he understood doom and its weight and complexion.

When finally the Foundling sank she shifted and settled as calmly as an animal curls down in the bush grass. Away over the waves two bobbing boats paused to witness this quiet death. It was a slow manoeuvre, altogether without the pageantry of uproar, but it flashed pallor into the faces of all men who saw it, and they groaned when they said, "There she goes!" Suddenly the captain whirled and knocked his hand on the gunwale. He sobbed for a time, and then he sobbed and swore also.

There was a dance at the Imperial Inn. During the evening some irresponsible young men came from the beach bringing the statement that several boatloads of people had been perceived off shore. It was a charming dance, and none cared to take time to believe this tale. The fountain in the court-yard splashed softly, and couple after couple paraded through the aisles of palms, where lamps with red shades threw a rose light upon the gleaming leaves. The band played its waltzes slumberously, and its music came faintly to the people among the palms.

Sometimes a woman said—"Oh, it is not really true, is it, that there was a wreck out at sea?"

A man usually said—"No, of course not."

At last, however, a youth came violently from the beach. He was triumphant in manner. "They're out there," he cried. "A whole boat-load!" He received eager attention, and he told all that he supposed. His news destroyed the dance. After a time the band was playing beautifully to space. The guests had hurried to the beach. One little girl cried, "Oh, mamma, may I go too?" Being refused permission she pouted.

As they came from the shelter of the great hotel, the wind was blowing swiftly from the sea, and at intervals a breaker shone livid. The women shuddered, and their bending companions seized the opportunity to draw the cloaks closer.

"Oh, dear!" said a girl; "supposin' they were out there drowning while we were dancing!"

"Oh, nonsense!" said her younger brother; "that don't happen."

"Well, it might, you know, Roger. How can you tell?"

A man who was not her brother gazed at her then with profound admiration. Later, she complained of the damp sand, and, drawing back her skirts, looked ruefully at her little feet.

A mother's son was venturing too near to the water in his interest and excitement. Occasionally she cautioned and reproached him from the background.

Save for the white glare of the breakers, the sea was a great wind-crossed void. From the throng of charming women floated the perfume of many flowers. Later there floated to them a body with a calm face of an Irish type. The expedition of the Foundling will never be historic.

HORSES

Richardson pulled up his horse, and looked back over the trail where the crimson serape of his servant flamed amid the dusk of the mesquit. The hills in the west were carved into peaks, and were painted the most profound blue. Above them the sky was of that marvellous tone of green—like still, sun-shot water—which people denounce in pictures.

José was muffled deep in his blanket, and his great toppling sombrero was drawn low over his brow. He shadowed his master along the dimming trail in the fashion of an assassin. A cold wind of the impending night swept over the wilderness of mesquit.

"Man," said Richardson in lame Mexican as the servant drew near, "I want eat! I want sleep! Understand—no? Quickly! Understand?"

"Si, señor," said José, nodding. He stretched one arm out of his blanket and pointed a yellow finger into the gloom. "Over there, small village. Si, señor."

They rode forward again. Once the American's horse shied and breathed quiveringly at something which he saw or imagined in the darkness, and the rider drew a steady, patient rein, and leaned over to speak tenderly as if he were addressing a frightened woman. The sky had faded to white over the mountains, and the plain was a vast, pointless ocean of black.

Suddenly some low houses appeared squatting amid the bushes. The horsemen rode into a hollow until the houses rose against the sombre sundown sky, and then up a small hillock, causing these habitations to sink like boats in the sea of shadow.

A beam of red firelight fell across the trail. Richardson sat sleepily on his horse while his servant quarrelled with somebody—a mere voice in the gloom—over the price of bed and board. The houses about him were for the most part like tombs in their whiteness and silence, but there were scudding black figures that seemed interested in his arrival.

José came at last to the horses' heads, and the American slid stiffly from his seat. He muttered a greeting, as with his spurred feet he clicked into the adobe house that confronted him. The brown stolid face of a woman shone in the light of the fire. He seated himself on the earthen floor and blinked drowsily at the blaze. He was aware that the woman was clinking earthenware, and hieing here and everywhere in the manoeuvres of the housewife. From a dark corner there came the sound of two or three snores twining together.

The woman handed him a bowl of tortillas. She was a submissive creature, timid and large-eyed. She gazed at his enormous silver spurs, his large and impressive revolver, with the interest and admiration of the highly-privileged cat of the adage. When he ate, she seemed transfixed off there in the gloom, her white teeth shining.

José entered, staggering under two Mexican saddles, large enough for building-sites. Richardson decided to smoke a cigarette, and then changed his mind. It would be much finer to go to sleep. His blanket hung over his left shoulder, furled into a long pipe of cloth, according to the Mexican fashion. By doffing his sombrero, unfastening his spurs and his revolver belt, he made himself ready for the slow, blissful twist into the blanket. Like a cautious man he lay close to the wall, and all his property was very near his hand.

The mesquit brush burned long. José threw two gigantic wings of shadow as he flapped his blanket about him—first across his chest under his arms, and then around his neck and across his chest again—this time over his arms, with the end tossed on his right shoulder. A Mexican thus snugly enveloped can nevertheless free his fighting arm in a beautifully brisk way, merely shrugging his shoulder as he grabs for the weapon at his belt. (They always wear their serapes in this manner.)

The firelight smothered the rays which, streaming from a moon as large as a drum-head, were struggling at the open door. Richardson heard from the plain the fine, rhythmical trample of the hoofs of hurried horses. He went to sleep wondering who rode so fast and so late. And in the deep silence the pale rays of the moon must have prevailed against the red spears of the fire until the room was slowly flooded to its middle with a rectangle of silver light.

308

Richardson was awakened by the sound of a guitar. It was badly played—in this land of Mexico, from which the romance of the instrument ascends to us like a perfume. The guitar was groaning and whining like a badgered soul. A noise of scuffling feet accompanied the music. Sometimes laughter arose, and often the voices of men saying bitter things to each other, but always the guitar cried on, the treble sounding as if some one were beating iron, and the bass humming like bees. "Damn it—they're having a dance," he muttered, fretfully. He heard two men quarrelling in short, sharp words, like pistol shots; they were calling each other worse names than common people know in other countries. He wondered why the noise was so loud. Raising his head from his saddle pillow, he saw, with the help of the valiant moonbeams, a blanket hanging flat against the wall at the further end of the room. Being of opinion that it concealed a door, and remembering that Mexican drink made men very drunk, he pulled his revolver closer to him and prepared for sudden disaster.

Richardson was dreaming of his far and beloved north.

"Well, I would kill him, then!"

"No, you must not!"

"Yes, I will kill him! Listen! I will ask this American beast for his beautiful pistol and spurs and money and saddle, and if he will not give them—you will see!"

"But these Americans—they are a strange people. Look out, señor."

Then twenty voices took part in the discussion. They rose in quavering shrillness, as from men badly drunk. Richardson felt the skin draw tight around his mouth, and his knee-joints turned to bread. He slowly came to a sitting posture, glaring at the motionless blanket at the far end of the room. This stiff and mechanical movement, accomplished entirely by the muscles of the waist, must have looked like the rising of a corpse in the wan moonlight, which gave everything a hue of the grave.

My friend, take my advice and never be executed by a hangman who doesn't talk the English language. It, or anything that resembles it, is the most difficult of deaths. The tumultuous emotions of Richardson's terror destroyed that slow and careful process of thought by means of which he understood Mexican. Then he used his instinctive comprehension of the first and universal language, which is tone. Still, it is disheartening not to be able to understand the detail of threats against the blood of your body.

Suddenly, the clamour of voices ceased. There was a silence—a silence of decision. The blanket was flung aside, and the red light of a torch flared into the room. It was held high by a fat, round-faced Mexican, whose little snake-like moustache was as black as his eyes, and whose eyes were black as jet. He was insane with the wild rage of a man whose liquor is dully burning at his brain. Five or six of his fellows crowded after him. The guitar, which had been thrummed doggedly during the time of the high words, now suddenly stopped. They contemplated each other. Richardson sat very straight and still, his right hand lost in his blanket. The Mexicans jostled in the light of the torch, their eyes blinking and glittering.

The fat one posed in the manner of a grandee. Presently his hand dropped to his belt, and from his lips there spun an epithet—a hideous word which often foreshadows knife-blows, a word peculiarly of Mexico, where people have to dig deep to find an insult that has not lost its savour. The American did not move. He was staring at the fat Mexican with a strange fixedness of gaze, not fearful, not dauntless, not anything that could be interpreted. He simply stared.

The fat Mexican must have been disconcerted, for he continued to pose as a grandee, with more and more sublimity, until it would have been easy for him to have fallen over backward. His companions were swaying very drunkenly. They still blinked their little beady eyes at Richardson. Ah, well, sirs, here was a mystery! At the approach of their menacing company, why did not this American cry out and turn pale, or run, or pray them mercy? The animal merely sat still, and stared, and waited for them to begin. Well, evidently he was a great fighter! Or perhaps he was an idiot? Indeed, this was an embarrassing situation, for who was going forward to discover whether he was a great fighter or an idiot?

To Richardson, whose nerves were tingling and twitching like live wires, and whose heart jolted inside him, this pause was a long horror; and for these men, who could so frighten him, there began to swell in him a fierce hatred—a hatred that made him long to be capable of fighting all of them, a hatred that made him capable of fighting all of them. A 44-calibre revolver can make a hole large enough for little boys to shoot marbles through; and there was a certain fat Mexican with a moustache like a snake who came extremely near to have eaten his last tomale merely because he frightened a man too much.

José had slept the first part of the night in his fashion, his body hunched into a heap, his legs crooked, his head touching his knees. Shadows had obscured him from the sight of the invaders. At this point he arose, and began to prowl quakingly over toward Richardson, as if he meant to hide behind him.

Of a sudden the fat Mexican gave a howl of glee. José had come within the torch's circle of light. With roars of ferocity the whole group of Mexicans pounced on the American's servant. He shrank shuddering away from them, beseeching by every device of word and gesture. They pushed him this way and that. They beat him with their fists. They stung him with their curses. As he grovelled on his knees, the fat Mexican took him by the throat and said—"I am going to kill you!" And continually they turned their eyes to see if they were to succeed in causing the initial demonstration by the American. But he looked on impassively. Under the blanket his fingers were clenched, as iron, upon the handle of his revolver.

Here suddenly two brilliant clashing chords from the guitar were heard, and a woman's voice, full of laughter and confidence, cried from without—"Hello! hello! Where are you?" The lurching company of Mexicans instantly paused and looked at the ground. One said, as he stood with his legs wide apart in order to balance himself—"It is the girls. They have come!" He screamed in answer to the question of the woman—"Here!" And without waiting he started on a pilgrimage toward the blanket-covered door. One could now hear a number of female voices giggling and chattering.

Two other Mexicans said—"Yes, it is the girls! Yes!" They also started quietly away. Even the fat Mexican's ferocity seemed to be affected. He looked uncertainly at the still immovable American. Two of his friends grasped him gaily—"Come, the girls are here! Come!" He cast another glower at Richardson. "But this——," he began. Laughing, his comrades hustled him toward the door. On its threshold, and holding back the blanket, with one hand, he turned his yellow face with a last challenging glare toward the American. José, bewailing his state in little sobs of utter despair and woe, crept to Richardson and huddled near his knee. Then the cries of the Mexicans meeting the girls were heard, and the guitar burst out in joyous humming.

The moon clouded, and but a faint square of light fell through the open main door of the house. The coals of the fire were silent, save for occasional sputters. Richardson did not change his position. He remained staring at the blanket which hid the strategic door in the far end. At his knees José was arguing, in a low, aggrieved tone, with the saints. Without, the Mexicans laughed and danced, and—it would appear from the sound—drank more.

In the stillness and the night Richardson sat wondering if some serpent-like Mexican were sliding towards him in the darkness, and if the first thing he knew of it would be the deadly sting of a knife. "Sssh," he whispered, to José. He drew his revolver from under the blanket, and held it on his leg. The blanket over the door fascinated him. It was a vague form, black and unmoving. Through the opening it shielded were to come, probably, threats, death. Sometimes he thought he saw it move. As grim white sheets, the black and silver of coffins, all the panoply of death, affect us, because of that which they hide, so this blanket, dangling before a hole in an adobe wall, was to Richardson a horrible emblem, and a horrible thing in itself. In his present mood he could not have been brought to touch it with his finger.

The celebrating Mexicans occasionally howled in song. The guitarist played with speed and enthusiasm. Richardson longed to run. But in this vibrating and threatening gloom his terror convinced him that a move on his part would be a signal for the pounce of death. José, crouching abjectly, mumbled now and again. Slowly, and ponderous as stars, the minutes went.

Suddenly Richardson thrilled and started. His breath for a moment left him. In sleep his nerveless fingers had allowed his revolver to fall and clang upon the hard floor. He grabbed it up hastily, and his glance swept apprehensively over the room. A chill blue light of dawn was in the place. Every outline was slowly growing; detail was following detail. The dread blanket did not move. The riotous company had gone or fallen silent. He felt the effect of this cold dawn in his blood. The candour of breaking day brought his nerve. He touched José. "Come," he said. His servant lifted his lined yellow face, and comprehended. Richardson buckled on his spurs and strode up; José obediently lifted the two great saddles. Richardson held two bridles and a blanket on his left arm; in his right hand he had his revolver. They sneaked toward the door.

The man who said that spurs jingled was insane. Spurs have a mellow clash—clash—clash. Walking in spurs—notably Mexican spurs—you remind yourself vaguely of a telegraphic linesman. Richardson was inexpressibly shocked when he came to walk. He sounded to himself like a pair of cymbals. He would have known of this if he had reflected; but then, he was escaping, not reflecting. He made a gesture of despair, and from under the two saddles José tried to make one of hopeless horror. Richardson stooped, and with shaking fingers unfastened the spurs. Taking them in his left hand, he picked up his revolver, and they slunk on toward the door. On the threshold he looked back. In a corner he saw, watching him with large eyes, the Indian man and woman who had been his hosts. Throughout the night they had made no sign, and now they neither spoke nor moved. Yet Richardson thought he detected meek satisfaction at his departure.

The street was still and deserted. In the eastern sky there was a lemon-coloured patch. José had picketed the horses at the side of the house. As the two men came round the corner Richardson's beast set up a whinny of welcome. The little horse had heard them coming. He stood facing them, his ears cocked forward, his eyes bright with welcome.

Richardson made a frantic gesture, but the horse, in his happiness at the appearance of his friends, whinnied with enthusiasm. The American felt that he could have strangled his well-beloved steed. Upon the threshold of safety, he was being betrayed by his horse, his friend! He felt the same hate that he would have felt for a dragon. And yet, as he glanced wildly about him, he could see nothing stirring in the street, nothing at the doors of the tomb-like houses.

José had his own saddle-girth and both bridles buckled in a moment. He curled the picket-ropes with a few sweeps of his arm. The American's fingers, however, were shaking so that he could hardly buckle the girth. His hands were in invisible mittens. He was wondering, calculating, hoping about his horse. He knew the little animal's willingness and courage under all circumstances up to this time; but then—here it was different. Who could tell if some wretched instance of equine perversity was not about to develop? Maybe the little fellow would not feel like smoking over the plain at express speed this morning, and so he would rebel, and kick, and be wicked. Maybe he would be without feeling of interest, and run listlessly. All riders who have had to hurry in the saddle know what it is to be on a horse who does not understand the dramatic situation. Riding a lame sheep is bliss to it. Richardson, fumbling furiously at the girth, thought of these things.

Presently he had it fastened. He swung into the saddle, and as he did so his horse made a mad jump forward. The spurs of José scratched and tore the flanks of his great black beast, and side by side the two horses raced down the village street. The American heard his horse breathe a quivering sigh of excitement. Those four feet skimmed. They were as light as fairy puff balls. The houses glided past in a moment, and the great, clear, silent plain appeared like a pale blue sea of mist and wet bushes. Above the mountains the colours of the sunlight were like the first tones, the opening chords of the mighty hymn of the morning.

The American looked down at his horse. He felt in his heart the first thrill of confidence. The little animal, unurged and quite tranquil, moving his ears this way and that way with an air of interest in the scenery, was nevertheless bounding into the eye of the breaking day with the speed of a frightened antelope. Richardson, looking down, saw the long, fine reach of forelimb as steady as steel machinery. As the ground reeled past, the long, dried grasses hissed, and cactus plants were dull blurs. A wind whirled the horse's mane over his rider's bridle hand.

José's profile was lined against the pale sky. It was as that of a man who swims alone in an ocean. His eyes glinted like metal, fastened on some unknown point ahead of him, some fabulous place of safety. Occasionally his mouth puckered in a little unheard cry; and his legs, bended back, worked spasmodically as his spurred heels sliced his charger's sides.

Richardson consulted the gloom in the west for signs of a hard-riding, yelling cavalcade. He knew that, whereas his friends the enemy had not attacked him when he had sat still and with apparent calmness confronted them, they would take furiously after him now that he had run from them—now that he had confessed himself the weaker. Their valour would grow like weeds in the spring, and upon discovering his escape they would ride forth dauntless warriors. Sometimes he was sure he saw them. Sometimes he was sure he heard them. Continually looking backward over his shoulder, he studied the purple expanses where the night was marching away. José rolled and shuddered in his saddle, persistently disturbing the stride of the black horse, fretting and worrying him until the white foam flew, and the great shoulders shone like satin from the sweat.

At last, Richardson drew his horse carefully down to a walk. José wished to rush insanely on, but the American spoke to him sternly. As the two paced forward side by side, Richardson's little horse thrust over his soft nose and inquired into the black's condition.

Riding with José was like riding with a corpse. His face resembled a cast in lead. Sometimes he swung forward and almost pitched from his seat. Richardson was too frightened himself to do anything but hate this man for his fear. Finally, he issued a mandate which nearly caused José's eyes to slide out of his head and fall to the ground, like two coins:—"Ride behind me— about fifty paces."

"Señor——" stuttered the servant. "Go," cried the American furiously. He glared at the other and laid his hand on his revolver. José looked at his master wildly. He made a piteous gesture. Then slowly he fell back, watching the hard face of the American for a sign of mercy. But Richardson had resolved in his rage that at any rate he was going to use the eyes and ears of extreme fear to detect the approach of danger; so he established his panic-stricken servant as a sort of outpost.

As they proceeded, he was obliged to watch sharply to see that the servant did not slink forward and join him. When José made beseeching circles in the air with his arm, he replied by menacingly gripping his revolver. José had a revolver too; nevertheless it was very clear in his mind that the revolver was distinctly an American weapon. He had been educated in the Rio Grande country.

Richardson lost the trail once. He was recalled to it by the loud sobs of his servant.

Then at last José came clattering forward, gesticulating and wailing. The little horse sprang to the shoulder of the black. They were off.

Richardson, again looking backward, could see a slanting flare of dust on the whitening plain. He thought that he could detect small moving figures in it.

José's moans and cries amounted to a university course in theology. They broke continually from his quivering lips. His spurs were as motors. They forced the black horse over the plain in great headlong leaps. But under Richardson there was a little insignificant rat-coloured beast who was running apparently with almost as much effort as it takes a bronze statue to stand still. The ground seemed merely something to be touched from time to time with hoofs that were as light as blown leaves. Occasionally Richardson lay back and pulled stoutly at the bridle to keep from abandoning his servant. José harried at his horse's mouth, flopped about in the saddle, and made his two heels beat like flails. The black ran like a horse in despair.

Crimson serapes in the distance resemble drops of blood on the great cloth of plain. Richardson began to dream of all possible chances. Although quite a humane man, he did not once think of his servant. José being a Mexican, it was natural that he should be killed in Mexico; but for himself, a New Yorker———! He remembered all the tales of such races for life, and he thought them badly written.

316

The great black horse was growing indifferent. The jabs of José's spurs no longer caused him to bound forward in wild leaps of pain. José had at last succeeded in teaching him that spurring was to be expected, speed or no speed, and now he took the pain of it dully and stolidly, as an animal who finds that doing his best gains him no respite. José was turned into a raving maniac. He bellowed and screamed, working his arms and his heels like one in a fit. He resembled a man on a sinking ship, who appeals to the ship. Richardson, too, cried madly to the black horse. The spirit of the horse responded to these calls, and quivering and breathing heavily he made a great effort, a sort of a final rush, not for himself apparently, but because he understood that his life's sacrifice, perhaps, had been invoked by these two men who cried to him in the universal tongue. Richardson had no sense of appreciation at this time— he was too frightened; but often now he remembers a certain black horse.

From the rear could be heard a yelling, and once a shot was fired—in the air, evidently. Richardson moaned as he looked back. He kept his hand on his revolver. He tried to imagine the brief tumult of his capture—the flurry of dust from the hoofs of horses pulled suddenly to their haunches, the shrill, biting curses of the men, the ring of the shots, his own last contortion. He wondered, too, if he could not somehow manage to pelt that fat Mexican, just to cure his abominable egotism.

It was José, the terror-stricken, who at last discovered safety. Suddenly he gave a howl of delight and astonished his horse into a new burst of speed. They were on a little ridge at the time, and the American at the top of it saw his servant gallop down the slope and into the arms, so to speak, of a small column of horsemen in grey and silver clothes. In the dim light of the early morning they were as vague as shadows, but Richardson knew them at once for a detachment of Rurales, that crack cavalry corps of the Mexican army which polices the plain so zealously, being of themselves the law and the arm of it—a fierce and swift-moving body that knows little of prevention but much of vengeance. They drew up suddenly, and the rows of great silver-trimmed sombreros bobbed in surprise.

Richardson saw José throw himself from his horse and begin to jabber at the leader. When he arrived he found that his servant had already outlined the entire situation, and was then engaged in describing him, Richardson, as an American señor of vast wealth, who was the friend of almost every governmental potentate within two hundred miles. This seemed profoundly to impress the officer. He bowed gravely to Richardson and smiled significantly at his men, who unslung their carbines.

The little ridge hid the pursuers from view, but the rapid thud of their horses' feet could be heard. Occasionally they yelled and called to each other. Then at last they swept over the brow of the hill, a wild mob of almost fifty drunken horsemen. When they discerned the pale-uniformed Rurales, they were sailing down the slope at top speed.

If toboggans half-way down a hill should suddenly make up their minds to turn round and go back, there would be an effect something like that produced by the drunken horsemen. Richardson saw the Rurales serenely swing their carbines forward, and, peculiar-minded person that he was, felt his heart leap into his throat at the prospective volley. But the officer rode forward alone.

It appeared that the man who owned the best horse in this astonished company was the fat Mexican with the snaky moustache, and, in consequence, this gentleman was quite a distance in the van. He tried to pull up, wheel his horse, and scuttle back over the hill as some of his companions had done, but the officer called to him in a voice harsh with rage. "——!" howled the officer. "This señor is my friend, the friend of my friends. Do you dare pursue him, ——?——!——!——!——!" These dashes represent terrible names, all different, used by the officer.

The fat Mexican simply grovelled on his horse's neck. His face was green: it could be seen that he expected death. The officer stormed with magnificent intensity: "——!——!——!" Finally he sprang from his saddle, and, running to the fat Mexican's side, yelled—"Go!" and kicked the horse in the belly with all his might. The animal gave a mighty leap into the air, and the fat Mexican, with one wretched glance at the contemplative Rurales, aimed his steed for the top of the ridge. Richardson gulped again in expectation of a volley, for— it is said—this is a favourite method for disposing of objectionable people.

The fat, green Mexican also thought that he was to be killed on the run, from the miserable look he cast at the troops. Nevertheless, he was allowed to vanish in a cloud of yellow dust at the ridge-top.

José was exultant, defiant, and, oh! bristling with courage. The black horse was drooping sadly, his nose to the ground. Richardson's little animal, with his ears bent forward, was staring at the horses of the Rurales as if in an intense study. Richardson longed for speech, but he could only bend forward and pat the shining, silken shoulders. The little horse turned his head and looked back gravely.

DEATH AND THE CHILD

I

The peasants who were streaming down the mountain trail had in their sharp terror evidently lost their ability to count. The cattle and the huge round bundles seemed to suffice to the minds of the crowd if there were now two in each case where there had been three. This brown stream poured on with a constant wastage of goods and beasts. A goat fell behind to scout the dried grass and its owner, howling, flogging his donkeys, passed far ahead. A colt, suddenly frightened, made a stumbling charge up the hill-side. The expenditure was always profligate and always unnamed, unnoted. It was as if fear was a river, and this horde had simply been caught in the torrent, man tumbling over beast, beast over man, as helpless in it as the logs that fall and shoulder grindingly through the gorges of a lumber country. It was a freshet that might sear the face of the tall quiet mountain; it might draw a livid line across the land, this downpour of fear with a thousand homes adrift in the current—men, women, babes, animals. From it there arose a constant babble of tongues, shrill, broken, and sometimes choking as from men drowning. Many made gestures, painting their agonies on the air with fingers that twirled swiftly.

The blue bay with its pointed ships and the white town lay below them, distant, flat, serene. There was upon this vista a peace that a bird knows when high in the air it surveys the world, a great calm thing rolling noiselessly toward the end of the mystery. Here on the height one felt the existence of the universe scornfully defining the pain in ten thousand minds. The sky was an arch of stolid sapphire. Even to the mountains raising their mighty shapes from the valley, this headlong rush of the fugitives was too minute. The sea, the sky, and the hills combined in their grandeur to term this misery inconsequent. Then too it sometimes happened that a face seen as it passed on the flood reflected curiously the spirit of them all and still more. One saw then a woman of the opinion of the vaults above the clouds. When a child cried it cried always because of some adjacent misfortune, some discomfort of a pack-saddle or rudeness of an encircling arm. In the dismal melody of this flight there were often sounding chords of apathy. Into these preoccupied countenances, one felt that needles could be thrust without purchasing a scream. The trail wound here and there as the sheep had willed in the making of it.

Although this throng seemed to prove that the whole of humanity was fleeing in one direction—with every tie severed that binds us to the soil—a young man was walking rapidly up the mountain, hastening to a side of the path from time to time to avoid some particularly wide rush of people and cattle. He looked at everything in agitation and pity. Frequently he called admonitions to maniacal fugitives, and at other moments he exchanged strange stares with the imperturbable ones. They seemed to him to wear merely the expressions of so many boulders rolling down the hill. He exhibited wonder and awe with his pitying glances.

Turning once toward the rear, he saw a man in the uniform of a lieutenant of infantry marching the same way. He waited then, subconsciously elate at a prospect of being able to make into words the emotion which heretofore had only been expressed in the flash of eyes and sensitive movements of his flexible mouth. He spoke to the officer in rapid French, waving his arms wildly, and often pointing with a dramatic finger. "Ah, this is too cruel, too cruel, too cruel. Is it not? I did not think it would be as bad as this. I did not think— God's mercy—I did not think at all. And yet I am a Greek. Or at least my father was a Greek. I did not come here to fight. I am really a correspondent, you see? I was to write for an Italian paper. I have been educated in Italy. I have spent nearly all my life in Italy. At the schools and universities! I knew nothing of war! I was a student—a student. I came here merely because my father was a Greek, and for his sake I thought of Greece—I loved Greece. But I did not dream——"

He paused, breathing heavily. His eyes glistened from that soft overflow which comes on occasion to the glance of a young woman. Eager, passionate, profoundly moved, his first words, while facing the procession of fugitives, had been an active definition of his own dimension, his personal relation to men, geography, life. Throughout he had preserved the fiery dignity of a

321

tragedian.

The officer's manner at once deferred to this outburst. "Yes," he said, polite but mournful, "these poor people! These poor people! I do not know what is to become of these poor people."

The young man declaimed again. "I had no dream—I had no dream that it would be like this! This is too cruel! Too cruel! Now I want to be a soldier. Now I want to fight. Now I want to do battle for the land of my father." He made a sweeping gesture into the north-west.

The officer was also a young man, but he was very bronzed and steady. Above his high military collar of crimson cloth with one silver star upon it, appeared a profile stern, quiet, and confident, respecting fate, fearing only opinion. His clothes were covered with dust; the only bright spot was the flame of the crimson collar. At the violent cries of his companion he smiled as if to himself, meanwhile keeping his eyes fixed in a glance ahead.

From a land toward which their faces were bent came a continuous boom of artillery fire. It was sounding in regular measures like the beating of a colossal clock, a clock that was counting the seconds in the lives of the stars, and men had time to die between the ticks. Solemn, oracular, inexorable, the great seconds tolled over the hills as if God fronted this dial rimmed by the horizon. The soldier and the correspondent found themselves silent. The latter in particular was sunk in a great mournfulness, as if he had resolved willy-nilly to swing to the bottom of the abyss where dwell secrets of his kind, and had learned beforehand that all to be met there was cruelty and hopelessness. A strap of his bright new leather leggings came unfastened, and he bowed over it slowly, impressively, as one bending over the grave of a child.

Then suddenly, the reverberations mingled until one could not separate an explosion from another, and into the hubbub came the drawling sound of a leisurely musketry fire. Instantly, for some reason of cadence, the noise was irritating, silly, infantile. This uproar was childish. It forced the nerves to object, to protest against this racket which was as idle as the din of a lad with a drum.

The lieutenant lifted his finger and pointed. He spoke in vexed tones, as if he held the other man personally responsible for the noise. "Well, there!" he said. "If you wish for war you now have an opportunity magnificent."

The correspondent raised himself upon his toes. He tapped his chest with gloomy pride. "Yes! There is war! There is the war I wish to enter. I fling myself in. I am a Greek, a Greek, you understand. I wish to fight for my country. You know the way. Lead me. I offer myself." Struck by a sudden thought he brought a case from his pocket, and extracting a card handed it to the officer with a bow. "My name is Peza," he said simply.

A strange smile passed over the soldier's face. There was pity and pride—the vanity of experience—and contempt in it. "Very well," he said, returning the bow. "If my company is in the middle of the fight I shall be glad for the honour of your companionship. If my company is not in the middle of the fight—I will make other arrangements for you."

Peza bowed once more, very stiffly, and correctly spoke his thanks. On the edge of what he took to be a great venture toward death, he discovered that he was annoyed at something in the lieutenant's tone. Things immediately assumed new and extraordinary proportions. The battle, the great carnival of woe, was sunk at once to an equation with a vexation by a stranger. He wanted to ask the lieutenant what was his meaning. He bowed again majestically; the lieutenant bowed. They flung a shadow of manners, of capering tinsel ceremony across a land that groaned, and it satisfied something within themselves completely.

In the meantime, the river of fleeing villagers had changed to simply a last dropping of belated creatures, who fled past stammering and flinging their hands high. The two men had come to the top of the great hill. Before them was a green plain as level as an inland sea. It swept northward, and merged finally into a length of silvery mist. Upon the near part of this plain, and upon two grey treeless mountains at the side of it, were little black lines from which floated slanting sheets of smoke. It was not a battle to the nerves. One could survey it with equanimity, as if it were a tea-table; but upon Peza's mind it struck a loud clanging blow. It was war. Edified, aghast, triumphant, he paused suddenly, his lips apart. He remembered the pageants of carnage that had marched through the dreams of his childhood. Love he knew that he had confronted, alone, isolated, wondering, an individual, an atom taking the hand of a titanic principle. But, like the faintest breeze on his forehead, he felt here the vibration from the hearts of forty thousand men.

The lieutenant's nostrils were moving. "I must go at once," he said. "I must go at once."

"I will go with you wherever you go," shouted Peza loudly.

A primitive track wound down the side of the mountain, and in their rush they bounded from here to there, choosing risks which in the ordinary caution of man would surely have seemed of remarkable danger. The ardour of the correspondent surpassed the full energy of the soldier. Several times he turned and shouted, "Come on! Come on!"

At the foot of the path they came to a wide road, which extended toward the battle in a yellow and straight line. Some men were trudging wearily to the rear. They were without rifles; their clumsy uniforms were dirty and all awry. They turned eyes dully aglow with fever upon the pair striding toward the battle. Others were bandaged with the triangular kerchief upon which one could still see through bloodstains the little explanatory pictures illustrating the ways to bind various wounds. "Fig. 1."—"Fig. 2."—"Fig. 7." Mingled with the pacing soldiers were peasants, indifferent, capable of smiling, gibbering about the battle, which was to them an ulterior drama. A man was leading a string of three donkeys to the rear, and at intervals he was accosted by wounded or fevered soldiers, from whom he defended his animals with ape-like cries and mad gesticulation. After much chattering they usually subsided gloomily, and allowed him to go with his sleek little beasts unburdened. Finally he encountered a soldier who walked slowly with the assistance of a staff. His head was bound with a wide bandage, grimey from blood and mud. He made application to the peasant, and immediately they were involved in a hideous Levantine discussion. The peasant whined and clamoured, sometimes spitting like a kitten. The wounded soldier jawed on thunderously, his great hands stretched in claw-like graspings over the peasant's head. Once he raised his staff and made threat with it. Then suddenly the row was at an end. The other sick men saw their comrade mount the leading donkey and at once begin to drum with his heels. None attempted to gain the backs of the remaining animals. They gazed after them dully. Finally they saw the caravan outlined for a moment against the sky. The soldier was still waving his arms passionately, having it out with the peasant.

Peza was alive with despair for these men who looked at him with such doleful, quiet eyes. "Ah, my God!" he cried to the lieutenant, "these poor souls! These poor souls!"

The officer faced about angrily. "If you are coming with me there is no time for this." Peza obeyed instantly and with a sudden meekness. In the moment some portion of egotism left him, and he modestly wondered if the universe took cognizance of him to an important degree. This theatre for slaughter, built by the inscrutable needs of the earth, was an enormous affair, and he reflected that the accidental destruction of an individual, Peza by name, would perhaps be nothing at all.

With the lieutenant he was soon walking along behind a series of little crescent-shape trenches, in which were soldiers, tranquilly interested, gossiping with the hum of a tea-party. Although these men were not at this time under fire, he concluded that they were fabulously brave. Else they would not be so comfortable, so at home in their sticky brown trenches. They were certain to be heavily attacked before the day was old. The universities had not taught him to understand this attitude.

At the passing of the young man in very nice tweed, with his new leggings, his new white helmet, his new field-glass case, his new revolver holster, the soiled soldiers turned with the same curiosity which a being in strange garb meets at the corners of streets. He might as well have been promenading a populous avenue. The soldiers volubly discussed his identity.

To Peza there was something awful in the absolute familiarity of each tone, expression, gesture. These men, menaced with battle, displayed the curiosity of the café. Then, on the verge of his great encounter toward death, he found himself extremely embarrassed, composing his face with difficulty, wondering what to do with his hands, like a gawk at a levée.

He felt ridiculous, and also he felt awed, aghast, at these men who could turn their faces from the ominous front and debate his clothes, his business. There was an element which was new born into his theory of war. He was not averse to the brisk pace at which the lieutenant moved along the line.

The roar of fighting was always in Peza's ears. It came from some short hills ahead and to the left. The road curved suddenly and entered a wood. The trees stretched their luxuriant and graceful branches over grassy slopes. A breeze made all this verdure gently rustle and speak in long silken sighs. Absorbed in listening to the hurricane racket from the front, he still remembered that these trees were growing, the grass-blades were extending according to their process. He inhaled a deep breath of moisture and fragrance from the grove, a wet odour which expressed all the opulent fecundity of unmoved nature, marching on with her million plans for multiple life, multiple death.

Further on, they came to a place where the Turkish shells were landing. There was a long hurtling sound in the air, and then one had sight of a shell. To Peza it was of the conical missiles which friendly officers had displayed to him on board warships. Curiously enough, too, this first shell smacked of the foundry, of men with smudged faces, of the blare of furnace fires. It brought machinery immediately into his mind. He thought that if he was killed there at that time it would be as romantic, to the old standards, as death by a bit of falling iron in a factory.

II

A child was playing on a mountain and disregarding a battle that was waging on the plain. Behind him was the little cobbled hut of his fled parents. It was now occupied by a pearl-coloured cow that stared out from the darkness thoughtful and tender-eyed. The child ran to and fro, fumbling with sticks and making great machinations with pebbles. By a striking exercise of artistic license the sticks were ponies, cows, and dogs, and the pebbles were sheep. He was managing large agricultural and herding affairs. He was too intent on them to pay much heed to the fight four miles away, which at that distance resembled in sound the beating of surf upon rocks. However, there were occasions when some louder outbreak of that thunder stirred him from his serious occupation, and he turned then a questioning eye upon the battle, a small stick poised in his hand, interrupted in the act of sending his dog after his sheep. His tranquillity in regard to the death on the plain was as invincible as that of the mountain on which he stood.

It was evident that fear had swept the parents away from their home in a manner that could make them forget this child, the first-born. Nevertheless, the hut was clean bare. The cow had committed no impropriety in billeting herself at the domicile of her masters. This smoke-coloured and odorous interior contained nothing as large as a humming-bird. Terror had operated on these runaway people in its sinister fashion, elevating details to enormous heights, causing a man to remember a button while he forgot a coat, overpowering every one with recollections of a broken coffee-cup, deluging them with fears for the safety of an old pipe, and causing them to forget their first-born. Meanwhile the child played soberly with his trinkets.

He was solitary; engrossed in his own pursuits, it was seldom that he lifted his head to inquire of the world why it made so much noise. The stick in his hand was much larger to him than was an army corps of the distance. It was too childish for the mind of the child. He was dealing with sticks.

The battle lines writhed at times in the agony of a sea-creature on the sands. These tentacles flung and waved in a supreme excitement of pain, and the struggles of the great outlined body brought it nearer and nearer to the child. Once he looked at the plain and saw some men running wildly across a field. He had seen people chasing obdurate beasts in such fashion, and it struck him immediately that it was a manly thing which he would incorporate in his game. Consequently he raced furiously at his stone sheep, flourishing a cudgel, crying the shepherd calls. He paused frequently to get a cue of manner from the soldiers fighting on the plain. He reproduced, to a degree, any movements which he accounted rational to his theory of sheep-herding, the business of men, the traditional and exalted living of his father.

III

It was as if Peza was a corpse walking on the bottom of the sea, and finding there fields of grain, groves, weeds, the faces of men, voices. War, a strange employment of the race, presented to him a scene crowded with

327

familiar objects which wore the livery of their commonness, placidly, undauntedly. He was smitten with keen astonishment; a spread of green grass lit with the flames of poppies was too old for the company of this new ogre. If he had been devoting the full lens of his mind to this phase, he would have known he was amazed that the trees, the flowers, the grass, all tender and peaceful nature had not taken to heels at once upon the outbreak of battle. He venerated the immovable poppies.

The road seemed to lead into the apex of an angle formed by the two defensive lines of the Greeks. There was a straggle of wounded men and of gunless and jaded men. These latter did not seem to be frightened. They remained very cool, walking with unhurried steps and busy in gossip. Peza tried to define them. Perhaps during the fight they had reached the limit of their mental storage, their capacity for excitement, for tragedy, and had then simply come away. Peza remembered his visit to a certain place of pictures, where he had found himself amid heavenly skies and diabolic midnights—the sunshine beating red upon desert sands, nude bodies flung to the shore in the green moon-glow, ghastly and starving men clawing at a wall in darkness, a girl at her bath with screened rays falling upon her pearly shoulders, a dance, a funeral, a review, an execution, all the strength of argus-eyed art: and he had whirled and whirled amid this universe with cries of woe and joy, sin and beauty piercing his ears until he had been obliged to simply come away. He remembered that as he had emerged he had lit a cigarette with unction and advanced promptly to a café. A great hollow quiet seemed to be upon the earth.

This was a different case, but in his thoughts he conceded the same causes to many of these gunless wanderers. They too may have dreamed at lightning speed until the capacity for it was overwhelmed. As he watched them, he again saw himself walking toward the café, puffing upon his cigarette. As if to reinforce his theory, a soldier stopped him with an eager but polite inquiry for a match. He watched the man light his little roll of tobacco and paper and begin to smoke ravenously.

Peza no longer was torn with sorrow at the sight of wounded men. Evidently he found that pity had a numerical limit, and when this was passed the emotion became another thing. Now, as he viewed them, he merely felt himself very lucky, and beseeched the continuance of his superior fortune. At the passing of these slouched and stained figures he now heard a reiteration of warning. A part of himself was appealing through the medium of these grim shapes. It was plucking at his sleeve and pointing, telling him to beware; and so it had come to pass that he cared for the implacable misery of these soldiers only as he would have cared for the harms of broken dolls. His whole vision was focussed upon his own chance.

The lieutenant suddenly halted. "Look," he said. "I find that my duty is in another direction. I must go another way. But if you wish to fight you have only to go forward, and any officer of the fighting line will give you opportunity." He raised his cap ceremoniously; Peza raised his new white helmet. The stranger to battles uttered thanks to his chaperon, the one who had presented him. They bowed punctiliously, staring at each other with civil eyes.

The lieutenant moved quietly away through a field. In an instant it flashed upon Peza's mind that this desertion was perfidious. He had been subjected to a criminal discourtesy. The officer had fetched him into the middle of the thing, and then left him to wander helplessly toward death. At one time he was upon the point of shouting at the officer.

In the vale there was an effect as if one was then beneath the battle. It was going on above somewhere. Alone, unguided, Peza felt like a man groping in a cellar. He reflected too that one should always see the beginning of a fight. It was too difficult to thus approach it when the affair was in full swing. The trees hid all movements of troops from him, and he thought he might be walking out to the very spot which chance had provided for the reception of a fool. He asked eager questions of passing soldiers. Some paid no heed to him; others shook their heads mournfully. They knew nothing save that war was hard work. If they talked at all it was in testimony of having fought well, savagely. They did not know if the army was going to advance, hold its ground, or retreat; they were weary.

A long pointed shell flashed through the air and struck near the base of a tree, with a fierce upheaval, compounded of earth and flames. Looking back, Peza could see the shattered tree quivering from head to foot. Its whole being underwent a convulsive tremor which was an exhibition of pain, and, furthermore, deep amazement. As he advanced through the vale, the shells continued to hiss and hurtle in long low flights, and the bullets purred in the air. The missiles were flying into the breast of an astounded nature. The landscape, bewildered, agonized, was suffering a rain of infamous shots, and Peza imagined a million eyes gazing at him with the gaze of startled antelopes.

There was a resolute crashing of musketry from the tall hill on the left, and from directly in front there was a mingled din of artillery and musketry firing. Peza felt that his pride was playing a great trick in forcing him forward in this manner under conditions of strangeness, isolation, and ignorance. But he recalled the manner of the lieutenant, the smile on the hill-top among the flying peasants. Peza blushed and pulled the peak of his helmet down on his forehead. He strode onward firmly. Nevertheless he hated the lieutenant, and he resolved that on some future occasion he would take much trouble to arrange a stinging social revenge upon that grinning jackanapes. It did not occur to him until later that he was now going to battle mainly because at a previous time a certain man had smiled.

IV

The road curved round the base of a little hill, and on this hill a battery of mountain guns was leisurely shelling something unseen. In the lee of the height the mules, contented under their heavy saddles, were quietly browsing the long grass. Peza ascended the hill by a slanting path. He felt his heart beat swiftly; once at the top of the hill he would be obliged to look this phenomenon in the face. He hurried, with a mysterious idea of preventing by this strategy the battle from making his appearance a signal for some tremendous renewal. This vague thought seemed logical at the time. Certainly this living thing had knowledge of his coming. He endowed it with the intelligence of a barbaric deity. And so he hurried; he wished to surprise war, this terrible emperor, when it was growling on its throne. The ferocious and horrible sovereign was not to be allowed to make the arrival a pretext for some fit of smoky rage and blood. In this half-lull, Peza had distinctly the sense of stealing upon the battle unawares.

The soldiers watching the mules did not seem to be impressed by anything august. Two of them sat side by side and talked comfortably; another lay flat upon his back staring dreamily at the sky; another cursed a mule for certain refractions. Despite their uniforms, their bandoliers and rifles, they were dwelling in the peace of hostlers. However, the long shells were whooping from time to time over the brow of the hill, and swirling in almost straight lines toward the vale of trees, flowers, and grass. Peza, hearing and seeing the shells, and seeing the pensive guardians of the mules, felt reassured. They were accepting the condition of war as easily as an old sailor accepts the chair behind the counter of a tobacco-shop. Or, it was merely that the farm-boy had gone to sea, and he had adjusted himself to the circumstances immediately, and with only the usual first misadventures in conduct. Peza was proud and ashamed that he was not of them, these stupid peasants, who, throughout the world, hold potentates on their thrones, make statesmen illustrious, provide generals with lasting victories, all with ignorance, indifference, or half-witted hatred, moving the world with the strength of their arms and getting their heads knocked together in the name of God, the king, or the Stock Exchange; immortal, dreaming, hopeless asses who surrender their reason to the care of a shining puppet, and persuade some toy to carry their lives in his purse. Peza mentally abased himself before them, and wished to stir them with furious kicks.

As his eyes ranged above the rim of the plateau, he saw a group of artillery officers talking busily. They turned at once and regarded his ascent. A moment later a row of infantry soldiers in a trench beyond the little guns all faced him. Peza bowed to the officers. He understood at the time that he had made a good and cool bow, and he wondered at it, for his breath was coming in gasps, he was stifling from sheer excitement. He felt like a tipsy man trying to conceal his muscular uncertainty from the people in the street. But the officers did not display any knowledge. They bowed. Behind them Peza saw the plain, glittering green, with three lines of black marked upon it heavily. The front of the first of these lines was frothy with smoke. To the left of this hill was a craggy mountain, from which came a continual dull rattle of musketry. Its summit was ringed with the white smoke. The black lines on the plain slowly moved. The shells that came from there passed overhead with the sound of great birds frantically flapping their wings. Peza thought of the first sight of the sea during a storm. He seemed to feel against his face the wind that races over the tops of cold and tumultuous billows.

He heard a voice afar off—"Sir, what would you?" He turned, and saw the dapper captain of the battery standing beside him. Only a moment had elapsed. "Pardon me, sir," said Peza, bowing again. The officer was evidently reserving his bows; he scanned the new-comer attentively. "Are you a correspondent?" he asked. Peza produced a card. "Yes, I came as a correspondent," he replied, "but now, sir, I have other thoughts. I wish to help. You see? I wish to help."

"What do you mean?" said the captain. "Are you a Greek? Do you wish to fight?"

"Yes, I am a Greek. I wish to fight." Peza's voice surprised him by coming from his lips in even and deliberate tones. He thought with gratification that he was behaving rather well. Another shell travelling from some unknown point on the plain whirled close and furiously in the air, pursuing an apparently horizontal course as if it were never going to touch the earth. The dark shape swished across the sky.

"Ah," cried the captain, now smiling, "I am not sure that we will be able to accommodate you with a fierce affair here just at this time, but——" He walked gaily to and fro behind the guns with Peza, pointing out to him the lines of the Greeks, and describing his opinion of the general plan of defence. He wore the air of an amiable host. Other officers questioned Peza in regard to the politics of the war. The king, the ministry, Germany, England, Russia, all these huge words were continually upon their tongues. "And the people in Athens? Were they——" Amid this vivacious babble Peza, seated upon an ammunition box, kept his glance high, watching the appearance of shell after shell. These officers were like men who had been lost for days in the forest. They were thirsty for any scrap of news. Nevertheless, one of them would occasionally dispute their informant courteously. What would Servia have to say to that? No, no, France and Russia could never allow it. Peza was elated. The shells killed no one; war was not so bad. He was simply having coffee in the smoking-room of some embassy where reverberate the names of nations.

A rumour had passed along the motley line of privates in the trench. The new arrival with the clean white helmet was a famous English cavalry officer come to assist the army with his counsel. They stared at the figure of him, surrounded by officers. Peza, gaining sense of the glances and whispers, felt that his coming was an event.

Later, he resolved that he could with temerity do something finer. He contemplated the mountain where the Greek infantry was engaged, and announced leisurely to the captain of the battery that he thought presently of going in that direction and getting into the fight. He re-affirmed the sentiments of a patriot. The captain seemed surprised. "Oh, there will be fighting here at this knoll in a few minutes," he said orientally. "That will be sufficient? You had better stay with us. Besides, I have been ordered to resume fire." The officers all tried to dissuade him from departing. It was really not worth the trouble. The battery would begin again directly. Then it would be amusing for him.

Peza felt that he was wandering with his protestations of high patriotism through a desert of sensible men. These officers gave no heed to his exalted declarations. They seemed too jaded. They were fighting the men who were fighting them. Palaver of the particular kind had subsided before their intense pre-occupation in war as a craft. Moreover, many men had talked in that manner and only talked.

Peza believed at first that they were treating him delicately. They were considerate of his inexperience. War had turned out to be such a gentle business that Peza concluded he could scorn this idea. He bade them a heroic farewell despite their objections.

However, when he reflected upon their ways afterward, he saw dimly that they were actuated principally by some universal childish desire for a spectator of their fine things. They were going into action, and they wished to be seen at war, precise and fearless.

V

Climbing slowly to the high infantry position, Peza was amazed to meet a soldier whose jaw had been half shot away, and who was being helped down the sheep track by two tearful comrades. The man's breast was drenched with blood, and from a cloth which he held to the wound drops were splashing wildly upon the stones of the path. He gazed at Peza for a moment. It was a mystic gaze, which Peza withstood with difficulty. He was exchanging looks with a spectre; all aspect of the man was somehow gone from this victim. As Peza went on, one of the unwounded soldiers loudly shouted to him to return and assist in this tragic march. But even Peza's fingers revolted; he was afraid of the spectre; he would not have dared to touch it. He was surely craven in the movement of refusal he made to them. He scrambled hastily on up the path. He was running away.

At the top of the hill he came immediately upon a part of the line that was in action. Another battery of mountain guns was here firing at the streaks of black on the plain. There were trenches filled with men lining parts of the crest, and near the base were other trenches, all crashing away mightily. The plain stretched as far as the eye can see, and from where silver mist ended this emerald ocean of grass, a great ridge of snow-topped mountains poised against a fleckless blue sky. Two knolls, green and yellow with grain, sat on the prairie confronting the dark hills of the Greek position. Between them were the lines of the enemy. A row of trees, a village, a stretch of road, showed faintly on this great canvas, this tremendous picture, but men, the Turkish battalions, were emphasized startlingly upon it. The ranks of troops between the knolls and the Greek position were as black as ink.

The first line of course was muffled in smoke, but at the rear of it battalions crawled up and to and fro plainer than beetles on a plate. Peza had never understood that masses of men were so declarative, so unmistakable, as if nature makes every arrangement to give information of the coming and the presence of destruction, the end, oblivion. The firing was full, complete, a roar of cataracts, and this pealing of connected volleys was adjusted to the grandeur of the far-off range of snowy mountains. Peza, breathless, pale, felt that he had been set upon a pillar and was surveying mankind, the world.

In the meantime dust had got in his eye. He took his handkerchief and mechanically administered to it.

An officer with a double stripe of purple on his trousers paced in the rear of the battery of howitzers. He waved a little cane. Sometimes he paused in his promenade to study the field through his glasses. "A fine scene, sir," he cried airily, upon the approach of Peza. It was like a blow in the chest to the wide-eyed volunteer. It revealed to him a point of view. "Yes, sir, it is a fine scene," he answered. They spoke in French. "I am happy to be able to entertain monsieur with a little practice," continued the officer. "I am firing upon that mass of troops you see there a little to the right. They are probably forming for another attack." Peza smiled; here again appeared manners, manners erect by the side of death.

The right-flank gun of the battery thundered; there was a belch of fire and smoke; the shell flung swiftly and afar was known only to the ear in which rang a broadening hooting wake of sound. The howitzer had thrown itself backward convulsively, and lay with its wheels moving in the air as a squad of men rushed toward it. And later, it seemed as if each little gun had made the supreme effort of its being in each particular shot. They roared with voices far too loud, and the thunderous effort caused a gun to bound as in a dying convulsion. And then occasionally one was hurled with wheels in air. These shuddering howitzers presented an appearance of so many cowards always longing to bolt to the rear, but being implacably held to their business by this throng of soldiers who ran in squads to drag them up again to their obligation. The guns were herded and cajoled and bullied interminably. One by one, in relentless program, they were dragged forward to contribute a profound vibration of steel and wood, a flash and a roar, to the important happiness of man.

The adjacent infantry celebrated a good shot with smiles and an outburst of gleeful talk.

"Look, sir," cried an officer to Peza. Thin smoke was drifting lazily before Peza, and dodging impatiently he brought his eyes to bear upon that part of the plain indicated by the officer's finger. The enemy's infantry was advancing to attack. From the black lines had come forth an inky mass which was shaped much like a human tongue. It advanced slowly, casually, without apparent spirit, but with an insolent confidence that was like a proclamation of the inevitable.

The impetuous part was all played by the defensive side. Officers called, men plucked each other by the sleeve; there were shouts, motions, all eyes were turned upon the inky mass which was flowing toward the base of the hills, heavily, languorously, as oily and thick as one of the streams that ooze through a swamp.

Peza was chattering a question at every one. In the way, pushed aside, or in the way again, he continued to repeat it. "Can they take the position? Can they take the position? Can they take the position?" He was apparently addressing an assemblage of deaf men. Every eye was busy watching every hand. The soldiers did not even seem to see the interesting stranger in the white helmet who was crying out so feverishly.

Finally, however, the hurried captain of the battery espied him and heeded his question. "No, sir! no, sir! It is impossible," he shouted angrily. His manner seemed to denote that if he had sufficient time he would have completely insulted Peza. The latter swallowed the crumb of news without regard to the coating of scorn, and, waving his hand in adieu, he began to run along the crest of the hill toward the part of the Greek line against which the attack was directed.

VI

Peza, as he ran along the crest of the mountain, believed that his action was receiving the wrathful attention of the hosts of the foe. To him then it was incredible foolhardiness thus to call to himself the stares of thousands of hateful eyes. He was like a lad induced by playmates to commit some indiscretion in a cathedral. He was abashed; perhaps he even blushed as he ran. It seemed to him that the whole solemn ceremony of war had paused during this commission. So he scrambled wildly over the rocks in his haste to end the embarrassing ordeal. When he came among the crowning rifle-pits filled with eager soldiers he wanted to yell with joy. None noticed him save a young officer of infantry, who said—"Sir, what do you want?" It was obvious that people had devoted some attention to their own affairs.

Peza asserted, in Greek, that he wished above everything to battle for the fatherland. The officer nodded; with a smile he pointed to some dead men covered with blankets, from which were thrust upturned dusty shoes.

"Yes, I know, I know," cried Peza. He thought the officer was poetically alluding to the danger.

"No," said the officer at once. "I mean cartridges—a bandolier. Take a bandolier from one of them."

Peza went cautiously toward a body. He moved a hand toward the corner of a blanket. There he hesitated, stuck, as if his arm had turned to plaster. Hearing a rustle behind him he spun quickly. Three soldiers of the close rank in the trench were regarding him. The officer came again and tapped him on the shoulder. "Have you any tobacco?" Peza looked at him in bewilderment. His hand was still extended toward the blanket which covered the dead soldier. "Yes," he said, "I have some tobacco." He gave the officer his pouch. As if in compensation, the other directed a soldier to strip the bandolier from the corpse. Peza, having crossed the long cartridge belt on his breast, felt that the dead man had flung his two arms around him.

A soldier with a polite nod and smile gave Peza a rifle, a relic of another dead man. Thus, he felt, besides the clutch of a corpse about his neck, that the rifle was as inhumanly horrible as a snake that lives in a tomb. He heard at his ear something that was in effect like the voices of those two dead men, their low voices speaking to him of bloody death, mutilation. The bandolier gripped him tighter; he wished to raise his hands to his throat like a man who is choking. The rifle was clammy; upon his palms he felt the movement of the sluggish currents of a serpent's life; it was crawling and frightful.

All about him were these peasants, with their interested countenances, gibbering of the fight. From time to time a soldier cried out in semi-humorous lamentations descriptive of his thirst. One bearded man sat munching a great bit of hard bread. Fat, greasy, squat, he was like an idol made of tallow. Peza felt dimly that there was a distinction between this man and a young student who could write sonnets and play the piano quite well. This old blockhead was coolly gnawing at the bread, while he, Peza, was being throttled by a dead man's arms.

He looked behind him, and saw that a head by some chance had been uncovered from its blanket. Two liquid-like eyes were staring into his face. The head was turned a little sideways as if to get better opportunity for the scrutiny. Peza could feel himself blanch; he was being drawn and drawn by these dead men slowly, firmly down as to some mystic chamber under the earth where they could walk, dreadful figures, swollen and blood-marked. He was bidden; they had commanded him; he was going, going, going.

When the man in the new white helmet bolted for the rear, many of the soldiers in the trench thought that he had been struck, but those who had been nearest to him knew better. Otherwise they would have heard the silken sliding tender noise of the bullet and the thud of its impact. They bawled after him curses, and also outbursts of self-congratulation and vanity. Despite the prominence of the cowardly part, they were enabled to see in this exhibition a fine comment upon their own fortitude. The other soldiers thought that Peza had been wounded somewhere in the neck, because as he ran he was tearing madly at the bandolier, the dead man's arms. The soldier with the bread paused in his eating and cynically remarked upon the speed of the runaway.

An officer's voice was suddenly heard calling out the calculation of the distance to the enemy, the readjustment of the sights. There was a stirring rattle along the line. The men turned their eyes to the front. Other trenches beneath them to the right were already heavily in action. The smoke was lifting toward the blue sky. The soldier with the bread placed it carefully on a bit of paper beside him as he turned to kneel in the trench.

VII

In the late afternoon, the child ceased his play on the mountain with his flocks and his dogs. Part of the battle had whirled very near to the base of his hill, and the noise was great. Sometimes he could see fantastic smoky shapes which resembled the curious figures in foam which one sees on the slant of a rough sea. The plain indeed was etched in white circles and whirligigs like the slope of a colossal wave. The child took seat on a stone and contemplated the fight. He was beginning to be astonished; he had never before seen cattle herded with such uproar. Lines of flame flashed out here and there. It was mystery.

Finally, without any preliminary indication, he began to weep. If the men struggling on the plain had had time and greater vision, they could have seen this strange tiny figure seated on a boulder, surveying them while the tears streamed. It was as simple as some powerful symbol.

As the magic clear light of day amid the mountains dimmed the distances, and the plain shone as a pallid blue cloth marked by the red threads of the firing, the child arose and moved off to the unwelcoming door of his home. He called softly for his mother, and complained of his hunger in the familiar formula. The pearl-coloured cow, grinding her jaws thoughtfully, stared at him with her large eyes. The peaceful gloom of evening was slowly draping the hills.

The child heard a rattle of loose stones on the hillside, and facing the sound, saw a moment later a man drag himself up to the crest of the hill and fall panting. Forgetting his mother and his hunger, filled with calm interest, the child walked forward and stood over the heaving form. His eyes too were now large and inscrutably wise and sad like those of the animal in the house.

After a silence he spoke inquiringly. "Are you a man?"

Peza rolled over quickly and gazed up into the fearless cherubic countenance. He did not attempt to reply. He breathed as if life was about to leave his body. He was covered with dust; his face had been cut in some way, and his cheek was ribboned with blood. All the spick of his former appearance had vanished in a general dishevelment, in which he resembled a creature that had been flung to and fro, up and down, by cliffs and prairies during an earthquake. He rolled his eye glassily at the child.

They remained thus until the child repeated his words. "Are you a man?"

Peza gasped in the manner of a fish. Palsied, windless, and abject, he confronted the primitive courage, the sovereign child, the brother of the mountains, the sky and the sea, and he knew that the definition of his misery could be written on a grass-blade.

Part II. Midnight Sketches

AN EXPERIMENT IN MISERY

(From the Press, New York.)

It was late at night, and a fine rain was swirling softly down, causing the pavements to glisten with hue of steel and blue and yellow in the rays of the innumerable lights. A youth was trudging slowly, without enthusiasm, with his hands buried deep in his trouser's pockets, towards the down-town places where beds can be hired for coppers. He was clothed in an aged and tattered suit, and his derby was a marvel of dust-covered crown and torn rim. He was going forth to eat as the wanderer may eat, and sleep as the homeless sleep. By the time he had reached City Hall Park he was so completely plastered with yells of "bum" and "hobo," and with various unholy epithets that small boys had applied to him at intervals, that he was in a state of the most profound dejection. The sifting rain saturated the old velvet collar of his overcoat, and as the wet cloth pressed against his neck, he felt that there no longer could be pleasure in life. He looked about him searching for an outcast of highest degree that they too might share miseries, but the lights threw a quivering glare over rows and circles of deserted benches that glistened damply, showing patches of wet sod behind them. It seemed that their usual freights had fled on this night to better things. There were only squads of well-dressed Brooklyn people who swarmed towards the bridge.

The young man loitered about for a time and then went shuffling off down Park Row. In the sudden descent in style of the dress of the crowd he felt relief, and as if he were at last in his own country. He began to see tatters that matched his tatters. In Chatham Square there were aimless men strewn in front of saloons and lodging-houses, standing sadly, patiently, reminding one vaguely of the attitudes of chickens in a storm. He aligned himself with these men, and turned slowly to occupy himself with the flowing life of the great street.

Through the mists of the cold and storming night, the cable cars went in silent procession, great affairs shining with red and brass, moving with formidable power, calm and irresistible, dangerful and gloomy, breaking silence only by the loud fierce cry of the gong. Two rivers of people swarmed along the side walks, spattered with black mud, which made each shoe leave a scar-like impression. Overhead elevated trains with a shrill grinding of the wheels stopped at the station, which upon its leg-like pillars seemed to resemble some monstrous kind of crab squatting over the street. The quick fat puffings of the engines could be heard. Down an alley there were sombre curtains of purple and black, on which street lamps dully glittered like embroidered flowers.

A saloon stood with a voracious air on a corner. A sign leaning against the front of the door-post announced "Free hot soup to-night!" The swing doors, snapping to and fro like ravenous lips, made gratified smacks as the saloon gorged itself with plump men, eating with astounding and endless appetite, smiling in some indescribable manner as the men came from all directions like sacrifices to a heathenish superstition.

Caught by the delectable sign the young man allowed himself to be swallowed. A bar-tender placed a schooner of dark and portentous beer on the bar. Its monumental form up-reared until the froth a-top was above the crown of the young man's brown derby.

"Soup over there, gents," said the bar-tender affably. A little yellow man in rags and the youth grasped their schooners and went with speed toward a lunch counter, where a man with oily but imposing whiskers ladled genially from a kettle until he had furnished his two mendicants with a soup that was steaming hot, and in which there were little floating suggestions of chicken. The young man, sipping his broth, felt the cordiality expressed by the warmth of the mixture, and he beamed at the man with oily but imposing whiskers, who was presiding like a priest behind an altar. "Have some more, gents?" he inquired of the two sorry figures before him. The little yellow man accepted with a swift gesture, but the youth shook his head and went out, following a man whose wondrous seediness promised that he would have a knowledge of cheap lodging-houses.

On the side-walk he accosted the seedy man. "Say, do you know a cheap place to sleep?"

The other hesitated for a time gazing sideways. Finally he nodded in the direction of the street, "I sleep up there," he said, "when I've got the price."

"How much?"

"Ten cents."

The young man shook his head dolefully. "That's too rich for me."

At that moment there approached the two a reeling man in strange garments. His head was a fuddle of bushy hair and whiskers, from which his eyes peered with a guilty slant. In a close scrutiny it was possible to distinguish the cruel lines of a mouth which looked as if its lips had just closed with satisfaction over some tender and piteous morsel. He appeared like an assassin steeped in crimes performed awkwardly.

But at this time his voice was tuned to the coaxing key of an affectionate puppy. He looked at the men with wheedling eyes, and began to sing a little melody for charity.

"Say, gents, can't yeh give a poor feller a couple of cents t' git a bed. I got five, and I gits anudder two I gits me a bed. Now, on th' square, gents, can't yeh jest gimme two cents t' git a bed? Now, yeh know how a respecter'ble gentlem'n feels when he's down on his luck, an' I——"

The seedy man, staring with imperturbable countenance at a train which clattered overhead, interrupted in an expressionless voice—"Ah, go t' h—!"

But the youth spoke to the prayerful assassin in tones of astonishment and inquiry. "Say, you must be crazy! Why don't yeh strike somebody that looks as if they had money?"

The assassin, tottering about on his uncertain legs, and at intervals brushing imaginary obstacles from before his nose, entered into a long explanation of the psychology of the situation. It was so profound that it was unintelligible.

When he had exhausted the subject, the young man said to him—

"Let's see th' five cents."

The assassin wore an expression of drunken woe at this sentence, filled with suspicion of him. With a deeply pained air he began to fumble in his clothing, his red hands trembling. Presently he announced in a voice of bitter grief, as if he had been betrayed—"There's on'y four."

"Four," said the young man thoughtfully. "Well, look-a-here, I'm a stranger here, an' if ye'll steer me to your cheap joint I'll find the other three."

The assassin's countenance became instantly radiant with joy. His whiskers quivered with the wealth of his alleged emotions. He seized the young man's hand in a transport of delight and friendliness.

"B' Gawd," he cried, "if ye'll do that, b' Gawd, I'd say yeh was a damned good fellow, I would, an' I'd remember yeh all m' life, I would, b' Gawd, an' if I ever got a chance I'd return the compliment"—he spoke with drunken dignity,—"b' Gawd, I'd treat yeh white, I would, an' I'd allus remember yeh."

The young man drew back, looking at the assassin coldly. "Oh, that's all right," he said. "You show me th' joint—that's all you've got t' do."

The assassin, gesticulating gratitude, led the young man along a dark street. Finally he stopped before a little dusty door. He raised his hand impressively. "Look-a-here," he said, and there was a thrill of deep and ancient wisdom upon his face, "I've brought yeh here, an' that's my part, ain't it? If th' place don't suit yeh, yeh needn't git mad at me, need yeh? There won't be no bad feelin', will there?"

"No," said the young man.

The assassin waved his arm tragically, and led the march up the steep stairway. On the way the young man furnished the assassin with three pennies. At the top a man with benevolent spectacles looked at them through a hole in a board. He collected their money, wrote some names on a register, and speedily was leading the two men along a gloom-shrouded corridor.

Shortly after the beginning of this journey the young man felt his liver turn white, for from the dark and secret places of the building there suddenly came to his nostrils strange and unspeakable odours, that assailed him like malignant diseases with wings. They seemed to be from human bodies closely packed in dens; the exhalations from a hundred pairs of reeking lips; the fumes from a thousand bygone debauches; the expression of a thousand present miseries.

A man, naked save for a little snuff-coloured undershirt, was parading sleepily along the corridor. He rubbed his eyes, and, giving vent to a prodigious yawn, demanded to be told the time.

"Half-past one."

The man yawned again. He opened a door, and for a moment his form was outlined against a black, opaque interior. To this door came the three men, and as it was again opened the unholy odours rushed out like fiends, so that the young man was obliged to struggle as against an overpowering wind.

It was some time before the youth's eyes were good in the intense gloom within, but the man with benevolent spectacles led him skilfully, pausing but a moment to deposit the limp assassin upon a cot. He took the youth to a cot that lay tranquilly by the window, and showing him a tall locker for clothes that stood near the head with the ominous air of a tombstone, left him.

The youth sat on his cot and peered about him. There was a gas-jet in a distant part of the room, that burned a small flickering orange-hued flame. It caused vast masses of tumbled shadows in all parts of the place, save where, immediately about it, there was a little grey haze. As the young man's eyes became used to the darkness, he could see upon the cots that thickly littered the floor the forms of men sprawled out, lying in death-like silence, or heaving and snoring with tremendous effort, like stabbed fish.

The youth locked his derby and his shoes in the mummy case near him, and then lay down with an old and familiar coat around his shoulders. A blanket he handed gingerly, drawing it over part of the coat. The cot was covered with leather, and as cold as melting snow. The youth was obliged to shiver for some time on this affair, which was like a slab. Presently, however, his chill gave him peace, and during this period of leisure from it he turned his head to stare at his friend the assassin, whom he could dimly discern where he lay sprawled on a cot in the abandon of a man filled with drink. He was snoring with incredible vigour. His wet hair and beard dimly glistened, and his inflamed nose shone with subdued lustre like a red light in a fog.

Within reach of the youth's hand was one who lay with yellow breast and shoulders bare to the cold drafts. One arm hung over the side of the cot, and the fingers lay full length upon the wet cement floor of the room. Beneath the inky brows could be seen the eyes of the man exposed by the partly opened lids. To the youth it seemed that he and this corpse-like being were exchanging a prolonged stare, and that the other threatened with his eyes. He drew back watching his neighbour from the shadows of his blanket edge. The man did not move once through the night, but lay in this stillness as of death like a body stretched out expectant of the surgeon's knife.

And all through the room could be seen the tawny hues of naked flesh, limbs thrust into the darkness, projecting beyond the cots; upreared knees, arms hanging long and thin over the cot edges. For the most part they were statuesque, carven, dead. With the curious lockers standing all about like tombstones, there was a strange effect of a graveyard where bodies were merely flung.

Yet occasionally could be seen limbs wildly tossing in fantastic nightmare gestures, accompanied by guttural cries, grunts, oaths. And there was one fellow off in a gloomy corner, who in his dreams was oppressed by some frightful calamity, for of a sudden he began to utter long wails that went almost like yells from a hound, echoing wailfully and weird through this chill place of tombstones where men lay like the dead.

The sound in its high piercing beginnings, that dwindled to final melancholy moans, expressed a red and grim tragedy of the unfathomable possibilities of the man's dreams. But to the youth these were not merely the shrieks of a vision-pierced man: they were an utterance of the meaning of the room and its occupants. It was to him the protest of the wretch who feels the touch of the imperturbable granite wheels, and who then cries with an impersonal eloquence, with a strength not from him, giving voice to the wail of a whole section, a class, a people. This, weaving into the young man's brain, and mingling with his views of the vast and sombre shadows that, like mighty black fingers, curled around the naked bodies, made the young man so that he did not sleep, but lay carving the biographies for these men from his meagre experience. At times the fellow in the corner howled in a writhing agony of his imaginations.

Finally a long lance-point of grey light shot through the dusty panes of the window. Without, the young man could see roofs drearily white in the dawning. The point of light yellowed and grew brighter, until the golden rays of the morning sun came in bravely and strong. They touched with radiant colour the form of a small fat man, who snored in stuttering fashion. His round and shiny bald head glowed suddenly with the valour of a decoration. He sat up, blinked at the sun, swore fretfully, and pulled his blanket over the ornamental splendours of his head.

The youth contentedly watched this rout of the shadows before the bright spears of the sun, and presently he slumbered. When he awoke he heard the voice of the assassin raised in valiant curses. Putting up his head, he perceived his comrade seated on the side of the cot engaged in scratching his neck with long finger-nails that rasped like files.

"Hully Jee, dis is a new breed. They've got can-openers on their feet." He continued in a violent tirade.

The young man hastily unlocked his closet and took out his shoes and hat. As he sat on the side of the cot lacing his shoes, he glanced about and saw that daylight had made the room comparatively common-place and uninteresting. The men, whose faces seemed stolid, serene or absent, were engaged in dressing, while a great crackle of bantering conversation arose.

A few were parading in unconcerned nakedness. Here and there were men of brawn, whose skins shone clear and ruddy. They took splendid poses,

347

standing massively like chiefs. When they had dressed in their ungainly garments there was an extraordinary change. They then showed bumps and deficiencies of all kinds.

There were others who exhibited many deformities. Shoulders were slanting, humped, pulled this way and pulled that way. And notable among these latter men was the little fat man, who had refused to allow his head to be glorified. His pudgy form, builded like a pear, bustled to and fro, while he swore in fish-wife fashion. It appeared that some article of his apparel had vanished.

The young man attired speedily, and went to his friend the assassin. At first the latter looked dazed at the sight of the youth. This face seemed to be appealing to him through the cloud wastes of his memory. He scratched his neck and reflected. At last he grinned, a broad smile gradually spreading until his countenance was a round illumination. "Hello, Willie," he cried cheerily.

"Hello," said the young man. "Are yeh ready t' fly?"

"Sure." The assassin tied his shoe carefully with some twine and came ambling.

When he reached the street the young man experienced no sudden relief from unholy atmospheres. He had forgotten all about them, and had been breathing naturally, and with no sensation of discomfort or distress.

He was thinking of these things as he walked along the street, when he was suddenly startled by feeling the assassin's hand, trembling with excitement, clutching his arm, and when the assassin spoke, his voice went into quavers from a supreme agitation.

"I'll be hully, bloomin' blowed if there wasn't a feller with a nightshirt on up there in that joint."

The youth was bewildered for a moment, but presently he turned to smile indulgently at the assassin's humour.

"Oh, you're a d——d liar," he merely said.

Whereupon the assassin began to gesture extravagantly, and take oath by strange gods. He frantically placed himself at the mercy of remarkable fates if his tale were not true.

"Yes, he did! I cross m'heart thousan' times!" he protested, and at the moment his eyes were large with amazement, his mouth wrinkled in unnatural glee.

"Yessir! A nightshirt! A hully white nightshirt!"

"You lie!"

"No, sir! I hope ter die b'fore I kin git anudder ball if there wasn't a jay wid a hully, bloomin' white nightshirt!"

His face was filled with the infinite wonder of it. "A hully white nightshirt," he continually repeated.

The young man saw the dark entrance to a basement restaurant. There was a sign which read "No mystery about our hash!" and there were other age-stained and world-battered legends which told him that the place was within his means. He stopped before it and spoke to the assassin. "I guess I'll git somethin' t' eat."

At this the assassin, for some reason, appeared to be quite embarrassed. He gazed at the seductive front of the eating place for a moment. Then he started slowly up the street. "Well, good-bye, Willie," he said bravely.

For an instant the youth studied the departing figure. Then he called out, "Hol' on a minnet." As they came together he spoke in a certain fierce way, as if he feared that the other would think him to be charitable. "Look-a-here, if yeh wanta git some breakfas' I'll lend yeh three cents t' do it with. But say, look-a-here, you've gota git out an' hustle. I ain't goin' t' support yeh, or I'll go broke b'fore night. I ain't no millionaire."

"I take me oath, Willie," said the assassin earnestly, "th' on'y thing I really needs is a ball. Me t'roat feels like a fryin'-pan. But as I can't get a ball, why, th' next bes' thing is breakfast, an' if yeh do that for me, b' Gawd, I say yeh was th' whitest lad I ever see."

They spent a few moments in dexterous exchanges of phrases, in which they each protested that the other was, as the assassin had originally said, "a respecter'ble gentlem'n." And they concluded with mutual assurances that they were the souls of intelligence and virtue. Then they went into the restaurant.

There was a long counter, dimly lighted from hidden sources. Two or three men in soiled white aprons rushed here and there.

The youth bought a bowl of coffee for two cents and a roll for one cent. The assassin purchased the same. The bowls were webbed with brown seams, and the tin spoons wore an air of having emerged from the first pyramid. Upon them were black moss-like encrustations of age, and they were bent and scarred from the attacks of long-forgotten teeth. But over their repast the wanderers waxed warm and mellow. The assassin grew affable as the hot mixture went soothingly down his parched throat, and the young man felt courage flow in his veins.

Memories began to throng in on the assassin, and he brought forth long tales, intricate, incoherent, delivered with a chattering swiftness as from an old woman. "—— great job out'n Orange. Boss keep yeh hustlin' though all time. I was there three days, and then I went an' ask 'im t' lend me a dollar. 'G-g-go ter the devil,' he ses, an' I lose me job."

"South no good. Damn niggers work for twenty-five an' thirty cents a day. Run white man out. Good grub though. Easy livin'."

"Yas; useter work little in Toledo, raftin' logs. Make two or three dollars er day in the spring. Lived high. Cold as ice though in the winter."

"I was raised in northern N'York. O-o-oh, yeh jest oughto live there. No beer ner whisky though, way off in the woods. But all th' good hot grub yeh can eat. B' Gawd, I hung around there long as I could till th' ol' man fired me. 'Git t' hell outa here, yeh wuthless skunk, git t' hell outa here, an' go die,' he ses. 'You're a hell of a father,' I ses, 'you are,' an' I quit 'im."

As they were passing from the dim eating place, they encountered an old man who was trying to steal forth with a tiny package of food, but a tall man with an indomitable moustache stood dragon fashion, barring the way of

350

escape. They heard the old man raise a plaintive protest. "Ah, you always want to know what I take out, and you never see that I usually bring a package in here from my place of business."

As the wanderers trudged slowly along Park Row, the assassin began to expand and grow blithe. "B' Gawd, we've been livin' like kings," he said, smacking appreciative lips.

"Look out, or we'll have t' pay fer it t'night," said the youth with gloomy warning.

But the assassin refused to turn his gaze toward the future. He went with a limping step, into which he injected a suggestion of lamblike gambols. His mouth was wreathed in a red grin.

In the City Hall Park the two wanderers sat down in the little circle of benches sanctified by traditions of their class. They huddled in their old garments, slumbrously conscious of the march of the hours which for them had no meaning.

The people of the street hurrying hither and thither made a blend of black figures changing yet frieze-like. They walked in their good clothes as upon important missions, giving no gaze to the two wanderers seated upon the benches. They expressed to the young man his infinite distance from all that he valued. Social position, comfort, the pleasures of living, were unconquerable kingdoms. He felt a sudden awe.

And in the background a multitude of buildings, of pitiless hues and sternly high, were to him emblematic of a nation forcing its regal head into the clouds, throwing no downward glances; in the sublimity of its aspirations ignoring the wretches who may flounder at its feet. The roar of the city in his ear was to him the confusion of strange tongues, babbling heedlessly; it was the clink of coin, the voice of the city's hopes which were to him no hopes.

He confessed himself an outcast, and his eyes from under the lowered rim of his hat began to glance guiltily, wearing the criminal expression that comes with certain convictions.

THE MEN IN THE STORM

The blizzard began to swirl great clouds of snow along the streets, sweeping it down from the roofs, and up from the pavements, until the faces of pedestrians tingled and burned as from a thousand needle-prickings. Those on the walks huddled their necks closely in the collars of their coats, and went along stooping like a race of aged people. The drivers of vehicles hurried their horses furiously on their way. They were made more cruel by the exposure of their position, aloft on high seats. The street cars, bound up town, went slowly, the horses slipping and straining in the spongy brown mass that lay between the rails. The drivers, muffled to the eyes, stood erect, facing the wind, models of grim philosophy. Overhead trains rumbled and roared, and the dark structure of the elevated railroad, stretching over the avenue, dripped little streams and drops of water upon the mud and snow beneath.

All the clatter of the street was softened by the masses that lay upon the cobbles, until, even to one who looked from a window, it became important music, a melody of life made necessary to the ear by the dreariness of the pitiless beat and sweep of the storm. Occasionally one could see black figures of men busily shovelling the white drifts from the walks. The sounds from their labour created new recollections of rural experiences which every man manages to have in a measure. Later, the immense windows of the shops became aglow with light, throwing great beams of orange and yellow upon the pavement. They were infinitely cheerful, yet in a way they accentuated the force and discomfort of the storm, and gave a meaning to the pace of the people and the vehicles, scores of pedestrians and drivers, wretched with cold faces, necks and feet, speeding for scores of unknown doors and entrances, scattering to an infinite variety of shelters, to places which the imagination made warm with the familiar colours of home.

There was an absolute expression of hot dinners in the pace of the people. If one dared to speculate upon the destination of those who came trooping, he lost himself in a maze of social calculation; he might fling a handful of sand and attempt to follow the flight of each particular grain. But as to the suggestion of hot dinners, he was in firm lines of thought, for it was upon every hurrying face. It is a matter of tradition; it is from the tales of childhood. It comes forth with every storm.

However, in a certain part of a dark west-side street, there was a collection of men to whom these things were as if they were not. In this street was located a charitable house, where for five cents the homeless of the city could get a bed at night, and in the morning coffee and bread.

During the afternoon of the storm, the whirling snows acted as drivers, as men with whips, and at half-past three the walk before the closed doors of the house was covered with wanderers of the street, waiting. For some distance on either side of the place they could be seen lurking in the doorways and behind projecting parts of buildings, gathering in close bunches in an effort to get warm. A covered wagon drawn up near the curb sheltered a dozen of them. Under the stairs that led to the elevated railway station, there were six or eight, their hands stuffed deep in their pockets, their shoulders stooped, jiggling their feet. Others always could be seen coming, a strange procession, some slouching along with the characteristic hopeless gait of professional strays, some coming with hesitating steps, wearing the air of men to whom this sort of thing was new.

It was an afternoon of incredible length. The snow, blowing in twisting clouds, sought out the men in their meagre hiding-places, and skilfully beat in among them, drenching their persons with showers of fine stinging flakes. They crowded together, muttering, and fumbling in their pockets to get their red inflamed wrists covered by the cloth.

New-comers usually halted at one end of the groups and addressed a question, perhaps much as a matter of form, "Is it open yet?"

Those who had been waiting inclined to take the questioner seriously and became contemptuous. "No; do yeh think we'd be standin' here?"

The gathering swelled in numbers steadily and persistently. One could always see them coming, trudging slowly through the storm.

Finally, the little snow plains in the street began to assume a leaden hue from the shadows of evening. The buildings upreared gloomily save where various windows became brilliant figures of light, that made shimmers and splashes of yellow on the snow. A street lamp on the curb struggled to illuminate, but it was reduced to impotent blindness by the swift gusts of sleet crusting its panes.

In this half-darkness, the men began to come from their shelter places and mass in front of the doors of charity. They were of all types, but the nationalities were mostly American, German, and Irish. Many were strong, healthy, clear-skinned fellows, with that stamp of countenance which is not frequently seen upon seekers after charity. There were men of undoubted patience, industry, and temperance, who, in time of ill-fortune, do not habitually turn to rail at the state of society, snarling at the arrogance of the rich, and bemoaning the cowardice of the poor, but who at these times are apt to wear a sudden and singular meekness, as if they saw the world's progress marching from them, and were trying to perceive where they had failed, what they had lacked, to be thus vanquished in the race. Then there were others of the shifting, Bowery element, who were used to paying ten cents for a place to sleep, but who now came here because it was cheaper.

But they were all mixed in one mass so thoroughly that one could not have discerned the different elements, but for the fact that the labouring men, for the most part, remained silent and impassive in the blizzard, their eyes fixed on the windows of the house, statues of patience.

The sidewalk soon became completely blocked by the bodies of the men. They pressed close to one another like sheep in a winter's gale, keeping one another warm by the heat of their bodies. The snow came down upon this compressed group of men until, directly from above, it might have appeared like a heap of snow-covered merchandise, if it were not for the fact that the crowd swayed gently with a unanimous, rhythmical motion. It was wonderful to see how the snow lay upon the heads and shoulders of these men, in little ridges an inch thick perhaps in places, the flakes steadily adding drop and drop, precisely as they fall upon the unresisting grass of the fields. The feet of the men were all wet and cold, and the wish to warm them accounted for the slow, gentle, rhythmical motion. Occasionally some man whose ear or nose tingled acutely from the cold winds would wriggle down until his head was protected by the shoulders of his companions.

There was a continuous murmuring discussion as to the probability of the doors being speedily opened. They persistently lifted their eyes towards the windows. One could hear little combats of opinion.

"There's a light in th' winder!"

"Naw; it's a reflection f'm across th' way."

"Well, didn't I see 'em light it?"

"You did?"

"I did!"

"Well, then, that settles it!"

As the time approached when they expected to be allowed to enter, the men crowded to the doors in an unspeakable crush, jamming and wedging in a way that it seemed would crack bones. They surged heavily against the building in a powerful wave of pushing shoulders. Once a rumour flitted among all the tossing heads.

"They can't open th' door! Th' fellers er smack up agin 'em."

Then a dull roar of rage came from the men on the outskirts; but all the time they strained and pushed until it appeared to be impossible for those that they cried out against to do anything but be crushed into pulp.

"Ah, git away f'm th' door!"

"Git outa that!"

"Throw 'em out!"

"Kill 'em!"

"Say, fellers, now, what th' 'ell? G've 'em a chance t' open th' door!"

"Yeh dam pigs, give 'em a chance t' open th' door!"

Men in the outskirts of the crowd occasionally yelled when a boot-heel of one of trampling feet crushed on their freezing extremities.

"Git off me feet, yeh clumsy tarrier!"

"Say, don't stand on me feet! Walk on th' ground!"

A man near the doors suddenly shouted—"O-o-oh! Le' me out—le' me out!" And another, a man of infinite valour, once twisted his head so as to half face those who were pushing behind him. "Quit yer shovin', yeh"—and he delivered a volley of the most powerful and singular invective, straight into the faces of the men behind him. It was as if he was hammering the noses of them with curses of triple brass. His face, red with rage, could be seen upon it, an expression of sublime disregard of consequences. But nobody cared to reply to his imprecations; it was too cold. Many of them snickered, and all continued to push.

In occasional pauses of the crowd's movement the men had opportunities to make jokes; usually grim things, and no doubt very uncouth. Nevertheless, they were notable—one does not expect to find the quality of humour in a heap of old clothes under a snow-drift.

The winds seemed to grow fiercer as time wore on. Some of the gusts of snow that came down on the close collection of heads, cut like knives and needles, and the men huddled, and swore, not like dark assassins, but in a sort of American fashion, grimly and desperately, it is true, but yet with a wondrous under-effect, indefinable and mystic, as if there was some kind of humour in this catastrophe, in this situation in a night of snow-laden winds.

Once the window of the huge dry-goods shop across the street furnished material for a few moments of forgetfulness. In the brilliantly-lighted space appeared the figure of a man. He was rather stout and very well clothed. His beard was fashioned charmingly after that of the Prince of Wales. He stood in an attitude of magnificent reflection. He slowly stroked his moustache with a certain grandeur of manner, and looked down at the snow-encrusted mob. From below, there was denoted a supreme complacence in him. It seemed that the sight operated inversely, and enabled him to more clearly regard his own delightful environment.

One of the mob chanced to turn his head, and perceived the figure in the window. "Hello, lookit 'is whiskers," he said genially.

Many of the men turned then, and a shout went up. They called to him in all strange keys. They addressed him in every manner, from familiar and cordial greetings, to carefully-worded advice concerning changes in his personal appearance. The man presently fled, and the mob chuckled ferociously, like ogres who had just devoured something.

They turned then to serious business. Often they addressed the stolid front of the house.

"Oh, let us in fer Gawd's sake!"

"Let us in, or we'll all drop dead!"

"Say, what's th' use o' keepin' us poor Indians out in th' cold?"

And always some one was saying, "Keep off my feet."

The crushing of the crowd grew terrific toward the last. The men, in keen pain from the blasts, began almost to fight. With the pitiless whirl of snow upon them, the battle for shelter was going to the strong. It became known that the basement door at the foot of a little steep flight of stairs was the one to be opened, and they jostled and heaved in this direction like labouring fiends. One could hear them panting and groaning in their fierce exertion.

Usually some one in the front ranks was protesting to those in the rear—"O-o-ow! Oh, say now, fellers, let up, will yeh? Do yeh wanta kill somebody!"

A policeman arrived and went into the midst of them, scolding and be-rating, occasionally threatening, but using no force but that of his hands and shoulders against these men who were only struggling to get in out of the storm. His decisive tones rang out sharply—"Stop that pushin' back there! Come, boys, don't push! Stop that! Here you, quit yer shovin'! Cheese that!"

When the door below was opened, a thick stream of men forced a way down the stairs, which were of an extraordinary narrowness, and seemed only wide enough for one at a time. Yet they somehow went down almost three abreast. It was a difficult and painful operation. The crowd was like a turbulent water forcing itself through one tiny outlet. The men in the rear, excited by the success of the others, made frantic exertions, for it seemed that this large band would more than fill the quarters, and that many would be left upon the pavements. It would be disastrous to be of the last, and accordingly men with the snow biting their faces, writhed and twisted with their might. One expected that from the tremendous pressure, the narrow passage to the basement door would be so choked and clogged with human limbs and bodies that movement would be impossible. Once indeed the crowd was forced to stop, and a cry went along that a man had been injured at the foot of the stairs. But presently the slow movement began again, and the policeman fought at the top of the flight to ease the pressure of those that were going down.

A reddish light from a window fell upon the faces of the men, when they, in turn, arrived at the last three steps, and were about to enter. One could then note a change of expression that had come over their features. As they stood thus upon the threshold of their hopes, they looked suddenly contented and complacent. The fire had passed from their eyes and the snarl had vanished from their lips. The very force of the crowd in the rear, which had previously vexed them, was regarded from another point of view, for it now made it inevitable that they should go through the little doors into the place that was cheery and warm with light.

The tossing crowd on the sidewalk grew smaller and smaller. The snow beat with merciless persistence upon the bowed heads of those who waited. The wind drove it up from the pavements in frantic forms of winding white, and it seethed in circles about the huddled forms passing in one by one, three by three, out of the storm.

THE DUEL THAT WAS NOT FOUGHT

Patsy Tulligan was not as wise as seven owls, but his courage could throw a shadow as long as the steeple of a cathedral. There were men on Cherry Street who had whipped him five times, but they all knew that Patsy would be as ready for the sixth time as if nothing had happened.

Once he and two friends had been away up on Eighth Avenue, far out of their country, and upon their return journey that evening they stopped frequently in saloons until they were as independent of their surroundings as eagles, and cared much less about thirty days on Blackwell's.

On Lower Sixth Avenue they paused in a saloon where there was a good deal of lamp-glare and polished wood to be seen from the outside, and within, the mellow light shone on much furbished brass and more polished wood. It was a better saloon than they were in the habit of seeing, but they did not mind it. They sat down at one of the little tables that were in a row parallel to the bar and ordered beer. They blinked stolidly at the decorations, the bartender, and the other customers. When anything transpired they discussed it with dazzling frankness, and what they said of it was as free as air to the other people in the place.

At midnight there were few people in the saloon. Patsy and his friends still sat drinking. Two well-dressed men were at another table, smoking cigars slowly and swinging back in their chairs. They occupied themselves with themselves in the usual manner, never betraying by a wink of an eyelid that they knew that other folk existed. At another table directly behind Patsy and his companions was a slim little Cuban, with miraculously small feet and hands, and with a youthful touch of down upon his lip. As he lifted his cigarette from time to time his little finger was bended in dainty fashion, and there was a green flash when a huge emerald ring caught the light. The bartender came often with his little brass tray. Occasionally Patsy and his two friends quarrelled.

Once this little Cuban happened to make some slight noise and Patsy turned his head to observe him. Then Patsy made a careless and rather loud comment to his two friends. He used a word which is no more than passing the time of day down in Cherry Street, but to the Cuban it was a dagger-point. There was a harsh scraping sound as a chair was pushed swiftly back.

The little Cuban was upon his feet. His eyes were shining with a rage that flashed there like sparks as he glared at Patsy. His olive face had turned a shade of grey from his anger. Withal his chest was thrust out in portentous dignity, and his hand, still grasping his wine-glass, was cool and steady, the little finger still bended, the great emerald gleaming upon it. The others, motionless, stared at him.

"Sir," he began ceremoniously. He spoke gravely and in a slow way, his tone coming in a marvel of self-possessed cadences from between those lips which quivered with wrath. "You have insult me. You are a dog, a hound, a cur. I spit upon you. I must have some of your blood."

Patsy looked at him over his shoulder.

"What's th' matter wi' che?" he demanded. He did not quite understand the words of this little man who glared at him steadily, but he knew that it was something about fighting. He snarled with the readiness of his class and heaved his shoulders contemptuously. "Ah, what's eatin' yeh? Take a walk! You h'ain't got nothin' t' do with me, have yeh? Well, den, go sit on yerself."

And his companions leaned back valorously in their chairs, and scrutinized this slim young fellow who was addressing Patsy.

"What's de little Dago chewin' about?"

"He wants t' scrap!"

"What!"

The Cuban listened with apparent composure. It was only when they laughed that his body cringed as if he was receiving lashes. Presently he put down his glass and walked over to their table. He proceeded always with the most impressive deliberation.

"Sir," he began again. "You have insult me. I must have s-s-satisfac-shone. I must have your body upon the point of my sword. In my country you would already be dead. I must have s-s-satisfac-shone."

Patsy had looked at the Cuban with a trifle of bewilderment. But at last his face began to grow dark with belligerency, his mouth curve in that wide sneer with which he would confront an angel of darkness. He arose suddenly in his seat and came towards the little Cuban. He was going to be impressive too.

"Say, young feller, if yeh go shootin' off fer face at me, I'll wipe d' joint wid yeh. What'cher gaffin' about, hey? Are yeh givin' me er jolly? Say, if yeh pick me up fer a cinch, I'll fool yeh. Dat's what! Don't take me fer no dead easy mug." And as he glowered at the little Cuban, he ended his oration with one eloquent word, "Nit!"

The bar-tender nervously polished his bar with a towel, and kept his eyes fastened upon the men. Occasionally he became transfixed with interest, leaning forward with one hand upon the edge of the bar and the other holding the towel grabbed in a lump, as if he had been turned into bronze when in the very act of polishing.

The Cuban did not move when Patsy came toward him and delivered his oration. At its conclusion he turned his livid face toward where, above him, Patsy was swaggering and heaving his shoulders in a consummate display of bravery and readiness. The Cuban, in his clear, tense tones, spoke one word. It was the bitter insult. It seemed to fairly spin from his lips and crackle in the air like breaking glass.

Every man save the little Cuban made an electric movement. Patsy roared a black oath and thrust himself forward until he towered almost directly above the other man. His fists were doubled into knots of bone and hard flesh. The Cuban had raised a steady finger.

"If you touch me wis your hand, I will keel you."

The two well-dressed men had come swiftly, uttering protesting cries. They suddenly intervened in this second of time in which Patsy had sprung forward and the Cuban had uttered his threat. The four men were now a tossing, arguing, violent group, one well-dressed man lecturing the Cuban, and the other holding off Patsy, who was now wild with rage, loudly repeating the Cuban's threat, and manoeuvring and struggling to get at him for revenge's sake.

The bar-tender, feverishly scouring away with his towel, and at times pacing to and fro with nervous and excited tread, shouted out—

"Say, for heaven's sake, don't fight in here. If yeh wanta fight, go out in the street and fight all yeh please. But don't fight in here."

Patsy knew only one thing, and this he kept repeating—

"Well, he wants t' scrap! I didn't begin dis! He wants t' scrap."

The well-dressed man confronting him continually replied—

"Oh, well, now, look here, he's only a lad. He don't know what he's doing. He's crazy mad. You wouldn't slug a kid like that."

Patsy and his aroused companions, who cursed and growled, were persistent with their argument. "Well, he wants t' scrap!" The whole affair was as plain as daylight when one saw this great fact. The interference and intolerable discussion brought the three of them forward, battleful and fierce.

"What's eatin' you, anyhow?" they demanded. "Dis ain't your business, is it? What business you got shootin' off your face?"

The other peacemaker was trying to restrain the little Cuban, who had grown shrill and violent.

"If he touch me wis his hand I will keel him. We must fight like gentlemen or else I keel him when he touch me wis his hand."

The man who was fending off Patsy comprehended these sentences that were screamed behind his back, and he explained to Patsy—

"But he wants to fight you with swords. With swords, you know."

The Cuban, dodging around the peacemakers, yelled in Patsy's face—

"Ah, if I could get you before me wis my sword! Ah! Ah! A-a-ah!" Patsy made a furious blow with a swift fist, but the peacemakers bucked against his body suddenly like football players.

Patsy was greatly puzzled. He continued doggedly to try to get near enough to the Cuban to punch him. To these attempts the Cuban replied savagely—

"If you touch me wis your hand, I will cut your heart in two piece."

At last Patsy said—"Well, if he's so dead stuck on fightin' wid swords, I'll fight 'im. Soitenly! I'll fight 'im." All this palaver had evidently tired him, and he now puffed out his lips with the air of a man who is willing to submit to any conditions if he can only bring on the row soon enough. He swaggered, "I'll fight 'im wid swords. Let 'im bring on his swords, an' I'll fight 'im 'til he's ready t' quit."

The two well-dressed men grinned. "Why, look here," they said to Patsy, "he'd punch you full of holes. Why, he's a fencer. You can't fight him with swords. He'd kill you in 'bout a minute."

"Well, I'll giv' 'im a go at it, anyhow," said Patsy, stout-hearted and resolute. "I'll giv' 'im a go at it, anyhow, an' I'll stay wid 'im long as I kin."

As for the Cuban, his lithe little body was quivering in an ecstasy of the muscles. His face radiant with a savage joy, he fastened his glance upon Patsy, his eyes gleaming with a gloating, murderous light. A most unspeakable, animal-like rage was in his expression.

"Ah! ah! He will fight me! Ah!" He bended unconsciously in the posture of a fencer. He had all the quick, springy movements of a skilful swordsman. "Ah, the b-r-r-rute! The b-r-r-rute! I will stick him like a pig!"

The two peacemakers, still grinning broadly, were having a great time with Patsy.

"Why, you infernal idiot, this man would slice you all up. You better jump off the bridge if you want to commit suicide. You wouldn't stand a ghost of a chance to live ten seconds."

Patsy was as unshaken as granite. "Well, if he wants t' fight wid swords, he'll get it. I'll giv' 'im a go at it, anyhow."

One man said—"Well, have you got a sword? Do you know what a sword is? Have you got a sword?"

"No, I ain't got none," said Patsy honestly, "but I kin git one." Then he added valiantly—"An' quick too."

The two men laughed. "Why, can't you understand it would be sure death to fight a sword duel with this fellow?"

"Dat's all right! See? I know me own business. If he wants t' fight one of dees d—n duels, I'm in it, understan'?"

"Have you ever fought one, you fool?"

"No, I ain't. But I will fight one, dough! I ain't no muff. If he want t' fight a duel, by Gawd, I'm wid 'im! D'yeh understan' dat!" Patsy cocked his hat and swaggered. He was getting very serious.

The little Cuban burst out—"Ah, come on, sirs: come on! We can take cab. Ah, you big cow, I will stick you, I will stick you. Ah, you will look very beautiful, very beautiful. Ah, come on, sirs. We will stop at hotel—my hotel. I there have weapons."

"Yeh will, will yeh? Yeh bloomin' little black Dago," cried Patsy in hoarse and maddened reply to the personal part of the Cuban's speech. He stepped forward. "Git yer d—n swords," he commanded. "Git yer swords. Git 'em quick! I'll fight wi' che! I'll fight wid anyting, too! See? I'll fight yeh wid a knife an' fork if yeh say so! I'll fight yer standin' up er sittin' down!" Patsy delivered this intense oration with sweeping, intensely emphatic gestures, his hands stretched out eloquently, his jaw thrust forward, his eyes glaring.

"Ah," cried the little Cuban joyously. "Ah, you are in very pretty temper. Ah, how I will cut your heart in two piece, my dear, d-e-a-r friend." His eyes, too, shone like carbuncles, with a swift, changing glitter, always fastened upon Patsy's face.

The two peacemakers were perspiring and in despair. One of them

364

blurted out—

"Well, I'll be blamed if this ain't the most ridiculous thing I ever saw."

The other said—"For ten dollars I'd be tempted to let these two infernal blockheads have their duel."

Patsy was strutting to and fro, and conferring grandly with his friends.

"He took me for a muff. He tought he was goin' t' bluff me out, talkin' 'bout swords. He'll get fooled." He addressed the Cuban—"You're a fine little dirty picter of a scrapper, ain't che? I'll chew yez up, dat's what I will."

There began then some rapid action. The patience of well-dressed men is not an eternal thing. It began to look as if it would at last be a fight with six corners to it. The faces of the men were shining red with anger. They jostled each other defiantly, and almost every one blazed out at three or four of the others. The bar-tender had given up protesting. He swore for a time, and banged his glasses. Then he jumped the bar and ran out of the saloon, cursing sullenly.

When he came back with a policeman, Patsy and the Cuban were preparing to depart together. Patsy was delivering his last oration—

"I'll fight yer wid swords! Sure I will! Come ahead, Dago! I'll fight yeh anywheres wid anyting! We'll have a large, juicy scrap, an' don't yeh forgit dat! I'm right wid yez. I ain't no muff! I scrap wid a man jest as soon as he ses scrap, an' if yeh wanta scrap, I'm yer kitten. Understan' dat?"

The policeman said sharply—"Come, now; what's all this?" He had a distinctly business air.

The little Cuban stepped forward calmly. "It is none of your business."

The policeman flushed to his ears. "What?"

One well-dressed man touched the other on the sleeve. "Here's the time to skip," he whispered. They halted a block away from the saloon and watched the policeman pull the Cuban through the door. There was a minute of scuffle on the sidewalk, and into this deserted street at midnight fifty people appeared at once as if from the sky to watch it.

At last the three Cherry Hill men came from the saloon, and swaggered with all their old valour toward the peacemakers.

"Ah," said Patsy to them, "he was so hot talkin' about this duel business, but I would a-given 'im a great scrap, an' don't yeh forgit it."

For Patsy was not as wise as seven owls, but his courage could throw a shadow as long as the steeple of a cathedral.

AN OMINOUS BABY

A baby was wandering in a strange country. He was a tattered child with a frowsled wealth of yellow hair. His dress, of a checked stuff, was soiled, and showed the marks of many conflicts, like the chain-shirt of a warrior. His sun-tanned knees shone above wrinkled stockings, which he pulled up occasionally with an impatient movement when they entangled his feet. From a gaping shoe there appeared an array of tiny toes.

He was toddling along an avenue between rows of stolid brown houses. He went slowly, with a look of absorbed interest on his small flushed face. His blue eyes stared curiously. Carriages went with a musical rumble over the smooth asphalt. A man with a chrysanthemum was going up steps. Two nursery maids chatted as they walked slowly, while their charges hobnobbed amiably between perambulators. A truck wagon roared thunderously in the distance.

The child from the poor district made his way along the brown street filled with dull grey shadows. High up, near the roofs, glancing sun-rays changed cornices to blazing gold and silvered the fronts of windows. The wandering baby stopped and stared at the two children laughing and playing in their carriages among the heaps of rugs and cushions. He braced his legs apart in an attitude of earnest attention. His lower jaw fell, and disclosed his small, even teeth. As they moved on, he followed the carriages with awe in his face as if contemplating a pageant. Once one of the babies, with twittering laughter, shook a gorgeous rattle at him. He smiled jovially in return.

Finally a nursery maid ceased conversation and, turning, made a gesture of annoyance.

"Go 'way, little boy," she said to him. "Go 'way. You're all dirty."

He gazed at her with infant tranquillity for a moment, and then went slowly off dragging behind him a bit of rope he had acquired in another street. He continued to investigate the new scenes. The people and houses struck him with interest as would flowers and trees. Passengers had to avoid the small, absorbed figure in the middle of the sidewalk. They glanced at the intent baby face covered with scratches and dust as with scars and with powder smoke.

After a time, the wanderer discovered upon the pavement a pretty child in fine clothes playing with a toy. It was a tiny fire-engine, painted brilliantly in crimson and gold. The wheels rattled as its small owner dragged it uproariously about by means of a string. The babe with his bit of rope trailing behind him paused and regarded the child and the toy. For a long while he remained motionless, save for his eyes, which followed all movements of the glittering thing. The owner paid no attention to the spectator, but continued his joyous imitations of phases of the career of a fire-engine. His gleeful baby laugh rang against the calm fronts of the houses. After a little the wandering baby began quietly to sidle nearer. His bit of rope, now forgotten, dropped at his feet. He removed his eyes from the toy and glanced expectantly at the other child.

"Say," he breathed softly.

The owner of the toy was running down the walk at top speed. His tongue was clanging like a bell and his legs were galloping. He did not look around at the coaxing call from the small tattered figure on the curb.

The wandering baby approached still nearer, and presently spoke again.

"Say," he murmured, "le' me play wif it?"

The other child interrupted some shrill tootings. He bended his head and spoke disdainfully over his shoulder.

"No," he said.

The wanderer retreated to the curb. He failed to notice the bit of rope, once treasured. His eyes followed as before the winding course of the engine, and his tender mouth twitched.

"Say," he ventured at last, "is dat yours?"

"Yes," said the other, tilting his round chin. He drew his property suddenly behind him as if it were menaced. "Yes," he repeated, "it's mine."

"Well, le' me play wif it?" said the wandering baby, with a trembling note of desire in his voice.

"No," cried the pretty child with determined lips. "It's mine. My ma-ma buyed it."

"Well, tan't I play wif it?" His voice was a sob. He stretched forth little covetous hands.

"No," the pretty child continued to repeat. "No, it's mine."

"Well, I want to play wif it," wailed the other. A sudden fierce frown mantled his baby face. He clenched his fat hands and advanced with a formidable gesture. He looked some wee battler in a war.

"It's mine! It's mine," cried the pretty child, his voice in the treble of outraged rights.

"I want it," roared the wanderer.

"It's mine! It's mine!"

"I want it!"

"It's mine!"

The pretty child retreated to the fence, and there paused at bay. He protected his property with outstretched arms. The small vandal made a charge. There was a short scuffle at the fence. Each grasped the string to the toy and tugged. Their faces were wrinkled with baby rage, the verge of tears. Finally, the child in tatters gave a supreme tug and wrenched the string from the other's hands. He set off rapidly down the street, bearing the toy in his arms. He was weeping with the air of a wronged one who has at last succeeded in achieving his rights. The other baby was squalling lustily. He seemed quite helpless. He rung his chubby hands and railed.

After the small barbarian had got some distance away, he paused and regarded his booty. His little form curved with pride. A soft, gleeful smile loomed through the storm of tears. With great care he prepared the toy for travelling. He stopped a moment on a corner and gazed at the pretty child, whose small figure was quivering with sobs. As the latter began to show signs of beginning pursuit, the little vandal turned and vanished down a dark side street as into a cavern.

A GREAT MISTAKE

An Italian kept a fruit-stand on a corner where he had good aim at the people who came down from the elevated station, and at those who went along two thronged streets. He sat most of the day in a backless chair that was placed strategically.

There was a babe living hard by, up five flights of stairs, who regarded this Italian as a tremendous being. The babe had investigated this fruit-stand. It had thrilled him as few things he had met with in his travels had thrilled him. The sweets of the world had laid there in dazzling rows, tumbled in luxurious heaps. When he gazed at this Italian seated amid such splendid treasures, his lower lip hung low and his eyes, raised to the vendor's face, were filled with deep respect, worship, as if he saw omnipotence.

The babe came often to this corner. He hovered about the stand and watched each detail of the business. He was fascinated by the tranquillity of the vendor, the majesty of power and possession. At times he was so engrossed in his contemplation that people, hurrying, had to use care to avoid bumping him down.

He had never ventured very near to the stand. It was his habit to hang warily about the curb. Even there he resembled a babe who looks unbidden at a feast of gods.

One day, however, as the baby was thus staring, the vendor arose, and going along the front of the stand, began to polish oranges with a red pocket handkerchief. The breathless spectator moved across the side walk until his small face almost touched the vendor's sleeve. His fingers were gripped in a fold of his dress.

At last, the Italian finished with the oranges and returned to his chair. He drew a newspaper printed in his language from behind a bunch of bananas. He settled himself in a comfortable position, and began to glare savagely at the print. The babe was left face to face with the massed joys of the world. For a time he was a simple worshipper at this golden shrine. Then tumultuous desires began to shake him. His dreams were of conquest. His lips moved. Presently into his head there came a little plan. He sidled nearer, throwing swift and cunning glances at the Italian. He strove to maintain his conventional manner, but the whole plot was written upon his countenance.

At last he had come near enough to touch the fruit. From the tattered skirt came slowly his small dirty hand. His eyes were still fixed upon the vendor. His features were set, save for the under lip, which had a faint fluttering movement. The hand went forward.

Elevated trains thundered to the station and the stairway poured people upon the sidewalks. There was a deep sea roar from feet and wheels going ceaselessly. None seemed to perceive the babe engaged in a great venture.

The Italian turned his paper. Sudden panic smote the babe. His hand dropped, and he gave vent to a cry of dismay. He remained for a moment staring at the vendor. There was evidently a great debate in his mind. His infant intellect had defined this Italian. The latter was undoubtedly a man who would eat babes that provoked him. And the alarm in the babe when this monarch had turned his newspaper brought vividly before him the consequences if he were detected. But at this moment the vendor gave a blissful grunt, and tilting his chair against a wall, closed his eyes. His paper dropped unheeded.

The babe ceased his scrutiny and again raised his hand. It was moved with supreme caution toward the fruit. The fingers were bent, claw-like, in the manner of great heart-shaking greed. Once he stopped and chattered convulsively, because the vendor moved in his sleep. The babe, with his eyes still upon the Italian, again put forth his hand, and the rapacious fingers closed over a round bulb.

And it was written that the Italian should at this moment open his eyes. He glared at the babe a fierce question. Thereupon the babe thrust the round bulb behind him, and with a face expressive of the deepest guilt, began a wild but elaborate series of gestures declaring his innocence. The Italian howled. He sprang to his feet, and with three steps overtook the babe. He whirled him fiercely, and took from the little fingers a lemon.

AN ELOQUENCE OF GRIEF

The windows were high and saintly, of the shape that is found in churches. From time to time a policeman at the door spoke sharply to some incoming person. "Take your hat off!" He displayed in his voice the horror of a priest when the sanctity of a chapel is defied or forgotten. The court-room was crowded with people who sloped back comfortably in their chairs, regarding with undeviating glances the procession and its attendant and guardian policemen that moved slowly inside the spear-topped railing. All persons connected with a case went close to the magistrate's desk before a word was spoken in the matter, and then their voices were toned to the ordinary talking strength. The crowd in the court-room could not hear a sentence; they could merely see shifting figures, men that gestured quietly, women that sometimes raised an eager eloquent arm. They could not always see the judge, although they were able to estimate his location by the tall stands surmounted by white globes that were at either hand of him. And so those who had come for curiosity's sweet sake wore an air of being in wait for a cry of anguish, some loud painful protestation that would bring the proper thrill to their jaded, world-weary nerves—wires that refused to vibrate for ordinary affairs.

Inside the railing the court officers shuffled the various groups with speed and skill; and behind the desk the magistrate patiently toiled his way through mazes of wonderful testimony.

In a corner of this space, devoted to those who had business before the judge, an officer in plain clothes stood with a girl that wept constantly. None seemed to notice the girl, and there was no reason why she should be noticed, if the curious in the body of the court-room were not interested in the devastation which tears bring upon some complexions. Her tears seemed to burn like acid, and they left fierce pink marks on her face. Occasionally the girl looked across the room, where two well-dressed young women and a man stood waiting with the serenity of people who are not concerned as to the interior fittings of a jail.

The business of the court progressed, and presently the girl, the officer, and the well-dressed contingent stood before the judge. Thereupon two lawyers engaged in some preliminary fire-wheels, which were endured generally in silence. The girl, it appeared, was accused of stealing fifty dollars' worth of silk clothing from the room of one of the well-dressed women. She had been a servant in the house.

In a clear way, and with none of the ferocity that an accuser often exhibits in a police-court, calmly and moderately, the two young women gave their testimony. Behind them stood their escort, always mute. His part, evidently, was to furnish the dignity, and he furnished it heavily, almost massively.

When they had finished, the girl told her part. She had full, almost Afric, lips, and they had turned quite white. The lawyer for the others asked some questions, which he did—be it said, in passing—with the air of a man throwing flower-pots at a stone house.

It was a short case and soon finished. At the end of it the judge said that, considering the evidence, he would have to commit the girl for trial. Instantly the quick-eyed court officer began to clear the way for the next case. The well-dressed women and their escort turned one way and the girl turned another, toward a door with an austere arch leading into a stone-paved passage. Then it was that a great cry rang through the court-room, the cry of this girl who believed that she was lost.

The loungers, many of them, underwent a spasmodic movement as if they had been knived. The court officers rallied quickly. The girl fell back opportunely for the arms of one of them, and her wild heels clicked twice on the floor. "I am innocent! Oh, I am innocent!"

People pity those who need none, and the guilty sob alone; but innocent or guilty, this girl's scream described such a profound depth of woe—it was so graphic of grief, that it slit with a dagger's sweep the curtain of common-place, and disclosed the gloom-shrouded spectre that sat in the young girl's heart so plainly, in so universal a tone of the mind, that a man heard expressed some far-off midnight terror of his own thought.

The cries died away down the stone-paved passage. A patrol-man leaned one arm composedly on the railing, and down below him stood an aged, almost toothless wanderer, tottering and grinning.

"Plase, yer honer," said the old man as the time arrived for him to speak, "if ye'll lave me go this time, I've niver been dhrunk befoor, sir."

A court officer lifted his hand to hide a smile.

THE AUCTION

Some said that Ferguson gave up sailoring because he was tired of the sea. Some said that it was because he loved a woman. In truth it was because he was tired of the sea and because he loved a woman.

He saw the woman once, and immediately she became for him the symbol of all things unconnected with the sea. He did not trouble to look again at the grey old goddess, the muttering slave of the moon. Her splendours, her treacheries, her smiles, her rages, her vanities, were no longer on his mind. He took heels after a little human being, and the woman made his thought spin at all times like a top; whereas the ocean had only made him think when he was on watch.

He developed a grin for the power of the sea, and, in derision, he wanted to sell the red and green parrot which had sailed four voyages with him. The woman, however, had a sentiment concerning the bird's plumage, and she commanded Ferguson to keep it in order, as it happened, that she might forget to put food in its cage.

The parrot did not attend the wedding. It stayed at home and blasphemed at a stock of furniture, bought on the installment plan, and arrayed for the reception of the bride and groom.

As a sailor, Ferguson had suffered the acute hankering for port; and being now always in port, he tried to force life to become an endless picnic. He was not an example of diligent and peaceful citizenship. Ablution became difficult in the little apartment, because Ferguson kept the wash-basin filled with ice and bottles of beer: and so, finally, the dealer in second-hand furniture agreed to auction the household goods on commission. Owing to an exceedingly liberal definition of a term, the parrot and cage were included. "On the level?" cried the parrot, "On the level? On the level? On the level?"

On the way to the sale, Ferguson's wife spoke hopefully. "You can't tell, Jim," she said. "Perhaps some of 'em will get to biddin', and we might get almost as much as we paid for the things."

The auction room was in a cellar. It was crowded with people and with house furniture; so that as the auctioneer's assistant moved from one piece to another he caused a great shuffling. There was an astounding number of old women in curious bonnets. The rickety stairway was thronged with men who wished to smoke and be free from the old women. Two lamps made all the faces appear yellow as parchment. Incidentally they could impart a lustre of value to very poor furniture.

The auctioneer was a fat, shrewd-looking individual, who seemed also to be a great bully. The assistant was the most imperturbable of beings, moving with the dignity of an image on rollers. As the Fergusons forced their way down the stair-way, the assistant roared: "Number twenty-one!"

"Number twenty-one!" cried the auctioneer. "Number twenty-one! A fine new handsome bureau! Two dollars? Two dollars is bid! Two and a half! Two and a half! Three? Three is bid. Four! Four dollars! A fine new handsome bureau at four dollars! Four dollars! Four dollars! F-o-u-r d-o-l-l-a-r-s! Sold at four dollars."

"On the level?" cried the parrot, muffled somewhere among furniture and carpets. "On the level? On the level?" Every one tittered.

Mrs. Ferguson had turned pale, and gripped her husband's arm. "Jim! Did you hear? The bureau—four dollars—"

Ferguson glowered at her with the swift brutality of a man afraid of a scene. "Shut up, can't you!"

Mrs. Ferguson took a seat upon the steps; and hidden there by the thick ranks of men, she began to softly sob. Through her tears appeared the yellowish mist of the lamplight, streaming about the monstrous shadows of the spectators. From time to time these latter whispered eagerly: "See, that went cheap!" In fact when anything was bought at a particularly low price, a murmur of admiration arose for the successful bidder.

The bedstead was sold for two dollars, the mattresses and springs for one dollar and sixty cents. This figure seemed to go through the woman's heart. There was derision in the sound of it. She bowed her head in her hands. "Oh, God, a dollar-sixty! Oh, God, a dollar-sixty!"

The parrot was evidently under heaps of carpet, but the dauntless bird still raised the cry, "On the level?"

Some of the men near Mrs. Ferguson moved timidly away upon hearing her low sobs. They perfectly understood that a woman in tears is formidable.

The shrill voice went like a hammer, beat and beat, upon the woman's heart. An odour of varnish, of the dust of old carpets, assailed her and seemed to possess a sinister meaning. The golden haze from the two lamps was an atmosphere of shame, sorrow, greed. But it was when the parrot called that a terror of the place and of the eyes of the people arose in her so strongly that she could not have lifted her head any more than if her neck had been of iron.

At last came the parrot's turn. The assistant fumbled until he found the ring of the cage, and the bird was drawn into view. It adjusted its feathers calmly and cast a rolling wicked eye over the crowd.

"Oh, the good ship Sarah sailed the seas,

And the wind it blew all day—"

This was the part of a ballad which Ferguson had tried to teach it. With a singular audacity and scorn, the parrot bawled these lines at the auctioneer as if it considered them to bear some particular insult.

The throng in the cellar burst into laughter. The auctioneer attempted to start the bidding, and the parrot interrupted with a repetition of the lines. It swaggered to and fro on its perch, and gazed at the faces of the crowd, with so much rowdy understanding and derision that even the auctioneer could not confront it. The auction was brought to a halt; a wild hilarity developed, and every one gave jeering advice.

Ferguson looked down at his wife and groaned. She had cowered against the wall, hiding her face. He touched her shoulder and she arose. They sneaked softly up the stairs with heads bowed.

Out in the street, Ferguson gripped his fists and said: "Oh, but wouldn't I like to strangle it!"

His wife cried in a voice of wild grief: "It—it m—made us a laughing-stock in—in front of all that crowd!"

For the auctioning of their household goods, the sale of their home—this financial calamity lost its power in the presence of the social shame contained in a crowd's laughter.

THE PACE OF YOUTH

I

Stimson stood in a corner and glowered. He was a fierce man and had indomitable whiskers, albeit he was very small.

"That young tarrier," he whispered to himself. "He wants to quit makin' eyes at Lizzie. This is too much of a good thing. First thing you know, he'll get fired."

His brow creased in a frown, he strode over to the huge open doors and looked at a sign. "Stimson's Mammoth Merry-Go-Round," it read, and the glory of it was great. Stimson stood and contemplated the sign. It was an enormous affair; the letters were as large as men. The glow of it, the grandeur of it was very apparent to Stimson. At the end of his contemplation, he shook his head thoughtfully, determinedly. "No, no," he muttered. "This is too much of a good thing. First thing you know, he'll get fired."

A soft booming sound of surf, mingled with the cries of bathers, came from the beach. There was a vista of sand and sky and sea that drew to a mystic point far away in the northward. In the mighty angle, a girl in a red dress was crawling slowly like some kind of a spider on the fabric of nature. A few flags hung lazily above where the bath-houses were marshalled in compact squares. Upon the edge of the sea stood a ship with its shadowy sails painted dimly upon the sky, and high overhead in the still, sun-shot air a great hawk swung and drifted slowly.

Within the Merry-Go-Round there was a whirling circle of ornamental lions, giraffes, camels, ponies, goats, glittering with varnish and metal that caught swift reflections from windows high above them. With stiff wooden legs, they swept on in a never-ending race, while a great orchestrion clamoured in wild speed. The summer sunlight sprinkled its gold upon the garnet canopies carried by the tireless racers and upon all the devices of decoration that made Stimson's machine magnificent and famous. A host of laughing children bestrode the animals, bending forward like charging cavalrymen, and shaking reins and whooping in glee. At intervals they leaned out perilously to clutch at iron rings that were tendered to them by a long wooden arm. At the intense moment before the swift grab for the rings one could see their little nervous bodies quiver with eagerness; the laughter rang shrill and excited. Down in the long rows of benches, crowds of people sat watching the game, while occasionally a father might arise and go near to shout encouragement, cautionary commands, or applause at his flying offspring. Frequently mothers called out: "Be careful, Georgie!" The orchestrion bellowed and thundered on its platform, filling the ears with its long monotonous song. Over in a corner, a man in a white apron and behind a counter roared above the tumult: "Pop corn! Pop corn!"

A young man stood upon a small, raised platform, erected in a manner of a pulpit, and just without the line of the circling figures. It was his duty to manipulate the wooden arm and affix the rings. When all were gone into the hands of the triumphant children, he held forth a basket, into which they returned all save the coveted brass one, which meant another ride free and made the holder very illustrious. The young man stood all day upon his narrow platform, affixing rings or holding forth the basket. He was a sort of general squire in these lists of childhood. He was very busy.

And yet Stimson, the astute, had noticed that the young man frequently found time to twist about on his platform and smile at a girl who shyly sold tickets behind a silvered netting. This, indeed, was the great reason of Stimson's glowering. The young man upon the raised platform had no manner of licence to smile at the girl behind the silvered netting. It was a most gigantic insolence. Stimson was amazed at it. "By Jiminy," he said to himself again, "that fellow is smiling at my daughter." Even in this tone of great wrath it could be discerned that Stimson was filled with wonder that any youth should dare smile at the daughter in the presence of the august father.

Often the dark-eyed girl peered between the shining wires, and, upon being detected by the young man, she usually turned her head away quickly to prove to him that she was not interested. At other times, however, her eyes seemed filled with a tender fear lest he should fall from that exceedingly dangerous platform. As for the young man, it was plain that these glances filled him with valour, and he stood carelessly upon his perch, as if he deemed it of no consequence that he might fall from it. In all the complexities of his daily life and duties he found opportunity to gaze ardently at the vision behind the netting.

This silent courtship was conducted over the heads of the crowd who thronged about the bright machine. The swift eloquent glances of the young man went noiselessly and unseen with their message. There had finally become established between the two in this manner a subtle understanding and companionship. They communicated accurately all that they felt. The boy told his love, his reverence, his hope in the changes of the future. The girl told him that she loved him, that she did not love him, that she did not know if she loved him, that she loved him. Sometimes a little sign saying "cashier" in gold letters, and hanging upon the silvered netting, got directly in range and interfered with the tender message.

The love affair had not continued without anger, unhappiness, despair. The girl had once smiled brightly upon a youth who came to buy some tickets for his little sister, and the young man upon the platform observing this smile had been filled with gloomy rage. He stood like a dark statue of vengeance upon his pedestal and thrust out the basket to the children with a gesture that was full of scorn for their hollow happiness, for their insecure and temporary joy. For five hours he did not once look at the girl when she was looking at him. He was going to crush her with his indifference; he was going to demonstrate that he had never been serious. However, when he narrowly observed her in secret he discovered that she seemed more blythe than was usual with her. When he found that his apparent indifference had not crushed her he suffered greatly. She did not love him, he concluded. If she had loved him she would have been crushed. For two days he lived a miserable existence upon his high perch. He consoled himself by thinking of how unhappy he was, and by swift, furtive glances at the loved face. At any rate he was in her presence, and he could get a good view from his perch when there was no interference by the little sign: "Cashier."

382

But suddenly, swiftly, these clouds vanished, and under the imperial blue sky of the restored confidence they dwelt in peace, a peace that was satisfaction, a peace that, like a babe, put its trust in the treachery of the future. This confidence endured until the next day, when she, for an unknown cause, suddenly refused to look at him. Mechanically he continued his task, his brain dazed, a tortured victim of doubt, fear, suspicion. With his eyes he supplicated her to telegraph an explanation. She replied with a stony glance that froze his blood. There was a great difference in their respective reasons for becoming angry. His were always foolish, but apparent, plain as the moon. Hers were subtle, feminine, as incomprehensible as the stars, as mysterious as the shadows at night.

They fell and soared, and soared and fell in this manner until they knew that to live without each other would be a wandering in deserts. They had grown so intent upon the uncertainties, the variations, the guessings of their affair that the world had become but a huge immaterial background. In time of peace their smiles were soft and prayerful, caresses confided to the air. In time of war, their youthful hearts, capable of profound agony, were wrung by the intricate emotions of doubt. They were the victims of the dread angel of affectionate speculation that forces the brain endlessly on roads that lead nowhere.

At night, the problem of whether she loved him confronted the young man like a spectre, looming as high as a hill and telling him not to delude himself. Upon the following day, this battle of the night displayed itself in the renewed fervour of his glances and in their increased number. Whenever he thought he could detect that she too was suffering, he felt a thrill of joy.

But there came a time when the young man looked back upon these contortions with contempt. He believed then that he had imagined his pain. This came about when the redoubtable Stimson marched forward to participate.

"This has got to stop," Stimson had said to himself, as he stood and watched them. They had grown careless of the light world that clattered about them; they were become so engrossed in their personal drama that the language of their eyes was almost as obvious as gestures. And Stimson, through his keenness, his wonderful, infallible penetration, suddenly came into possession of these obvious facts. "Well, of all the nerves," he said, regarding with a new interest the young man upon the perch.

He was a resolute man. He never hesitated to grapple with a crisis. He decided to overturn everything at once, for, although small, he was very fierce and impetuous. He resolved to crush this dreaming.

He strode over to the silvered netting. "Say, you want to quit your everlasting grinning at that idiot," he said, grimly.

The girl cast down her eyes and made a little heap of quarters into a stack. She was unable to withstand the terrible scrutiny of her small and fierce father.

Stimson turned from his daughter and went to a spot beneath the platform. He fixed his eyes upon the young man and said—

"I've been speakin' to Lizzie. You better attend strictly to your own business or there'll be a new man here next week." It was as if he had blazed away with a shot-gun. The young man reeled upon his perch. At last he in a measure regained his composure and managed to stammer: "A—all right, sir." He knew that denials would be futile with the terrible Stimson. He agitatedly began to rattle the rings in the basket, and pretend that he was obliged to count them or inspect them in some way. He, too, was unable to face the great Stimson.

For a moment, Stimson stood in fine satisfaction and gloated over the effect of his threat.

"I've fixed them," he said complacently, and went out to smoke a cigar and revel in himself. Through his mind went the proud reflection that people who came in contact with his granite will usually ended in quick and abject submission.

II

One evening, a week after Stimson had indulged in the proud reflection that people who came in contact with his granite will usually ended in quick and abject submission, a young feminine friend of the girl behind the silvered netting came to her there and asked her to walk on the beach after "Stimson's Mammoth Merry-Go-Round" was closed for the night. The girl assented with a nod.

The young man upon the perch holding the rings saw this nod and judged its meaning. Into his mind came an idea of defeating the watchfulness of the redoubtable Stimson.

When the Merry-Go-Round was closed and the two girls started for the beach, he wandered off aimlessly in another direction, but he kept them in view, and as soon as he was assured that he had escaped the vigilance of Stimson, he followed them.

The electric lights on the beach made a broad band of tremoring light, extending parallel to the sea, and upon the wide walk there slowly paraded a great crowd, intermingling, intertwining, sometimes colliding. In the darkness stretched the vast purple expanse of the ocean, and the deep indigo sky above was peopled with yellow stars. Occasionally out upon the water a whirling mass of froth suddenly flashed into view, like a great ghostly robe appearing, and then vanished, leaving the sea in its darkness, from whence came those bass tones of the water's unknown emotion. A wind, cool, reminiscent of the wave wastes, made the women hold their wraps about their throats, and caused the men to grip the rims of their straw hats. It carried the noise of the band in the pavilion in gusts. Sometimes people unable to hear the music, glanced up at the pavilion and were reassured upon beholding the distant leader still gesticulating and bobbing, and the other members of the band with their lips glued to their instruments. High in the sky soared an unassuming moon, faintly silver.

For a time the young man was afraid to approach the two girls; he followed them at a distance and called himself a coward. At last, however, he saw them stop on the outer edge of the crowd and stand silently listening to the voices of the sea. When he came to where they stood, he was trembling in his agitation. They had not seen him.

"Lizzie," he began. "I——"

The girl wheeled instantly and put her hand to her throat.

"Oh, Frank, how you frightened me," she said—inevitably.

"Well, you know I—I——" he stuttered.

But the other girl was one of those beings who are born to attend at tragedies. She had for love a reverence, an admiration that was greater the more that she contemplated the fact that she knew nothing of it. This couple, with their emotions, awed her and made her humbly wish that she might be destined to be of some service to them. She was very homely.

When the young man faltered before them, she, in her sympathy, actually over-estimated the crisis, and felt that he might fall dying at their feet. Shyly, but with courage, she marched to the rescue.

"Won't you come and walk on the beach with us?" she said.

The young woman gave her a glance of deep gratitude which was not without the patronage which a man in his condition naturally feels for one who pities it. The three walked on.

Finally, the being who was born to attend at this tragedy, said that she wished to sit down and gaze at the sea, alone.

They politely urged her to walk on with them, but she was obstinate. She wished to gaze at the sea, alone. The young man swore to himself that he would be her friend until he died.

And so the two young lovers went on without her. They turned once to look at her.

"Jennie's awful nice," said the girl.

"You bet she is," replied the young man, ardently.

They were silent for a little time.

At last the girl said—

"You were angry at me yesterday."

"No, I wasn't."

"Yes, you were, too. You wouldn't look at me once all day."

"No, I wasn't angry. I was only putting on."

Though she had, of course, known it, this confession seemed to make her very indignant. She flashed a resentful glance at him.

"Oh, were you, indeed?" she said with a great air.

For a few minutes she was so haughty with him that he loved her to madness. And directly this poem, which stuck at his lips, came forth lamely in fragments.

When they walked back toward the other girl and saw the patience of her attitude, their hearts swelled in a patronizing and secondary tenderness for her.

They were very happy. If they had been miserable they would have charged this fairy scene of the night with a criminal heartlessness; but as they were joyous, they vaguely wondered how the purple sea, the yellow stars, the changing crowds under the electric lights could be so phlegmatic and stolid.

They walked home by the lake-side way, and out upon the water those gay paper lanterns, flashing, fleeting, and careering, sang to them, sang a chorus of red and violet, and green and gold; a song of mystic bands of the future.

One day, when business paused during a dull sultry afternoon, Stimson went up town. Upon his return, he found that the popcorn man, from his stand over in a corner, was keeping an eye upon the cashier's cage, and that nobody at all was attending to the wooden arm and the iron rings. He strode forward like a sergeant of grenadiers.

"Where in thunder is Lizzie?" he demanded, a cloud of rage in his eyes.

The popcorn man, although associated long with Stimson, had never got over being dazed.

"They've—they've—gone round to th'—th'—house," he said with difficulty, as if he had just been stunned.

"Whose house?" snapped Stimson.

"Your—your house, I 'spose," said the popcorn man.

Stimson marched round to his home. Kingly denunciations surged, already formulated, to the tip of his tongue, and he bided the moment when his anger could fall upon the heads of that pair of children. He found his wife convulsive and in tears.

"Where's Lizzie?"

And then she burst forth—"Oh—John—John-they've run away, I know they have. They drove by here not three minutes ago. They must have done it on purpose to bid me good-bye, for Lizzie waved her hand sad-like; and then, before I could get out to ask where they were going or what, Frank whipped up the horse."

Stimson gave vent to a dreadful roar.

"Get my revolver—get a hack—get my revolver, do you hear—what the devil——" His voice became incoherent.

He had always ordered his wife about as if she were a battalion of infantry, and despite her misery, the training of years forced her to spring mechanically to obey; but suddenly she turned to him with a shrill appeal.

"Oh, John—not—the—revolver."

"Confound it, let go of me," he roared again, and shook her from him.

He ran hatless upon the street. There were a multitude of hacks at the summer resort, but it was ages to him before he could find one. Then he charged it like a bull.

"Uptown," he yelled, as he tumbled into the rear seat.

The hackman thought of severed arteries. His galloping horse distanced a large number of citizens who had been running to find what caused such contortions by the little hatless man.

It chanced as the bouncing hack went along near the lake, Stimson gazed across the calm grey expanse and recognized a colour in a bonnet and a pose of a head. A buggy was travelling along a highway that led to Sorington. Stimson bellowed—"There—there—there they are—in that buggy."

The hackman became inspired with the full knowledge of the situation. He struck a delirious blow with the whip. His mouth expanded in a grin of excitement and joy. It came to pass that this old vehicle, with its drowsy horse and its dusty-eyed and tranquil driver, seemed suddenly to awaken, to become animated and fleet. The horse ceased to ruminate on his state, his air of reflection vanished. He became intent upon his aged legs and spread them in quaint and ridiculous devices for speed. The driver, his eyes shining, sat critically in his seat. He watched each motion of this rattling machine down before him. He resembled an engineer. He used the whip with judgment and deliberation as the engineer would have used coal or oil. The horse clacked swiftly upon the macadam, the wheels hummed, the body of the vehicle wheezed and groaned.

Stimson, in the rear seat, was erect in that impassive attitude that comes sometimes to the furious man when he is obliged to leave the battle to others. Frequently, however, the tempest in his breast came to his face and he howled—

"Go it—go it—you're gaining; pound 'im! Thump the life out of 'im; hit 'im hard, you fool." His hand grasped the rod that supported the carriage top, and it was clenched so that the nails were faintly blue.

Ahead, that other carriage had been flying with speed, as from realization of the menace in the rear. It bowled away rapidly, drawn by the eager spirit of a young and modern horse. Stimson could see the buggy-top bobbing, bobbing. That little pane, like an eye, was a derision to him. Once he leaned forward and bawled angry sentences. He began to feel impotent; his whole expedition was a tottering of an old man upon a trail of birds. A sense of age made him choke again with wrath. That other vehicle, that was youth, with youth's pace; it was swift-flying with the hope of dreams. He began to comprehend those two children ahead of him, and he knew a sudden and strange awe, because he understood the power of their young blood, the power to fly strongly into the future and feel and hope again, even at that time when his bones must be laid in the earth. The dust rose easily from the hot road and stifled the nostrils of Stimson.

The highway vanished far away in a point with a suggestion of intolerable length. The other vehicle was becoming so small that Stimson could no longer see the derisive eye.

At last the hackman drew rein to his horse and turned to look at Stimson.

"No use, I guess," he said.

Stimson made a gesture of acquiescence, rage, despair. As the hackman turned his dripping horse about, Stimson sank back with the astonishment and grief of a man who has been defied by the universe. He had been in a great perspiration, and now his bald head felt cool and uncomfortable. He put up his hand with a sudden recollection that he had forgotten his hat.

At last he made a gesture. It meant that at any rate he was not responsible.

A DETAIL

The tiny old lady in the black dress and curious little black bonnet had at first seemed alarmed at the sound made by her feet upon the stone pavements. But later she forgot about it, for she suddenly came into the tempest of the Sixth Avenue shopping district, where from the streams of people and vehicles went up a roar like that from headlong mountain torrents.

She seemed then like a chip that catches, recoils, turns and wheels, a reluctant thing in the clutch of the impetuous river. She hesitated, faltered, debated with herself. Frequently she seemed about to address people; then of a sudden she would evidently lose her courage. Meanwhile the torrent jostled her, swung her this and that way.

At last, however, she saw two young women gazing in at a shop-window. They were well-dressed girls; they wore gowns with enormous sleeves that made them look like full-rigged ships with all sails set. They seemed to have plenty of time; they leisurely scanned the goods in the window. Other people had made the tiny old woman much afraid because obviously they were speeding to keep such tremendously important engagements. She went close to the girls and peered in at the same window. She watched them furtively for a time. Then finally she said—

"Excuse me!"

The girls looked down at this old face with its two large eyes turned towards them.

"Excuse me, can you tell me where I can get any work?"

For an instant the two girls stared. Then they seemed about to exchange a smile, but, at the last moment, they checked it. The tiny old lady's eyes were upon them. She was quaintly serious, silently expectant. She made one marvel that in that face the wrinkles showed no trace of experience, knowledge; they were simply little, soft, innocent creases. As for her glance, it had the trustfulness of ignorance and the candour of babyhood.

"I want to get something to do, because I need the money," she continued since, in their astonishment, they had not replied to her first question. "Of course I'm not strong and I couldn't do very much, but I can sew well; and in a house where there was a good many men folks, I could do all the mending. Do you know any place where they would like me to come?"

The young women did then exchange a smile, but it was a subtle tender smile, the edge of personal grief.

"Well, no, madame," hesitatingly said one of them at last; "I don't think I know any one."

A shade passed over the tiny old lady's face, a shadow of the wing of disappointment.

"Don't you?" she said, with a little struggle to be brave, in her voice.

Then the girl hastily continued—"But if you will give me your address, I may find some one, and if I do, I will surely let you know of it."

The tiny old lady dictated her address, bending over to watch the girl write on a visiting card with a little silver pencil. Then she said—

"I thank you very much." She bowed to them, smiling, and went on down the avenue.

As for the two girls, they walked to the curb and watched this aged figure, small and frail, in its black gown and curious black bonnet. At last, the crowd, the innumerable wagons, intermingling and changing with uproar and riot, suddenly engulfed it.

About Author

Stephen Crane (November 1, 1871 – June 5, 1900) was an American poet, novelist, and short story writer. Prolific throughout his short life, he wrote notable works in the Realist tradition as well as early examples of American Naturalism and Impressionism. He is recognized by modern critics as one of the most innovative writers of his generation.

The ninth surviving child of Methodist parents, Crane began writing at the age of four and had published several articles by the age of 16. Having little interest in university studies though he was active in a fraternity, he left Syracuse University in 1891 to work as a reporter and writer. Crane's first novel was the 1893 Bowery tale Maggie: A Girl of the Streets, generally considered by critics to be the first work of American literary Naturalism. He won international acclaim in 1895 for his Civil War novel The Red Badge of Courage, which he wrote without having any battle experience.

In 1896, Crane endured a highly publicized scandal after appearing as a witness in the trial of a suspected prostitute, an acquaintance named Dora Clark. Late that year he accepted an offer to travel to Cuba as a war correspondent. As he waited in Jacksonville, Florida for passage, he met Cora Taylor, with whom he began a lasting relationship. En route to Cuba, Crane's vessel the SS Commodore sank off the coast of Florida, leaving him and others adrift for 30 hours in a dinghy. Crane described the ordeal in "The Open Boat". During the final years of his life, he covered conflicts in Greece (accompanied by Cora, recognized as the first woman war correspondent) and later lived in England with her. He was befriended by writers such as Joseph Conrad and H. G. Wells. Plagued by financial difficulties and ill health, Crane died of tuberculosis in a Black Forest sanatorium in Germany at the age of 28.

At the time of his death, Crane was considered an important figure in American literature. After he was nearly forgotten for two decades, critics revived interest in his life and work. Crane's writing is characterized by vivid intensity, distinctive dialects, and irony. Common themes involve fear, spiritual crises and social isolation. Although recognized primarily for The Red Badge of Courage, which has become an American classic, Crane is also known for his poetry, journalism, and short stories such as "The Open Boat", "The Blue Hotel", "The Bride Comes to Yellow Sky", and The Monster. His writing made a deep impression on 20th-century writers, most prominent among them Ernest Hemingway, and is thought to have inspired the Modernists and the Imagists.

Biography

Early years

Stephen Crane was born on November 1, 1871, in Newark, New Jersey, to Jonathan Townley Crane, a minister in the Methodist Episcopal church, and Mary Helen Peck Crane, daughter of a clergyman, George Peck. He was the fourteenth and last child born to the couple. At 45, Helen Crane had suffered the early deaths of her previous four children, each of whom died within one year of birth. Nicknamed "Stevie" by the family, he joined eight surviving brothers and sisters—Mary Helen, George Peck, Jonathan Townley, William Howe, Agnes Elizabeth, Edmund Byran, Wilbur Fiske, and Luther.

The Cranes were descended from Jaspar Crane, a founder of New Haven Colony, who had migrated there from England in 1639. Stephen was named for a putative founder of Elizabethtown, New Jersey, who had, according to family tradition, come from England or Wales in 1665, as well as his great-great-grandfather Stephen Crane (1709–1780), a Revolutionary War patriot who served as New Jersey delegate to the First Continental Congress in Philadelphia. Crane later wrote that his father, Dr. Crane, "was a great, fine, simple mind," who had written numerous tracts on theology. Although his mother was a popular spokeswoman for the Woman's Christian Temperance Union and a highly religious woman, Crane wrote that he did not believe "she was as narrow as most of her friends or family." The young Stephen was raised primarily by his sister Agnes, who was 15 years his senior. The family moved to Port Jervis, New York, in 1876, where Dr. Crane became the pastor of Drew Methodist Church, a position that he retained until his death.

As a child, Stephen was often sickly and afflicted by constant colds.

When the boy was almost two, his father wrote in his diary that his youngest son became "so sick that we are anxious about him." Despite his fragile nature, Crane was an intelligent child who taught himself to read before the age of four. His first known inquiry, recorded by his father, dealt with writing; at the age of three, while imitating his brother Townley's writing, he asked his mother, "how do you spell O?" In December 1879, Crane wrote a poem about wanting a dog for Christmas. Entitled "I'd Rather Have –", it is his first surviving poem. Stephen was not regularly enrolled in school until January 1880, but he had no difficulty in completing two grades in six weeks. Recalling this feat, he wrote that it "sounds like the lie of a fond mother at a teaparty, but I do remember that I got ahead very fast and that father was very pleased with me."

Dr. Crane died on February 16, 1880, at the age of 60; Stephen was eight years old. Some 1,400 people mourned Dr. Crane at his funeral, more than double the size of his congregation. After her husband's death, Mrs. Crane moved to Roseville, near Newark, leaving Stephen in the care of his older brother Edmund, with whom the young boy lived with cousins in Sussex County. He next lived with his brother William, a lawyer, in Port Jervis for several years.

His older sister Helen took him to Asbury Park to be with their brother Townley and his wife, Fannie. Townley was a professional journalist; he headed the Long Branch department of both the New-York Tribune and the Associated Press, and also served as editor of the Asbury Park Shore Press. Agnes, another Crane sister, joined the siblings in New Jersey. She took a position at Asbury Park's intermediate school and moved in with Helen to care for the young Stephen.

Within a couple of years, the Crane family suffered more losses. First, Townley and his wife lost their two young children. His wife Fannie died of Bright's disease in November 1883. Agnes Crane became ill and died on June 10, 1884, of meningitis at the age of 28.

Schooling

Crane wrote his first known story, "Uncle Jake and the Bell Handle", when he was 14. In late 1885, he enrolled at Pennington Seminary, a ministry-focused coeducational boarding school 7 miles (11 km) north of Trenton. His father had been principal there from 1849 to 1858. Soon after her youngest son left for school, Mrs. Crane began suffering what the Asbury Park Shore Press reported as "a temporary aberration of the mind." She had apparently recovered by early 1886, but later that year, her son, 23-year-old Luther Crane, died after falling in front of an oncoming train while working as a flagman for the Erie Railroad. It was the fourth death in six years among Stephen's immediate family.

After two years, Crane left Pennington for Claverack College, a quasi-military school. He later looked back on his time at Claverack as "the happiest period of my life although I was not aware of it." A classmate remembered him as a highly literate but erratic student, lucky to pass examinations in math and science, and yet "far in advance of his fellow students in his knowledge of History and Literature", his favorite subjects. While he held an impressive record on the drill field and baseball diamond, Crane generally did not excel in the classroom. Not having a middle name, as was customary among other students, he took to signing his name "Stephen T. Crane" in order "to win recognition as a regular fellow". Crane was seen as friendly, but also moody and rebellious. He sometimes skipped class in order to play baseball, a game in which he starred as catcher. He was also greatly interested in the school's military training program. He rose rapidly in the ranks of the student battalion. One classmate described him as "indeed physically attractive without being handsome", but he was aloof, reserved and not generally popular at Claverack. Although academically weak, Crane gained experience at Claverack that provided background (and likely some anecdotes from the Civil War veterans on the staff) that proved useful when he came to write The Red Badge of Courage.

In mid-1888, Crane became his brother Townley's assistant at a New Jersey shore news bureau, working there every summer until 1892. Crane's first publication under his byline was an article on the explorer Henry M. Stanley's famous quest to find the Scottish missionary David Livingstone in Africa. It appeared in the February 1890 Claverack College Vidette. Within a few months, Crane was persuaded by his family to forgo a military career and transfer to Lafayette College in Easton, Pennsylvania, in order to pursue a mining engineering degree. He registered at Lafayette on September 12, and promptly became involved in extracurricular activities; he took up baseball again and joined the largest fraternity, Delta Upsilon. He also joined both rival literary societies, named for (George) Washington and (Benjamin) Franklin. Crane infrequently attended classes and ended the semester with grades for four of the seven courses he had taken.

After one semester, Crane transferred to Syracuse University, where he enrolled as a non-degree candidate in the College of Liberal Arts. He roomed in the Delta Upsilon fraternity house and joined the baseball team. Attending just one class (English Literature) during the middle trimester, he remained in residence while taking no courses in the third semester.

Concentrating on his writing, Crane began to experiment with tone and style while trying out different subjects. He published his fictional story, "Great Bugs of Onondaga," simultaneously in the Syracuse Daily Standard and the New York Tribune. Declaring college "a waste of time", Crane decided to become a full-time writer and reporter. He attended a Delta Upsilon chapter meeting on June 12, 1891, but shortly afterward left college for good.

Full-time writer

In the summer of 1891, Crane often camped with friends in the nearby area of Sullivan County, New York, where his brother Edmund occupied a house obtained as part of their brother William's Hartwood Club (Association) land dealings. He used this area as the geographic setting for several short stories, which were posthumously published in a collection under the title Stephen Crane: Sullivan County Tales and Sketches. Crane showed two of these works to Tribune editor Willis Fletcher Johnson, a friend of the family, who accepted them for the publication. "Hunting Wild Dogs" and "The Last of the Mohicans" were the first of fourteen unsigned Sullivan County sketches and tales that were published in the Tribune between February and July 1892. Crane also showed Johnson an early draft of his first novel, Maggie: A Girl of the Streets.

Later that summer, Crane met and befriended author Hamlin Garland, who had been lecturing locally on American literature and the expressive arts; on August 17 he gave a talk on novelist William Dean Howells, which Crane wrote up for the Tribune. Garland became a mentor for and champion of the young writer, whose intellectual honesty impressed him. Their relationship suffered in later years, however, because Garland disapproved of Crane's alleged immorality, related to his living with a woman married to another man.

Stephen moved into his brother Edmund's house in Lakeview, a suburb of Paterson, New Jersey, in the fall of 1891. From here he made frequent trips into New York City, writing and reporting particularly on its impoverished tenement districts. Crane focused particularly on The Bowery, a small and once prosperous neighborhood in the southern part of Manhattan. After the Civil War, Bowery shops and mansions had given way to saloons, dance halls, brothels and flophouses, all of which Crane frequented. He later said he did so for research. He was attracted to the human nature found in the slums, considering it "open and plain, with nothing hidden". Believing nothing honest and unsentimental had been written about the Bowery, Crane became determined to do so himself; this was the setting of his first novel. On December 7, 1891, Crane's mother died at the age of 64, and the 20-year-old appointed Edmund as his guardian.

Despite being frail, undernourished and suffering from a hacking cough, which did not prevent him from smoking cigarettes, in the spring of 1892 Crane began a romance with Lily Brandon Munroe, a married woman who was estranged from her husband. Although Munroe later said Crane "was not a handsome man", she admired his "remarkable almond-shaped gray eyes." He begged her to elope with him, but her family opposed the match because Crane lacked money and prospects, and she declined. Their last meeting likely occurred in April 1898, when he again asked her to run away with him and she again refused.

Between July 2 and September 11, 1892, Crane published at least ten news reports on Asbury Park affairs. Although a Tribune colleague stated that Crane "was not highly distinguished above any other boy of twenty who had gained a reputation for saying and writing bright things," that summer his reporting took on a more skeptical, hypocrisy-deflating tone. A storm of controversy erupted over a report he wrote on the Junior Order of United American Mechanics' American Day Parade, entitled "Parades and Entertainments". Published on August 21, the report juxtaposes the "bronzed, slope-shouldered, uncouth" marching men "begrimed with dust" and the spectators dressed in "summer gowns, lace parasols, tennis trousers, straw hats and indifferent smiles". Believing they were being ridiculed, some JOUAM marchers were outraged and wrote to the editor. The owner of the Tribune, Whitelaw Reid, was that year's Republican vice-presidential candidate, and this likely increased the sensitivity of the paper's management to the issue. Although Townley wrote a piece for the Asbury Park Daily Press in his brother's defense, the Tribune quickly apologized to its readers, calling Stephen Crane's piece "a bit of random correspondence, passed inadvertently by the copy editor". Hamlin Garland and biographer John Barry attested that Crane told them he had been dismissed by the Tribune, although Willis Fletcher Johnson later denied this. The paper did not publish any of Crane's work after 1892.

> Such an assemblage of the spraddle-legged men of the middle class, whose hands were bent and shoulders stooped from delving and constructing, had never appeared to an Asbury Park summer crowd, and the latter was vaguely amused.

> — Stephen Crane, account of the JOUAM parade as it appeared in the Tribune.

Life in New York

Crane struggled to make a living as a free-lance writer, contributing sketches and feature articles to various New York newspapers. In October 1892, he moved into a rooming house in Manhattan whose boarders were a group of medical students. During this time, he expanded or entirely reworked Maggie: A Girl of the Streets, which is about a girl who "blossoms in a mud-puddle" and becomes a pitiful victim of circumstance. In the winter of 1893, Crane took the manuscript of Maggie to Richard Watson Gilder, who rejected it for publication in The Century Magazine.

Crane decided to publish it privately, with money he had inherited from his mother. The novel was published in late February or early March 1893 by a small printing shop that usually printed medical books and religious tracts. The typewritten title page for the Library of Congress copyright application read simply: "A Girl of the Streets, / A Story of New York. / —By—/Stephen Crane." The name "Maggie" was added to the title later. Crane used the pseudonym "Johnston Smith" for the novel's initial publication, later telling friend and artist Corwin Knapp Linson that the nom de plume was the "commonest name I could think of. I had an editor friend named Johnson, and put in the "t", and no one could find me in the mob of Smiths." Hamlin Garland reviewed the work in the June 1893 issue of The Arena, calling it "the most truthful and unhackneyed study of the slums I have yet read, fragment though it is." Despite this early praise, Crane became depressed and destitute from having spent $869 for 1,100 copies of a novel that did not sell; he ended up giving a hundred copies away. He would later remember "how I looked forward to publication and pictured the sensation I thought it would make. It fell flat. Nobody seemed to notice it or care for it... Poor Maggie! She was one of my first loves."

In March 1893, Crane spent hours lounging in Linson's studio while having his portrait painted. He became fascinated with issues of the Century that were largely devoted to famous battles and military leaders from the Civil War. Frustrated with the dryly written stories, Crane stated, "I wonder that some of those fellows don't tell how they felt in those scraps. They spout enough of what they did, but they're as emotionless as rocks." Crane returned to these magazines during subsequent visits to Linson's studio, and eventually the idea of writing a war novel overtook him. He would later state that he "had been unconsciously working the detail of the story out through most of his boyhood" and had imagined "war stories ever since he was out of knickerbockers." This novel would ultimately become The Red Badge of Courage.

A river, amber-tinted in the shadow of its banks, purled at the army's feet; and at night, when the stream had become of a sorrowful blackness, one could see across it the red, eyelike gleam of hostile campfires set in the low brows of distant hills.

— Stephen Crane, The Red Badge of Courage

From the beginning, Crane wished to show how it felt to be in a war by writing "a psychological portrayal of fear." Conceiving his story from the point of view of a young private who is at first filled with boyish dreams of the glory of war and then quickly becomes disillusioned by war's reality, Crane borrowed the private's surname, "Fleming", from his sister-in-law's maiden name. He later said that the first paragraphs came to him with "every word in place, every comma, every period fixed." Working mostly nights, he wrote from around midnight until four or five in the morning. Because he could not afford a typewriter, he wrote carefully in ink on legal-sized paper, seldom crossing through or interlining a word. If he did change something, he would rewrite the whole page.

While working on his second novel, Crane remained prolific, concentrating on publishing stories to stave off poverty; "An Experiment in Misery", based on Crane's experiences in the Bowery, was printed by the New York Press. He also wrote five or six poems a day. In early 1894, he showed some of his poems or "lines" as he called them, to Hamlin Garland, who said he read "some thirty in all" with "growing wonder." Although Garland and William Dean Howells encouraged him to submit his poetry for publication, Crane's free verse was too unconventional for most. After brief wrangling between poet and publisher, Copeland & Day accepted Crane's first book of poems, The Black Riders and Other Lines, although it would not be published until after The Red Badge of Courage. He received a 10 percent royalty and the publisher assured him that the book would be in a form "more severely classic than any book ever yet issued in America."

In the spring of 1894, Crane offered the finished manuscript of The Red Badge of Courage to McClure's Magazine, which had become the foremost magazine for Civil War literature. While McClure's delayed giving him an answer on his novel, they offered him an assignment writing about the Pennsylvania coal mines. "In the Depths of a Coal Mine", a story with pictures by Linson, was syndicated by McClure's in a number of newspapers, heavily edited. Crane was reportedly disgusted by the cuts, asking Linson: "Why the hell did they send me up there then? Do they want the public to think the coal mines gilded ball-rooms with the miners eating ice-cream in boiled shirt-fronts?"

Sources report that following an encounter with a male prostitute that spring, Crane began a novel on the subject entitled Flowers of Asphalt, which he later abandoned. The manuscript has never been recovered.

After discovering that McClure's could not afford to pay him, Crane took his war novel to Irving Bacheller of the Bacheller-Johnson Newspaper Syndicate, which agreed to publish The Red Badge of Courage in serial form. Between the third and the ninth of December 1894, The Red Badge of Courage was published in some half-dozen newspapers in the United States. Although it was greatly cut for syndication, Bacheller attested to its causing a stir, saying "its quality [was] immediately felt and recognized." The lead editorial in the Philadelphia Press of December 7 said that Crane "is a new name now and unknown, but everybody will be talking about him if he goes on as he has begun".

Travels and fame

At the end of January 1895, Crane left on what he called "a very long and circuitous newspaper trip" to the west. While writing feature articles for the Bacheller syndicate, he traveled to Saint Louis, Missouri, Nebraska, New Orleans, Galveston, Texas and then Mexico City. Irving Bacheller would later state that he "sent Crane to Mexico for new color", which the author found in the form of Mexican slum life. Whereas he found the lower class in New York pitiful, he was impressed by the "superiority" of the Mexican peasants' contentment and "even refuse[d] to pity them."

Returning to New York five months later, Crane joined the Lantern (alternately spelled "Lanthom" or "Lanthorne") Club organized by a group of young writers and journalists. The Club, located on the roof of an old house on William Street near the Brooklyn Bridge, served as a drinking establishment of sorts and was decorated to look like a ship's cabin. There Crane ate one good meal a day, although friends were troubled by his "constant smoking, too much coffee, lack of food and poor teeth", as Nelson Greene put it. Living in near-poverty and greatly anticipating the publication of his books, Crane began work on two more novels: The Third Violet and George's Mother.

The Black Riders was published by Copeland & Day shortly before his return to New York in May, but it received mostly criticism, if not abuse, for the poems' unconventional style and use of free verse. A piece in the Bookman called Crane "the Aubrey Beardsley of poetry," and a commentator from the Chicago Daily Inter-Ocean stated that "there is not a line of poetry from the opening to the closing page. Whitman's Leaves of Grass were luminous in comparison. Poetic lunacy would be a better name for the book." In June, the New York Tribune dismissed the book as "so much trash." Crane was pleased that the book was "making some stir".

In contrast to the reception for Crane's poetry, The Red Badge of Courage was welcomed with acclaim after its publication by Appleton in September 1895. For the next four months, the book was in the top six on various bestseller lists around the country. It arrived on the literary scene "like a flash of lightning out of a clear winter sky", according to H. L. Mencken, who was about 15 at the time. The novel also became popular in Britain; Joseph Conrad, a future friend of Crane, wrote that the novel "detonated... with the impact and force of a twelve-inch shell charged with a very high explosive." Appleton published two, possibly three, printings in 1895 and as many as eleven more in 1896. Although some critics considered the work overly graphic and profane, it was widely heralded for its realistic portrayal of war and unique writing style. The Detroit Free Press declared that The Red Badge would give readers "so vivid a picture of the emotions and the horrors of the battlefield that you will pray your eyes may never look upon the reality."

Wanting to capitalize on the success of The Red Badge, McClure Syndicate offered Crane a contract to write a series on Civil War battlefields. Because it was a wish of his to "visit the battlefield—which I was to describe—at the time of year when it was fought", Crane agreed to take the assignment. Visiting battlefields in Northern Virginia, including Fredericksburg, he would later produce five more Civil War tales: "Three Miraculous Soldiers",

"The Veteran", "An Indiana Campaign", "An Episode of War" and The Little Regiment.

Scandal

At the age of 24, Crane, who was reveling in his success, became involved in a highly publicized case involving a suspected prostitute named Dora Clark. At 2 a.m. on September 16, 1896, he escorted two chorus girls and Clark from New York City's Broadway Garden, a popular "resort" where he had interviewed the women for a series he was writing. As Crane saw one woman safely to a streetcar, a plainclothes policeman named Charles Becker arrested the other two for solicitation; Crane was threatened with arrest when he tried to interfere. One of the women was released after Crane confirmed her erroneous claim that she was his wife, but Clark was charged and taken to the precinct. Against the advice of the arresting sergeant, Crane made a statement confirming Dora Clark's innocence, stating that "I only know that while with me she acted respectably, and that the policeman's charge was false." On the basis of Crane's testimony, Clark was discharged. The media seized upon the story; news spread to Philadelphia, Boston and beyond, with papers focusing on Crane's courage. The Stephen Crane story, as it became known, soon became a source for ridicule; the Chicago Dispatch in particular quipped that "Stephen Crane is respectfully informed that association with women in scarlet is not necessarily a 'Red Badge of Courage' ".

A couple of weeks after her trial, Clark pressed charges of false arrest against the officer who had arrested her. The next day, the officer physically attacked Clark in the presence of witnesses for having brought charges against him. Crane, who initially went briefly to Philadelphia to escape the pressure of publicity, returned to New York to give testimony at Becker's trial despite advice given to him from Theodore Roosevelt, who was Police Commissioner at the time and a new acquaintance of Crane. The defense targeted Crane: police raided his apartment and interviewed people who knew him, trying to find incriminating evidence in order to lessen the effect of his testimony. A vigorous cross-examination took place that sought to portray Crane as a man of dubious morals; while the prosecution proved that he frequented brothels, Crane claimed this was merely for research purposes. After the trial ended on

October 16, the arresting officer was exonerated, and Crane's reputation was ruined.

Cora Taylor and the Commodore shipwreck

> None of them knew the color of the sky. Their eyes glanced level and were fastened upon the waves that swept toward them. These waves were of the hue of slate, save for the tops, which were of foaming white, and all of the men knew the colors of the sea.

— Stephen Crane, "The Open Boat"

Given $700 in Spanish gold by the Bacheller-Johnson syndicate to work as a war correspondent in Cuba as the Spanish–American War was pending, the 25-year-old Crane left New York on November 27, 1896, on a train bound for Jacksonville, Florida. Upon arrival in Jacksonville, he registered at the St. James Hotel under the alias of Samuel Carleton to maintain anonymity while seeking passage to Cuba. While waiting for a boat, he toured the city and visited the local brothels. Within days he met 31-year-old Cora Taylor, proprietor of the downtown bawdy house Hotel de Dream. Born into a respectable Boston family, Taylor (whose legal name was Cora Ethel Stewart) had already had two brief marriages; her first husband, Vinton Murphy, divorced her on grounds of adultery. In 1889, she had married British Captain Donald William Stewart. She left him in 1892 for another man, but was still legally married. By the time Crane arrived, Taylor had been in Jacksonville for two years. She lived a bohemian lifestyle, owned a hotel of assignation, and was a well-known and respected local figure. The two spent much time together while Crane awaited his departure. He was finally cleared to leave for the Cuban port of Cienfuegos on New Year's Eve aboard the SS Commodore.

The ship sailed from Jacksonville with 27 or 28 men and a cargo of supplies and ammunition for the Cuban rebels. On the St. Johns River and less than 2 miles (3.2 km) from Jacksonville, Commodore struck a sandbar in a dense fog and damaged its hull. Although towed off the sandbar the following day, it was beached again in Mayport and again damaged. A leak began in the boiler room that evening and, as a result of malfunctioning water pumps, the ship came to a standstill about 16 miles (26 km) from Mosquito Inlet. As the ship took on more water, Crane described the engine room as resembling "a scene at this time taken from the middle kitchen of hades." Commodore's lifeboats were lowered in the early hours of the morning on January 2, 1897 and the ship ultimately sank at 7 a.m. Crane was one of the last to leave the ship in a 10-foot (3.0 m) dinghy. In an ordeal that he recounted in the short story "The Open Boat", Crane and three other men (including the ship's Captain) foundered off the coast of Florida for a day and a half before trying to land the dinghy at Daytona Beach. The small boat overturned in the surf, forcing the exhausted men to swim to shore; one of them died. Having lost the gold given to him for his journey, Crane wired Cora Taylor for help. She traveled to Daytona and returned to Jacksonville with Crane the next day, only four days after he had left on the Commodore.

The disaster was reported on the front pages of newspapers across the country. Rumors that the ship had been sabotaged were widely circulated but never substantiated. Portrayed favorably and heroically by the press, Crane emerged from the ordeal with his reputation enhanced, if not restored, after the battering he had received in the Dora Clark affair. Meanwhile, Crane's affair with Taylor blossomed.

Three seasons of archaeological investigation were conducted in 2002-04 to examine and document the exposed remains of a wreck near Ponce Inlet, FL conjectured to be that of the SS Commodore. The collected data, and other accumulated evidence, finally substantiated the identification of the Commodore beyond a reasonable doubt.

Greco-Turkish War

Despite contentment in Jacksonville and the need for rest after his ordeal, Crane became restless. He left Jacksonville on January 11 for New York City, where he applied for a passport to Cuba, Mexico and the West Indies. Spending three weeks in New York, he completed "The Open Boat" and periodically visited Port Jervis to see family. By this time, however, blockades had formed along the Florida coast as tensions rose with Spain, and Crane concluded that he would never be able to travel to Cuba. He sold "The Open

408

Boat" to Scribner's for $300 in early March. Determined to work as a war correspondent, Crane signed on with William Randolph Hearst's New York Journal to cover the impending Greco-Turkish conflict. He brought along Taylor, who had sold the Hotel de Dream in order to follow him.

On March 20, they sailed first to England, where Crane was warmly received. They arrived in Athens in early April; between April 17 (when Turkey declared war on Greece) and April 22, Crane wrote his first published report of the war, "An Impression of the 'Concert' ". When he left for Epirus in the northwest, Taylor remained in Athens, where she became the Greek war's first woman war correspondent. She wrote under the pseudonym "Imogene Carter" for the New York Journal, a job that Crane had secured for her. They wrote frequently, traveling throughout the country separately and together. The first large battle that Crane witnessed was the Turks' assault on General Constantine Smolenski's Greek forces at Velestino. Crane wrote, "It is a great thing to survey the army of the enemy. Just where and how it takes hold upon the heart is difficult of description." During this battle, Crane encountered "a fat waddling puppy" that he immediately claimed, dubbing it "Velestino, the Journal dog". Greece and Turkey signed an armistice on May 20, ending the 30-day war; Crane and Taylor left Greece for England, taking two Greek brothers as servants and Velestino the dog with them.

Spanish–American War

After staying in Limpsfield, Surrey, for a few days, Crane and Taylor settled in Ravensbrook, a plain brick villa in Oxted. Referring to themselves as Mr. and Mrs. Crane, the couple lived openly in England, but Crane concealed the relationship from his friends and family in the United States. Admired in England, Crane thought himself attacked back home: "There seem so many of them in America who want to kill, bury and forget me purely out of unkindness and envy and—my unworthiness, if you choose", he wrote. Velestino the dog sickened and died soon after their arrival in England, on August 1. Crane, who had a great love for dogs, wrote an emotional letter to a friend an hour after the dog's death, stating that "for eleven days we fought death for him, thinking nothing of anything but his life." The Limpsfield-Oxted area was home to members of the socialist Fabian

Society and a magnet for writers such as Edmund Gosse, Ford Madox Ford and Edward Garnett. Crane also met the Polish-born novelist Joseph Conrad in October 1897, with whom he would have what Crane called a "warm and endless friendship".

Although Crane was confident among peers, strong negative reviews of the recently published The Third Violet were causing his literary reputation to dwindle. Reviewers were also highly critical of Crane's war letters, deeming them self-centered. Although The Red Badge of Courage had by this time gone through fourteen printings in the United States and six in England, Crane was running out of money. To survive financially, he worked at a feverish pitch, writing prolifically for both the English and the American markets. He wrote in quick succession stories such as The Monster, "The Bride Comes to Yellow Sky", "Death and the Child" and "The Blue Hotel". Crane began to attach price tags to his new works of fiction, hoping that "The Bride", for example, would fetch $175.

As 1897 ended, Crane's money crisis worsened. Amy Leslie, a reporter from Chicago and a former lover, sued him for $550. The New York Times reported that Leslie gave him $800 in November 1896 but that he'd repaid only a quarter of the sum. In February he was summoned to answer Leslie's claim. The claim was apparently settled out of court, because no record of adjudication exists. Meanwhile, Crane felt "heavy with troubles" and "chased to the wall" by expenses. He confided to his agent that he was $2,000 in debt but that he would "beat it" with more literary output.

Soon after the USS Maine exploded in Havana Harbor on February 15, 1898, under suspicious circumstances, Crane was offered a £60 advance by Blackwood's Magazine for articles "from the seat of war in the event of a war breaking out" between the United States and Spain. His health was failing, and it is believed that signs of his pulmonary tuberculosis, which he may have contracted in childhood, became apparent. With almost no money coming in from his finished stories, Crane accepted the assignment and left Oxted for New York. Taylor and the rest of the household stayed behind to fend off local creditors. Crane applied for a passport and left New York for Key West two days before Congress declared war. While the war idled, he interviewed people and produced occasional copy.

In early June, he observed the establishment of an American base in Cuba when Marines seized Guantánamo Bay. He went ashore with the Marines, planning "to gather impressions and write them as the spirit moved." Although he wrote honestly about his fear in battle, others observed his calmness and composure. He would later recall "this prolonged tragedy of the night" in the war tale "Marines Signaling Under Fire at Guantanamo". After showing a willingness to serve during fighting at Cuzco, Cuba, by carrying messages to company commanders, Crane was officially cited for his "material aid during the action".

He continued to report upon various battles and the worsening military conditions and praised Theodore Roosevelt's Rough Riders, despite past tensions with the Commissioner. In early July, Crane was sent to the United States for medical treatment for a high fever. He was diagnosed with yellow fever, then malaria. Upon arrival in Old Point Comfort, Virginia, he spent a few weeks resting in a hotel. Although Crane had filed more than twenty dispatches in the three months he had covered the war, the World's business manager believed that the paper had not received its money's worth and fired him. In retaliation, Crane signed with Hearst's New York Journal with the wish to return to Cuba. He traveled first to Puerto Rico and then to Havana. In September, rumors began to spread that Crane, who was working anonymously, had either been killed or disappeared. He sporadically sent out dispatches and stories; he wrote about the mood in Havana, the crowded city sidewalks, and other topics, but he was soon desperate for money again. Taylor, left alone in England, was also penniless. She became frantic with worry over her lover's whereabouts; they were not in direct communication until the end of the year. Crane left Havana and arrived in England on January 11, 1899.

Death

Rent on Ravensbrook had not been paid for a year. Upon returning to England, Crane secured a solicitor to act as guarantor for their debts, after which Crane and Taylor relocated to Brede Place. This manor in Sussex, which dated to the 14th century and had neither electricity nor indoor plumbing, was offered to them by friends at a modest rent. The relocation appeared to give hope to Crane, but his money problems continued. Deciding that he could no longer afford to write for American publications, he concentrated on publishing in English magazines.

Crane pushed himself to write feverishly during the first months at Brede; he told his publisher that he was "doing more work now than I have at any other period in my life". His health worsened, and by late 1899 he was asking friends about health resorts. The Monster and Other Stories was in production and War Is Kind, his second collection of poems, was published in the United States in May. None of his books after The Red Badge of Courage had sold well, and he bought a typewriter to spur output. Active Service, a novella based on Crane's correspondence experience, was published in October. The New York Times reviewer questioned "whether the author of 'Active Service' himself really sees anything remarkable in his newspapery hero."

In December, the couple held an elaborate Christmas party at Brede, attended by Conrad, Henry James, H. G. Wells and other friends; it lasted several days. On December 29 Crane suffered a severe pulmonary hemorrhage. In January 1900 he'd recovered sufficiently to work on a new novel, The O'Ruddy, completing 25 of the 33 chapters. Plans were made for him to travel as a correspondent to Gibraltar to write sketches from Saint Helena, the site of a Boer prison, but at the end of March and in early April he suffered two more hemorrhages. Taylor took over most of Crane's correspondence while he was ill, writing to friends for monetary aid. The couple planned to travel on the continent, but Conrad, upon visiting Crane for the last time, remarked that his friend's "wasted face was enough to tell me that it was the most forlorn of all hopes."

On May 28, the couple arrived at Badenweiler, Germany, a health spa on the edge of the Black Forest. Despite his weakened condition, Crane continued to dictate fragmentary episodes for the completion of The O'Ruddy. He died on June 5, 1900, at the age of 28. In his will he left everything to Taylor, who took his body to New Jersey for burial. Crane was interred in Evergreen Cemetery in what is now Hillside, New Jersey.

Fiction and poetry

Style and technique

Stephen Crane's fiction is typically categorized as representative of Naturalism, American realism, Impressionism or a mixture of the three. Critic Sergio Perosa, for example, wrote in his essay, "Stephen Crane fra naturalismo e impressionismo," that the work presents a "symbiosis" of Naturalistic ideals and Impressionistic methods. When asked whether or not he would write an autobiography in 1896, Crane responded that he "dare not say that I am honest. I merely say that I am as nearly honest as a weak mental machinery will allow." Similarities between the stylistic techniques in Crane's writing and Impressionist painting—including the use of color and chiaroscuro—are often cited to support the theory that Crane was not only an Impressionist but also influenced by the movement. H. G. Wells remarked upon "the great influence of the studio" on Crane's work, quoting a passage from The Red Badge of Courage as an example: "At nightfall the column broke into regimental pieces, and the fragments went into the fields to camp. Tents sprang up like strange plants. Camp fires, like red, peculiar blossoms, dotted the night.... From this little distance the many fires, with the black forms of men passing to and fro before the crimson rays, made weird and satanic effects." Although no direct evidence exists that Crane formulated a precise theory of his craft, he vehemently rejected sentimentality, asserting that "a story should be logical in its action and faithful to character. Truth to life itself was the only test, the greatest artists were the simplest, and simple because they were true."

Poet and biographer John Berryman suggested that there were three basic variations, or "norms", of Crane's narrative style. The first, being "flexible, swift, abrupt and nervous", is best exemplified in The Red Badge of Courage, while the second ("supple majesty") is believed to relate to "The Open Boat", and the third ("much more closed, circumstantial and 'normal' in feeling and syntax") to later works such as The Monster. Crane's work, however, cannot be determined by style solely on chronology. Not only does his fiction not take place in any particular region with similar characters, but it varies from serious in tone to reportorial writing and light fiction. Crane's writing, both fiction and nonfiction, is consistently driven by immediacy and is at once concentrated, vivid and intense. The novels and short stories contain poetic characteristics such as shorthand prose, suggestibility, shifts in perspective and ellipses between and within sentences. Similarly, omission plays a large part in Crane's work; the names of his protagonists are not commonly used and sometimes they are not named at all.

Crane was often criticized by early reviewers for his frequent incorporation of everyday speech into dialogue, mimicking the regional accents of his characters with colloquial stylization. This is apparent in his first novel, in which Crane ignored the romantic, sentimental approach of slum fiction; he instead concentrated on the cruelty and sordid aspects of poverty, expressed by the brashness of the Bowery's crude dialect and profanity, which he used lavishly. The distinct dialect of his Bowery characters is apparent at the beginning of the text; the title character admonishes her brother saying: "Yeh knows it puts mudder out when yes comes home half dead, an' it's like we'll all get a poundin'."

Major themes

Crane's work is often thematically driven by Naturalistic and Realistic concerns, including ideals versus realities, spiritual crises and fear. These themes are particularly evident in Crane's first three novels, Maggie: A Girl of the Streets, The Red Badge of Courage and George's Mother. The three main characters search for a way to make their dreams come true, but ultimately suffer from crises of identity. Crane was fascinated by war and death, as well as fire, disfigurement, fear and courage, all of which inspired him to write many works based on these concepts. In The Red Badge of Courage, the main character both longs for the heroics of battle but ultimately fears it, demonstrating the dichotomy of courage and cowardice. He experiences the threat of death, misery and a loss of self.

Extreme isolation from society and community is also apparent in Crane's work. During the most intense battle scenes in The Red Badge of Courage, for example, the story's focus is mainly "on the inner responses of

414

a self unaware of others". In "The Open Boat", "An Experiment in Misery" and other stories, Crane uses light, motion and color to express degrees of epistemological uncertainty. Similar to other Naturalistic writers, Crane scrutinizes the position of man, who has been isolated not only from society, but also from God and nature. "The Open Boat", for example, distances itself from Romantic optimism and affirmation of man's place in the world by concentrating on the characters' isolation.

While he lived, Stephen Crane was denominated by critical readers a realist, a naturalist, an impressionist, symbolist, Symboliste, expressionist and ironist; his posthumous life was enriched by critics who read him as nihilistic, existentialist, a neo-Romantic, a sentimentalist, protomodernist, pointilliste, visionist, imagist and, by his most recent biographer, a "bleak naturalist." At midcentury he was a "predisciple of the New Criticism"; by its end he was "a proto-deconstructionist anti-artist hero" who had "leapfrogged modernism, landing on postmodernist ground." Or, as Sergio Perosa wrote in 1964, "The critic wanders in a labyrinth of possibilities, which every new turn taken by Crane's fiction seems to explode or deny."

One undeniable fact about Crane's work, as Anthony Splendora noted in 2015, is that Death haunts it; like a threatening eclipse it overshadows his best efforts, each of which features the signal demise of a main character. Allegorically, "The Blue Hotel," at the pinnacle of the short story form, may even be an autothanatography, the author's intentional exteriorization or objectification, in this case for the purpose of purgation, of his own impending death. Crane's "Swede" in that story can be taken, following current psychoanalytical theory, as a surrogative, sacrificial victim, ritually to be purged.

Transcending this "dark circumstance of composition," Crane had a particular telos and impetus for his creation: beyond the tautologies that all art is alterity and to some formal extent mimesis, Crane sought and obviously found "a form of catharsis" in writing. This view accounts for his uniqueness, especially as operative through his notorious "disgust" with his family's religion, their "vacuous, futile psalm-singing". His favorite book, for example, was Mark Twain's Life on the Mississippi, in which God is mentioned only twice—once as irony and once as "a swindle." Not only did Crane call out God specifically with the lines "Well then I hate thee / righteous image" in "The Black Riders" (1895), but even his most hopeful tropes, such as the "comradeship" of his "Open Boat" survivors, make no mention of deity, specifying only "indifferent nature." His antitheism is most evident in his characterization of the human race as "lice clinging to a space-lost bulb," a climax-nearing speech in "The Blue Hotel," Ch. VI. It is possible that Crane utilized religion's formal psychic space, now suddenly available resulting from the recent "Death of God", as a milieu for his compensative art.

Novels

Beginning with the publication of Maggie: A Girl of the Streets in 1893, Crane was recognized by critics mainly as a novelist. Maggie was initially rejected by numerous publishers because of its atypical and true-to-life depictions of class warfare, which clashed with the sentimental tales of that time. Rather than focusing on the very rich or middle class, the novel's characters are lower-class denizens of New York's Bowery. The main character, Maggie, descends into prostitution after being led astray by her lover. Although the novel's plot is simple, its dramatic mood, quick pace and portrayal of Bowery life have made it memorable. Maggie is not merely an account of slum life, but also represents eternal symbols. In his first draft, Crane did not give his characters proper names. Instead, they were identified by epithets: Maggie, for example, was the girl who "blossomed in a mud-puddle" and Pete, her seducer, was a "knight". The novel is dominated by bitter irony and anger, as well as destructive morality and treacherous sentiment. Critics would later call the novel "the first dark flower of American Naturalism" for its distinctive elements of naturalistic fiction.

Written thirty years after the end of the Civil War and before Crane had any experience of battle, The Red Badge of Courage was innovative stylistically as well as psychologically. Often described as a war novel, it focuses less on battle and more on the main character's psyche and his reactions and responses in war. It is believed that Crane based the fictional battle in the novel on that of Chancellorsville; he may also have interviewed veterans of the 124th New York Volunteer Infantry Regiment, commonly known

416

as the Orange Blossoms, in Port Jervis, New York. Told in a third-person limited point of view, it reflects the private experience of Henry Fleming, a young soldier who flees from combat. The Red Badge of Courage is notable in its vivid descriptions and well-cadenced prose, both of which help create suspense within the story. Similarly, by substituting epithets for characters' names ("the youth", "the tattered soldier"), Crane injects an allegorical quality into his work, making his characters point to a specific characteristic of man. Like Crane's first novel, The Red Badge of Courage has a deeply ironic tone which increases in severity as the novel progresses. The title of the work is ironic; Henry wishes "that he, too, had a wound, a red badge of courage", echoing a wish to have been wounded in battle. The wound he does receive (from the rifle butt of a fleeing Union soldier) is not a badge of courage but a badge of shame.

The novel expresses a strong connection between humankind and nature, a frequent and prominent concern in Crane's fiction and poetry throughout his career. Whereas contemporary writers (Ralph Waldo Emerson, Nathaniel Hawthorne, Henry David Thoreau) focused on a sympathetic bond on the two elements, Crane wrote from the perspective that human consciousness distanced humans from nature. In The Red Badge of Courage, this distance is paired with a great number of references to animals, and men with animalistic characteristics: people "howl", "squawk", "growl", or "snarl".

Since the resurgence of Crane's popularity in the 1920s, The Red Badge of Courage has been deemed a major American text. The novel has been anthologized numerous times, including in the 1942 collection Men at War: The Best War Stories of All Time, edited by Ernest Hemingway. In the introduction, Hemingway wrote that the novel "is one of the finest books of our literature, and I include it entire because it is all as much of a piece as a great poem is."

Crane's later novels have not received as much critical praise. After the success of The Red Badge of Courage, Crane wrote another tale set in the Bowery. George's Mother is less allegorical and more personal than his two previous novels, and it focuses on the conflict between a church-going, temperance-adhering woman (thought to be based on Crane's mother) and her single remaining offspring, who is a naive dreamer. Critical response to the novel was mixed. The Third Violet, a romance that he wrote quickly after publishing The Red Badge of Courage, is typically considered as Crane's attempt to appeal to popular audiences. Crane considered it a "quiet little story." Although it contained autobiographical details, the characters have been deemed inauthentic and stereotypical. Crane's second to last novel, Active Service, revolves around the Greco-Turkish War of 1897, with which the author was familiar. Although noted for its satirical take on the melodramatic and highly passionate works that were popular of the nineteenth century, the novel was not successful. It is generally accepted by critics that Crane's work suffered at this point due to the speed which he wrote in order to meet his high expenses. His last novel, a suspenseful and picaresque work entitled The O'Ruddy, was finished posthumously by Robert Barr and published in 1903.

Short fiction

Crane wrote many different types of fictional pieces while indiscriminately applying to them terms such as "story", "tale" and "sketch". For this reason, critics have found clear-cut classification of Crane's work problematic. While "The Open Boat" and "The Bride Comes to Yellow Sky" are often considered short stories, others are variously identified.

In an 1896 interview with Herbert P. Williams, a reporter for the Boston Herald, Crane said that he did "not find that short stories are utterly different in character from other fiction. It seems to me that short stories are the easiest things we write." During his brief literary career, he wrote more than a hundred short stories and fictional sketches. Crane's early fiction was based in camping expeditions in his teen years; these stories eventually became known as The Sullivan County Tales and Sketches. He considered these "sketches", which are mostly humorous and not of the same caliber of work as his later fiction, to be "articles of many kinds," in that they are part fiction and part journalism.

The subject matter for his stories varied extensively. His early New York City sketches and Bowery tales accurately described the results of industrialization, immigration and the growth of cities and their slums. His collection of six short stories, The Little Regiment, covered familiar ground with the American Civil War, a subject for which he became famous with The Red Badge of Courage. Although similar to Crane's noted novel, The Little Regiment was believed to lack vigor and originality. Realizing the limitations of these tales, Crane wrote: "I have invented the sum of my invention with regard to war and this story keeps me in internal despair."

The Open Boat and Other Tales of Adventure (1898) contains thirteen short stories that deal with three periods in Crane's life: his Asbury Park boyhood, his trip to the West and Mexico in 1895, and his Cuban adventure in 1897. This collection was well received and included several of his most critically successful works. His 1899 collection, The Monster and Other Stories, was similarly well received.

Two posthumously published collections were not as successful. In August 1900 The Whilomville Stories were published, a collection of thirteen stories that Crane wrote during the last year of his life. The work deals almost exclusively with boyhood, and the stories are drawn from events occurring in Port Jervis, where Crane lived from the age of six to eleven.Focusing on small-town America, the stories tend toward sentimentality, but remain perceptive of the lives of children. Wounds in the Rain, published in September 1900, contains fictional tales based on Crane's reports for the World and the Journal during the Spanish–American War. These stories, which Crane wrote while desperately ill, include "The Price of the Harness" and "The Lone Charge of William B. Perkins" and are dramatic, ironic and sometimes humorous.

Despite Crane's prolific output, only four stories--"The Open Boat", "The Blue Hotel", "The Bride Comes to Yellow Sky", and The Monster— have received extensive attention from scholars. H. G. Wells considered "The Open Boat" to be "beyond all question, the crown of all his work", and it is one of the most frequently discussed of Crane's works.

Poetry

> Many red devils ran from my heart
>
> And out upon the page.

They were so tiny

The pen could mash them.

And many struggled in the ink.

It was strange

To write in this red muck

Of things from my heart.

— Stephen Crane

Crane's poems, which he preferred to call "lines", are typically not given as much scholarly attention as his fiction; no anthology contained Crane's verse until 1926. Although it is not certain when Crane began to write poetry seriously, he once said that his overall poetic aim was "to give my ideas of life as a whole, so far as I know it". The poetic style used in both of his books of poetry, The Black Riders and Other Lines and War is Kind, was unconventional for the time in that it was written in free verse without rhyme, meter, or even titles for individual works. They are typically short in length; although several poems, such as "Do not weep, maiden, for war is kind", use stanzas and refrains, most do not. Crane also differed from his peers and poets of later generations in that his work contains allegory, dialectic and narrative situations.

Critic Ruth Miller claimed that Crane wrote "an intellectual poetry rather than a poetry that evokes feeling, a poetry that stimulates the mind rather than arouses the heart". In the most complexly organized poems, the significance of the states of mind or feelings is ambiguous, but Crane's poems tend to affirm certain elemental attitudes, beliefs, opinions and stances toward God, man and the universe. The Black Riders in particular is essentially a dramatic concept and the poems provide continuity within the dramatic structure. There is also a dramatic interplay in which there is frequently a major voice reporting an incident seen ("In the desert / I saw a creature, naked, bestial") or experienced ("A learned man came to me once"). The second voice or additional voices represent a point of view which is revealed to be inferior; when these clash, a dominant attitude emerges.

Legacy

In four years, Crane published five novels, two volumes of poetry, three short story collections, two books of war stories, and numerous works of short fiction and reporting. Today he is mainly remembered for The Red Badge of Courage, which is regarded as an American classic. The novel has been adapted several times for the screen, including John Huston's 1951 version. By the time of his death, Crane had become one of the best known writers of his generation. His eccentric lifestyle, frequent newspaper reporting, association with other famous authors, and expatriate status made him somewhat of an international celebrity. Although most stories about his life tended toward the romantic, rumors about his alleged drug use and alcoholism persisted long after his death.

By the early 1920s, Crane and his work were nearly forgotten. It was not until Thomas Beer published his biography in 1923, which was followed by editor Wilson Follett's The Work of Stephen Crane (1925–1927), that Crane's writing came to the attention of a scholarly audience. Crane's reputation was then enhanced by faithful support from writer friends such as Joseph Conrad, H. G. Wells and Ford Madox Ford, all of whom either published recollections or commented upon their time with Crane. John Berryman's 1950 biography of Crane further established him as an important American author. Since 1951 there has been a steady outpouring of articles, monographs and reprints in Crane scholarship.

Today, Crane is considered one of the most innovative writers of the 1890s. His peers, including Conrad and James, as well as later writers such as Robert Frost, Ezra Pound and Willa Cather, hailed Crane as one of the finest creative spirits of his time. His work was described by Wells as "the first expression of the opening mind of a new period, or, at least, the early emphatic phase of a new initiative." Wells said that "beyond dispute", Crane was "the best writer of our generation, and his untimely death was an irreparable loss to our literature." Conrad wrote that Crane was an "artist" and "a seer with a gift for rendering the significant on the surface of things and with an incomparable insight into primitive emotions". Crane's work has proved inspirational for future writers; not only have scholars drawn similarities between Hemingway's A Farewell to Arms and The Red Badge of Courage, but Crane's fiction is thought to have been an important inspiration for Hemingway and his fellow Modernists. In 1936, Hemingway wrote in The Green Hills of Africa that "The good writers are Henry James, Stephen Crane, and Mark Twain. That's not the order they're good in. There is no order for good writers." Crane's poetry is thought to have been a precursor to the Imagist movement, and his short fiction has also influenced American literature. "The Open Boat", "The Blue Hotel", The Monster and "The Bride Comes to Yellow Sky" are generally considered by critics to be examples of Crane's best work.

Several institutions and places have endeavored to keep Crane's legacy alive. Badenweiler and the house where he died became something of a tourist attraction for its fleeting association with the American author; Alexander Woollcott attested to the fact that, long after Crane's death, tourists would be directed to the room where he died. Columbia University Rare Book and Manuscript Library has a collection of Crane and Taylor's personal correspondence dating from 1895 to 1908. Near his brother Edmund's Sullivan County home in New York, where Crane stayed for a short time, a pond is named after him. The Stephen Crane House in Asbury Park, New Jersey, where the author lived with his siblings for nine years, is operated as a museum dedicated to his life and work. Syracuse University has an annual Stephen Crane Lecture Series which is sponsored by the Dikaia Foundation.

Columbia University purchased much of the Stephen Crane materials held by Cora Crane at her death. The Crane Collection is one of the largest in the nation of his materials. Columbia University had an exhibit: 'The Tall Swift Shadow of a Ship at Night': Stephen and Cora Crane, November 2, 1995 through February 16, 1996, about the lives of the couple, featuring letters and other documents and memorabilia. (Source : Wikipedia)

NOTABLE WORKS

NOVELS

Maggie: A Girl of the Streets, 1893.

The Red Badge of Courage, 1895.

George's Mother, 1896.

The Third Violet, 1897.

Active Service, 1899.

Crane, Stephen and Robert Barr. The O'Ruddy, 1903.

The Black Riders and Other Lines, 1895.

The Open Boat and Other Tales of Adventure, 1898

War is Kind, 1899

The Monster and Other Stories, 1899

Wounds in the Rain, 1900

Great Battles of the World, 1901

The O'Ruddy, 1903

SHORT STORY COLLECTIONS

The Little Regiment and Other Episodes from the American Civil War, 1896.

The Open Boat and Other Tales of Adventure, 1898.

The Monster and Other Stories, 1899.

Whilomville Stories, 1900.

Wounds in the Rain: War Stories, 1900.

Great Battles of the World, 1901.

The Monster,1901.

Last Words, 1902.

POETRY COLLECTIONS

The Black Riders and Other Lines, 1895.

War is Kind, 1899.

UNFINISHED WORKS

Sources report that following an encounter with a male prostitute in the spring of 1894, Crane began a novel on the subject entitled Flowers of Asphalt. He reportedly abandoned the project and the manuscript has never been recovered.

CPSIA information can be obtained
at www.ICGtesting.com
Printed in the USA
LVHW010108210720
661156LV00012B/458